BASKETFUL OF HEADS

JOE HILL WRITER **LEOMACS** ARTIST

RICCARDO LA BELLA ADDITIONAL PENCILS, *BASKETFUL OF HEADS* #5

DAVE STEWART COLORIST **DERON BENNETT** LETTERER

REIKO MURAKAMI COLLECTION COVER ARTIST

BASKETFUL OF HEADS CREATED BY **JOE HILL**

BASKETFUL OF HEADS

PUBLISHED BY DC COMICS. COMPILATION AND ALL NEW MATERIAL COPYRIGHT © 2020 JOE HILL. ALL RIGHTS RESERVED. ORIGINALLY PUBLISHED IN SINGLE MAGAZINE FORM IN *BASKETFUL OF HEADS* 1-7. COPYRIGHT © 2019, 2020 JOE HILL. ALL RIGHTS RESERVED. ALL CHARACTERS, THEIR DISTINCTIVE LIKENESSES, AND RELATED ELEMENTS FEATURED IN THIS PUBLICATION ARE TRADEMARKS OF JOE HILL. HILL HOUSE COMICS IS A TRADEMARK OF DC COMICS. THE STORIES, CHARACTERS, AND INCIDENTS FEATURED IN THIS PUBLICATION ARE ENTIRELY FICTIONAL. DC COMICS DOES NOT READ OR ACCEPT UNSOLICITED SUBMISSIONS OF IDEAS, STORIES, OR ARTWORK. DC – A WARNERMEDIA COMPANY.

DC COMICS, 2900 WEST ALAMEDA AVE., BURBANK, CA 91505
PRINTED BY TRANSCONTINENTAL INTERGLOBE, BEAUCEVILLE, QC, CANADA. 7/31/20.
ISBN: 978-1-77950-297-1

LIBRARY OF CONGRESS CATALOGING-IN-PUBLICATION DATA IS AVAILABLE.

PEFC Certified

This product is from sustainably managed forests and controlled sources

PEFC/01-31-106   www.pefc.org

MARK DOYLE, AMEDEO TURTURRO EDITORS – ORIGINAL SERIES
JEB WOODARD GROUP EDITOR – COLLECTED EDITIONS
ERIKA ROTHBERG EDITOR – COLLECTED EDITION
STEVE COOK DESIGN DIRECTOR – BOOKS
LOUIS PRANDI PUBLICATION DESIGN
SUZANNAH ROWNTREE PUBLICATION PRODUCTION

BOB HARRAS SENIOR VP – EDITOR-IN-CHIEF, DC COMICS

JIM LEE PUBLISHER & CHIEF CREATIVE OFFICER
BOBBIE CHASE VP – GLOBAL PUBLISHING INITIATIVES & DIGITAL STRATEGY
DON FALLETTI VP – MANUFACTURING OPERATIONS & WORKFLOW MANAGEMENT
LAWRENCE GANEM VP – TALENT SERVICES
ALISON GILL SENIOR VP – MANUFACTURING & OPERATIONS
HANK KANALZ SENIOR VP – PUBLISHING STRATEGY & SUPPORT SERVICES
DAN MIRON VP – PUBLISHING OPERATIONS
NICK J. NAPOLITANO VP – MANUFACTURING ADMINISTRATION & DESIGN
NANCY SPEARS VP – SALES
JONAH WEILAND VP – MARKETING & CREATIVE SERVICES
MICHELE R. WELLS VP & EXECUTIVE EDITOR, YOUNG READER

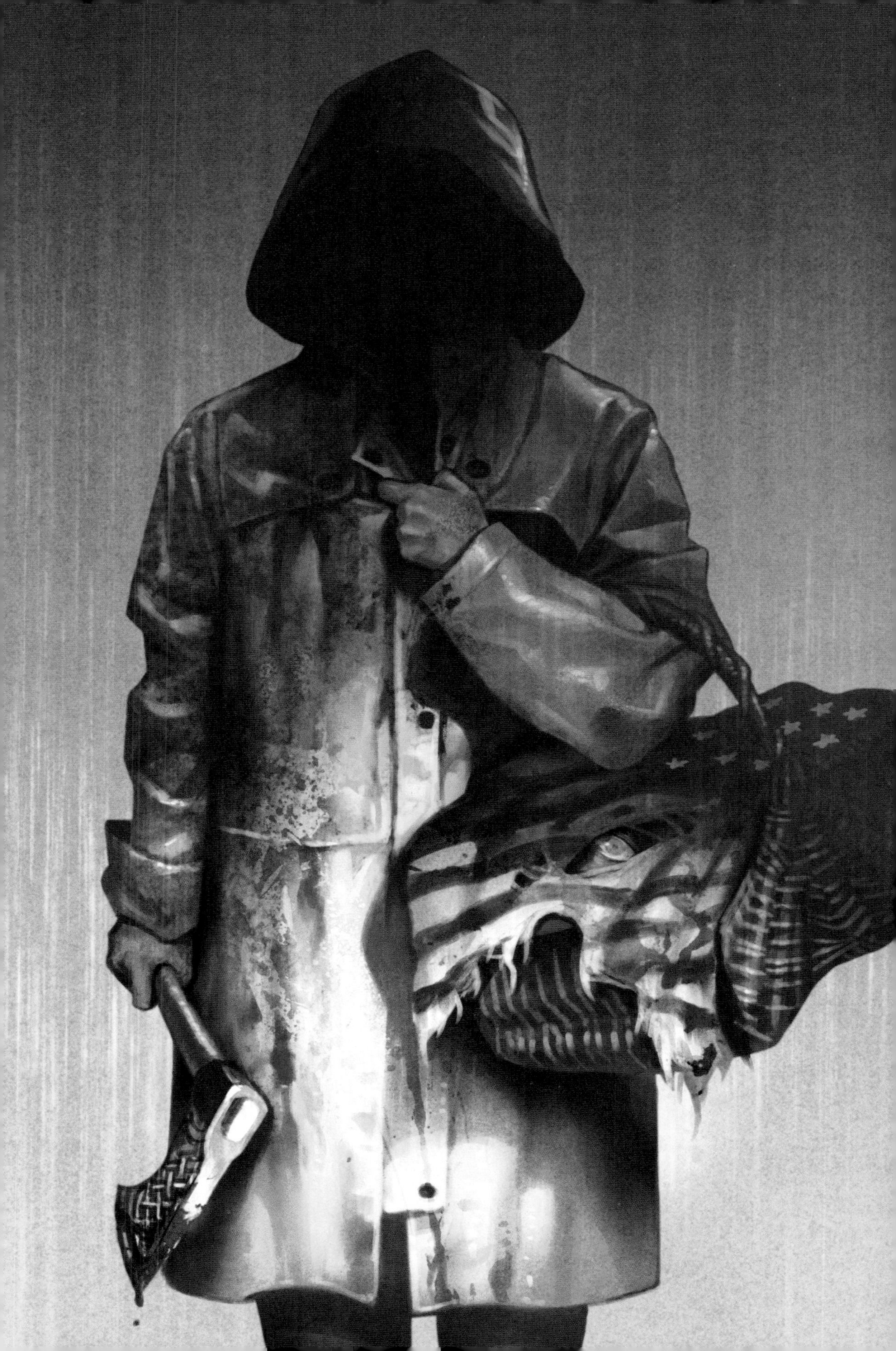

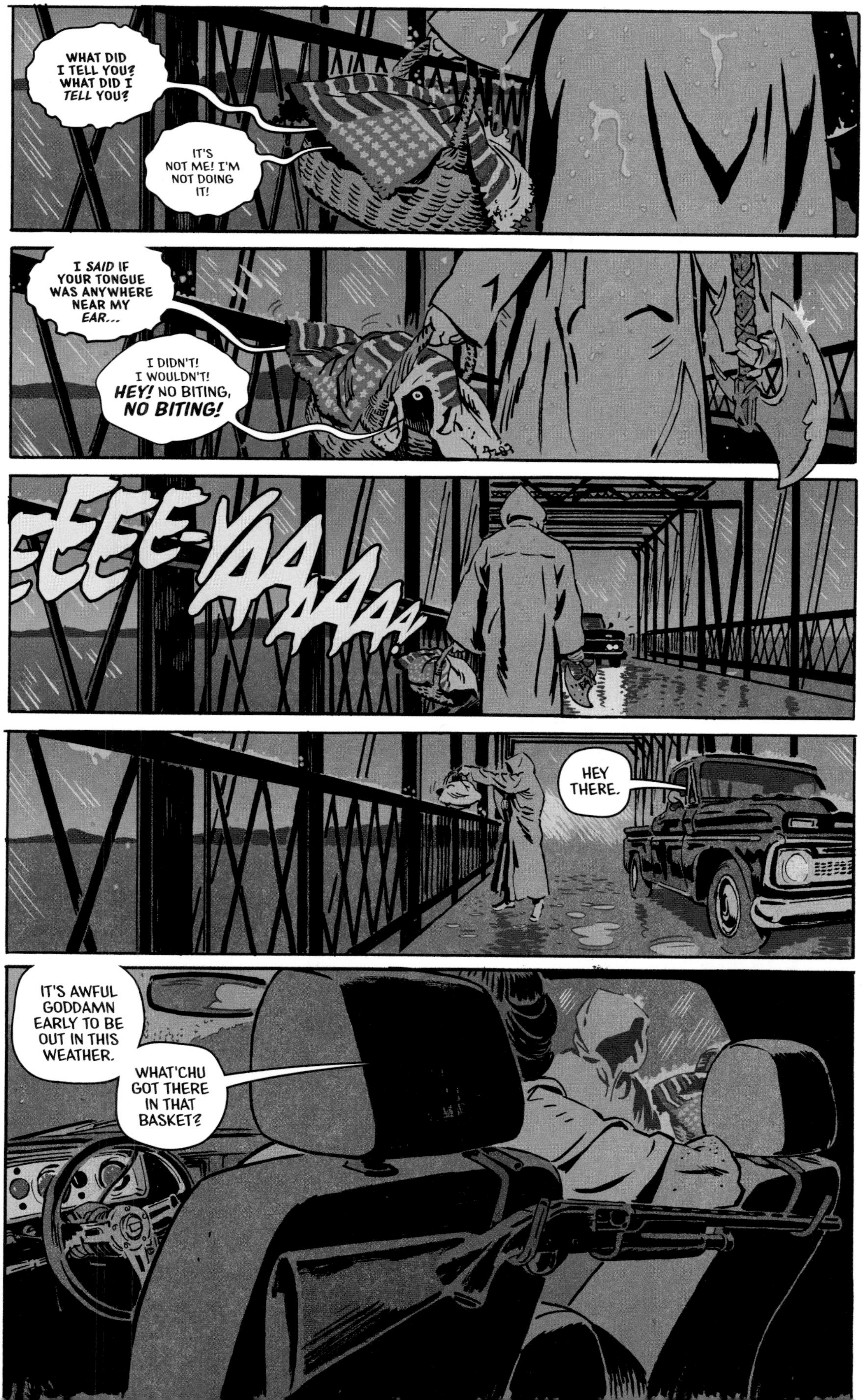
WHAT DID I TELL YOU? WHAT DID I *TELL* YOU?
IT'S NOT ME! I'M NOT DOING IT!
I *SAID* IF YOUR TONGUE WAS ANYWHERE NEAR MY *EAR*...
I DIDN'T! I WOULDN'T! **HEY!** NO BITING, **NO BITING!**
EEEE-YAAAAAAA!
HEY THERE.
IT'S AWFUL GODDAMN EARLY TO BE OUT IN THIS WEATHER.
WHAT'CHU GOT THERE IN THAT BASKET?

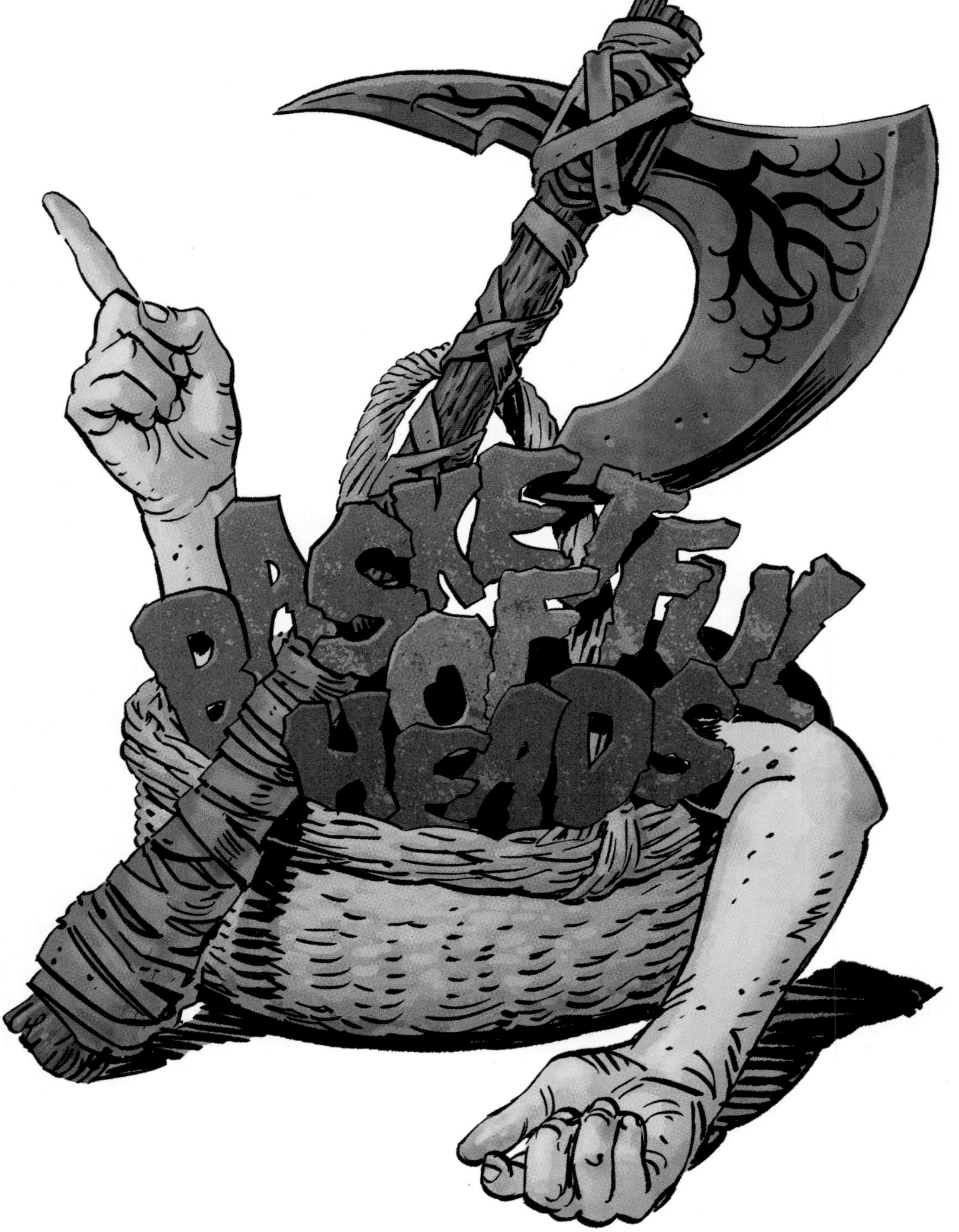
BASKETFUL OF HEADS

Written by JOE HILL Illustrated by LEOMACS
Colored by DAVE STEWART Lettered by DERON BENNETT
Cover by REIKO MURAKAMI
Edited by MARK DOYLE & AMEDEO TURTURRO

BEFORE.

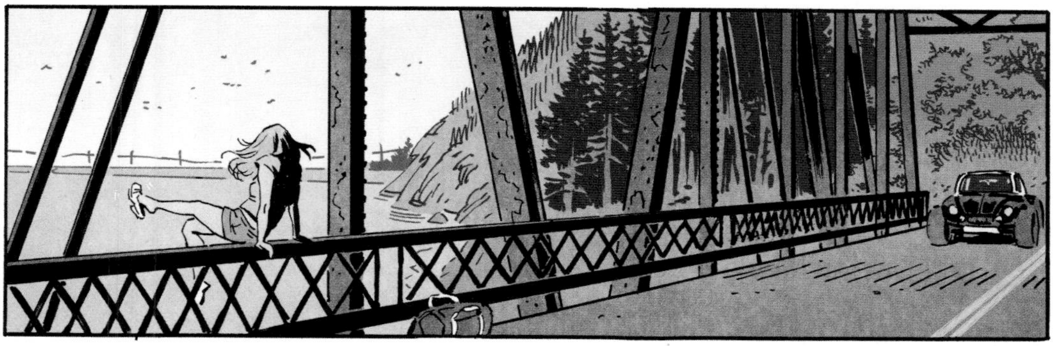

BRODY ISLAND, MAINE.

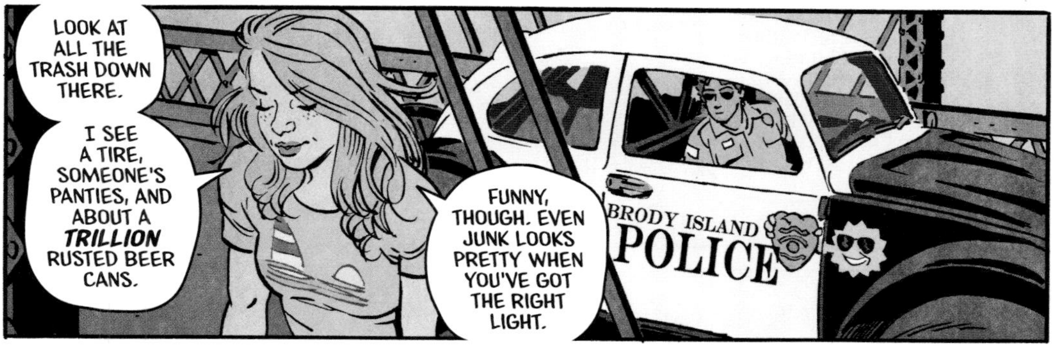
LOOK AT ALL THE TRASH DOWN THERE.
I SEE A TIRE, SOMEONE'S PANTIES, AND ABOUT A ***TRILLION*** RUSTED BEER CANS.
FUNNY, THOUGH. EVEN JUNK LOOKS PRETTY WHEN YOU'VE GOT THE RIGHT LIGHT.
BRODY ISLAND
POLICE

SEPTEMBER 1983.

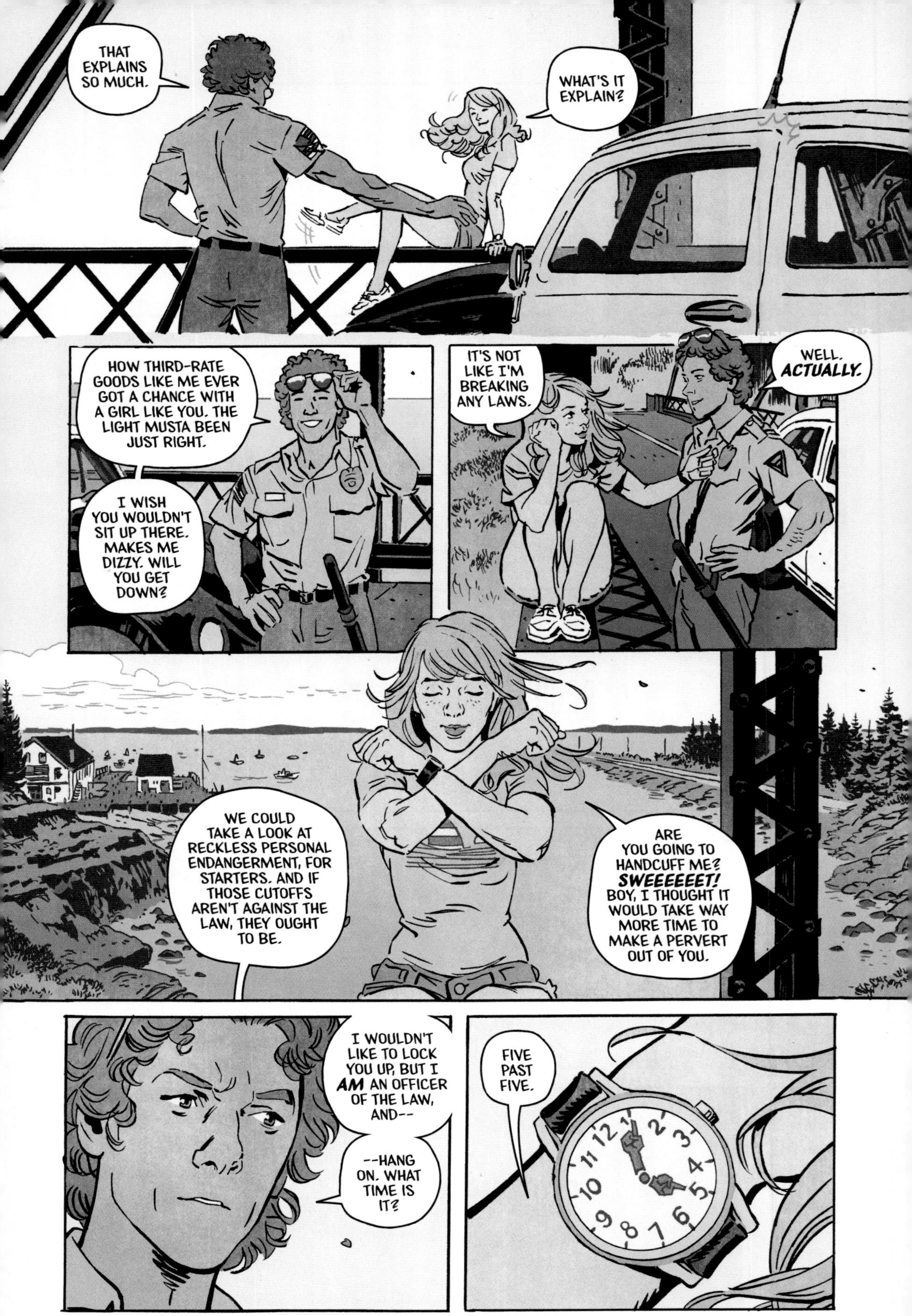
THAT EXPLAINS SO MUCH.
WHAT'S IT EXPLAIN?
HOW THIRD-RATE GOODS LIKE ME EVER GOT A CHANCE WITH A GIRL LIKE YOU. THE LIGHT MUSTA BEEN JUST RIGHT.
I WISH YOU WOULDN'T SIT UP THERE. MAKES ME DIZZY. WILL YOU GET DOWN?
IT'S NOT LIKE I'M BREAKING ANY LAWS.
WELL. ACTUALLY.
WE COULD TAKE A LOOK AT RECKLESS PERSONAL ENDANGERMENT, FOR STARTERS. AND IF THOSE CUTOFFS AREN'T AGAINST THE LAW, THEY OUGHT TO BE.
ARE YOU GOING TO HANDCUFF ME? SWEEEEEET! BOY, I THOUGHT IT WOULD TAKE WAY MORE TIME TO MAKE A PERVERT OUT OF YOU.
I WOULDN'T LIKE TO LOCK YOU UP, BUT I AM AN OFFICER OF THE LAW, AND--
--HANG ON. WHAT TIME IS IT?
FIVE PAST FIVE.

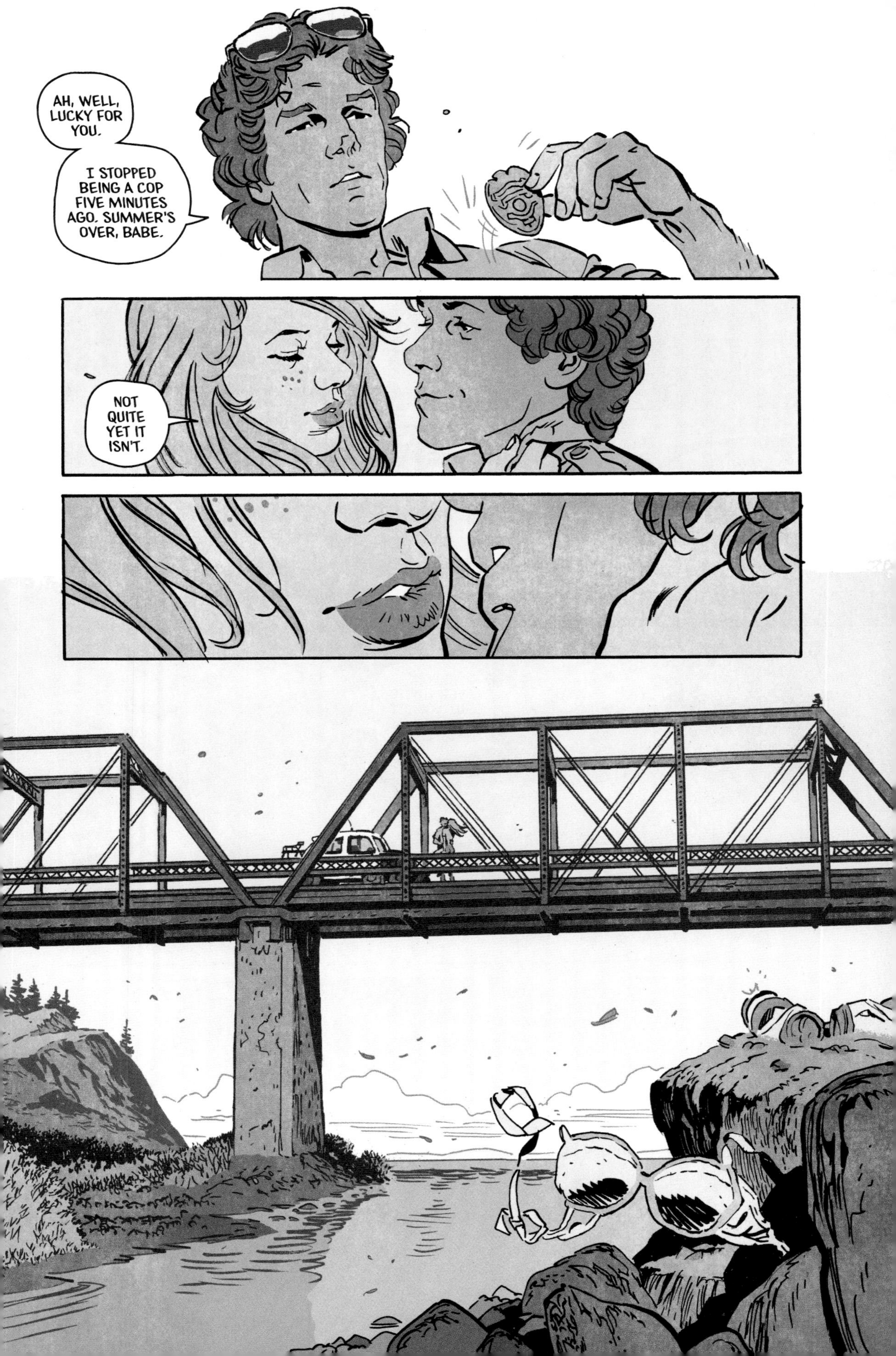
AH, WELL, LUCKY FOR YOU.
I STOPPED BEING A COP FIVE MINUTES AGO. SUMMER'S OVER, BABE.
NOT QUITE YET IT ISN'T.

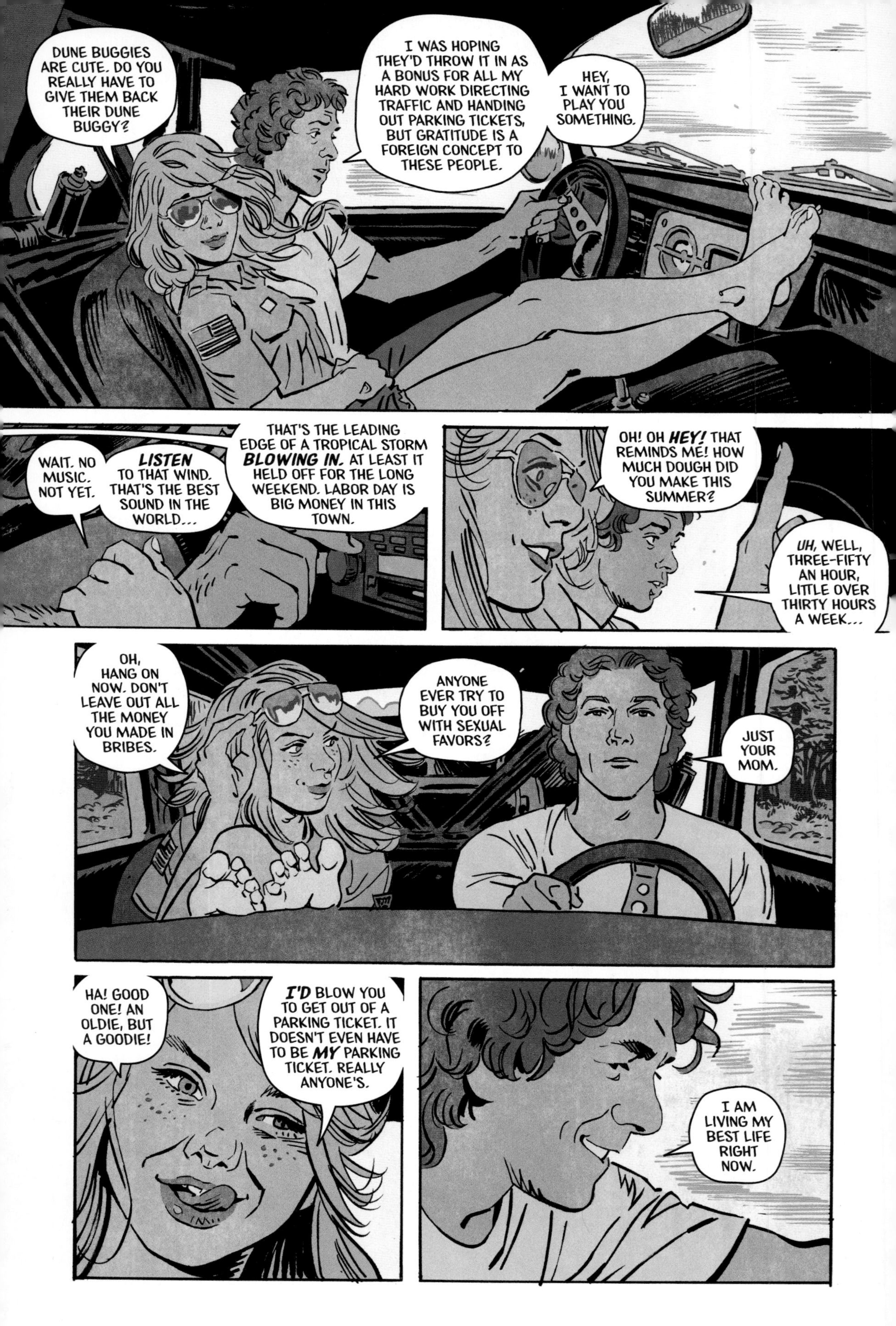
DUNE BUGGIES ARE CUTE. DO YOU REALLY HAVE TO GIVE THEM BACK THEIR DUNE BUGGY?
I WAS HOPING THEY'D THROW IT IN AS A BONUS FOR ALL MY HARD WORK DIRECTING TRAFFIC AND HANDING OUT PARKING TICKETS, BUT GRATITUDE IS A FOREIGN CONCEPT TO THESE PEOPLE.
HEY, I WANT TO PLAY YOU SOMETHING.
WAIT. NO MUSIC. NOT YET.
LISTEN TO THAT WIND. THAT'S THE BEST SOUND IN THE WORLD...
THAT'S THE LEADING EDGE OF A TROPICAL STORM BLOWING IN. AT LEAST IT HELD OFF FOR THE LONG WEEKEND. LABOR DAY IS BIG MONEY IN THIS TOWN.
OH! OH HEY! THAT REMINDS ME! HOW MUCH DOUGH DID YOU MAKE THIS SUMMER?
UH, WELL, THREE-FIFTY AN HOUR, LITTLE OVER THIRTY HOURS A WEEK...
OH, HANG ON NOW. DON'T LEAVE OUT ALL THE MONEY YOU MADE IN BRIBES.
ANYONE EVER TRY TO BUY YOU OFF WITH SEXUAL FAVORS?
JUST YOUR MOM.
HA! GOOD ONE! AN OLDIE, BUT A GOODIE!
I'D BLOW YOU TO GET OUT OF A PARKING TICKET. IT DOESN'T EVEN HAVE TO BE MY PARKING TICKET. REALLY ANYONE'S.
I AM LIVING MY BEST LIFE RIGHT NOW.

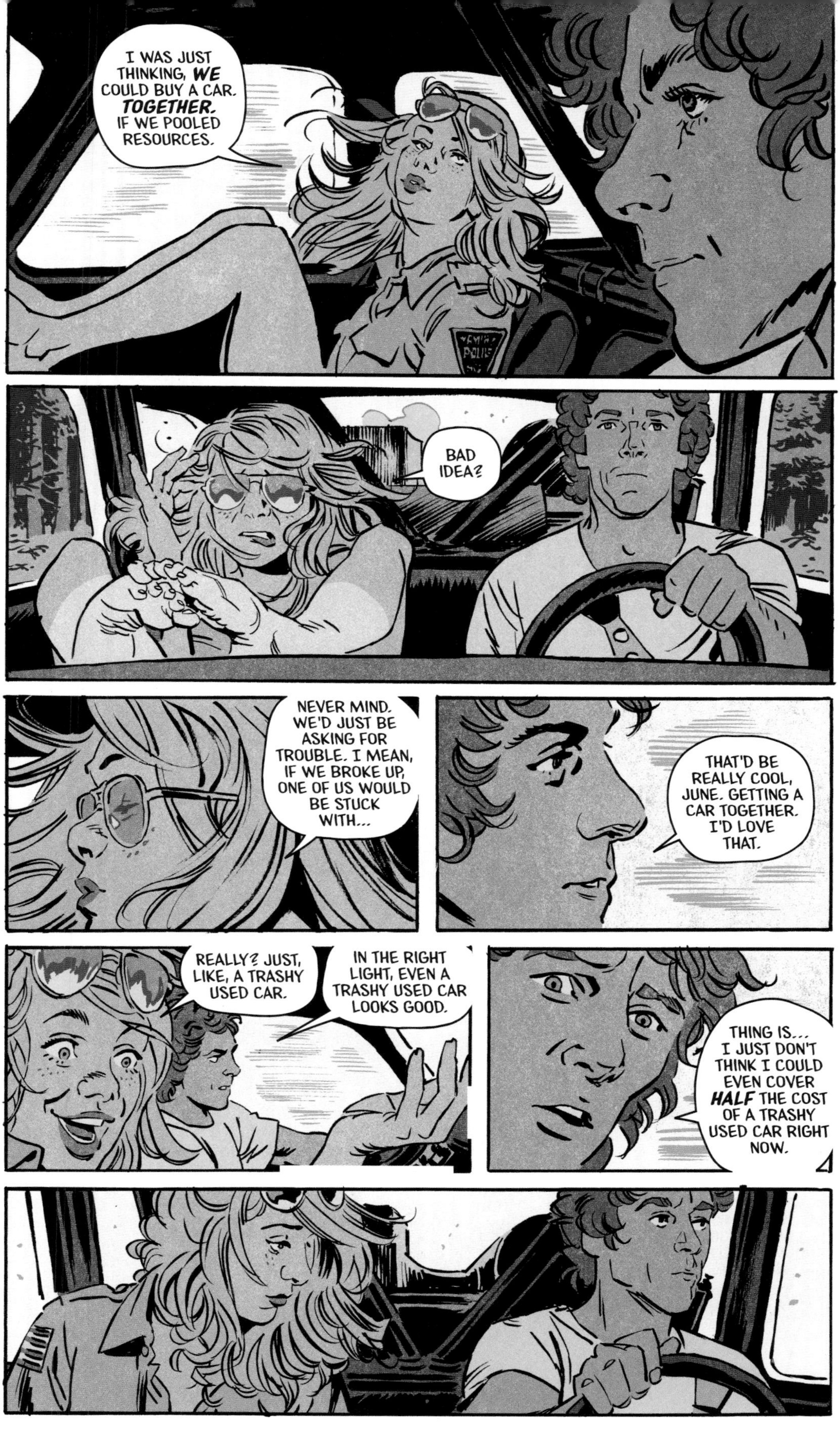
I WAS JUST THINKING, WE COULD BUY A CAR. TOGETHER. IF WE POOLED RESOURCES.
BAD IDEA?
NEVER MIND. WE'D JUST BE ASKING FOR TROUBLE. I MEAN, IF WE BROKE UP, ONE OF US WOULD BE STUCK WITH...
THAT'D BE REALLY COOL, JUNE. GETTING A CAR TOGETHER. I'D LOVE THAT.
REALLY? JUST, LIKE, A TRASHY USED CAR.
IN THE RIGHT LIGHT, EVEN A TRASHY USED CAR LOOKS GOOD.
THING IS... I JUST DON'T THINK I COULD EVEN COVER HALF THE COST OF A TRASHY USED CAR RIGHT NOW.

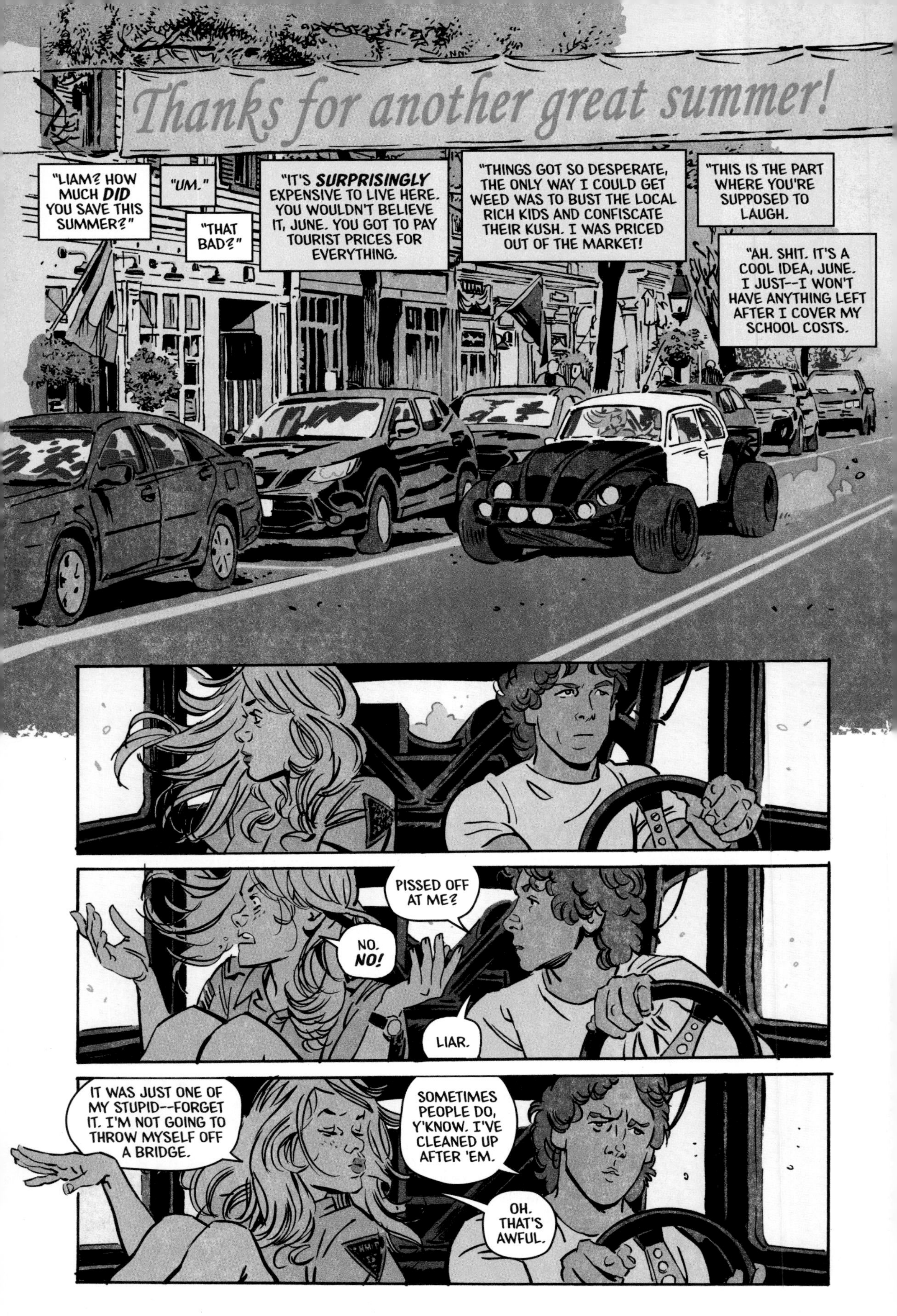
Thanks for another great summer!
"LIAM? HOW MUCH DID YOU SAVE THIS SUMMER?"
"UM."
"THAT BAD?"
"IT'S SURPRISINGLY EXPENSIVE TO LIVE HERE. YOU WOULDN'T BELIEVE IT, JUNE. YOU GOT TO PAY TOURIST PRICES FOR EVERYTHING.
"THINGS GOT SO DESPERATE, THE ONLY WAY I COULD GET WEED WAS TO BUST THE LOCAL RICH KIDS AND CONFISCATE THEIR KUSH. I WAS PRICED OUT OF THE MARKET!
"THIS IS THE PART WHERE YOU'RE SUPPOSED TO LAUGH.
"AH. SHIT. IT'S A COOL IDEA, JUNE. I JUST--I WON'T HAVE ANYTHING LEFT AFTER I COVER MY SCHOOL COSTS.
PISSED OFF AT ME?
NO. NO!
LIAR.
IT WAS JUST ONE OF MY STUPID--FORGET IT. I'M NOT GOING TO THROW MYSELF OFF A BRIDGE.
SOMETIMES PEOPLE DO, Y'KNOW. I'VE CLEANED UP AFTER 'EM.
OH. THAT'S AWFUL.

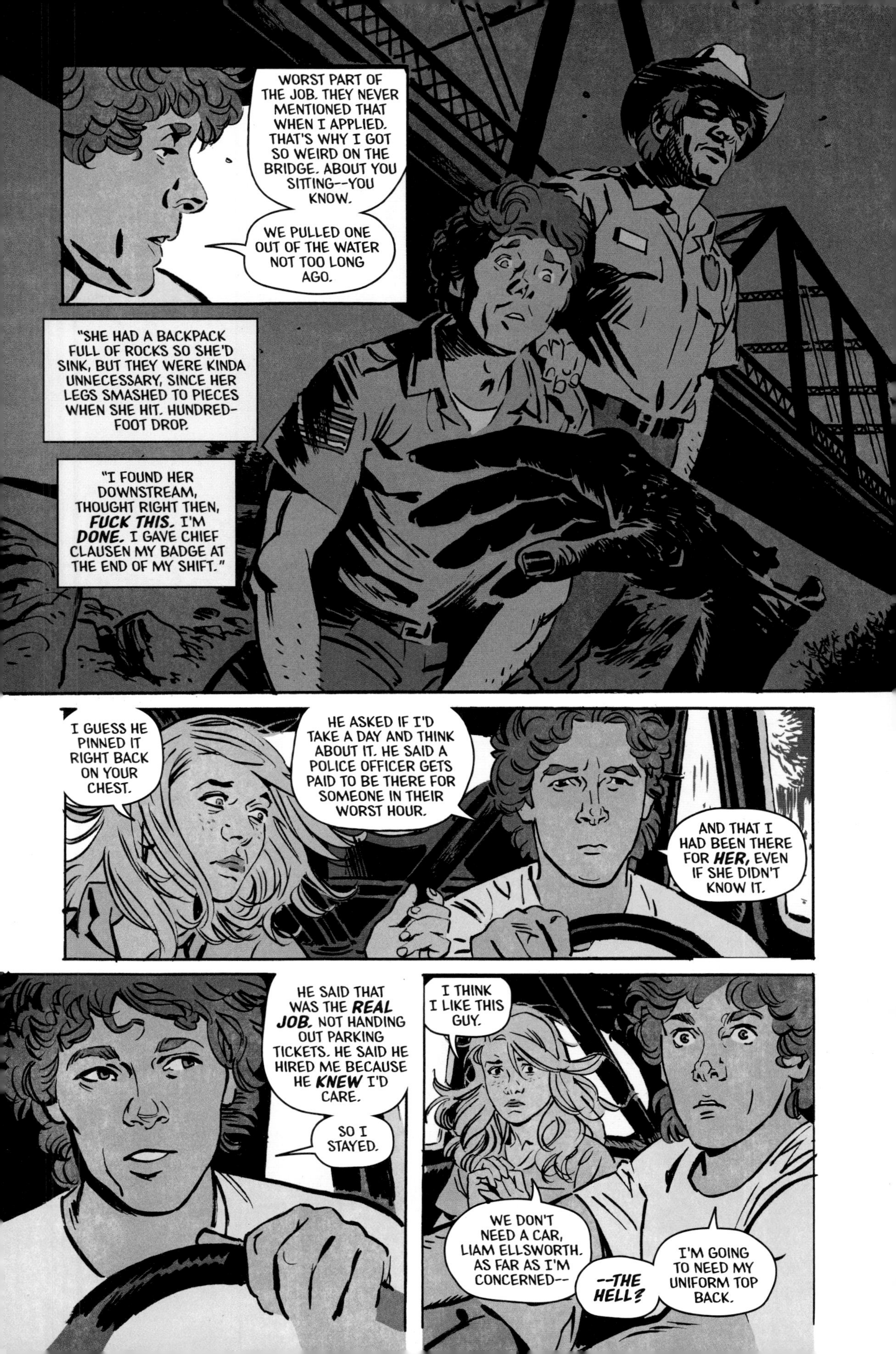
WORST PART OF THE JOB. THEY NEVER MENTIONED THAT WHEN I APPLIED. THAT'S WHY I GOT SO WEIRD ON THE BRIDGE. ABOUT YOU SITTING--YOU KNOW.
WE PULLED ONE OUT OF THE WATER NOT TOO LONG AGO.
"SHE HAD A BACKPACK FULL OF ROCKS SO SHE'D SINK, BUT THEY WERE KINDA UNNECESSARY, SINCE HER LEGS SMASHED TO PIECES WHEN SHE HIT. HUNDRED-FOOT DROP.
"I FOUND HER DOWNSTREAM, THOUGHT RIGHT THEN, ***FUCK THIS.*** I'M ***DONE.*** I GAVE CHIEF CLAUSEN MY BADGE AT THE END OF MY SHIFT."
I GUESS HE PINNED IT RIGHT BACK ON YOUR CHEST.
HE ASKED IF I'D TAKE A DAY AND THINK ABOUT IT. HE SAID A POLICE OFFICER GETS PAID TO BE THERE FOR SOMEONE IN THEIR WORST HOUR.
AND THAT I HAD BEEN THERE FOR ***HER,*** EVEN IF SHE DIDN'T KNOW IT.
HE SAID THAT WAS THE ***REAL JOB.*** NOT HANDING OUT PARKING TICKETS. HE SAID HE HIRED ME BECAUSE HE ***KNEW*** I'D CARE.
SO I STAYED.
I THINK I LIKE THIS GUY.
WE DON'T NEED A CAR, LIAM ELLSWORTH. AS FAR AS I'M CONCERNED--
--THE HELL?
I'M GOING TO NEED MY UNIFORM TOP BACK.

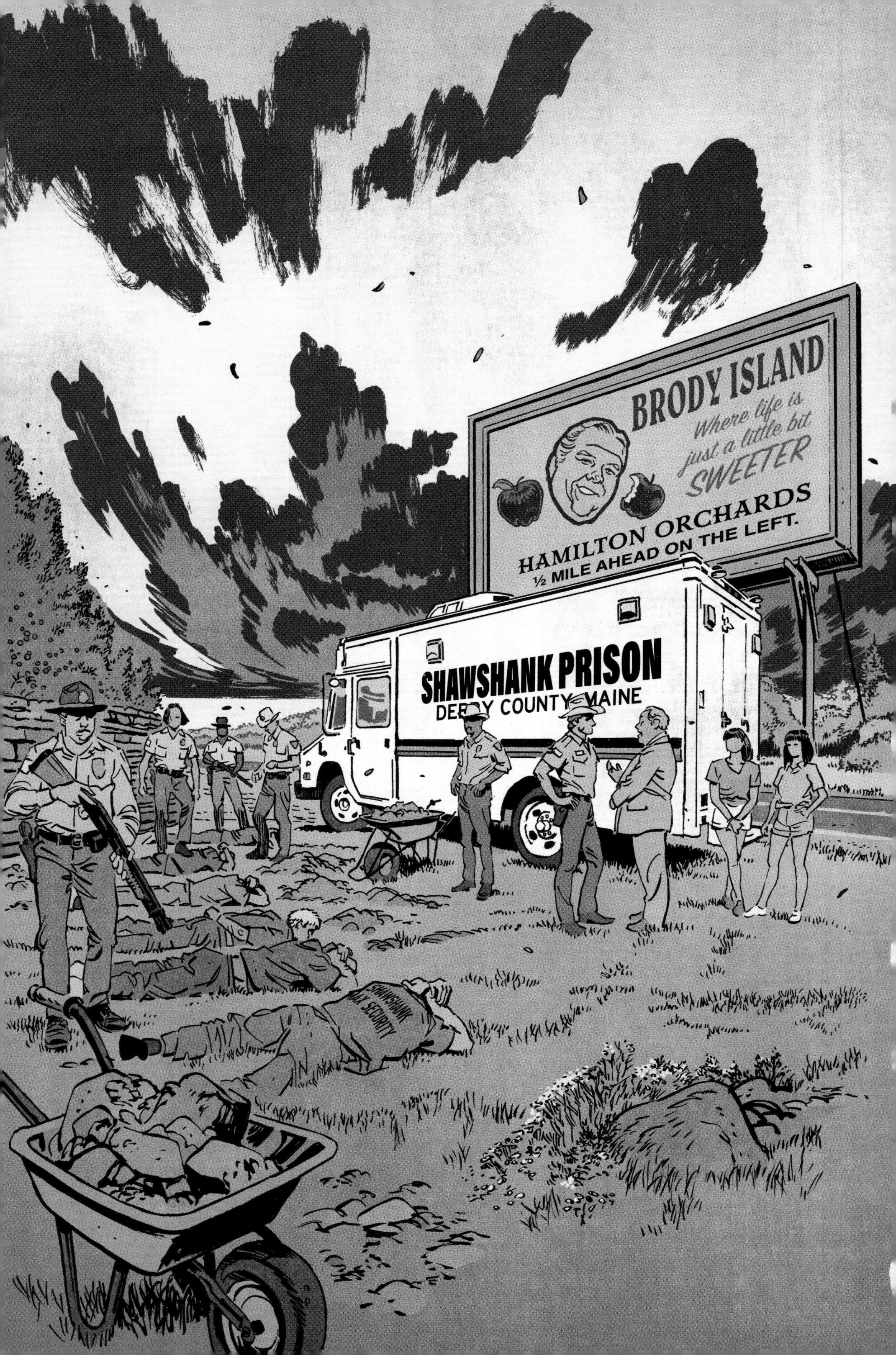
BRODY ISLAND
Where life is just a little bit SWEETER
HAMILTON ORCHARDS
½ MILE AHEAD ON THE LEFT.
SHAWSHANK PRISON

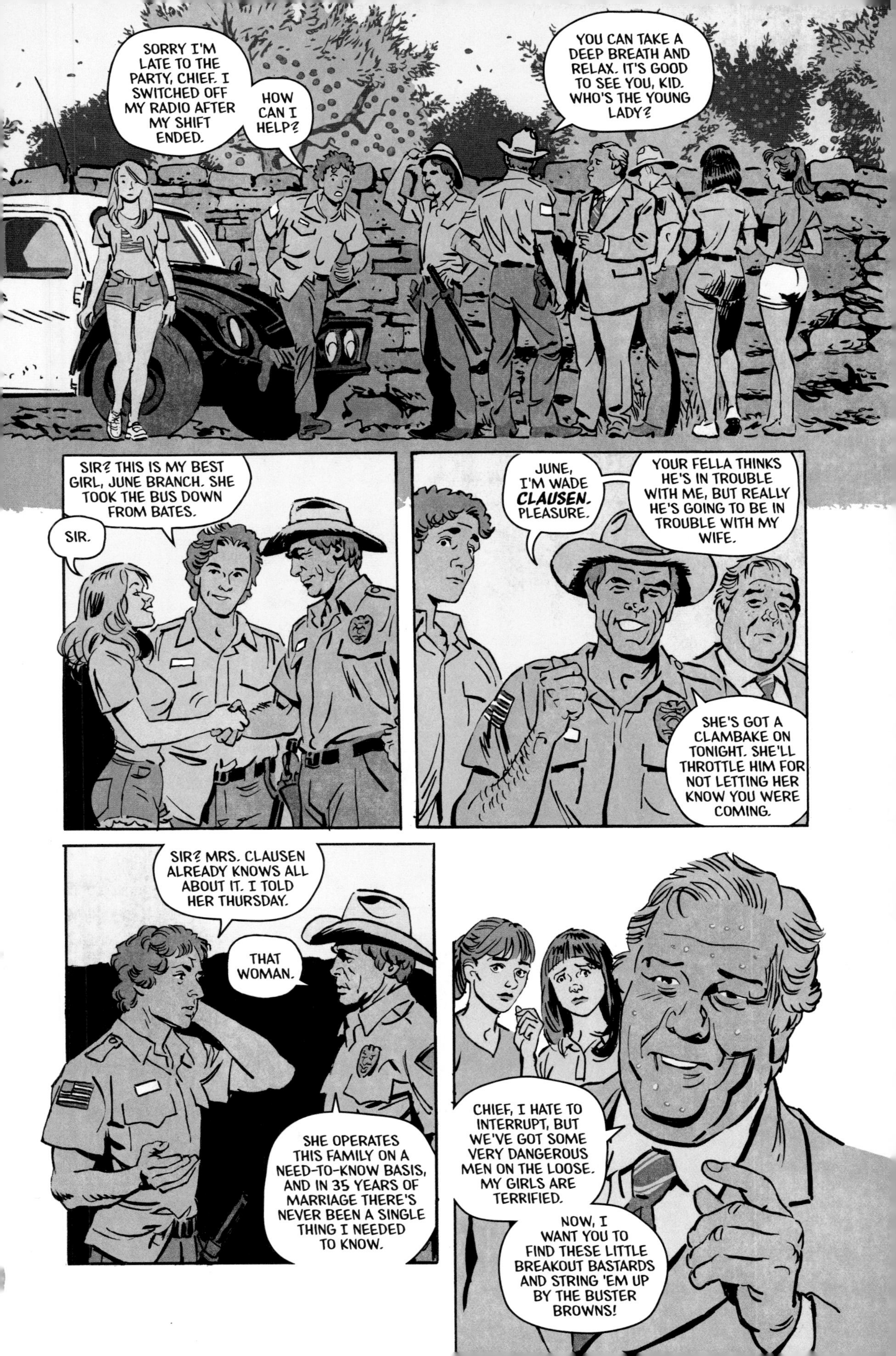
SORRY I'M LATE TO THE PARTY, CHIEF. I SWITCHED OFF MY RADIO AFTER MY SHIFT ENDED.
HOW CAN I HELP?
YOU CAN TAKE A DEEP BREATH AND RELAX. IT'S GOOD TO SEE YOU, KID. WHO'S THE YOUNG LADY?
SIR? THIS IS MY BEST GIRL, JUNE BRANCH. SHE TOOK THE BUS DOWN FROM BATES.
SIR.
JUNE, I'M WADE CLAUSEN. PLEASURE.
YOUR FELLA THINKS HE'S IN TROUBLE WITH ME, BUT REALLY HE'S GOING TO BE IN TROUBLE WITH MY WIFE.
SHE'S GOT A CLAMBAKE ON TONIGHT. SHE'LL THROTTLE HIM FOR NOT LETTING HER KNOW YOU WERE COMING.
SIR? MRS. CLAUSEN ALREADY KNOWS ALL ABOUT IT. I TOLD HER THURSDAY.
THAT WOMAN.
SHE OPERATES THIS FAMILY ON A NEED-TO-KNOW BASIS, AND IN 35 YEARS OF MARRIAGE THERE'S NEVER BEEN A SINGLE THING I NEEDED TO KNOW.
CHIEF, I HATE TO INTERRUPT, BUT WE'VE GOT SOME VERY DANGEROUS MEN ON THE LOOSE. MY GIRLS ARE TERRIFIED.
NOW, I WANT YOU TO FIND THESE LITTLE BREAKOUT BASTARDS AND STRING 'EM UP BY THE BUSTER BROWNS!

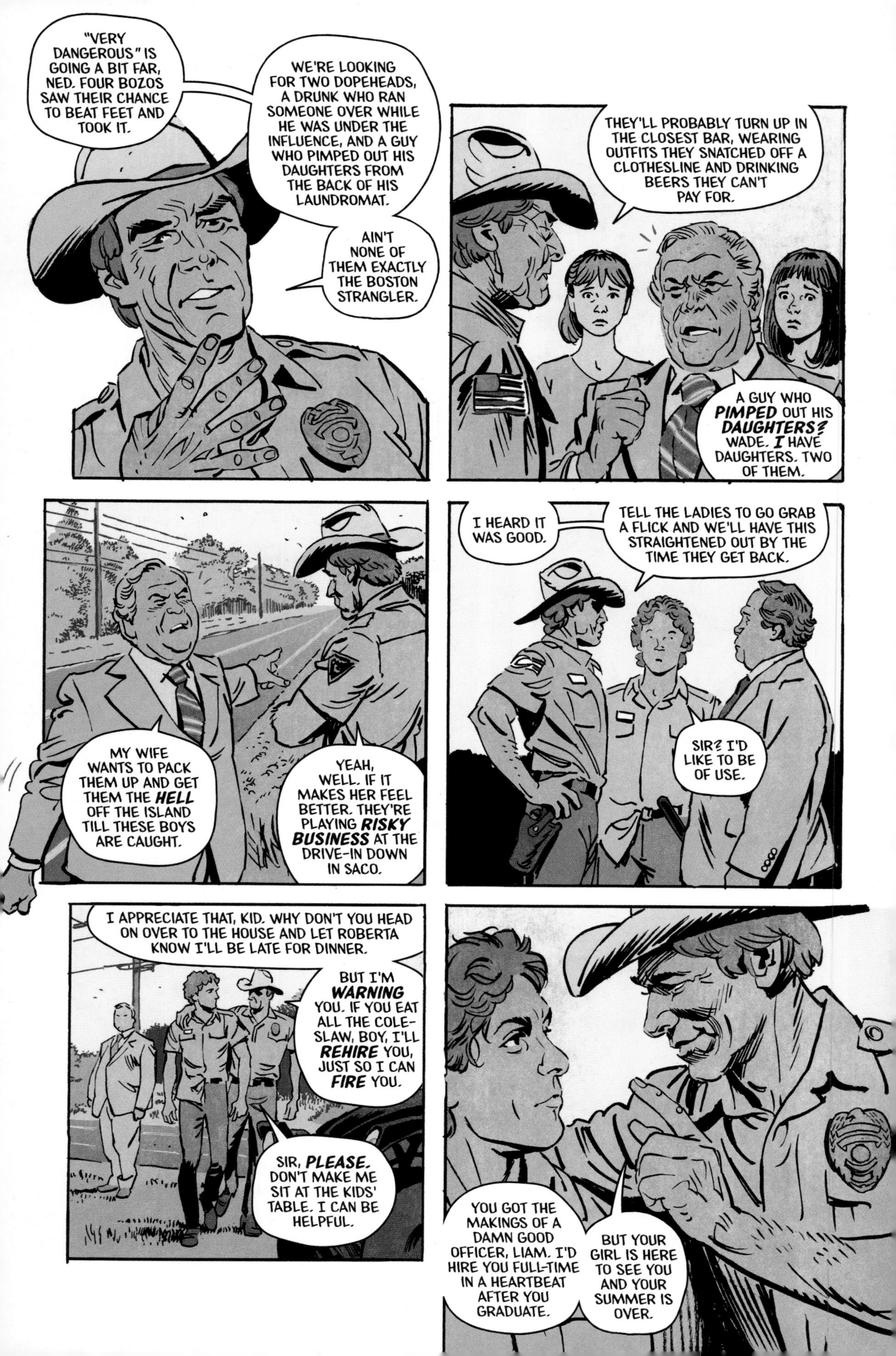
"VERY DANGEROUS" IS GOING A BIT FAR, NED. FOUR BOZOS SAW THEIR CHANCE TO BEAT FEET AND TOOK IT.
WE'RE LOOKING FOR TWO DOPEHEADS, A DRUNK WHO RAN SOMEONE OVER WHILE HE WAS UNDER THE INFLUENCE, AND A GUY WHO PIMPED OUT HIS DAUGHTERS FROM THE BACK OF HIS LAUNDROMAT.
AIN'T NONE OF THEM EXACTLY THE BOSTON STRANGLER.
THEY'LL PROBABLY TURN UP IN THE CLOSEST BAR, WEARING OUTFITS THEY SNATCHED OFF A CLOTHESLINE AND DRINKING BEERS THEY CAN'T PAY FOR.
A GUY WHO PIMPED OUT HIS DAUGHTERS? WADE. I HAVE DAUGHTERS. TWO OF THEM.
MY WIFE WANTS TO PACK THEM UP AND GET THEM THE HELL OFF THE ISLAND TILL THESE BOYS ARE CAUGHT.
YEAH, WELL. IF IT MAKES HER FEEL BETTER, THEY'RE PLAYING RISKY BUSINESS AT THE DRIVE-IN DOWN IN SACO.
I HEARD IT WAS GOOD.
TELL THE LADIES TO GO GRAB A FLICK AND WE'LL HAVE THIS STRAIGHTENED OUT BY THE TIME THEY GET BACK.
SIR? I'D LIKE TO BE OF USE.
I APPRECIATE THAT, KID. WHY DON'T YOU HEAD ON OVER TO THE HOUSE AND LET ROBERTA KNOW I'LL BE LATE FOR DINNER.
BUT I'M WARNING YOU. IF YOU EAT ALL THE COLE-SLAW, BOY, I'LL REHIRE YOU, JUST SO I CAN FIRE YOU.
SIR, PLEASE. DON'T MAKE ME SIT AT THE KIDS' TABLE. I CAN BE HELPFUL.
YOU GOT THE MAKINGS OF A DAMN GOOD OFFICER, LIAM. I'D HIRE YOU FULL-TIME IN A HEARTBEAT AFTER YOU GRADUATE.
BUT YOUR GIRL IS HERE TO SEE YOU AND YOUR SUMMER IS OVER.

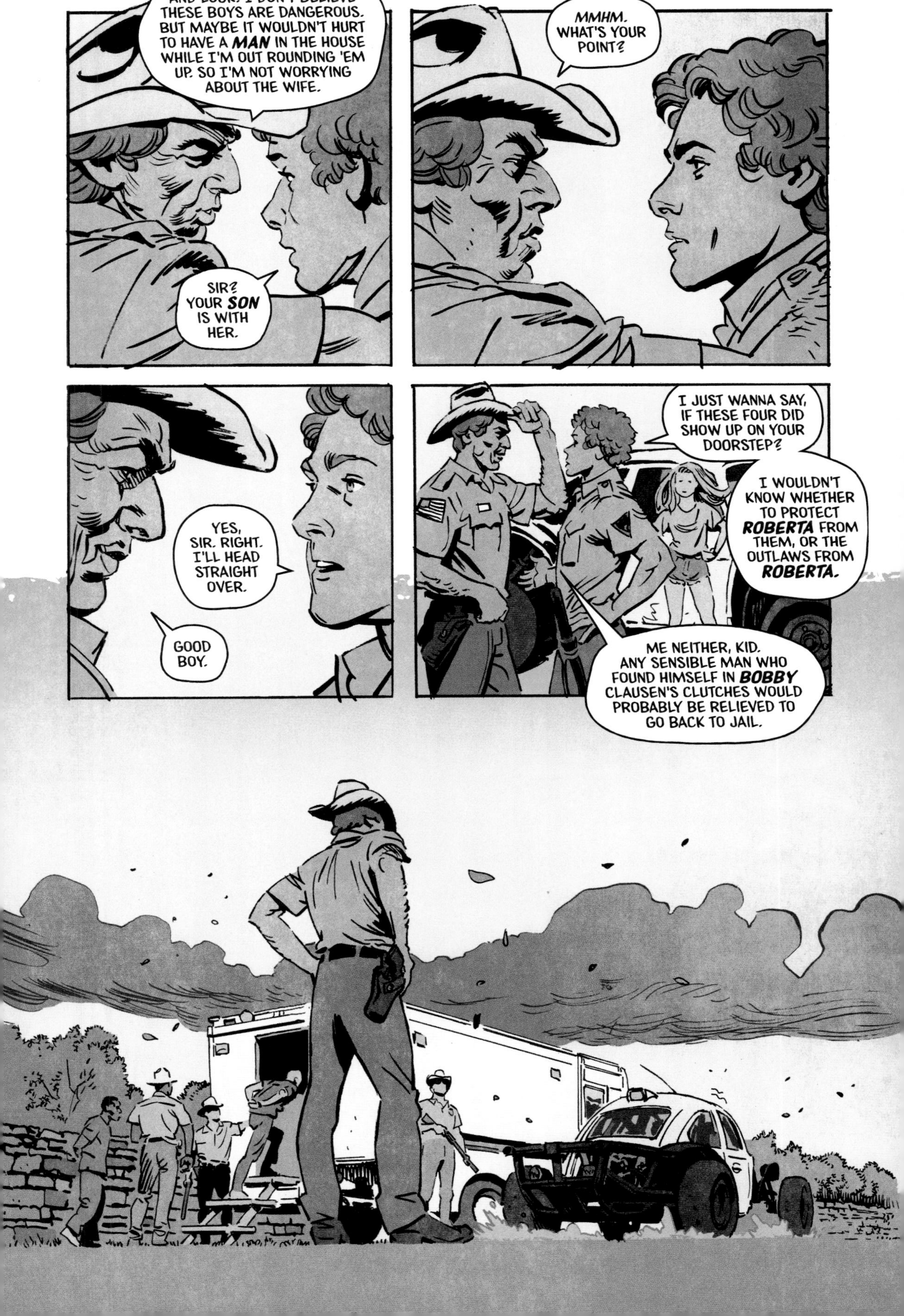
AND LOOK. I DON'T BELIEVE THESE BOYS ARE DANGEROUS. BUT MAYBE IT WOULDN'T HURT TO HAVE A MAN IN THE HOUSE WHILE I'M OUT ROUNDING 'EM UP. SO I'M NOT WORRYING ABOUT THE WIFE.
SIR? YOUR SON IS WITH HER.
MMHM. WHAT'S YOUR POINT?
YES, SIR. RIGHT. I'LL HEAD STRAIGHT OVER.
GOOD BOY.
I JUST WANNA SAY, IF THESE FOUR DID SHOW UP ON YOUR DOORSTEP?
I WOULDN'T KNOW WHETHER TO PROTECT ROBERTA FROM THEM, OR THE OUTLAWS FROM ROBERTA.
ME NEITHER, KID. ANY SENSIBLE MAN WHO FOUND HIMSELF IN BOBBY CLAUSEN'S CLUTCHES WOULD PROBABLY BE RELIEVED TO GO BACK TO JAIL.

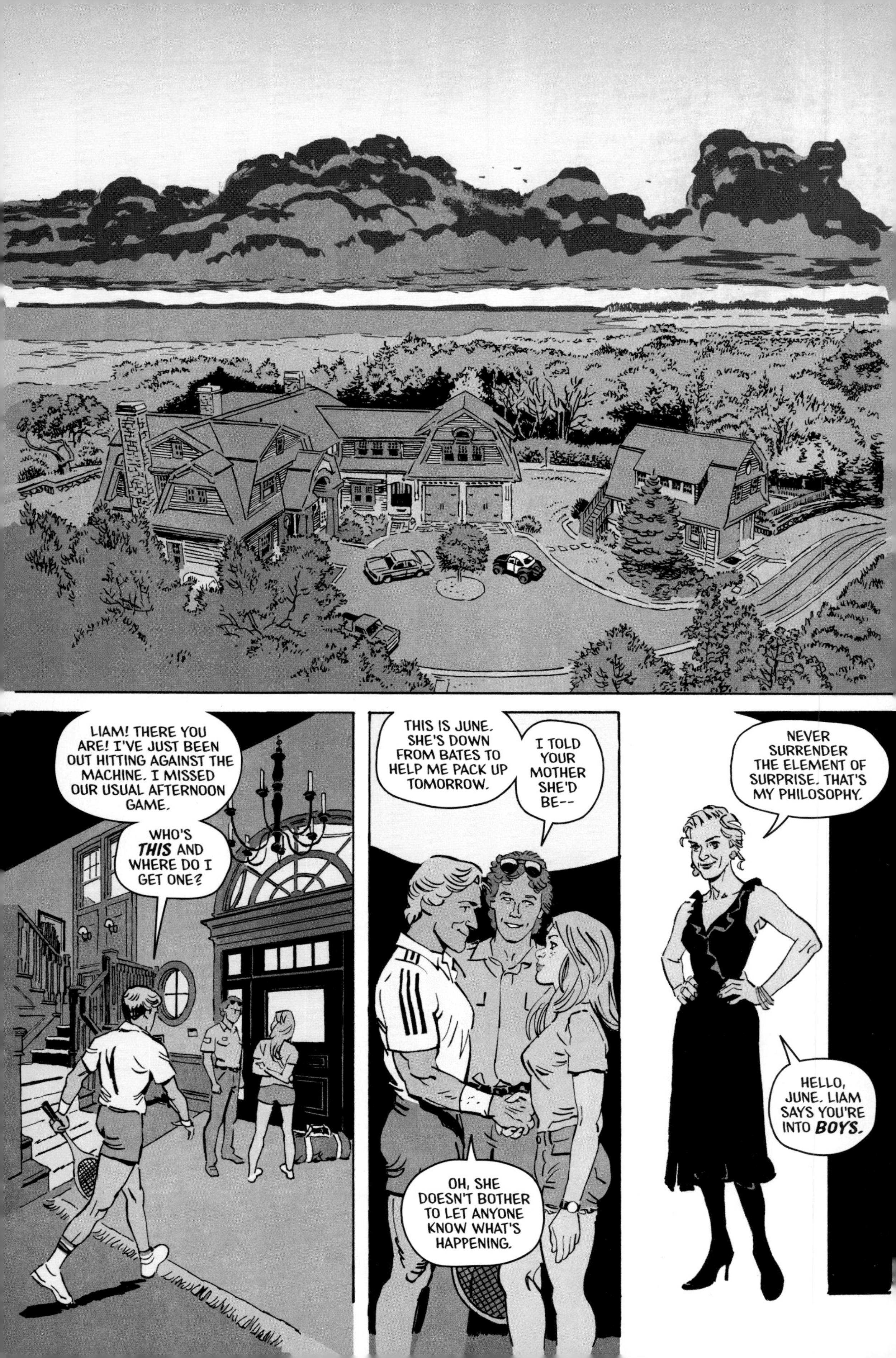
LIAM! THERE YOU ARE! I'VE JUST BEEN OUT HITTING AGAINST THE MACHINE. I MISSED OUR USUAL AFTERNOON GAME.
WHO'S THIS AND WHERE DO I GET ONE?
THIS IS JUNE. SHE'S DOWN FROM BATES TO HELP ME PACK UP TOMORROW.
I TOLD YOUR MOTHER SHE'D BE--
OH, SHE DOESN'T BOTHER TO LET ANYONE KNOW WHAT'S HAPPENING.
NEVER SURRENDER THE ELEMENT OF SURPRISE. THAT'S MY PHILOSOPHY.
HELLO, JUNE. LIAM SAYS YOU'RE INTO BOYS.

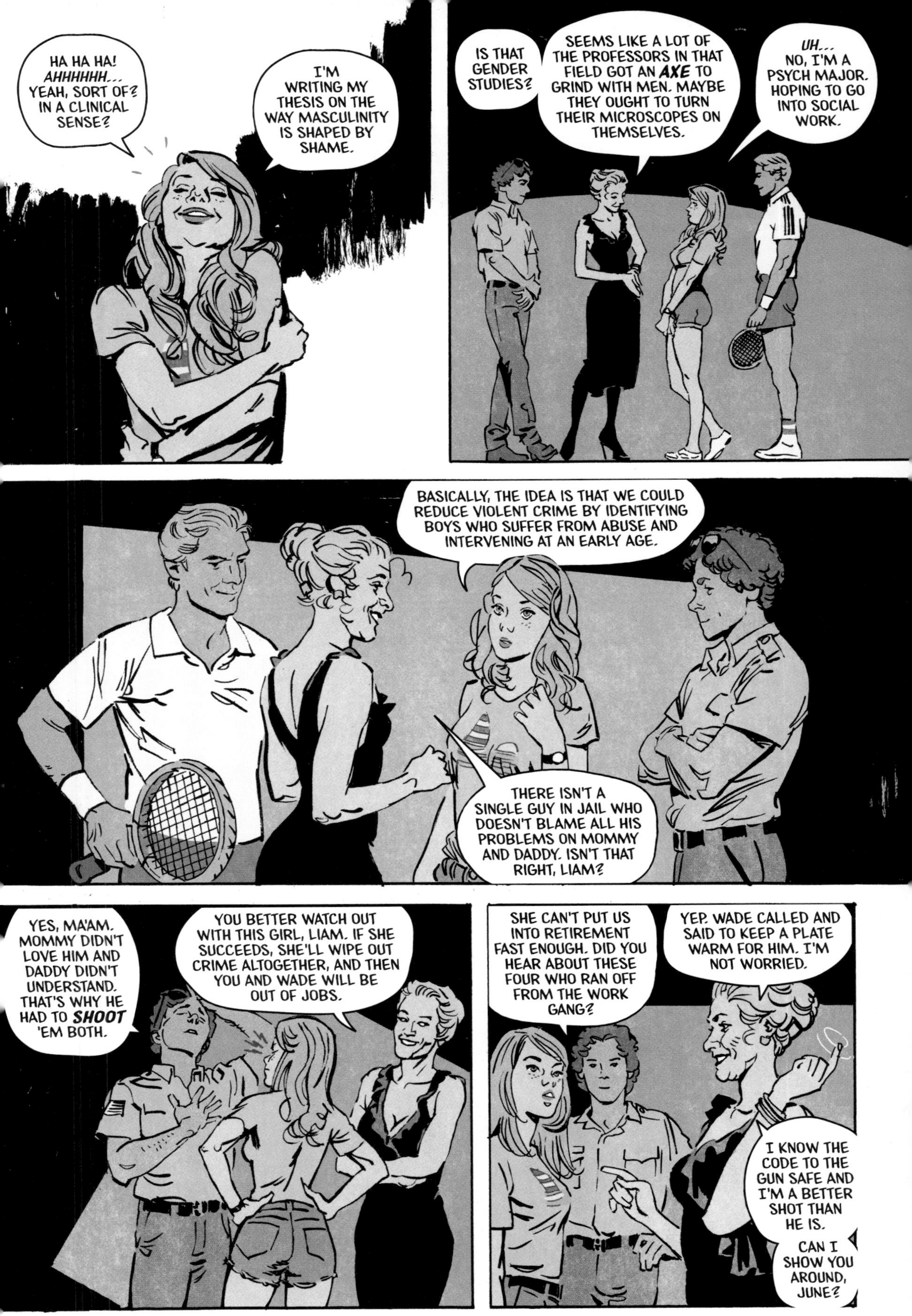
HA HA HA! AHHHHHH... YEAH, SORT OF? IN A CLINICAL SENSE?
I'M WRITING MY THESIS ON THE WAY MASCULINITY IS SHAPED BY SHAME.
IS THAT GENDER STUDIES?
SEEMS LIKE A LOT OF THE PROFESSORS IN THAT FIELD GOT AN AXE TO GRIND WITH MEN. MAYBE THEY OUGHT TO TURN THEIR MICROSCOPES ON THEMSELVES.
UH... NO, I'M A PSYCH MAJOR. HOPING TO GO INTO SOCIAL WORK.
BASICALLY, THE IDEA IS THAT WE COULD REDUCE VIOLENT CRIME BY IDENTIFYING BOYS WHO SUFFER FROM ABUSE AND INTERVENING AT AN EARLY AGE.
THERE ISN'T A SINGLE GUY IN JAIL WHO DOESN'T BLAME ALL HIS PROBLEMS ON MOMMY AND DADDY. ISN'T THAT RIGHT, LIAM?
YES, MA'AM. MOMMY DIDN'T LOVE HIM AND DADDY DIDN'T UNDERSTAND. THAT'S WHY HE HAD TO SHOOT 'EM BOTH.
YOU BETTER WATCH OUT WITH THIS GIRL, LIAM. IF SHE SUCCEEDS, SHE'LL WIPE OUT CRIME ALTOGETHER, AND THEN YOU AND WADE WILL BE OUT OF JOBS.
SHE CAN'T PUT US INTO RETIREMENT FAST ENOUGH. DID YOU HEAR ABOUT THESE FOUR WHO RAN OFF FROM THE WORK GANG?
YEP. WADE CALLED AND SAID TO KEEP A PLATE WARM FOR HIM. I'M NOT WORRIED.
I KNOW THE CODE TO THE GUN SAFE AND I'M A BETTER SHOT THAN HE IS.
CAN I SHOW YOU AROUND, JUNE?

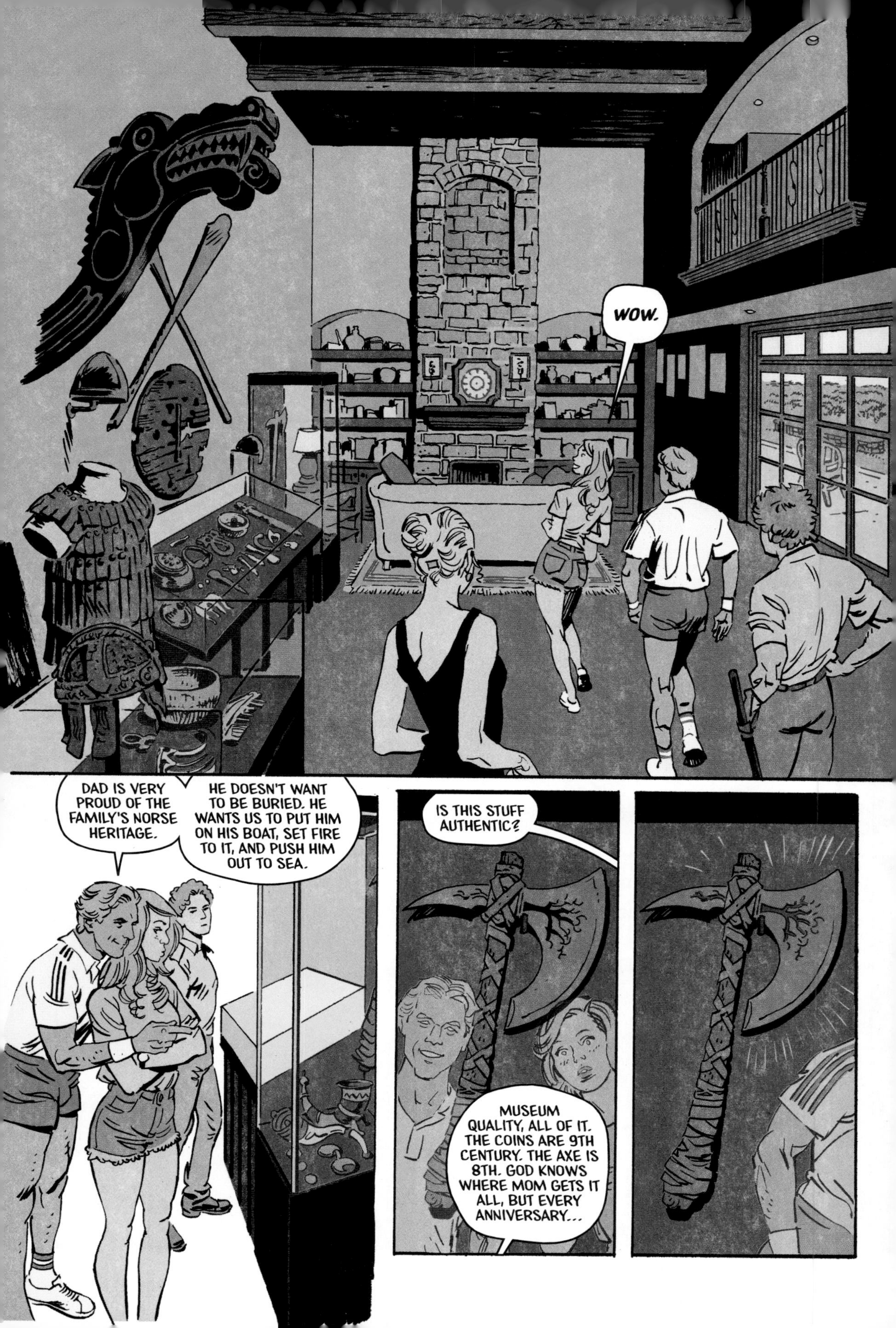
WOW.
DAD IS VERY PROUD OF THE FAMILY'S NORSE HERITAGE.
HE DOESN'T WANT TO BE BURIED. HE WANTS US TO PUT HIM ON HIS BOAT, SET FIRE TO IT, AND PUSH HIM OUT TO SEA.
IS THIS STUFF AUTHENTIC?
MUSEUM QUALITY, ALL OF IT. THE COINS ARE 9TH CENTURY. THE AXE IS 8TH. GOD KNOWS WHERE MOM GETS IT ALL, BUT EVERY ANNIVERSARY...

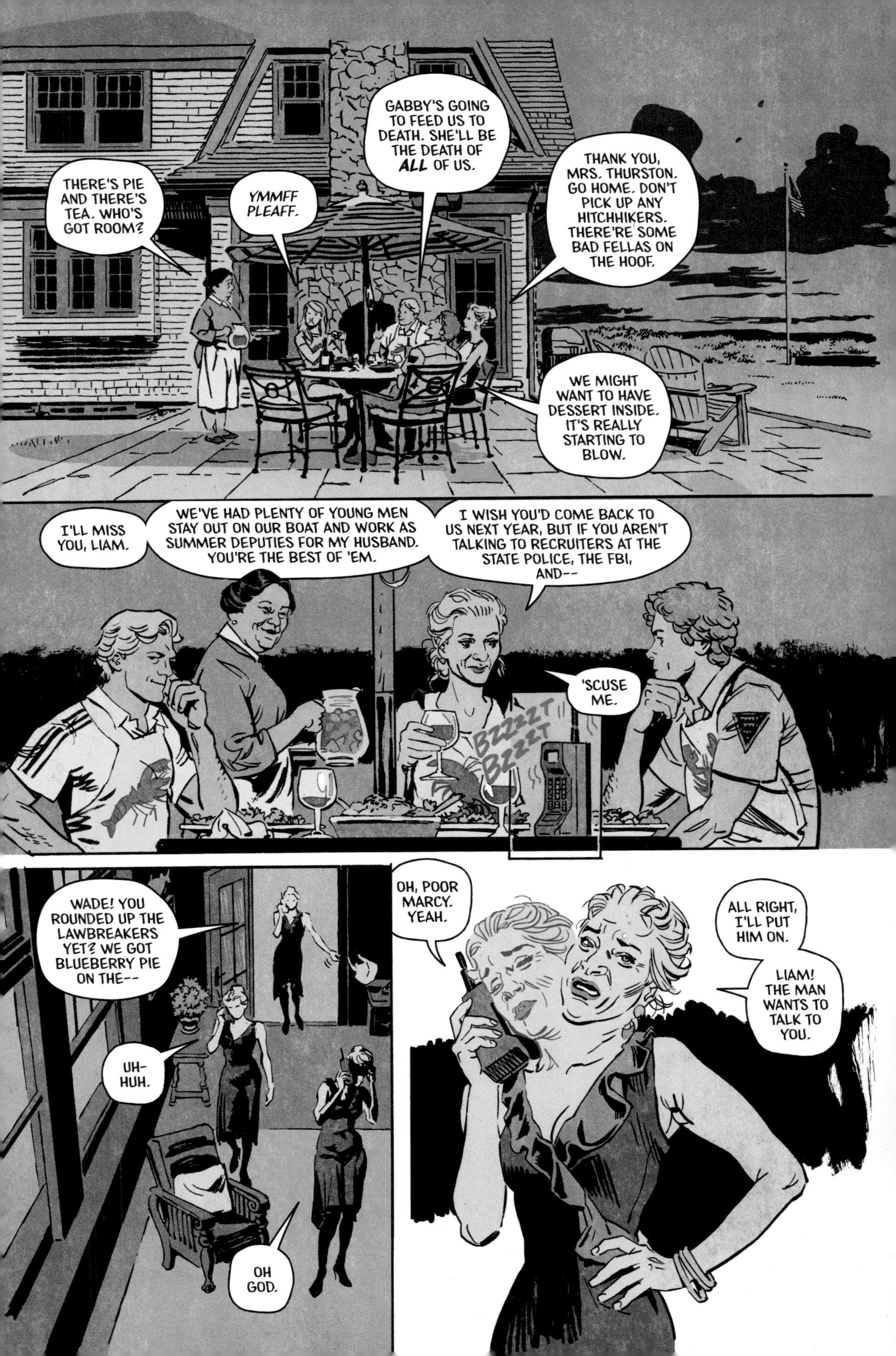
THERE'S PIE AND THERE'S TEA. WHO'S GOT ROOM?
YMMFF PLEAFF.
GABBY'S GOING TO FEED US TO DEATH. SHE'LL BE THE DEATH OF ***ALL*** OF US.
THANK YOU, MRS. THURSTON. GO HOME. DON'T PICK UP ANY HITCHHIKERS. THERE'RE SOME BAD FELLAS ON THE HOOF.
WE MIGHT WANT TO HAVE DESSERT INSIDE. IT'S REALLY STARTING TO BLOW.
I'LL MISS YOU, LIAM.
WE'VE HAD PLENTY OF YOUNG MEN STAY OUT ON OUR BOAT AND WORK AS SUMMER DEPUTIES FOR MY HUSBAND. YOU'RE THE BEST OF 'EM.
I WISH YOU'D COME BACK TO US NEXT YEAR, BUT IF YOU AREN'T TALKING TO RECRUITERS AT THE STATE POLICE, THE FBI, AND--
BZZZZT BZZZZT
'SCUSE ME.
WADE! YOU ROUNDED UP THE LAWBREAKERS YET? WE GOT BLUEBERRY PIE ON THE--
UH-HUH.
OH GOD.
OH, POOR MARCY. YEAH.
ALL RIGHT, I'LL PUT HIM ON.
LIAM! THE MAN WANTS TO TALK TO YOU.

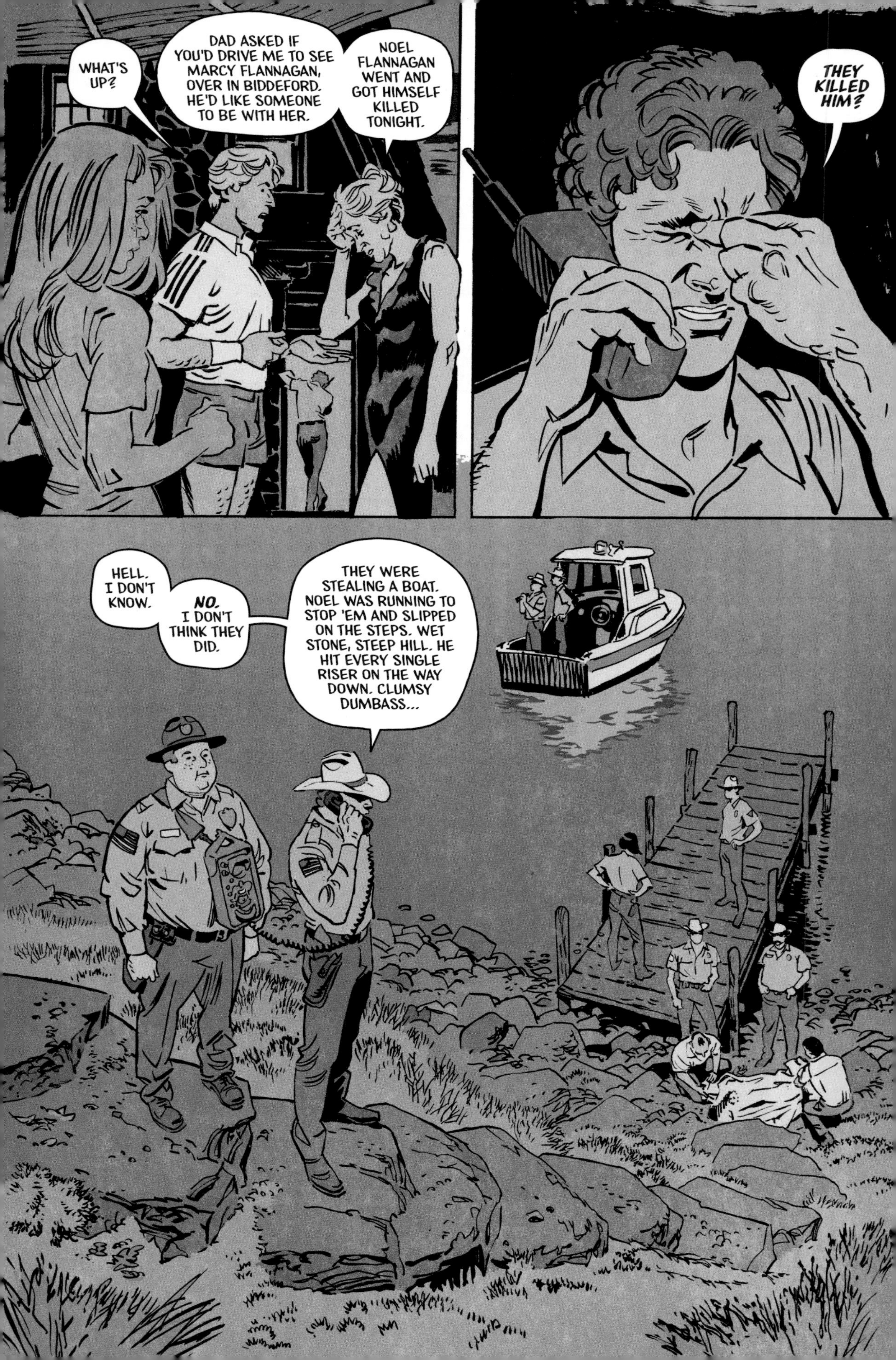
WHAT'S UP?
DAD ASKED IF YOU'D DRIVE ME TO SEE MARCY FLANNAGAN, OVER IN BIDDEFORD. HE'D LIKE SOMEONE TO BE WITH HER.
NOEL FLANNAGAN WENT AND GOT HIMSELF KILLED TONIGHT.
THEY KILLED HIM?
HELL. I DON'T KNOW.
NO. I DON'T THINK THEY DID.
THEY WERE STEALING A BOAT. NOEL WAS RUNNING TO STOP 'EM AND SLIPPED ON THE STEPS. WET STONE, STEEP HILL. HE HIT EVERY SINGLE RISER ON THE WAY DOWN. CLUMSY DUMBASS...

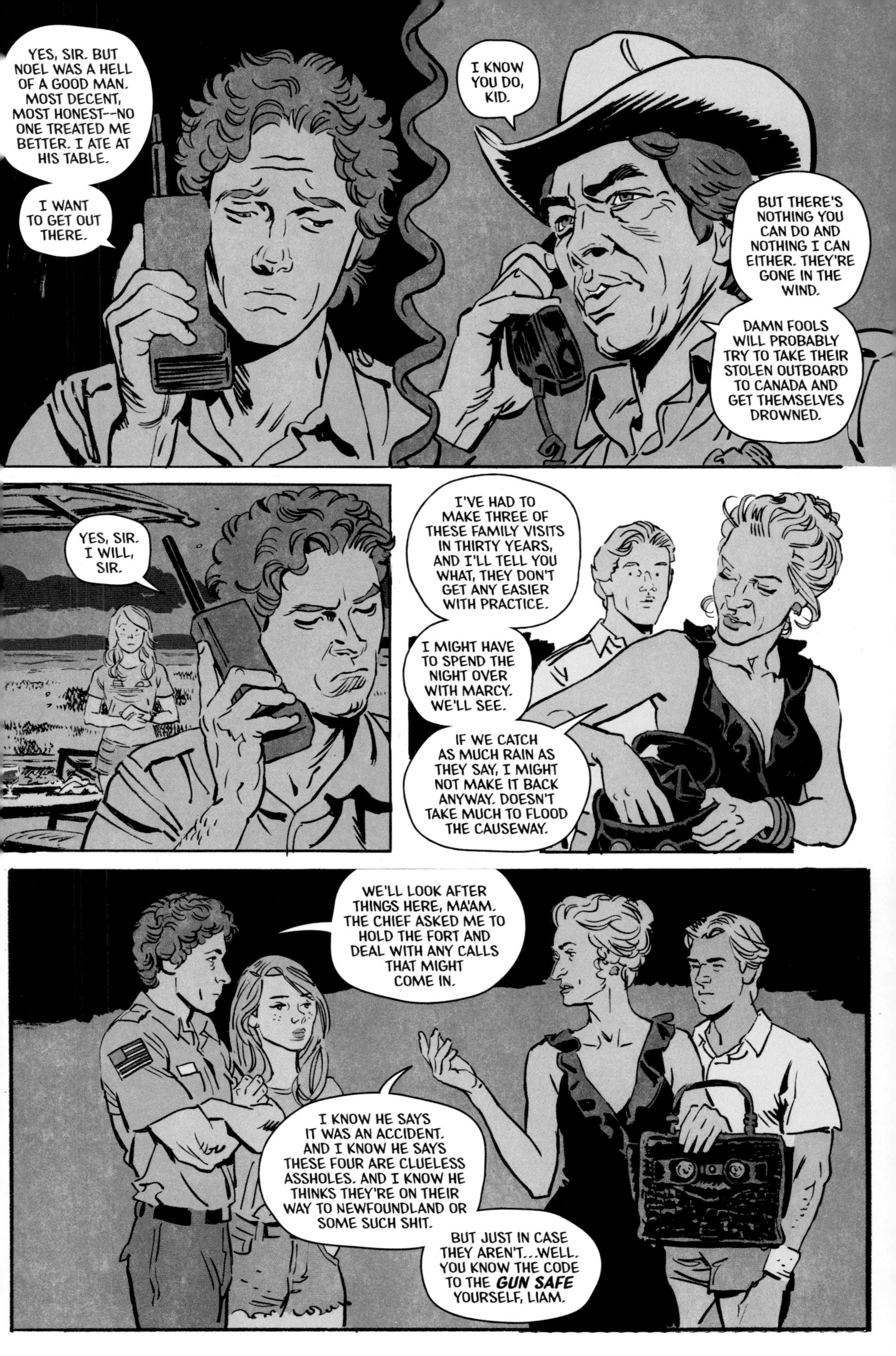
YES, SIR. BUT NOEL WAS A HELL OF A GOOD MAN. MOST DECENT, MOST HONEST--NO ONE TREATED ME BETTER. I ATE AT HIS TABLE.
I WANT TO GET OUT THERE.
I KNOW YOU DO, KID.
BUT THERE'S NOTHING YOU CAN DO AND NOTHING I CAN EITHER. THEY'RE GONE IN THE WIND.
DAMN FOOLS WILL PROBABLY TRY TO TAKE THEIR STOLEN OUTBOARD TO CANADA AND GET THEMSELVES DROWNED.
YES, SIR. I WILL, SIR.
I'VE HAD TO MAKE THREE OF THESE FAMILY VISITS IN THIRTY YEARS, AND I'LL TELL YOU WHAT, THEY DON'T GET ANY EASIER WITH PRACTICE.
I MIGHT HAVE TO SPEND THE NIGHT OVER WITH MARCY. WE'LL SEE.
IF WE CATCH AS MUCH RAIN AS THEY SAY, I MIGHT NOT MAKE IT BACK ANYWAY. DOESN'T TAKE MUCH TO FLOOD THE CAUSEWAY.
WE'LL LOOK AFTER THINGS HERE, MA'AM. THE CHIEF ASKED ME TO HOLD THE FORT AND DEAL WITH ANY CALLS THAT MIGHT COME IN.
I KNOW HE SAYS IT WAS AN ACCIDENT. AND I KNOW HE SAYS THESE FOUR ARE CLUELESS ASSHOLES. AND I KNOW HE THINKS THEY'RE ON THEIR WAY TO NEWFOUNDLAND OR SOME SUCH SHIT.
BUT JUST IN CASE THEY AREN'T...WELL. YOU KNOW THE CODE TO THE GUN SAFE YOURSELF, LIAM.

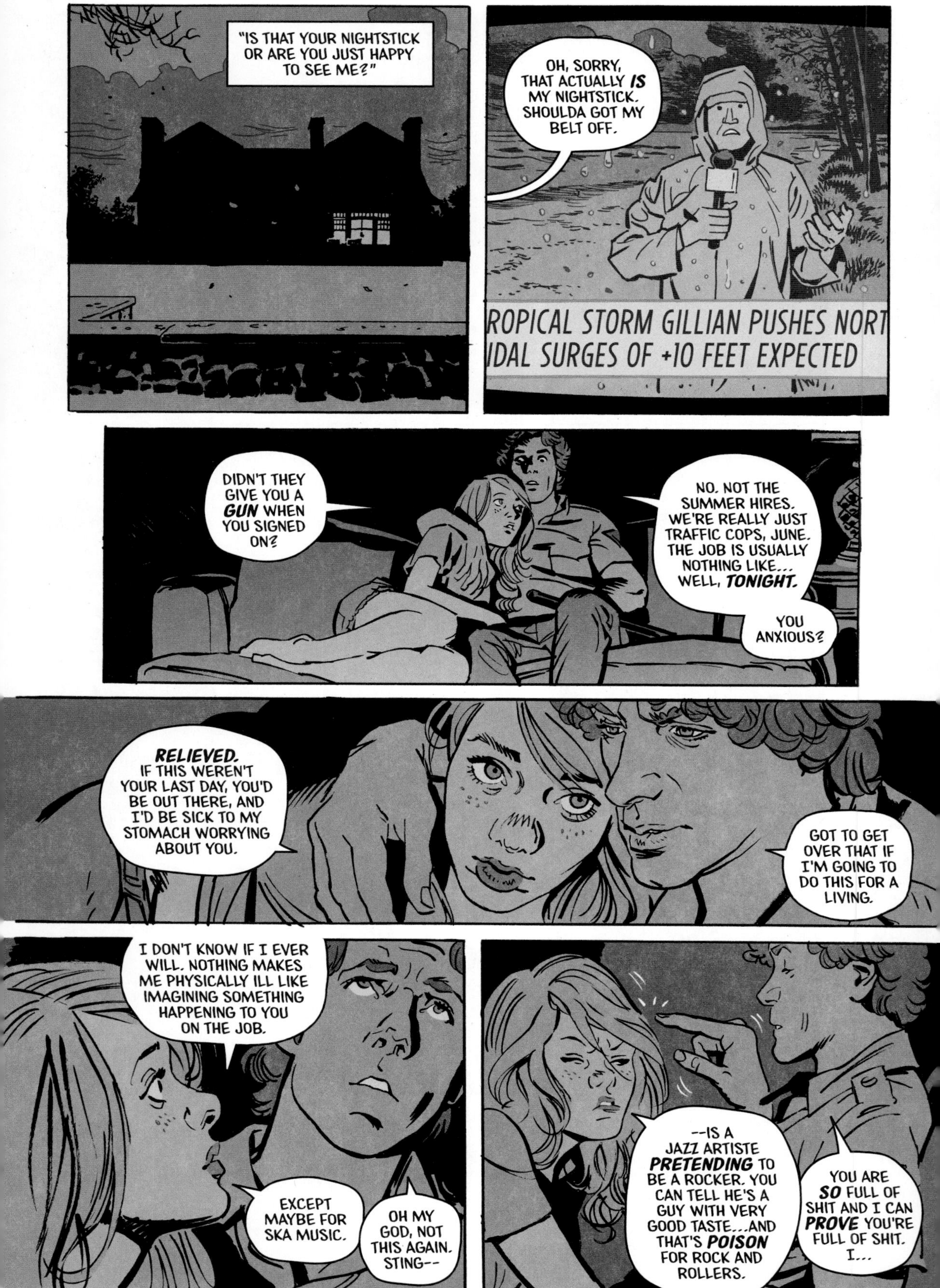
"IS THAT YOUR NIGHTSTICK OR ARE YOU JUST HAPPY TO SEE ME?"
OH, SORRY, THAT ACTUALLY IS MY NIGHTSTICK. SHOULDA GOT MY BELT OFF.
ROPICAL STORM GILLIAN PUSHES NORT
IDAL SURGES OF +10 FEET EXPECTED
DIDN'T THEY GIVE YOU A GUN WHEN YOU SIGNED ON?
NO. NOT THE SUMMER HIRES. WE'RE REALLY JUST TRAFFIC COPS, JUNE. THE JOB IS USUALLY NOTHING LIKE... WELL, TONIGHT.
YOU ANXIOUS?
RELIEVED. IF THIS WEREN'T YOUR LAST DAY, YOU'D BE OUT THERE, AND I'D BE SICK TO MY STOMACH WORRYING ABOUT YOU.
GOT TO GET OVER THAT IF I'M GOING TO DO THIS FOR A LIVING.
I DON'T KNOW IF I EVER WILL. NOTHING MAKES ME PHYSICALLY ILL LIKE IMAGINING SOMETHING HAPPENING TO YOU ON THE JOB.
EXCEPT MAYBE FOR SKA MUSIC.
OH MY GOD, NOT THIS AGAIN. STING--
--IS A JAZZ ARTISTE PRETENDING TO BE A ROCKER. YOU CAN TELL HE'S A GUY WITH VERY GOOD TASTE...AND THAT'S POISON FOR ROCK AND ROLLERS.
YOU ARE SO FULL OF SHIT AND I CAN PROVE YOU'RE FULL OF SHIT. I...

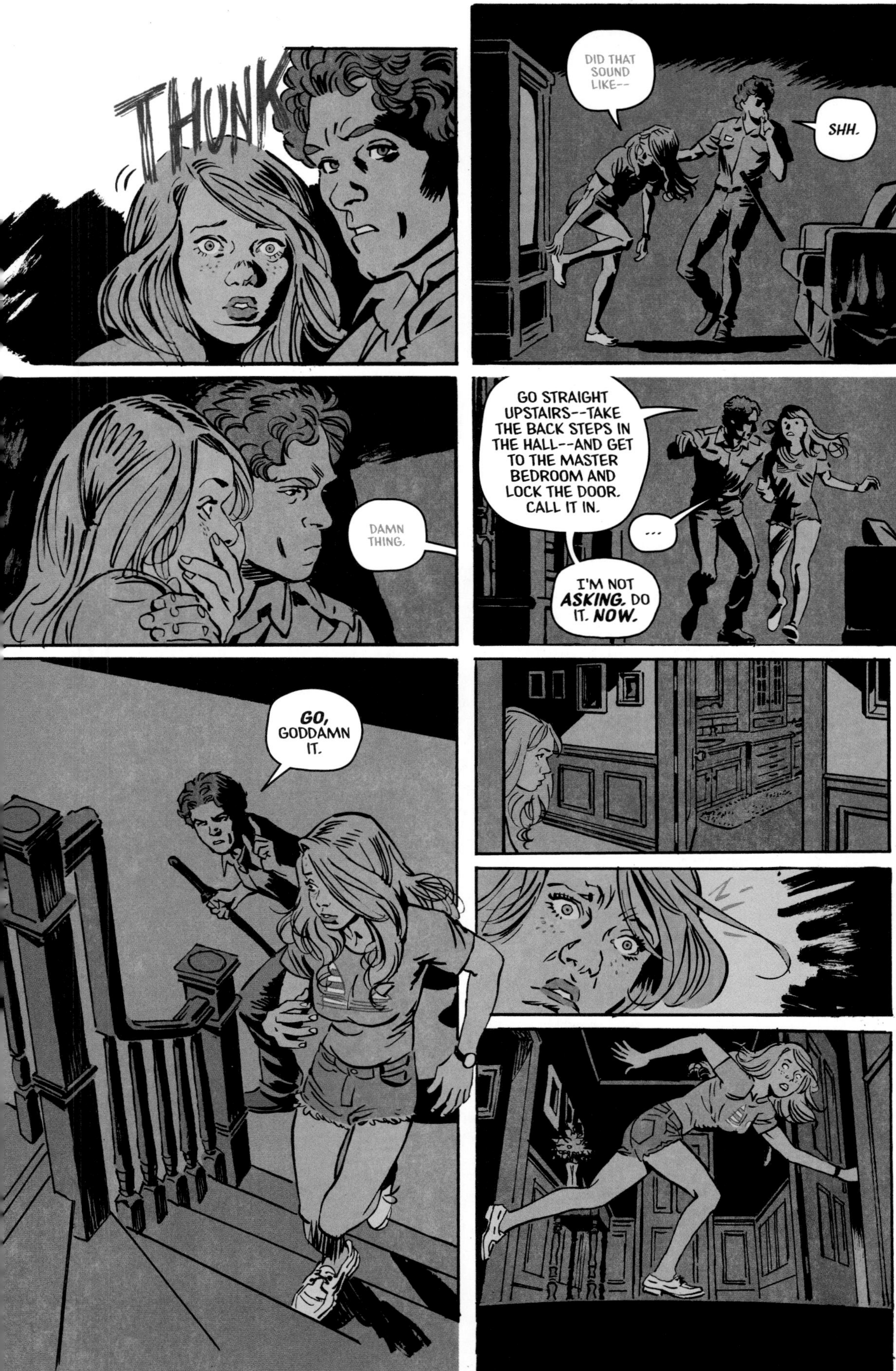
THUNK
DID THAT SOUND LIKE--
SHH.
DAMN THING.
GO STRAIGHT UPSTAIRS--TAKE THE BACK STEPS IN THE HALL--AND GET TO THE MASTER BEDROOM AND LOCK THE DOOR. CALL IT IN.
...
I'M NOT ASKING. DO IT. NOW.
GO, GODDAMN IT.

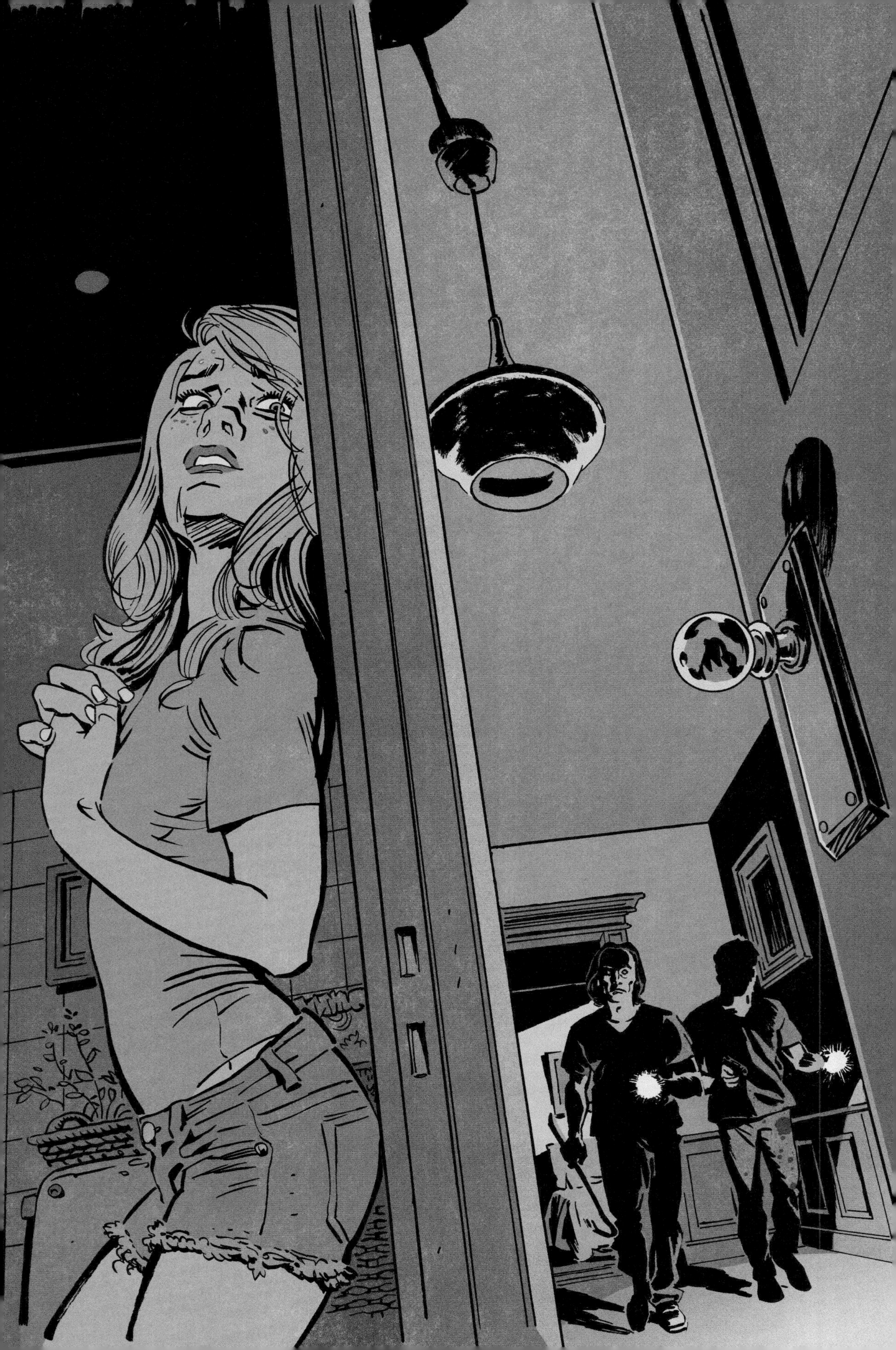

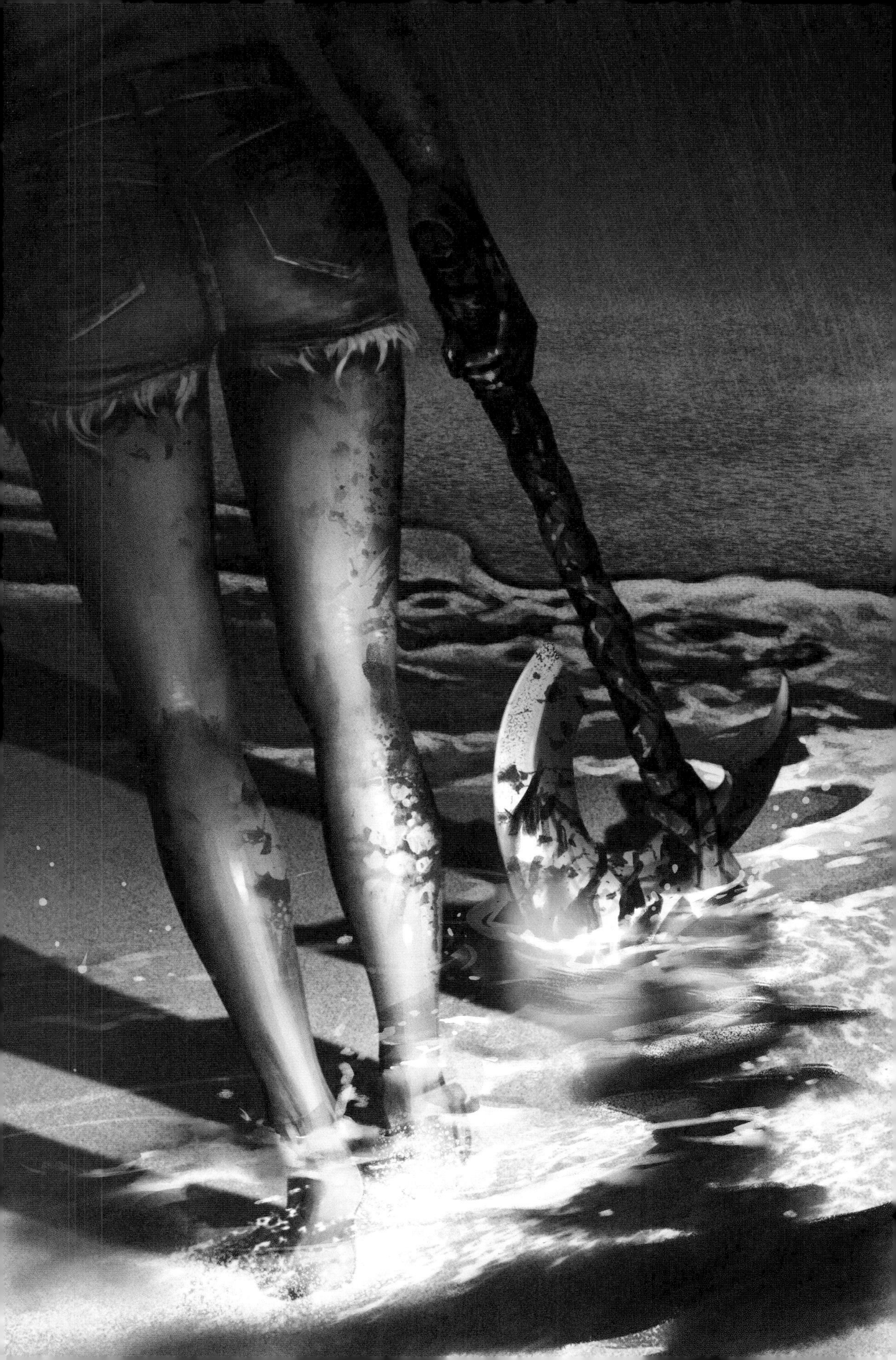

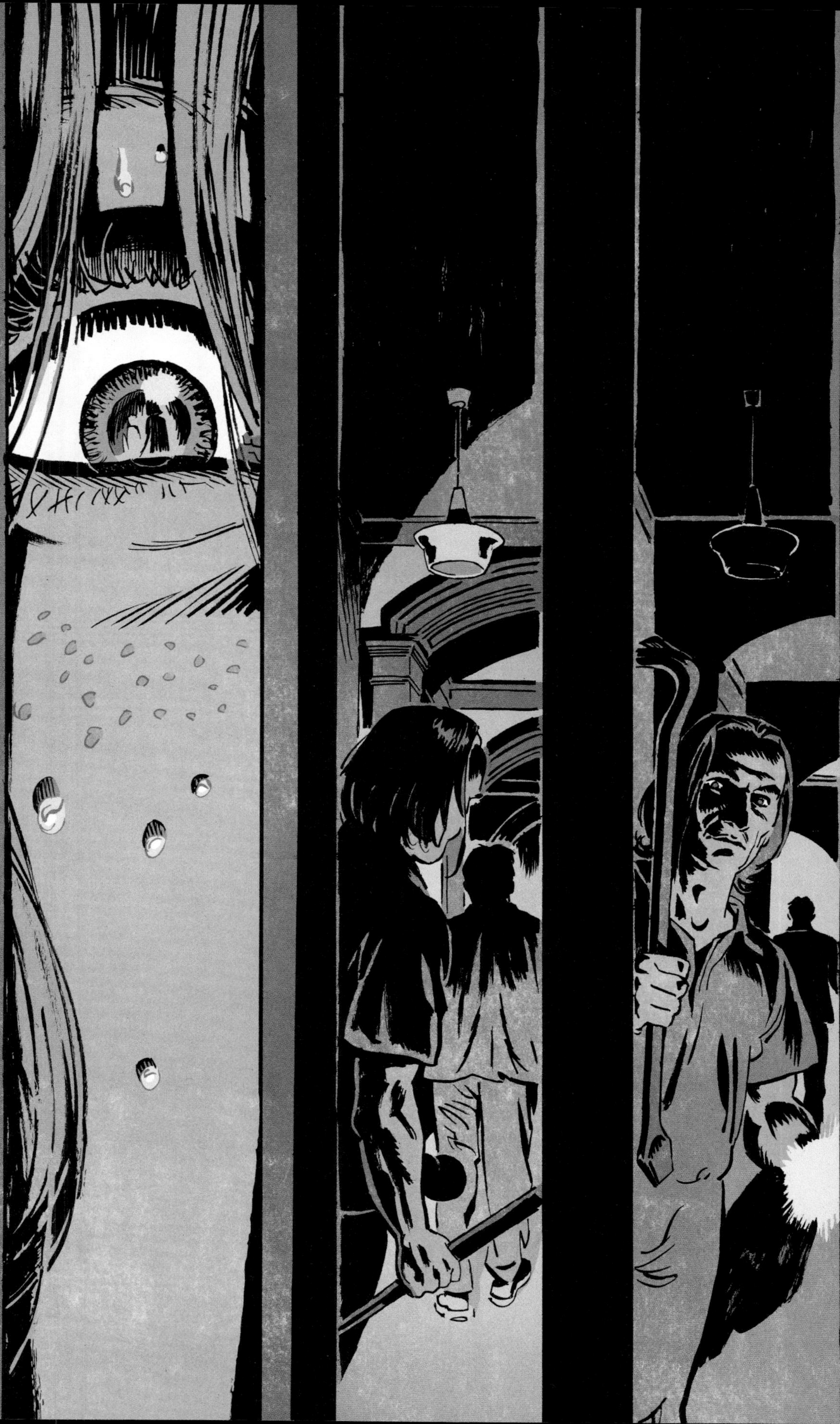

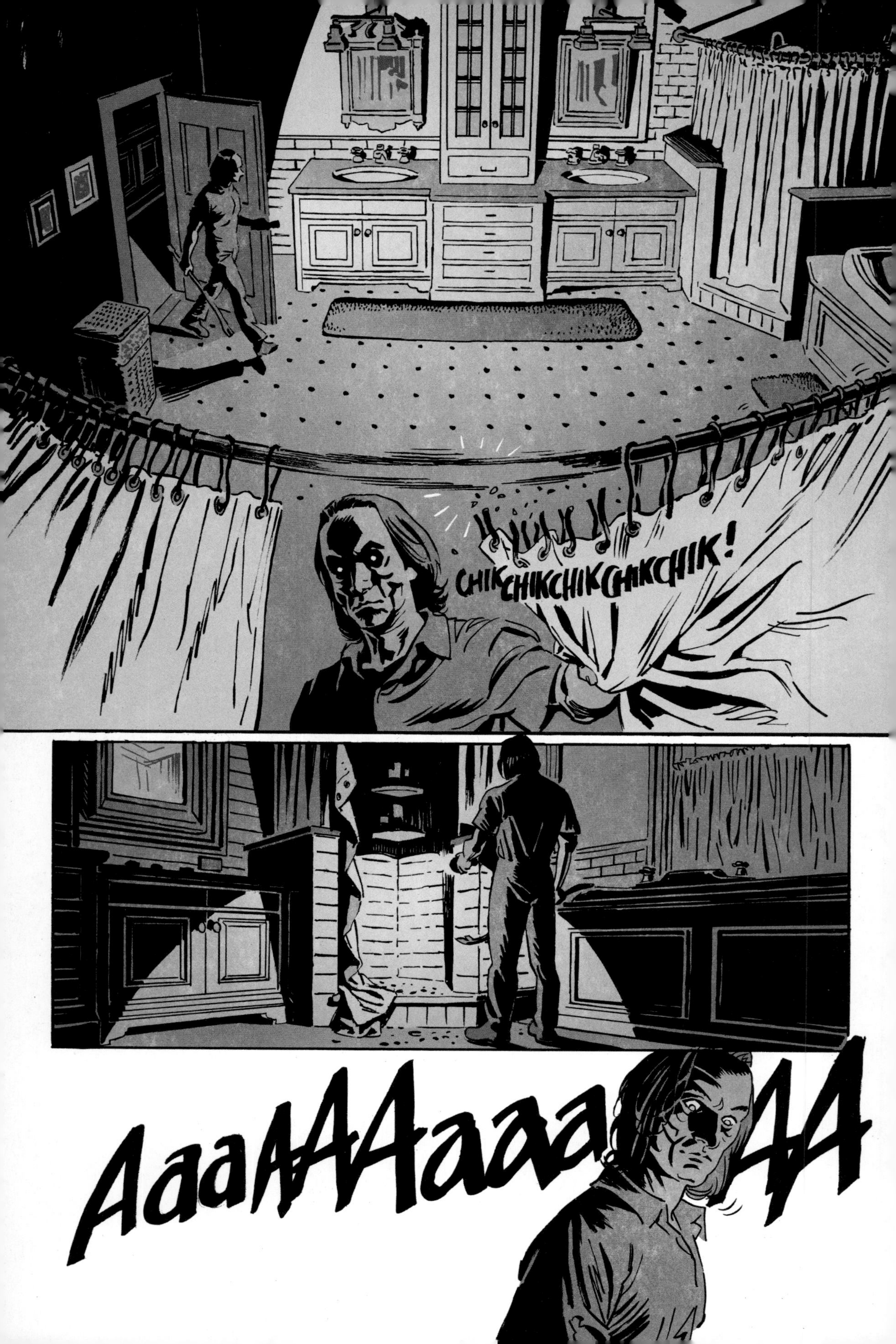
CHIKCHIKCHIKCHIKCHIK!
AaaAAAaaaAAA

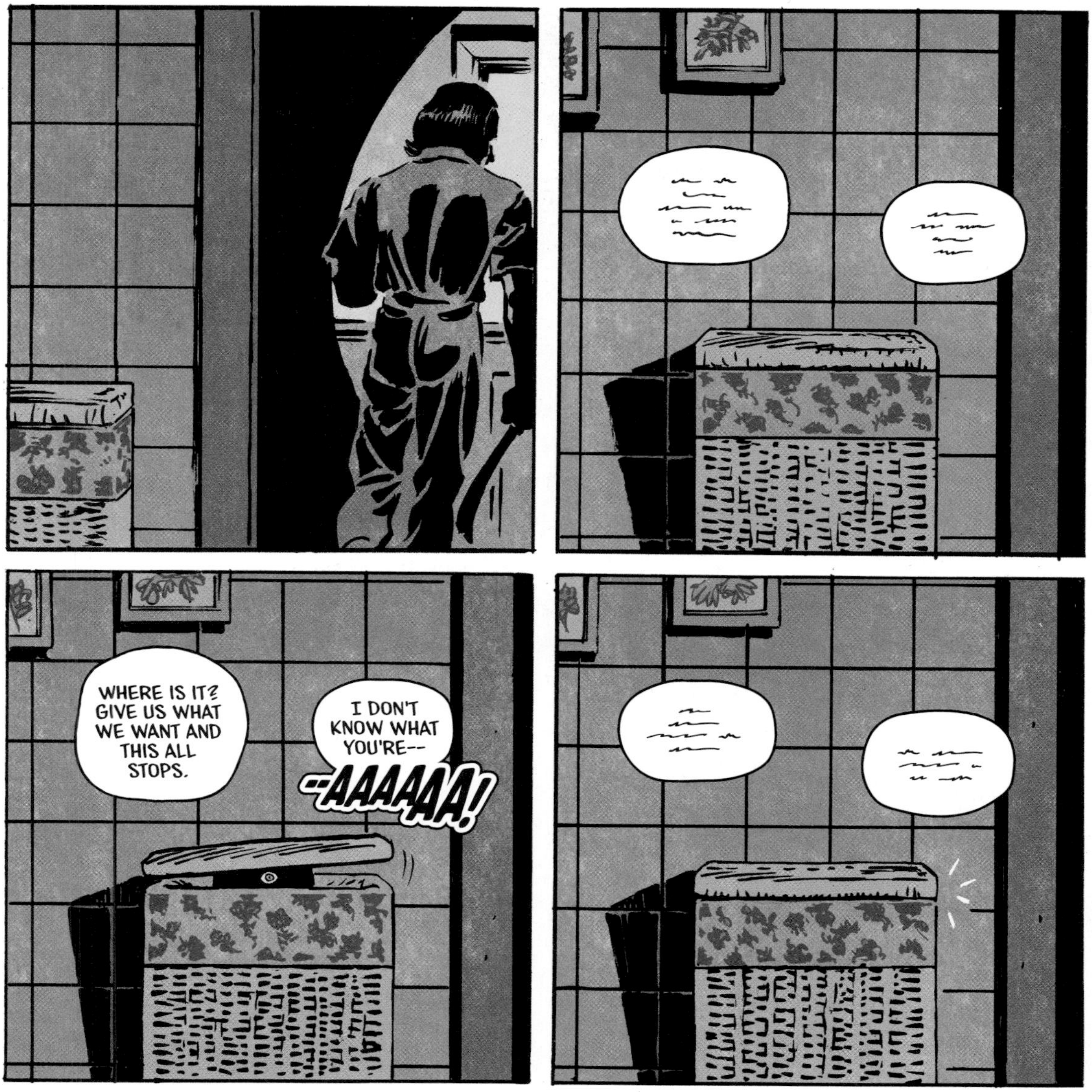
WHERE IS IT? GIVE US WHAT WE WANT AND THIS ALL STOPS.
I DON'T KNOW WHAT YOU'RE--
--AAAAAA!

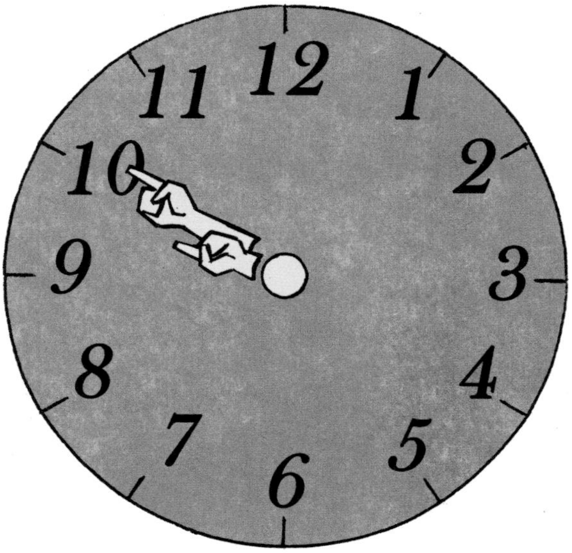

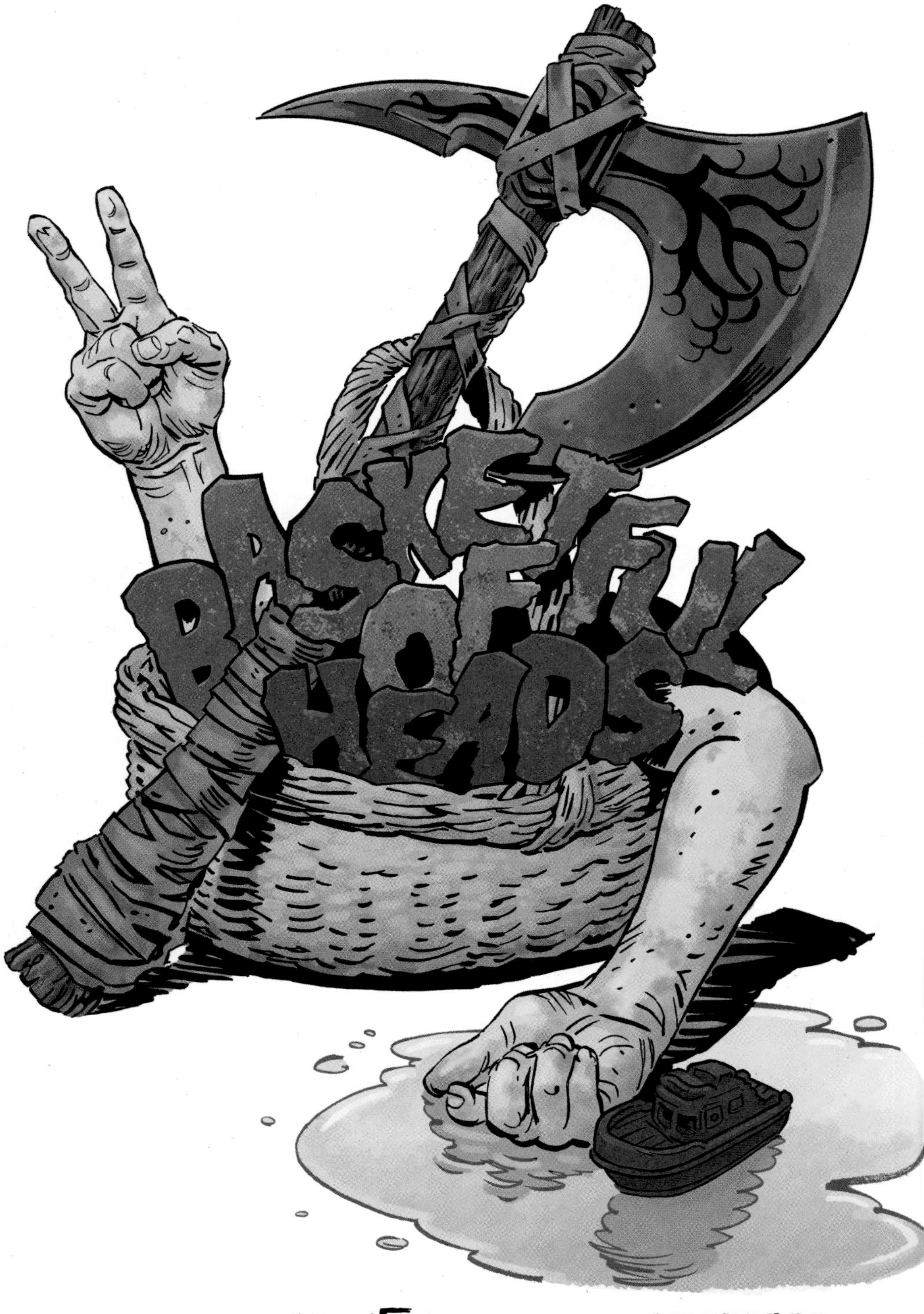
BASKETFUL OF HEADS

Written by JOE HILL Illustrated by LEOMACS
Colored by DAVE STEWART Lettered by DERON BENNETT
Cover by REIKO MURAKAMI
Edited by MARK DOYLE & AMEDEO TURTURRO

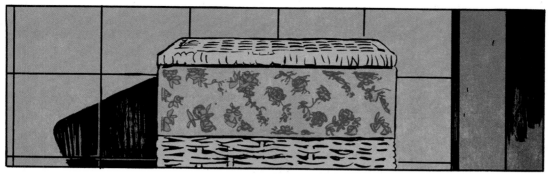

CLAUSEN'S HOUSE--BRODY ISLAND.

PLEASE BE GONE...

...PLEASE, *PLEASE* LET HIM BE ALL RIGHT.

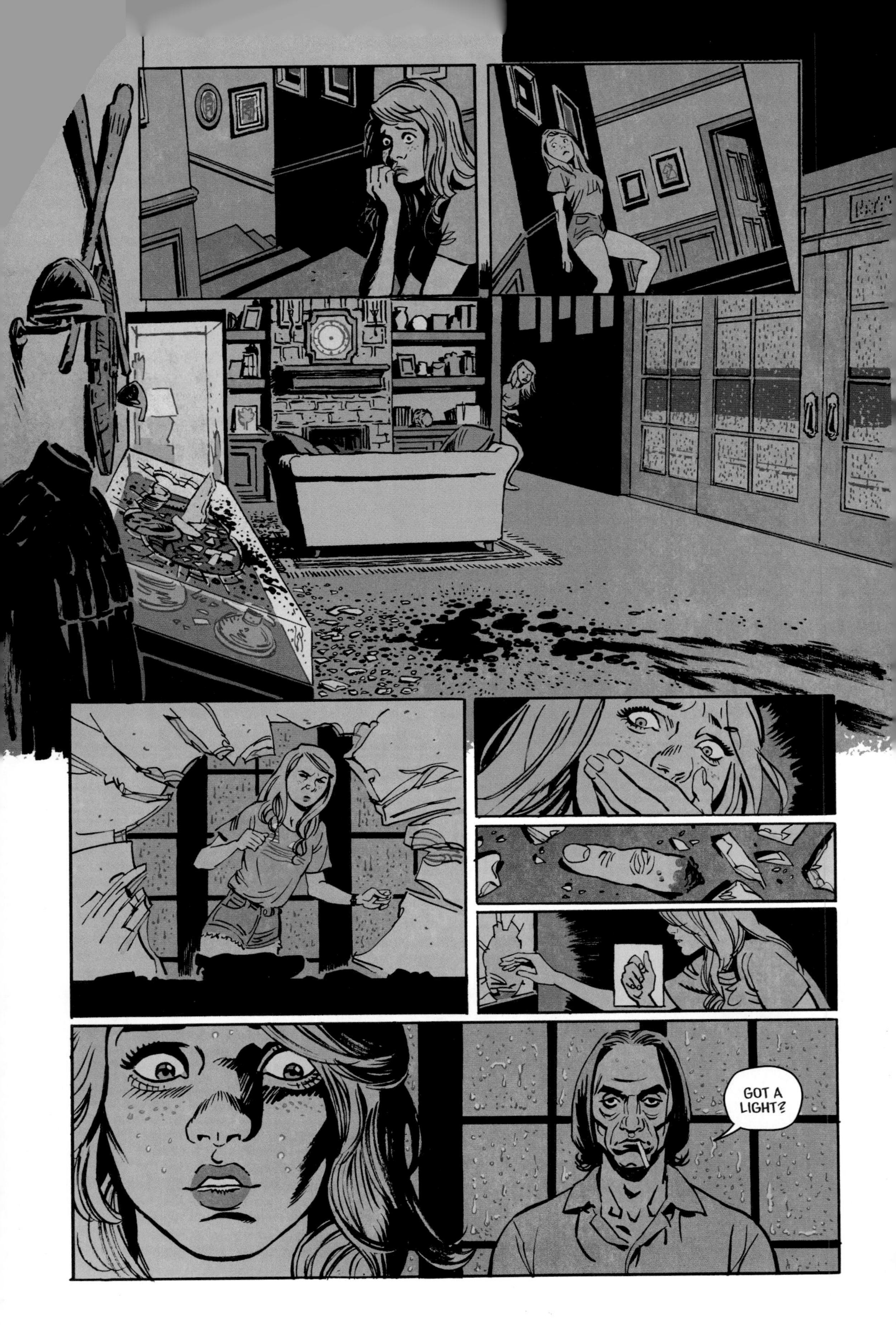
GOT A LIGHT?

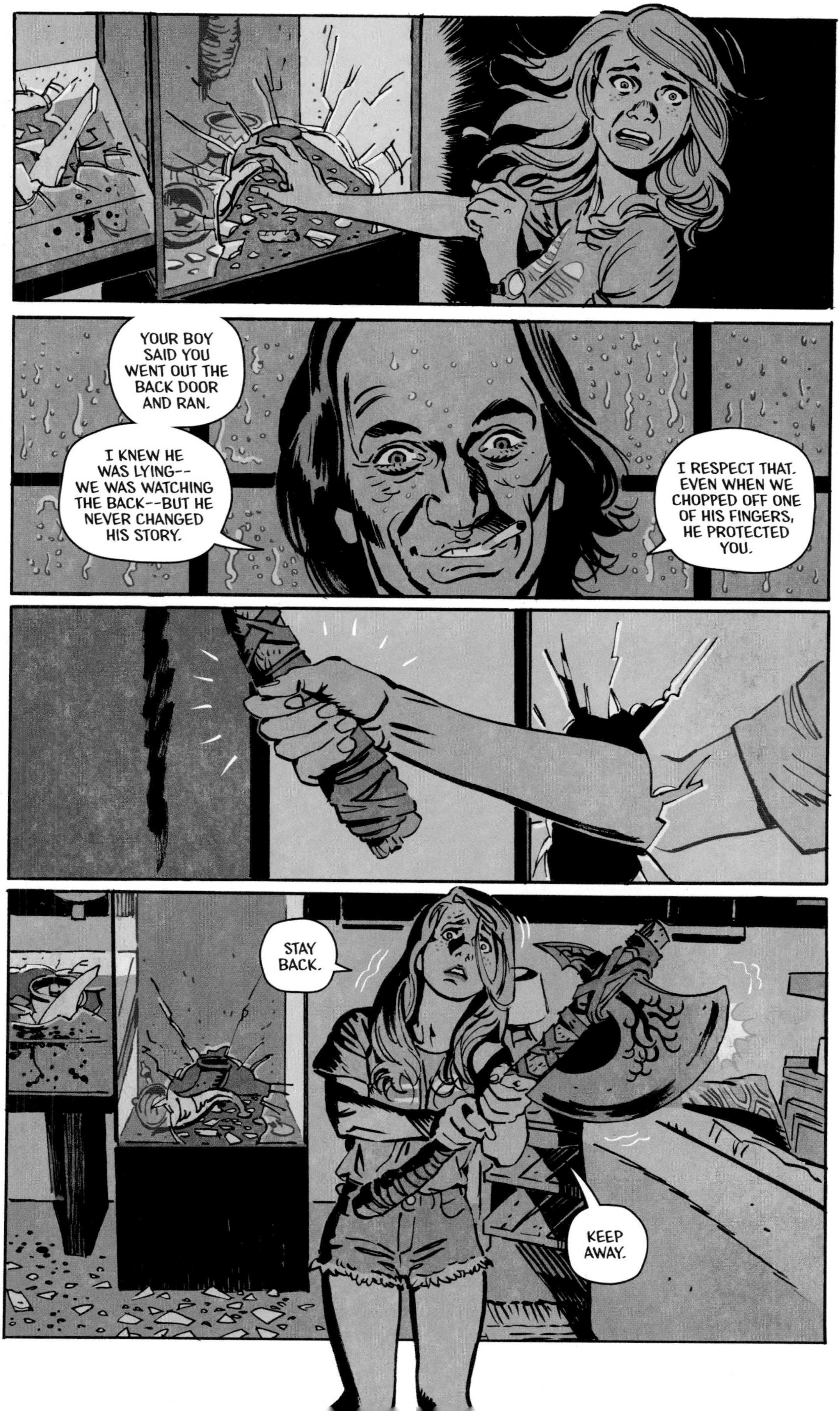
YOUR BOY SAID YOU WENT OUT THE BACK DOOR AND RAN.
I KNEW HE WAS LYING-- WE WAS WATCHING THE BACK--BUT HE NEVER CHANGED HIS STORY.
I RESPECT THAT. EVEN WHEN WE CHOPPED OFF ONE OF HIS FINGERS, HE PROTECTED YOU.
STAY BACK.
KEEP AWAY.

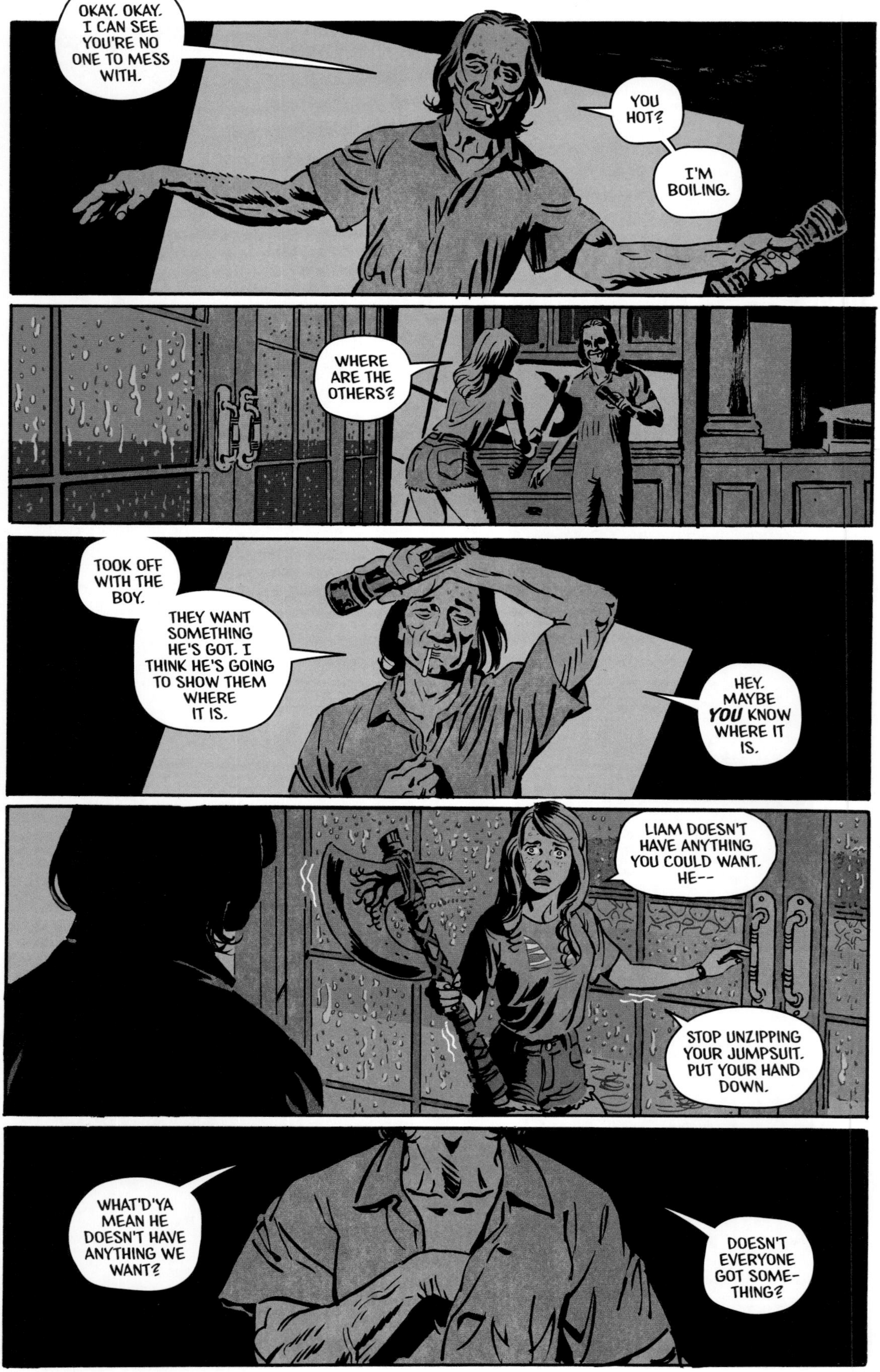

OKAY. OKAY. I CAN SEE YOU'RE NO ONE TO MESS WITH.
YOU HOT?
I'M BOILING.
WHERE ARE THE OTHERS?
TOOK OFF WITH THE BOY.
THEY WANT SOMETHING HE'S GOT. I THINK HE'S GOING TO SHOW THEM WHERE IT IS.
HEY. MAYBE *YOU* KNOW WHERE IT IS.
LIAM DOESN'T HAVE ANYTHING YOU COULD WANT. HE--
STOP UNZIPPING YOUR JUMPSUIT. PUT YOUR HAND DOWN.
WHAT'D'YA MEAN HE DOESN'T HAVE ANYTHING WE WANT?
DOESN'T EVERYONE GOT SOME-THING?

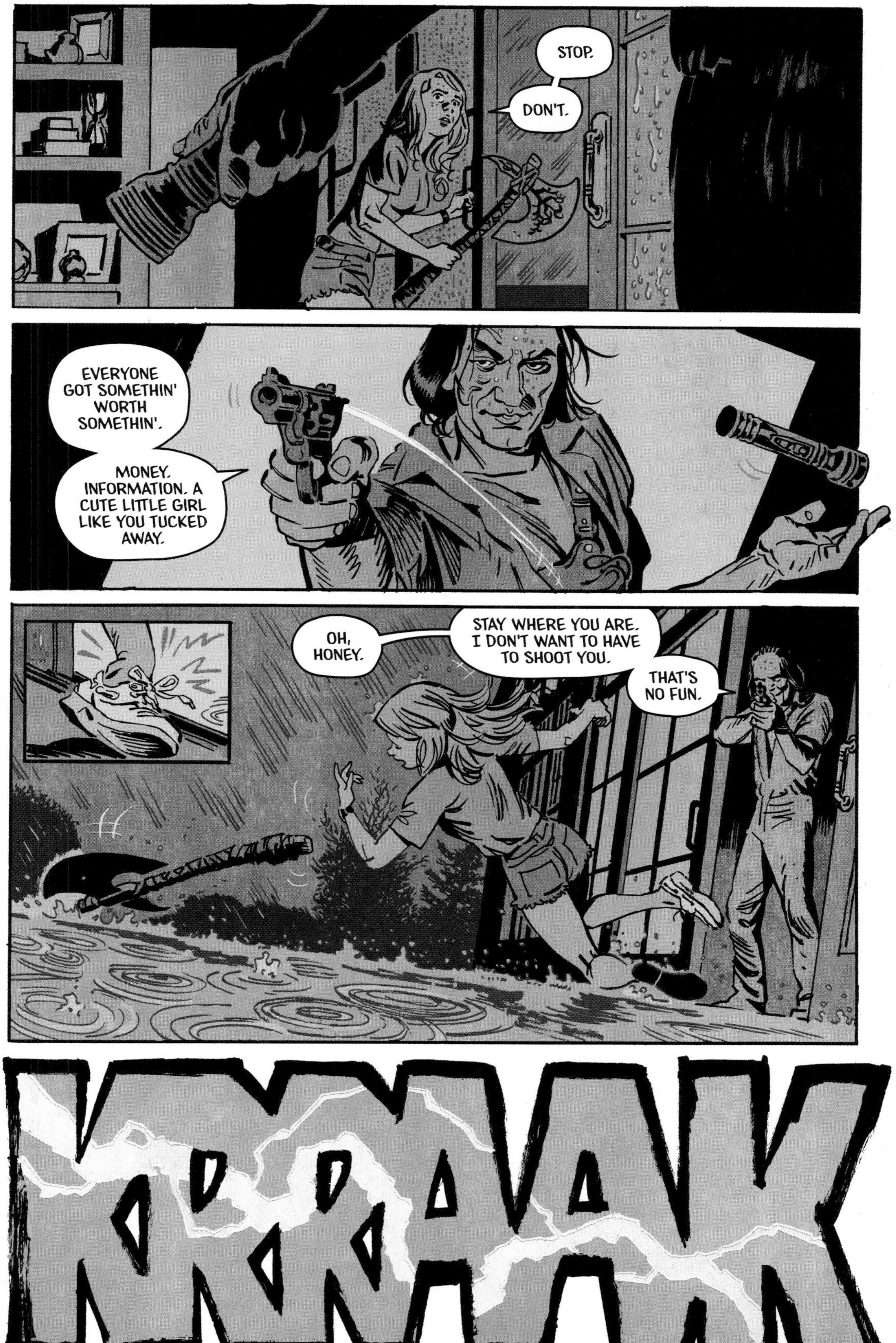
STOP.
DON'T.
EVERYONE GOT SOMETHIN' WORTH SOMETHIN'.
MONEY. INFORMATION. A CUTE LITTLE GIRL LIKE YOU TUCKED AWAY.
OH, HONEY.
STAY WHERE YOU ARE. I DON'T WANT TO HAVE TO SHOOT YOU.
THAT'S NO FUN.
KRAAK

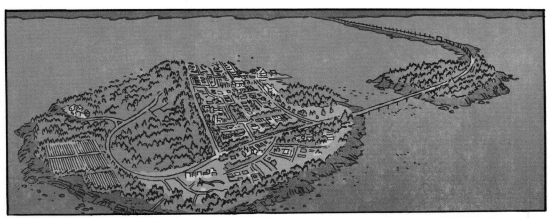

IT'S NOT TOO LATE...
THERE'S STILL TIME
TO TURN AROUND
AND COME BACK TO
BRODY ISLAND!
A TOP 10 YANK MAGAZINE
HIDDEN TREASURE (1980)!

IT'S NOT TOO LATE...
THERE'S STILL TIME
TO TURN AROUND
AND COME BACK TO
BRODY ISLAND!
A TOP 10 YANK MAGAZINE
HIDDEN TREASURE (1980)!

IT'S NOT TOO LATE...
THERE'S STILL TIME
TO TURN AROUND
AND COME BACK TO
BRODY ISLAND!
A TOP 10 YANK MAGAZINE
HIDDEN TREASURE (1980)!

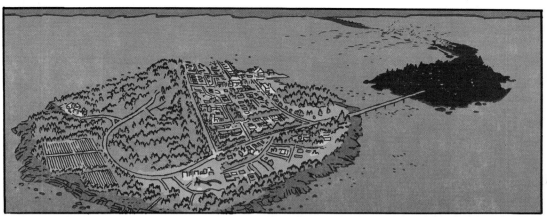

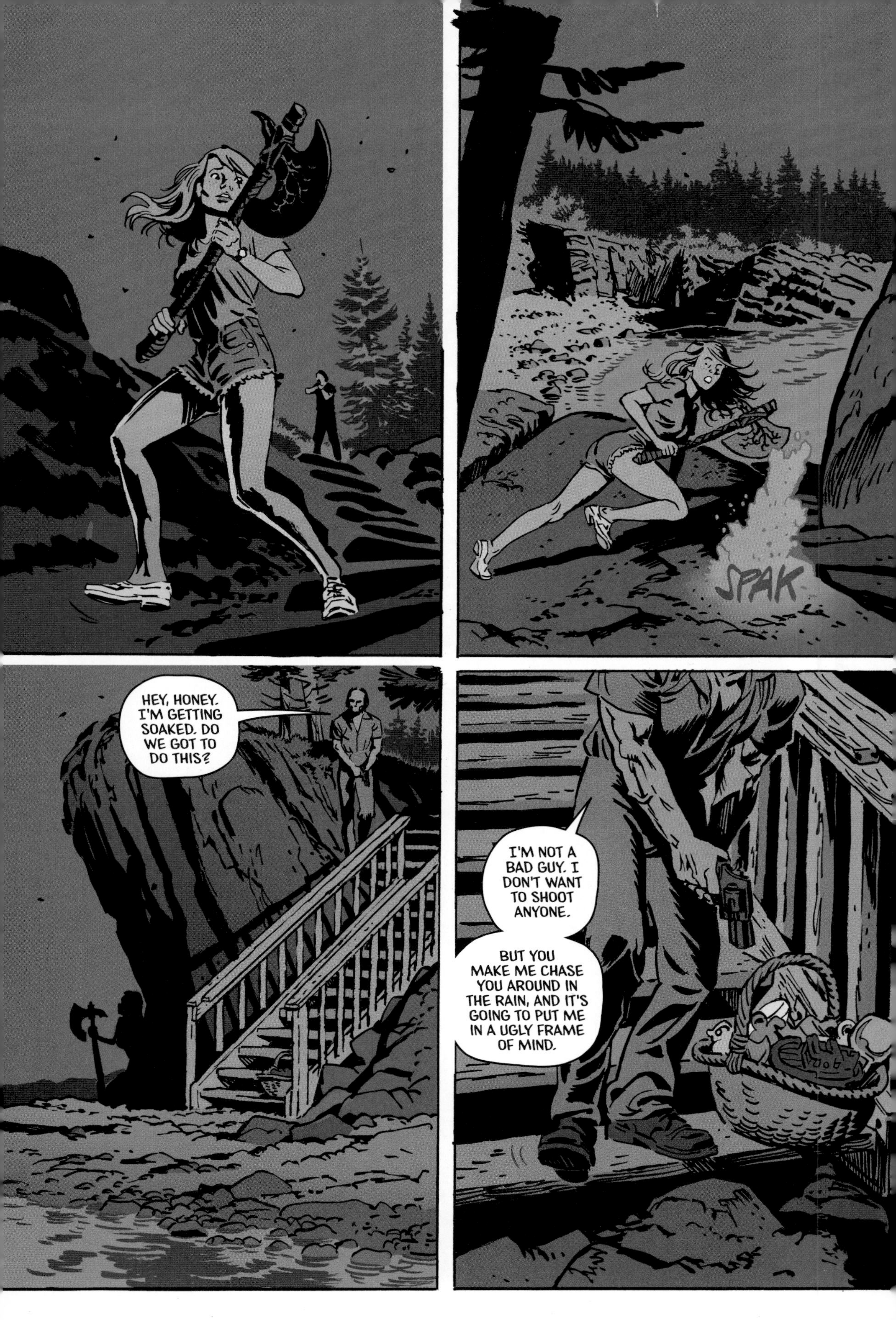
SPAK
HEY, HONEY. I'M GETTING SOAKED. DO WE GOT TO DO THIS?
I'M NOT A BAD GUY. I DON'T WANT TO SHOOT ANYONE.
BUT YOU MAKE ME CHASE YOU AROUND IN THE RAIN, AND IT'S GOING TO PUT ME IN A UGLY FRAME OF MIND.

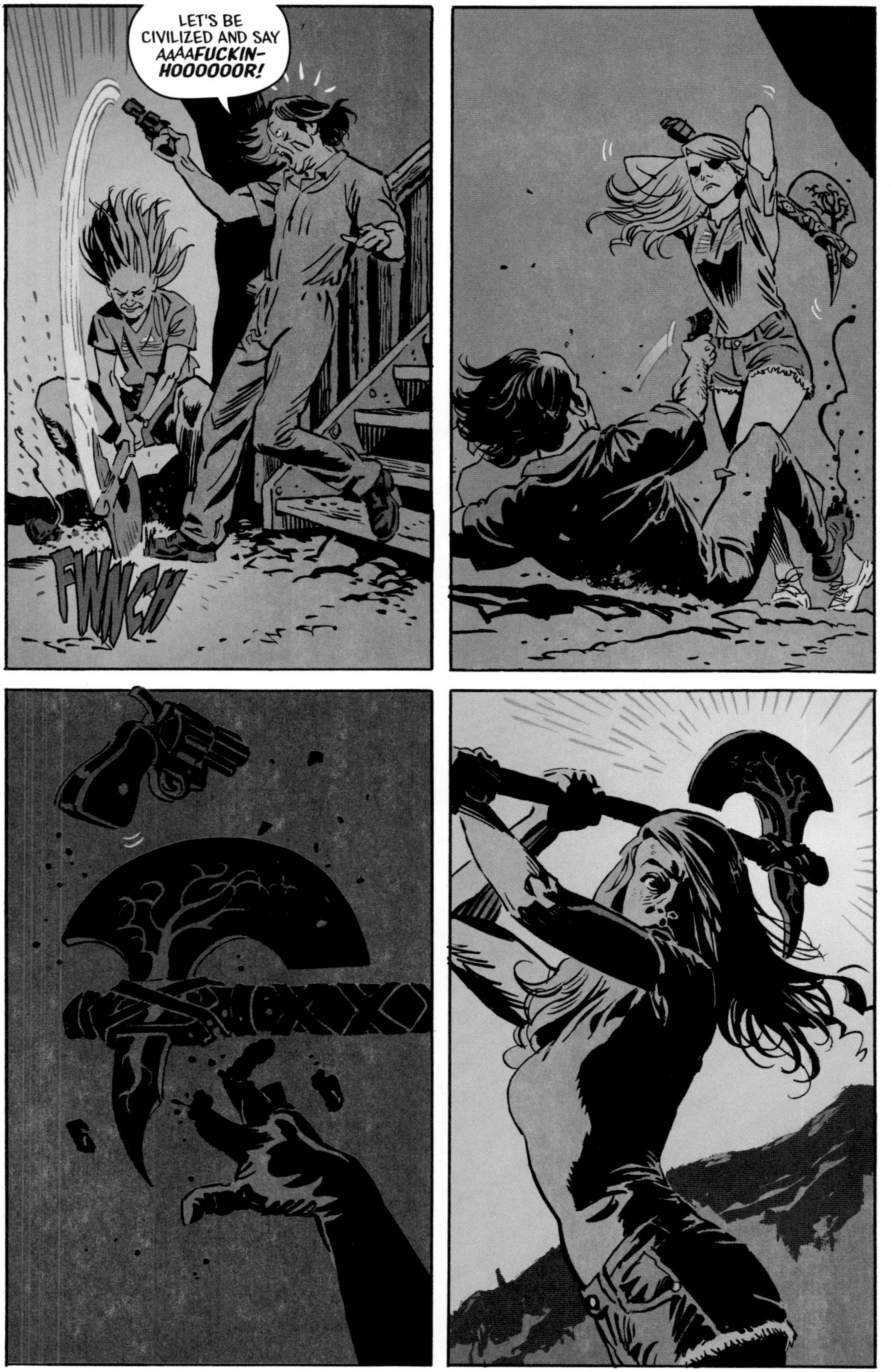
LET'S BE CIVILIZED AND SAY AAAAFUCKIN-HOOOOOOR!
FWNCH

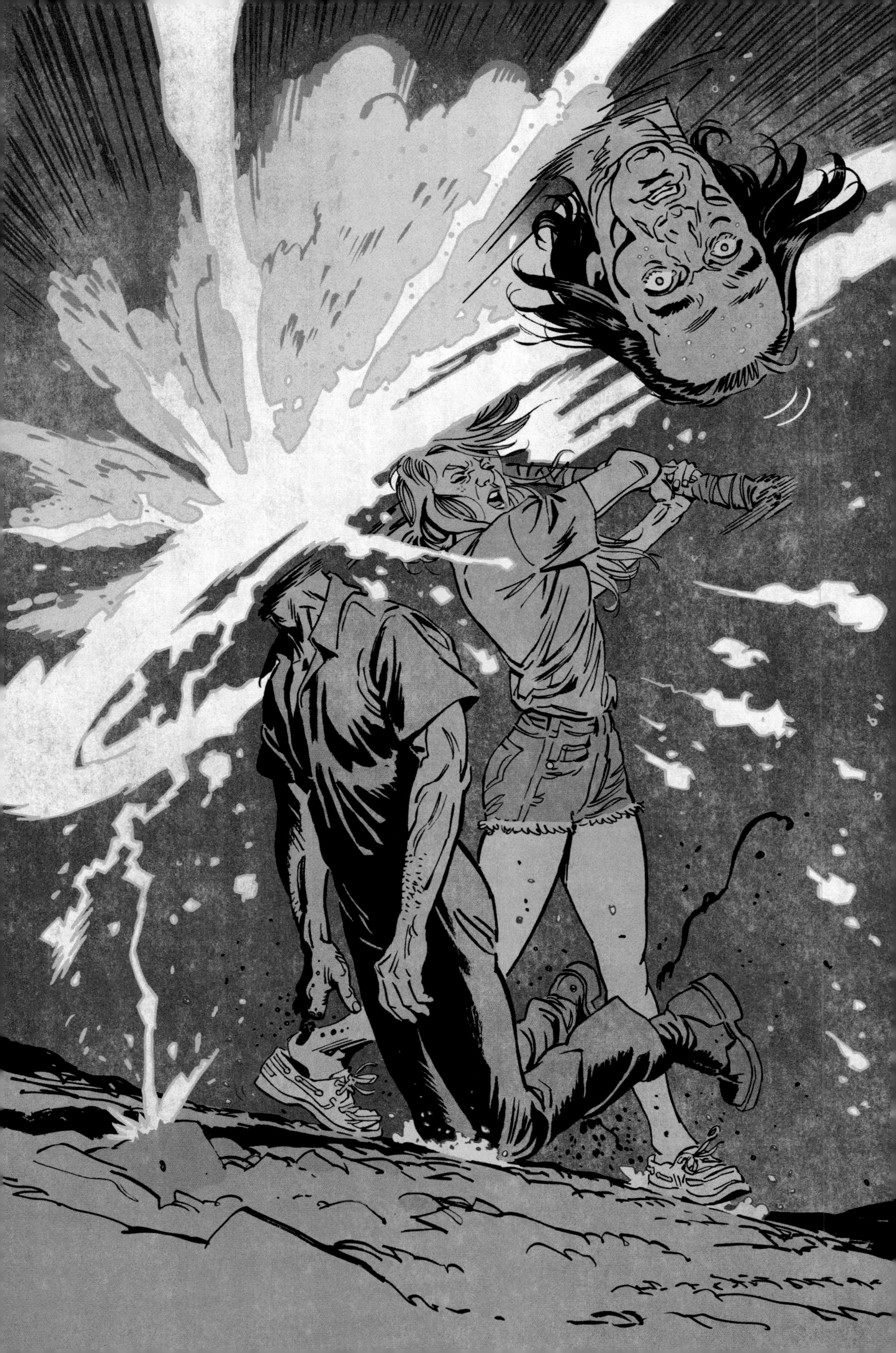

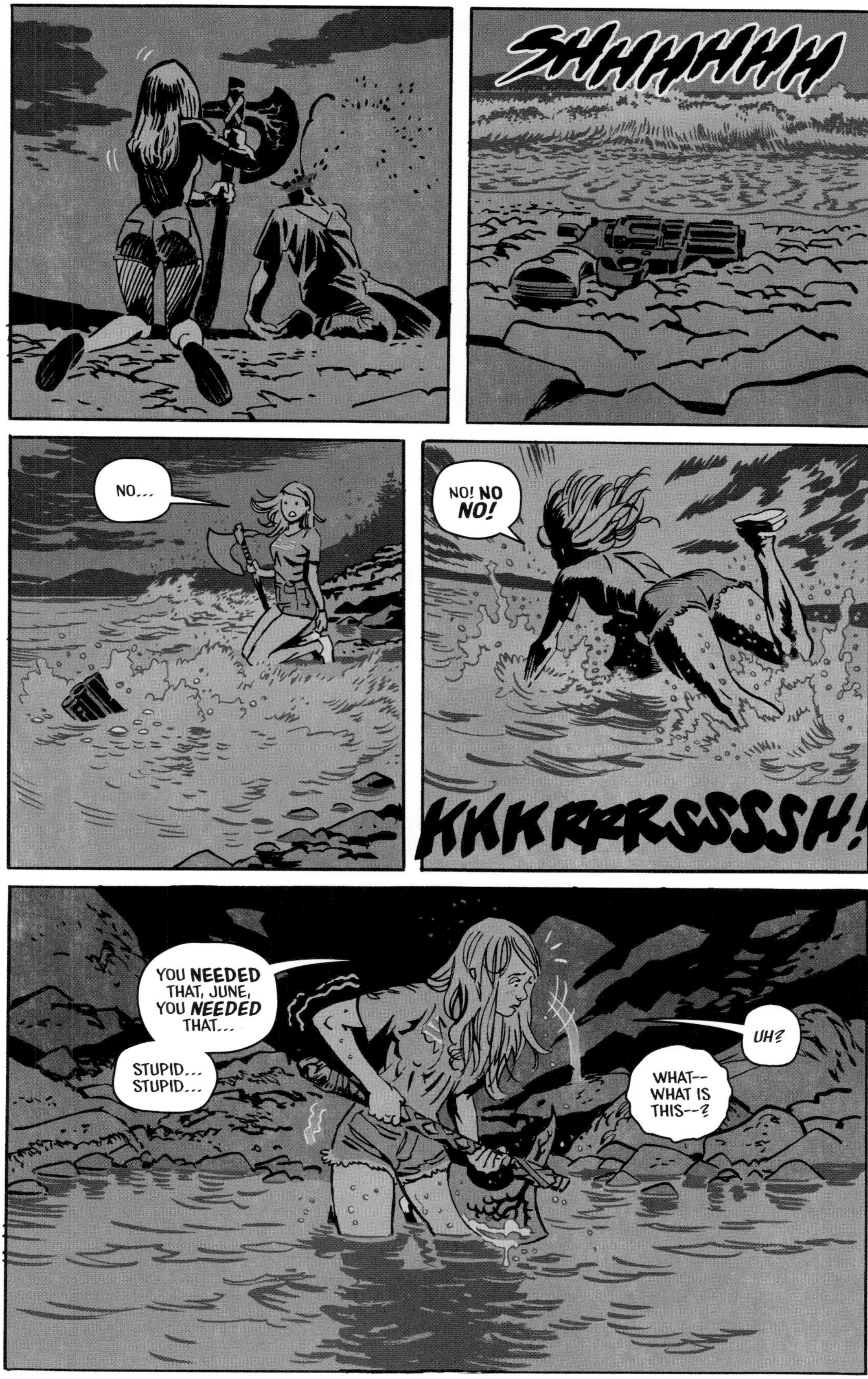
SHHHHHH
NO...
NO! NO NO!
KKKRRRSSSSH!
YOU NEEDED THAT, JUNE, YOU NEEDED THAT...
STUPID... STUPID...
UH?
WHAT-- WHAT IS THIS--?

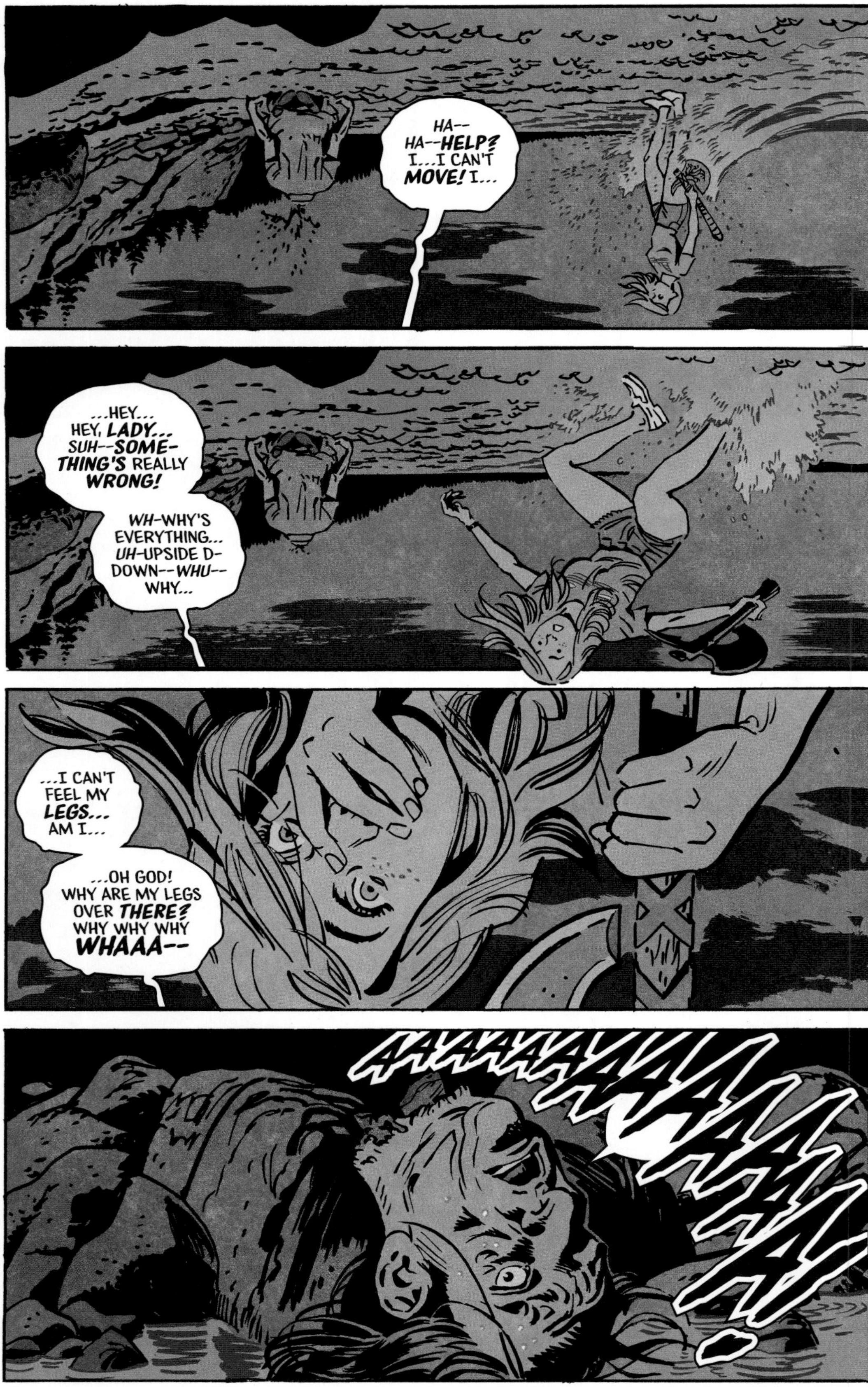
HA-- HA--HELP? I...I CAN'T MOVE! I...
...HEY... HEY, LADY... SUH--SOMETHING'S REALLY WRONG!
WH-WHY'S EVERYTHING... UH-UPSIDE D-DOWN--WHU--WHY...
...I CAN'T FEEL MY LEGS... AM I...
...OH GOD! WHY ARE MY LEGS OVER THERE? WHY WHY WHY WHAAA--
AAAAAAAAAAAAAAAAH!

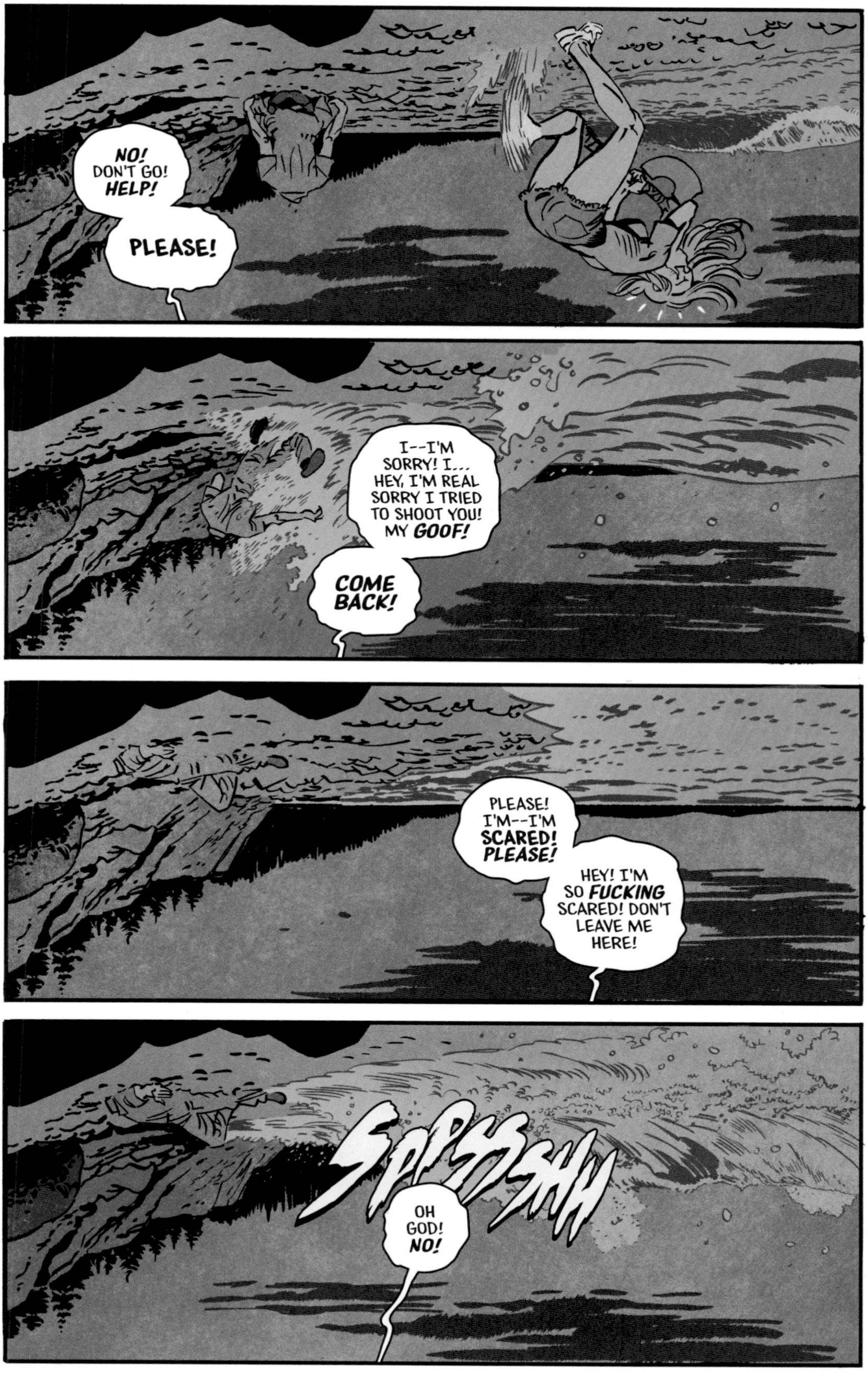
NO! DON'T GO! HELP!
PLEASE!
I--I'M SORRY! I... HEY, I'M REAL SORRY I TRIED TO SHOOT YOU! MY GOOF!
COME BACK!
PLEASE! I'M--I'M SCARED! PLEASE!
HEY! I'M SO FUCKING SCARED! DON'T LEAVE ME HERE!
SPPSSSHH
OH GOD! NO!

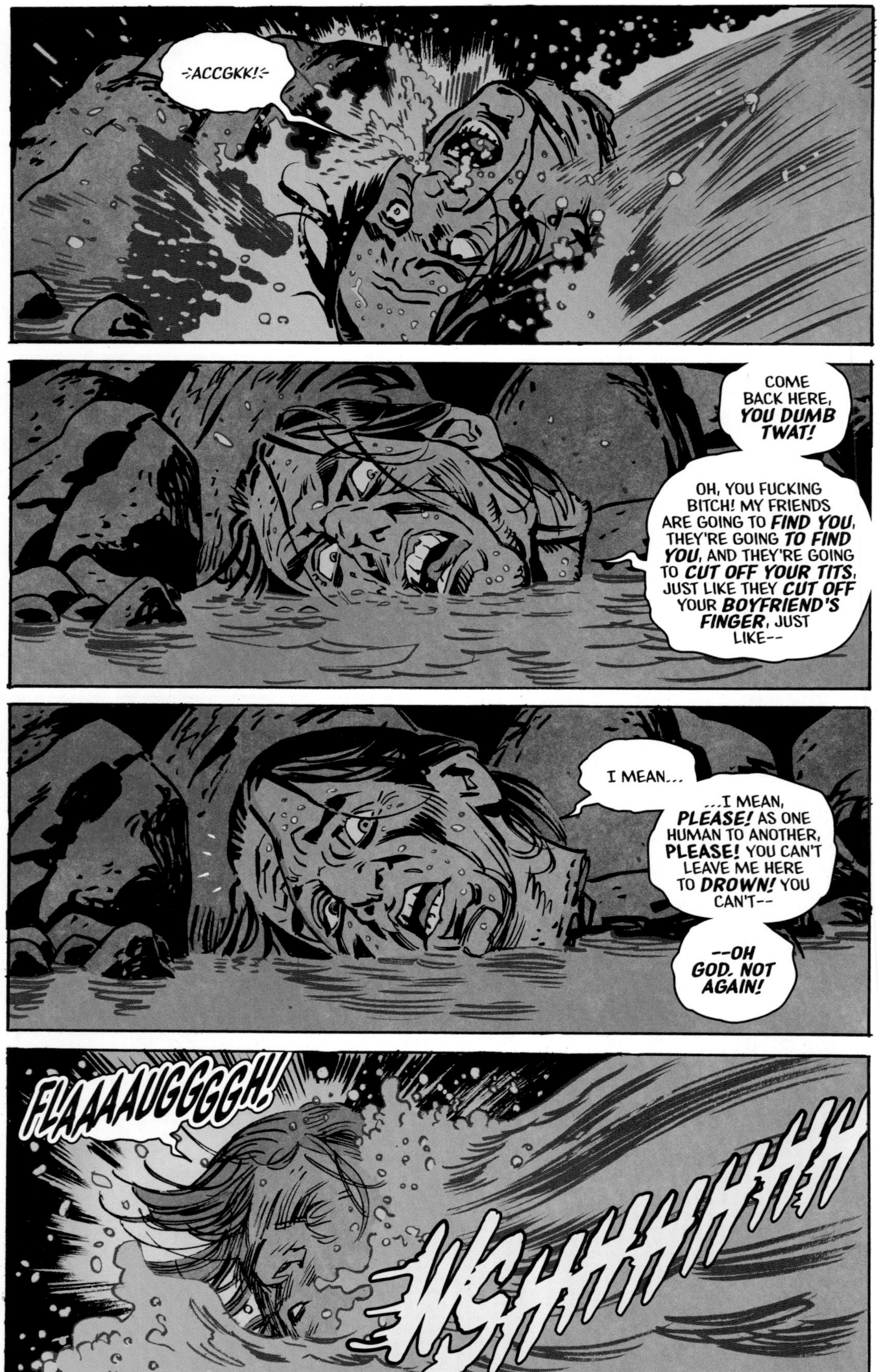
ACCGKK!
COME BACK HERE, YOU DUMB TWAT!
OH, YOU FUCKING BITCH! MY FRIENDS ARE GOING TO FIND YOU, THEY'RE GOING TO FIND YOU, AND THEY'RE GOING TO CUT OFF YOUR TITS, JUST LIKE THEY CUT OFF YOUR BOYFRIEND'S FINGER, JUST LIKE--
I MEAN...
...I MEAN, PLEASE! AS ONE HUMAN TO ANOTHER, PLEASE! YOU CAN'T LEAVE ME HERE TO DROWN! YOU CAN'T--
--OH GOD, NOT AGAIN!
FLAAAAUGGGGH!
WSHHHHHHHH

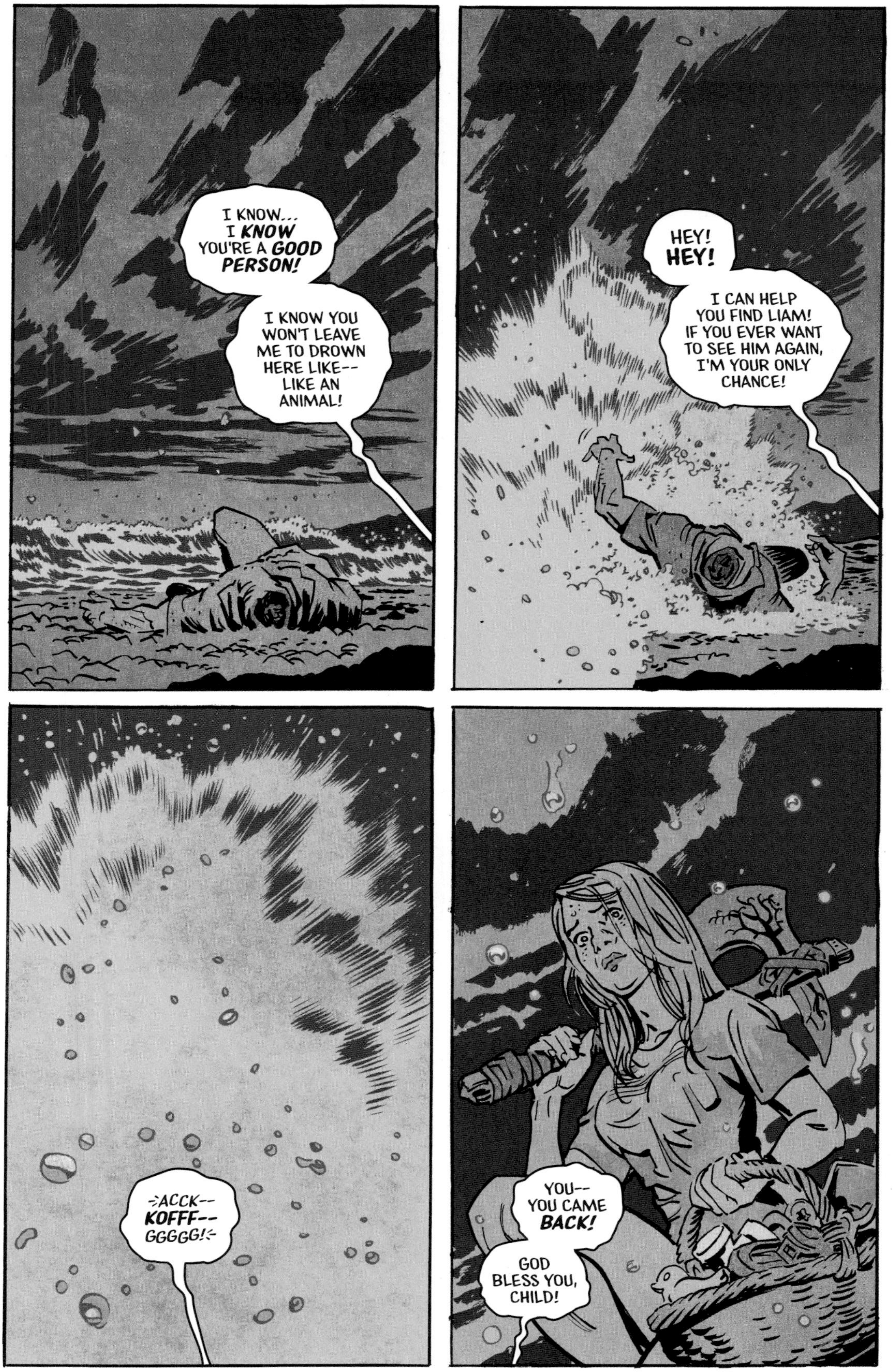

I KNOW... I KNOW YOU'RE A GOOD PERSON!
I KNOW YOU WON'T LEAVE ME TO DROWN HERE LIKE-- LIKE AN ANIMAL!
HEY! HEY!
I CAN HELP YOU FIND LIAM! IF YOU EVER WANT TO SEE HIM AGAIN, I'M YOUR ONLY CHANCE!
ACCK-- KOFFF-- GGGGG!
YOU-- YOU CAME BACK!
GOD BLESS YOU, CHILD!

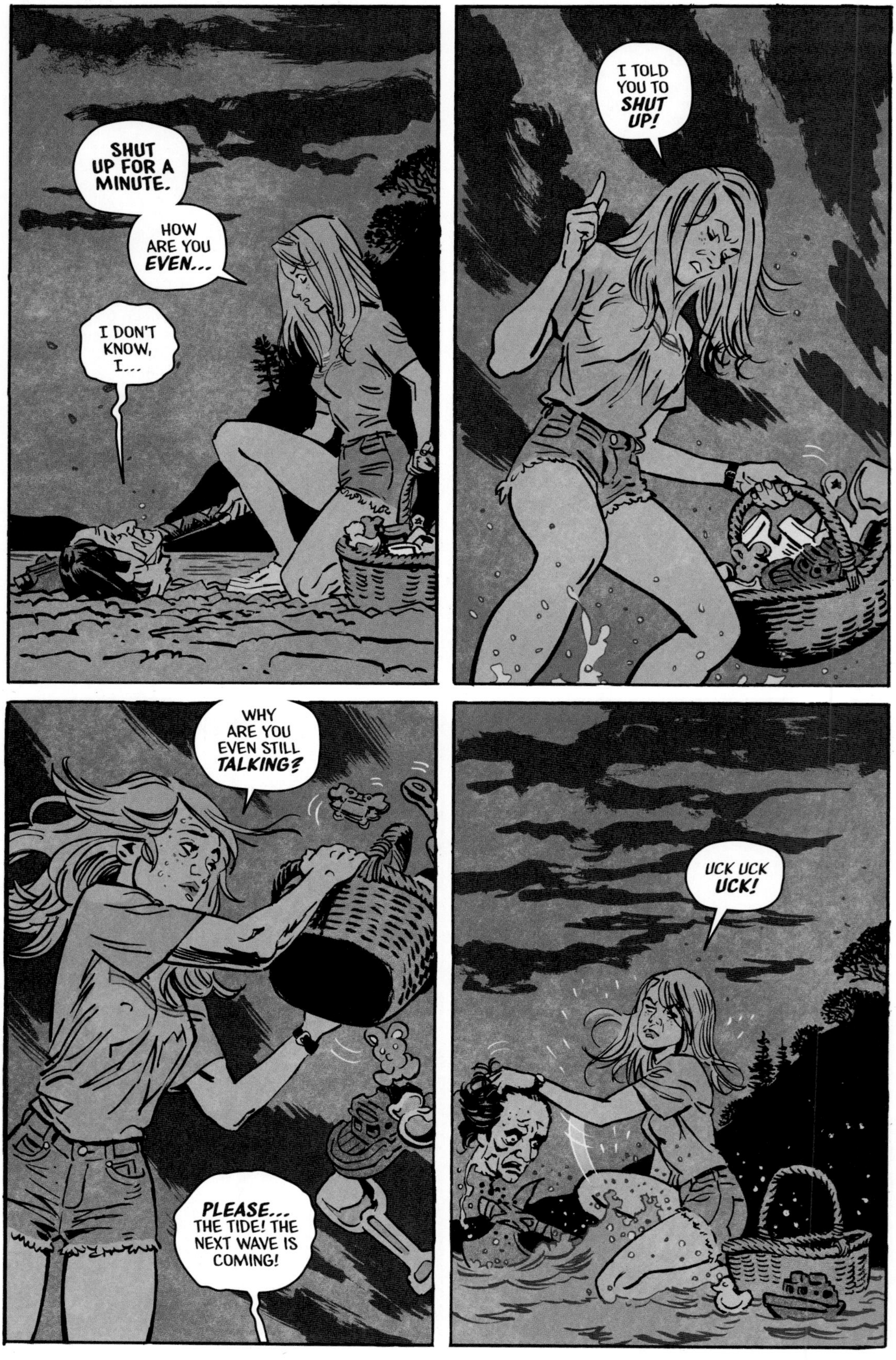
SHUT UP FOR A MINUTE.
HOW ARE YOU EVEN...
I DON'T KNOW, I...
I TOLD YOU TO SHUT UP!
WHY ARE YOU EVEN STILL TALKING?
PLEASE... THE TIDE! THE NEXT WAVE IS COMING!
UCK UCK UCK!

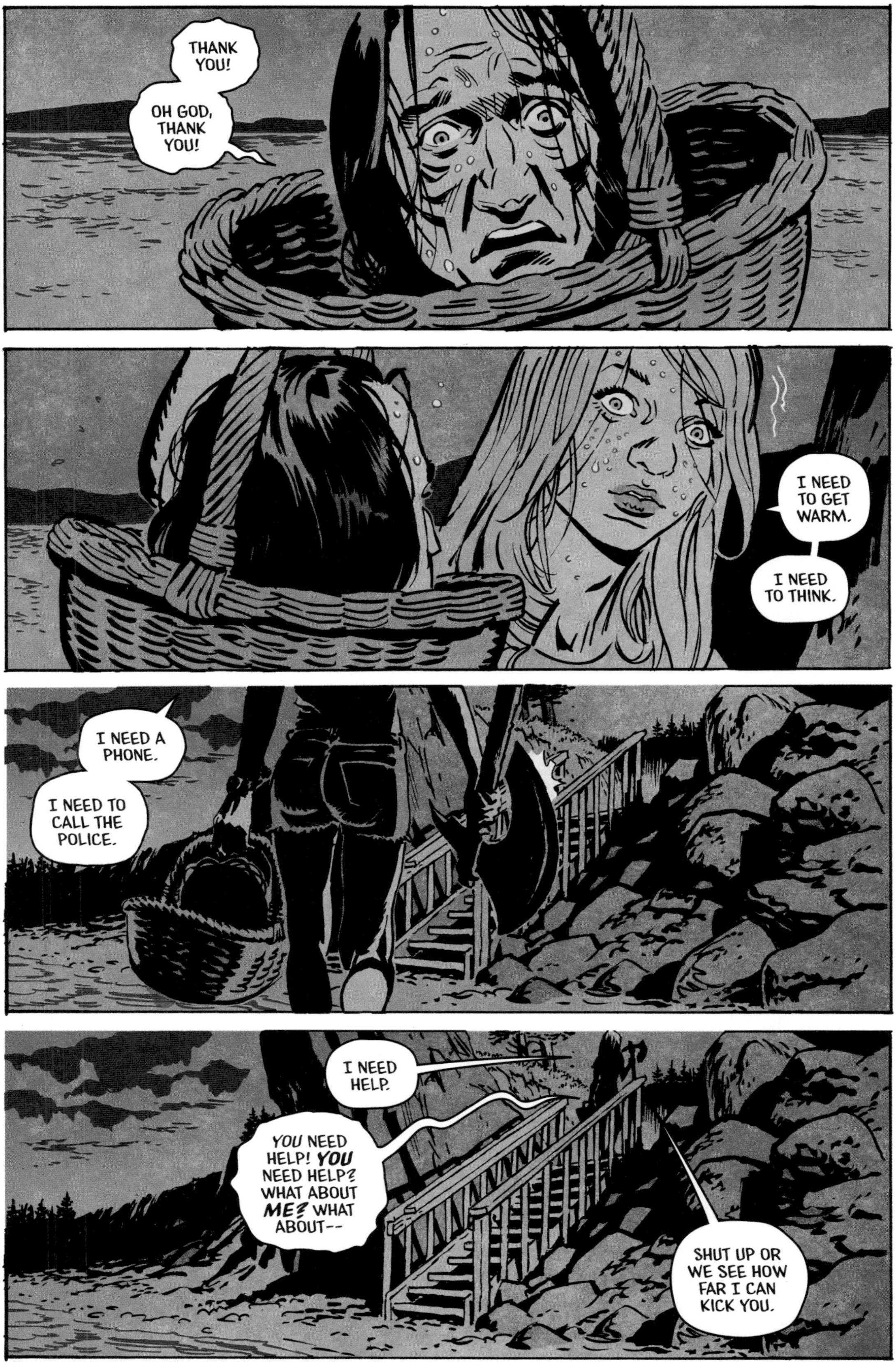
THANK YOU!
OH GOD, THANK YOU!
I NEED TO GET WARM.
I NEED TO THINK.
I NEED A PHONE.
I NEED TO CALL THE POLICE.
I NEED HELP.
YOU NEED HELP! YOU NEED HELP? WHAT ABOUT ME? WHAT ABOUT--
SHUT UP OR WE SEE HOW FAR I CAN KICK YOU.

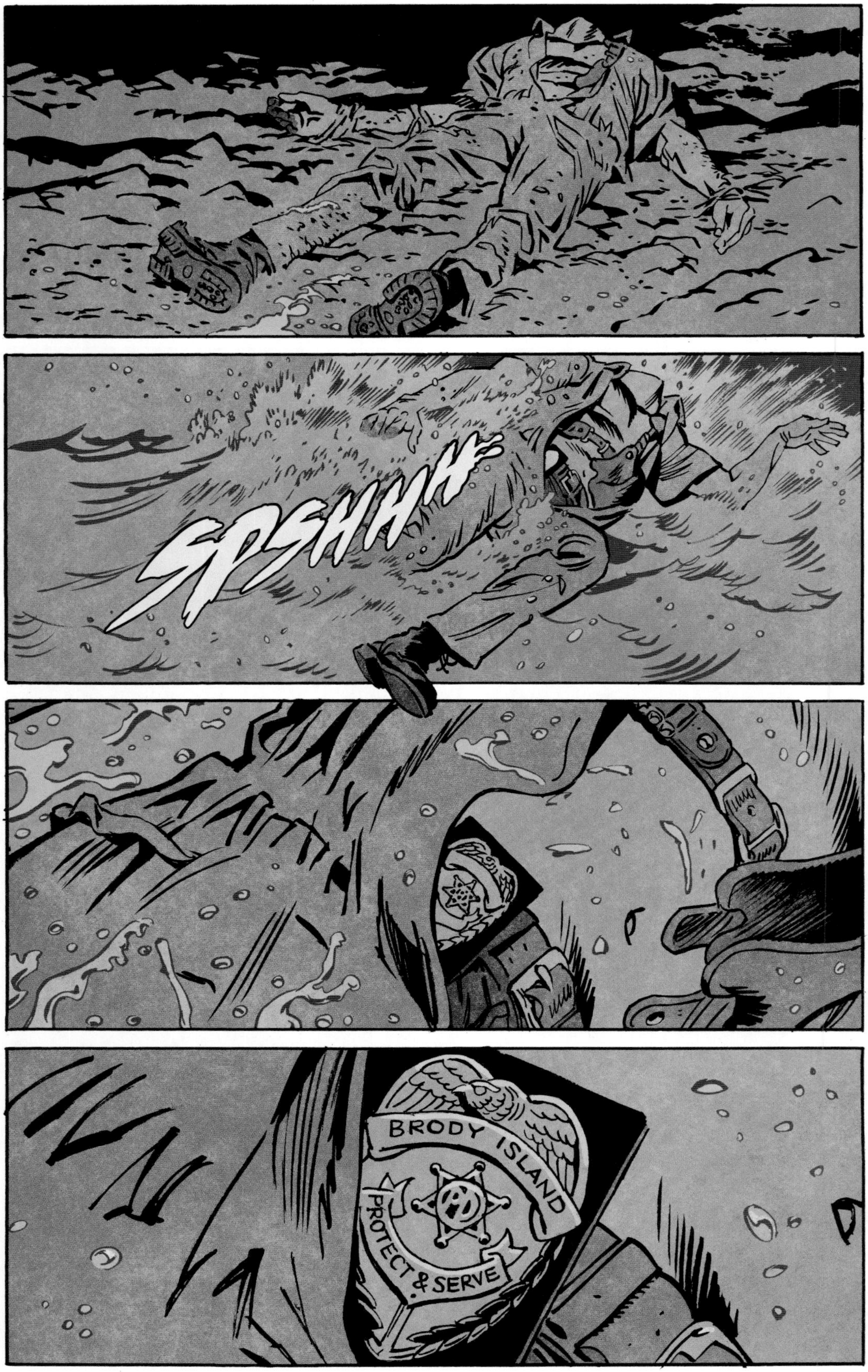
SPSHHH
BRODY ISLAND
PD
PROTECT & SERVE

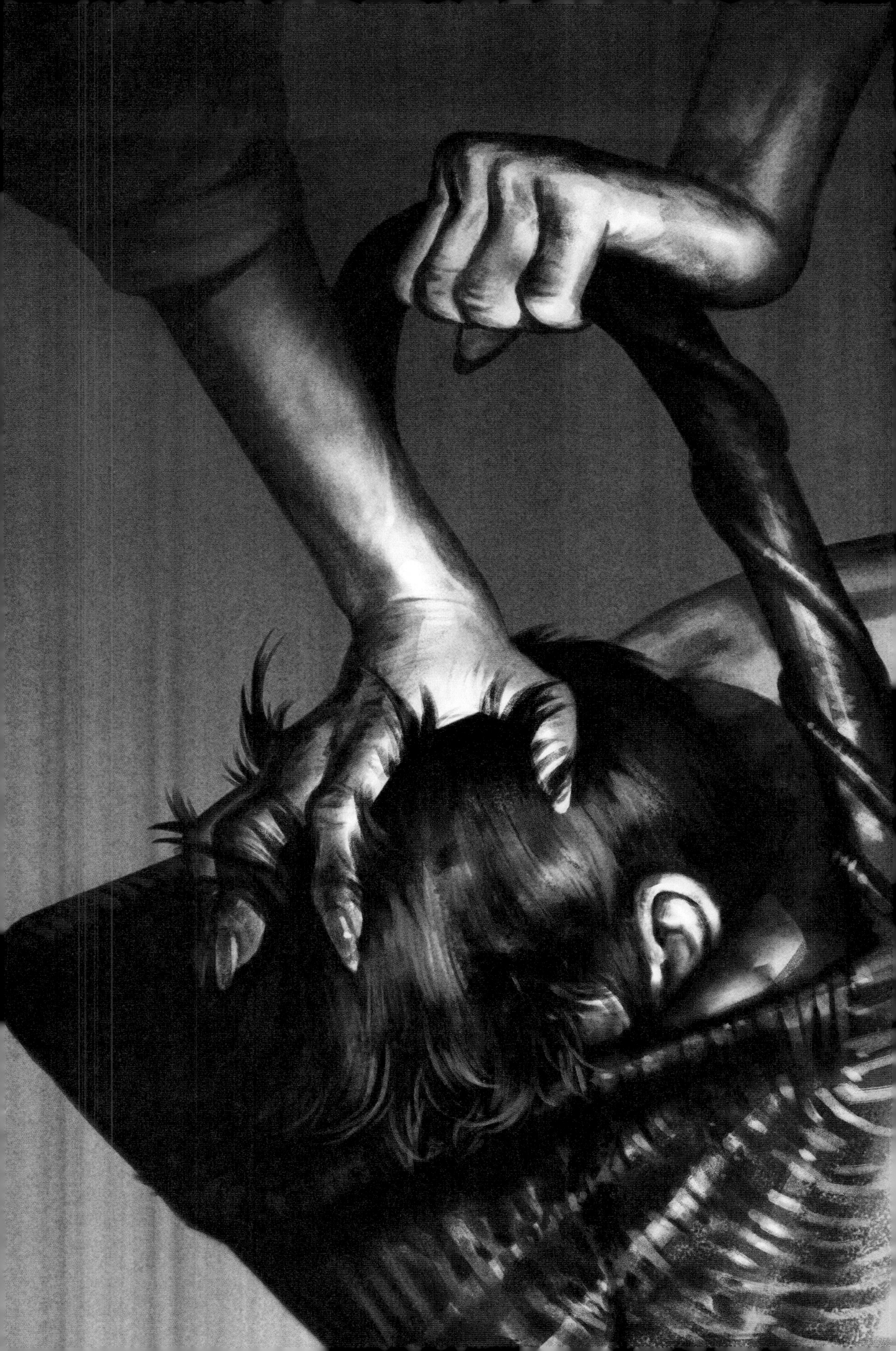

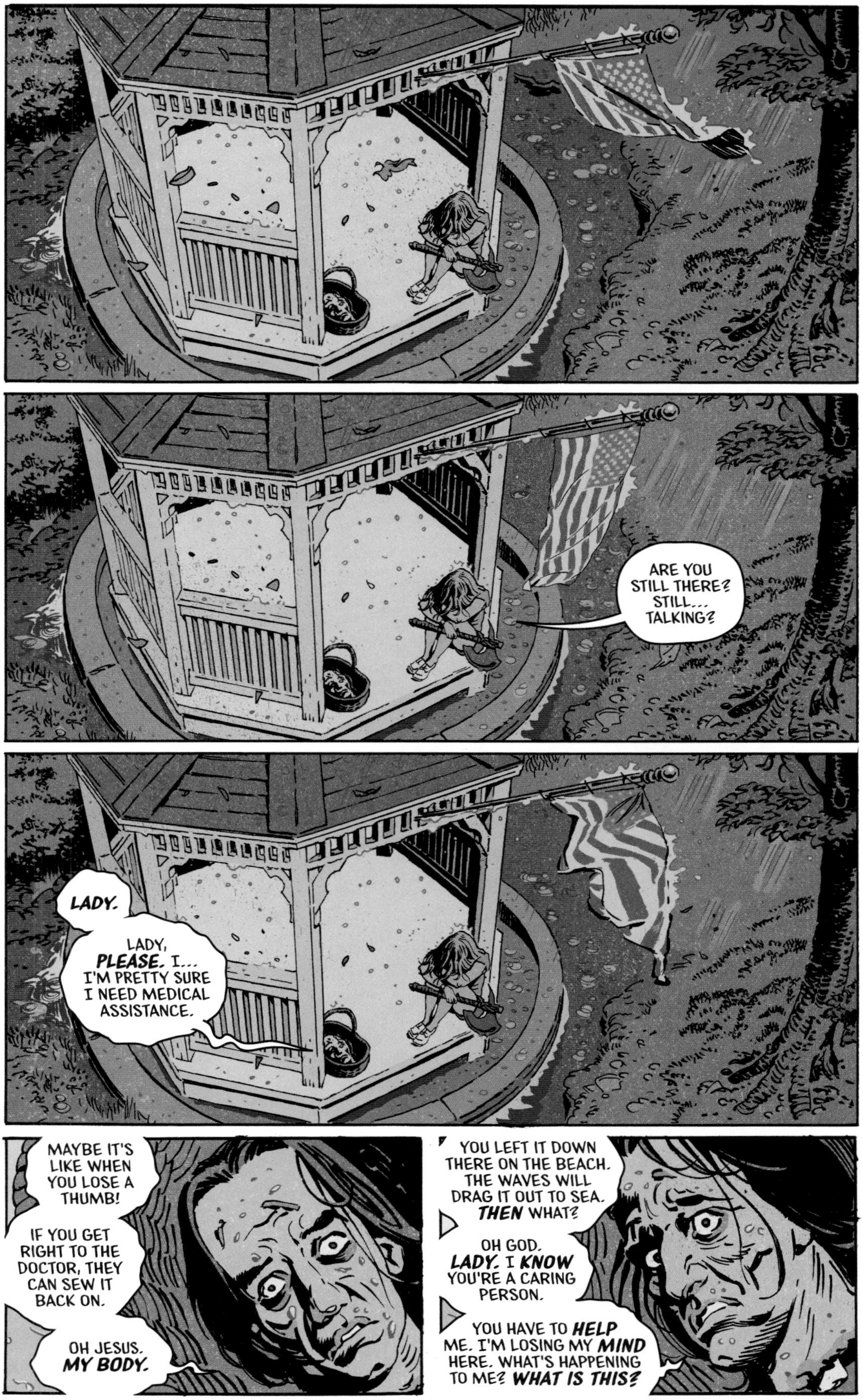

ARE YOU STILL THERE? STILL... TALKING?
LADY.
LADY, PLEASE. I... I'M PRETTY SURE I NEED MEDICAL ASSISTANCE.
MAYBE IT'S LIKE WHEN YOU LOSE A THUMB!
IF YOU GET RIGHT TO THE DOCTOR, THEY CAN SEW IT BACK ON.
OH JESUS. MY BODY.
YOU LEFT IT DOWN THERE ON THE BEACH. THE WAVES WILL DRAG IT OUT TO SEA. THEN WHAT?
OH GOD. LADY. I KNOW YOU'RE A CARING PERSON.
YOU HAVE TO HELP ME. I'M LOSING MY MIND HERE. WHAT'S HAPPENING TO ME? WHAT IS THIS?

Written by **JOE HILL**   Illustrated by **LEOMACS**
Colored by **DAVE STEWART** lettered by **DERON BENNETT**
Edited by **MARK DOYLE & AMEDEO TURTURRO**
Cover by **REIKO MURAKAMI**

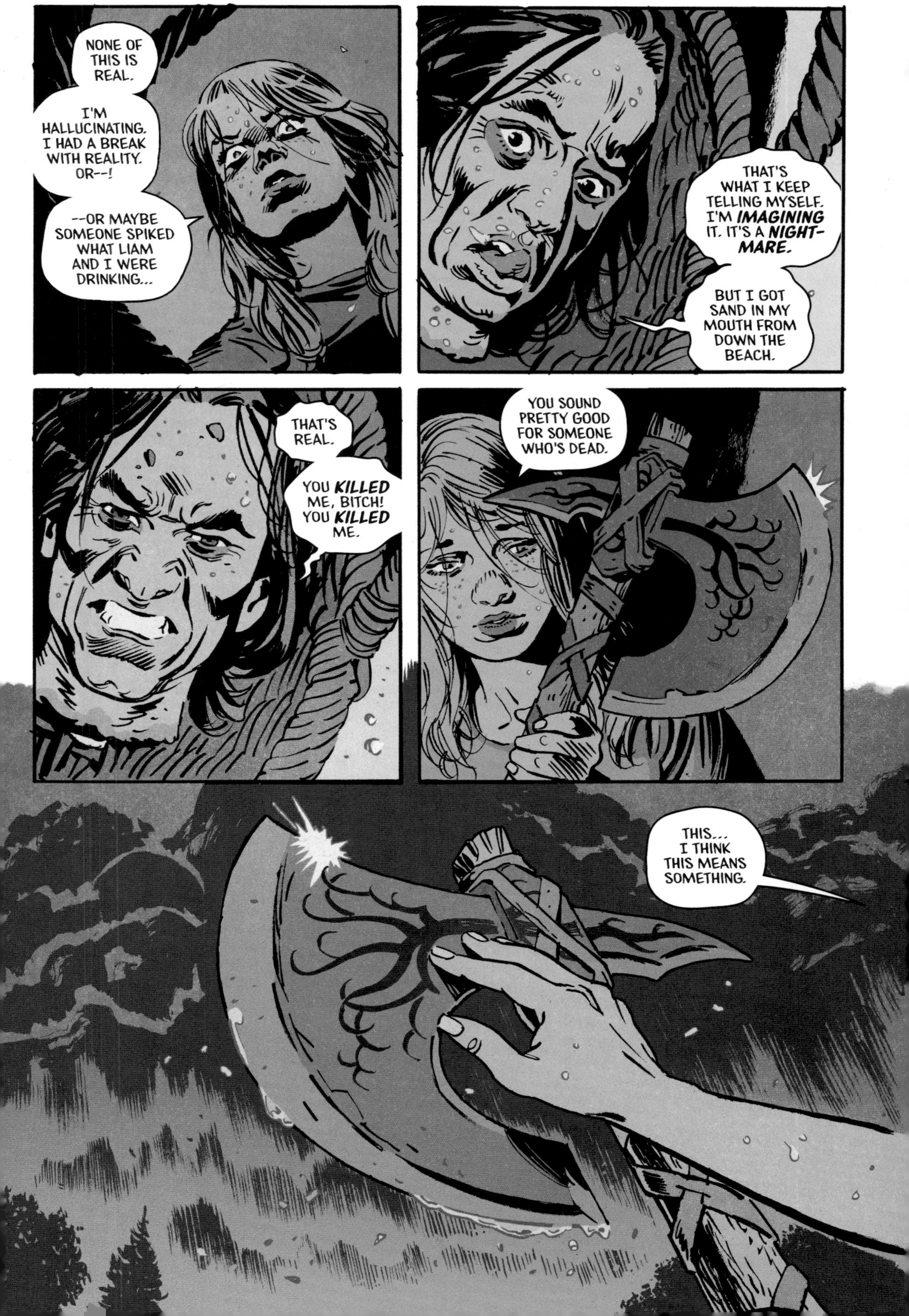
NONE OF THIS IS REAL.
I'M HALLUCINATING. I HAD A BREAK WITH REALITY. OR--!
--OR MAYBE SOMEONE SPIKED WHAT LIAM AND I WERE DRINKING...
THAT'S WHAT I KEEP TELLING MYSELF. I'M *IMAGINING* IT. IT'S A *NIGHT-MARE.*
BUT I GOT SAND IN MY MOUTH FROM DOWN THE BEACH.
THAT'S REAL.
YOU *KILLED* ME, BITCH! YOU *KILLED* ME.
YOU SOUND PRETTY GOOD FOR SOMEONE WHO'S DEAD.
THIS... I THINK THIS MEANS SOMETHING.

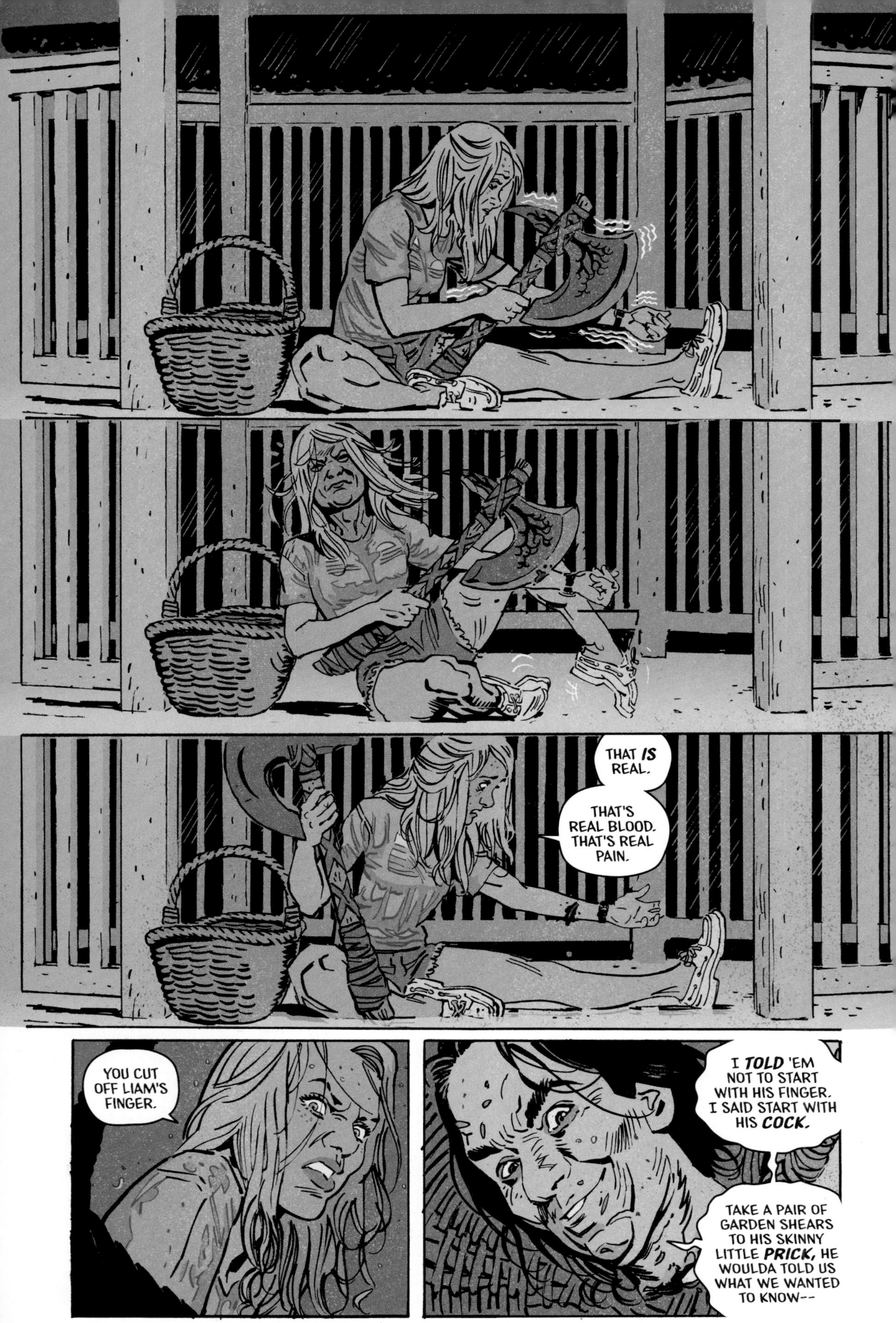
THAT *IS* REAL.
THAT'S REAL BLOOD. THAT'S REAL PAIN.
YOU CUT OFF LIAM'S FINGER.
I *TOLD* 'EM NOT TO START WITH HIS FINGER. I SAID START WITH HIS *COCK.*
TAKE A PAIR OF GARDEN SHEARS TO HIS SKINNY LITTLE *PRICK,* HE WOULDA TOLD US WHAT WE WANTED TO KNOW--

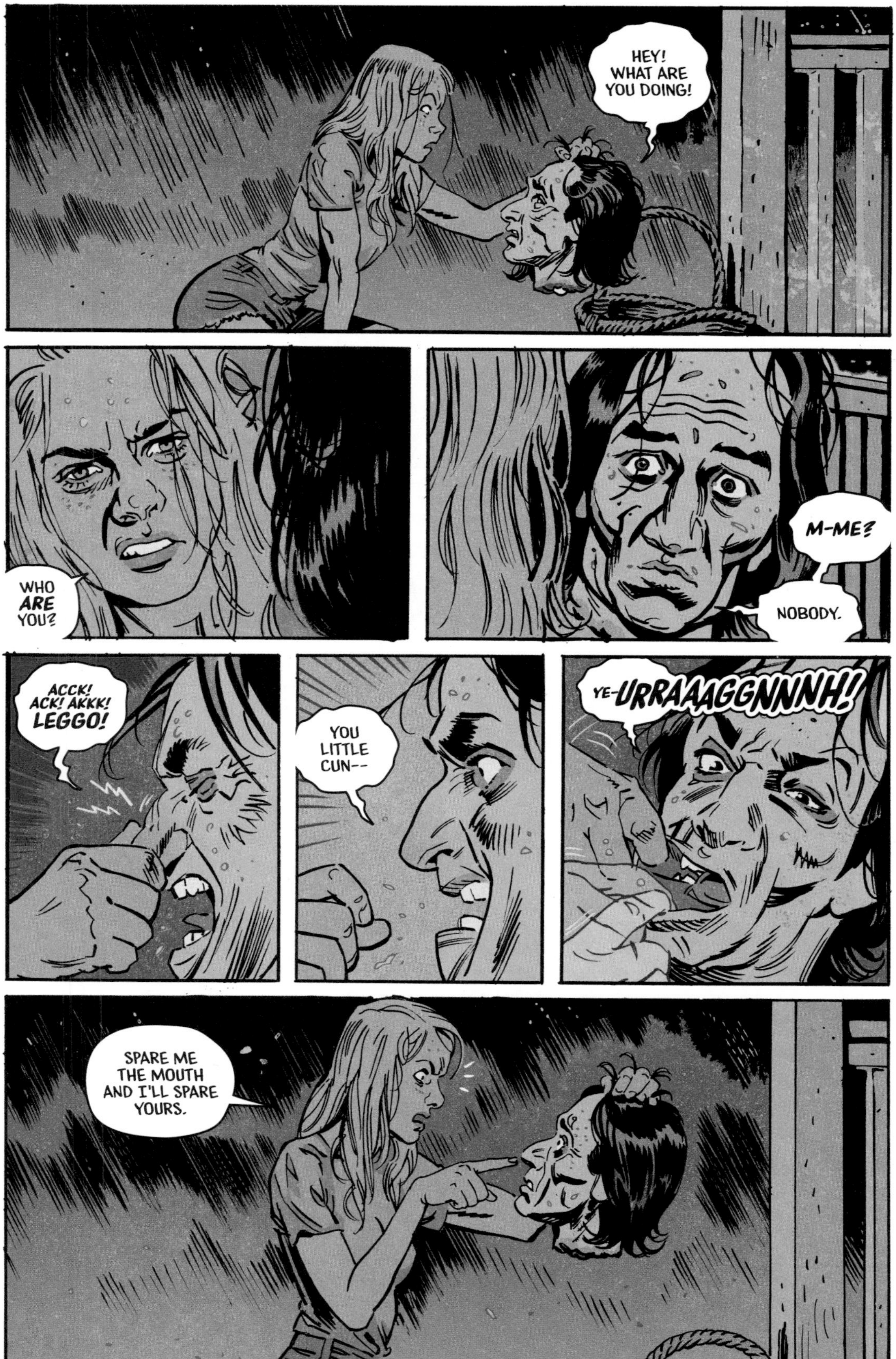
HEY! WHAT ARE YOU DOING!
WHO ARE YOU?
M-ME?
NOBODY.
ACCK! ACK! AKKK! LEGGO!
YOU LITTLE CUN--
YE-URRAAAGGNNNH!
SPARE ME THE MOUTH AND I'LL SPARE YOURS.

YOU'RE ONE OF THE ESCAPEES. WHICH ONE? YOU THE ONE WHO PIMPED HIS DAUGHTERS?

I HOPE YOU'RE THAT ONE. I'LL PLAY SOCCER WITH YOUR FACE, DIRTBAG.

NO! *NO! JESUS!* I SLUNG A LITTLE *DOPE,* THAT'S ALL. I DIDN'T EVEN WANT TO ESCAPE. THE OTHER GUYS *MADE* ME GO WITH 'EM!

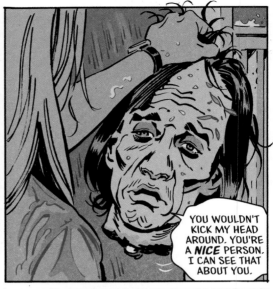

YOU WOULDN'T KICK MY HEAD AROUND. YOU'RE A *NICE* PERSON. I CAN SEE THAT ABOUT YOU.

YEAH? YOU CAN? WHAT GAVE IT AWAY? HOW NICE I AM?

WAS IT WHEN I WHACKED OFF YOUR TOES, OR WHEN I CUT OFF YOUR HEAD?

I WANT MY BOYFRIEND BACK.

WHERE ARE THEY GOING WITH HIM? WHY WOULD THEY-- *WAITAMINUTE.* WHAT DO THEY EVEN *WANT* FROM HIM?

WHAT DO THEY--

THEY CUT OFF HIS FINGER TO MAKE HIM TALK.

TALK ABOUT WHAT?

ABOUT--*UH?* ABOUT YOU! WE KNEW HE HAD A GIRL OVER. I DUNNO, MAYBE ONE OF THE OTHER GUYS WANTED A LITTLE QUIM.

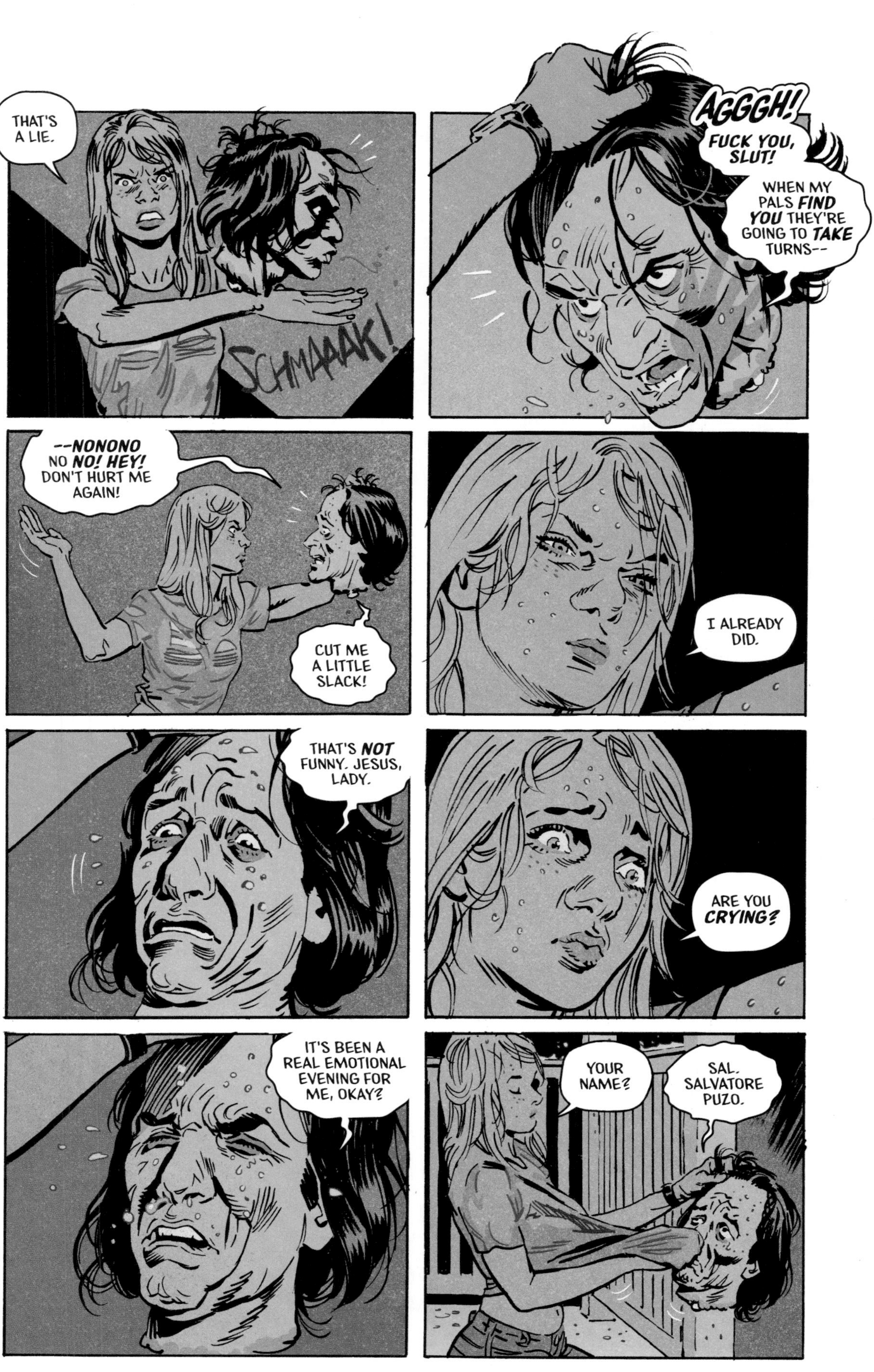
THAT'S A LIE.
SCHMAAAK!
AGGGH!
FUCK YOU, SLUT!
WHEN MY PALS FIND YOU THEY'RE GOING TO TAKE TURNS--
--NONONO NO NO! HEY! DON'T HURT ME AGAIN!
CUT ME A LITTLE SLACK!
I ALREADY DID.
THAT'S NOT FUNNY. JESUS, LADY.
ARE YOU CRYING?
IT'S BEEN A REAL EMOTIONAL EVENING FOR ME, OKAY?
YOUR NAME?
SAL. SALVATORE PUZO.

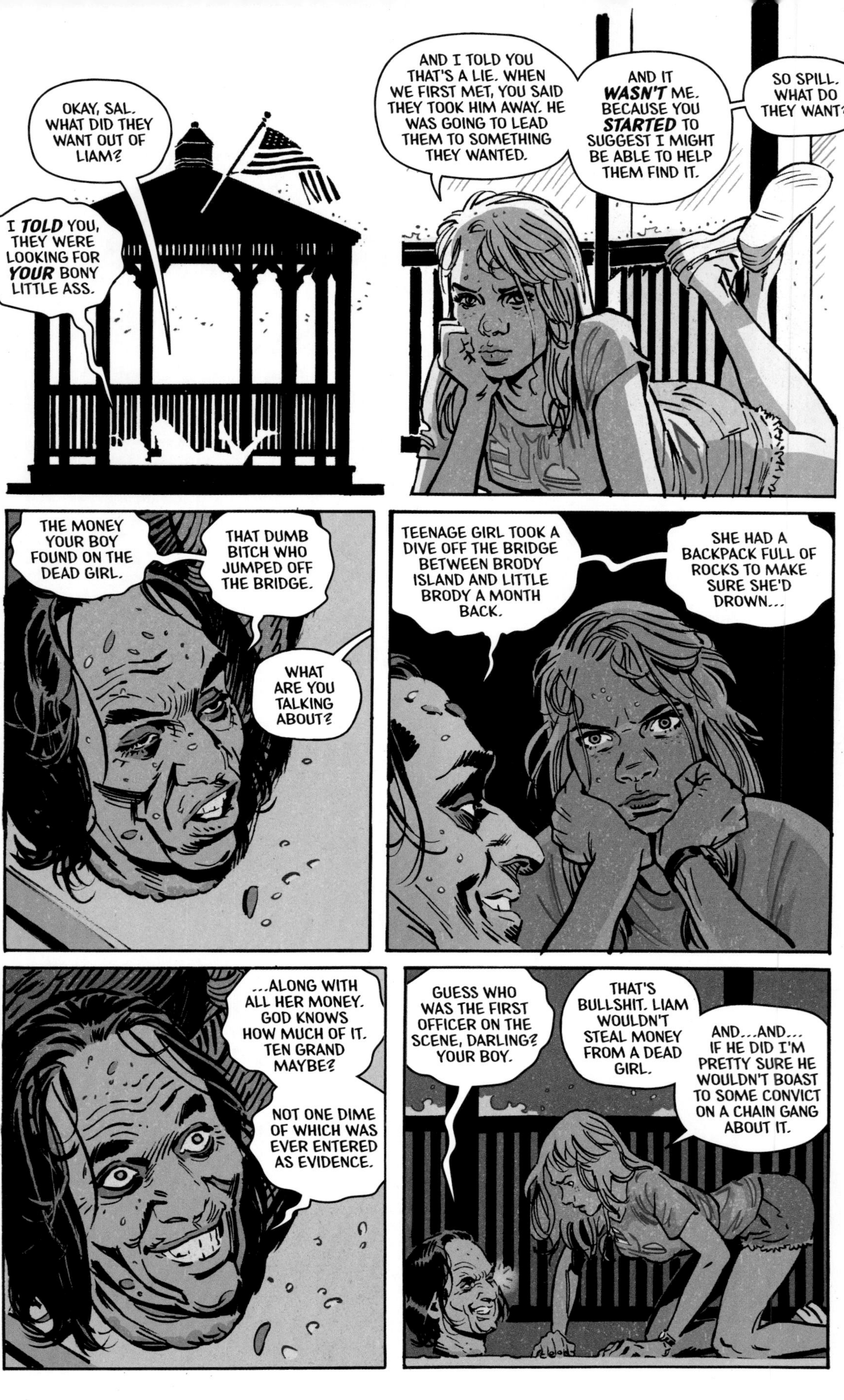
OKAY, SAL. WHAT DID THEY WANT OUT OF LIAM?
I TOLD YOU, THEY WERE LOOKING FOR YOUR BONY LITTLE ASS.
AND I TOLD YOU THAT'S A LIE. WHEN WE FIRST MET, YOU SAID THEY TOOK HIM AWAY. HE WAS GOING TO LEAD THEM TO SOMETHING THEY WANTED.
AND IT WASN'T ME. BECAUSE YOU STARTED TO SUGGEST I MIGHT BE ABLE TO HELP THEM FIND IT.
SO SPILL. WHAT DO THEY WANT?
THE MONEY YOUR BOY FOUND ON THE DEAD GIRL.
THAT DUMB BITCH WHO JUMPED OFF THE BRIDGE.
WHAT ARE YOU TALKING ABOUT?
TEENAGE GIRL TOOK A DIVE OFF THE BRIDGE BETWEEN BRODY ISLAND AND LITTLE BRODY A MONTH BACK.
SHE HAD A BACKPACK FULL OF ROCKS TO MAKE SURE SHE'D DROWN...
...ALONG WITH ALL HER MONEY. GOD KNOWS HOW MUCH OF IT. TEN GRAND MAYBE?
NOT ONE DIME OF WHICH WAS EVER ENTERED AS EVIDENCE.
GUESS WHO WAS THE FIRST OFFICER ON THE SCENE, DARLING? YOUR BOY.
THAT'S BULLSHIT. LIAM WOULDN'T STEAL MONEY FROM A DEAD GIRL.
AND...AND... IF HE DID I'M PRETTY SURE HE WOULDN'T BOAST TO SOME CONVICT ON A CHAIN GANG ABOUT IT.

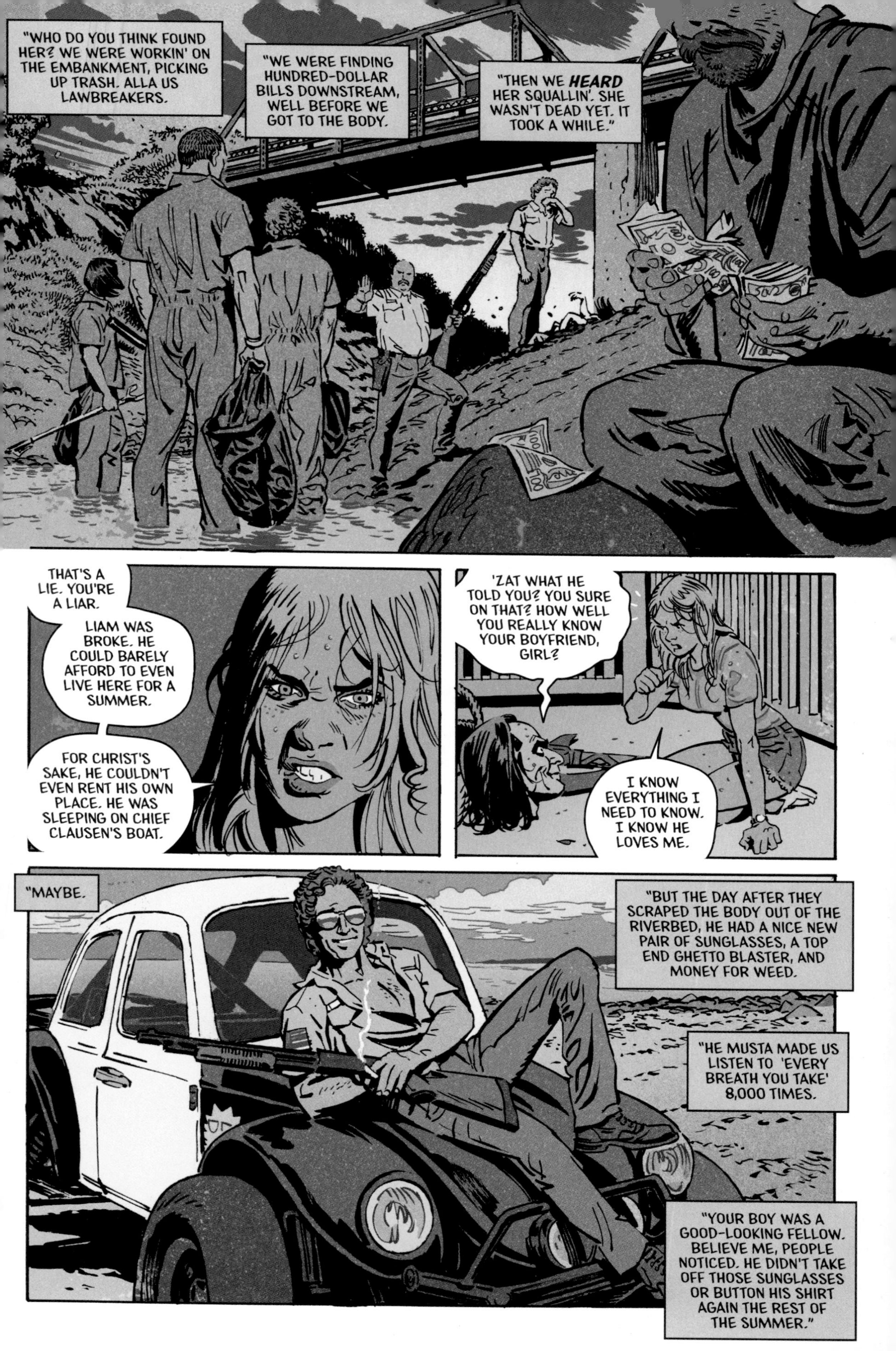
"WHO DO YOU THINK FOUND HER? WE WERE WORKIN' ON THE EMBANKMENT, PICKING UP TRASH. ALLA US LAWBREAKERS.
"WE WERE FINDING HUNDRED-DOLLAR BILLS DOWNSTREAM, WELL BEFORE WE GOT TO THE BODY.
"THEN WE **HEARD** HER SQUALLIN'. SHE WASN'T DEAD YET. IT TOOK A WHILE."
THAT'S A LIE. YOU'RE A LIAR.
LIAM WAS BROKE. HE COULD BARELY AFFORD TO EVEN LIVE HERE FOR A SUMMER.
FOR CHRIST'S SAKE, HE COULDN'T EVEN RENT HIS OWN PLACE. HE WAS SLEEPING ON CHIEF CLAUSEN'S BOAT.
'ZAT WHAT HE TOLD YOU? YOU SURE ON THAT? HOW WELL YOU REALLY KNOW YOUR BOYFRIEND, GIRL?
I KNOW EVERYTHING I NEED TO KNOW. I KNOW HE LOVES ME.
"MAYBE.
"BUT THE DAY AFTER THEY SCRAPED THE BODY OUT OF THE RIVERBED, HE HAD A NICE NEW PAIR OF SUNGLASSES, A TOP END GHETTO BLASTER, AND MONEY FOR WEED.
"HE MUSTA MADE US LISTEN TO 'EVERY BREATH YOU TAKE' 8,000 TIMES.
"YOUR BOY WAS A GOOD-LOOKING FELLOW. BELIEVE ME, PEOPLE NOTICED. HE DIDN'T TAKE OFF THOSE SUNGLASSES OR BUTTON HIS SHIRT AGAIN THE REST OF THE SUMMER."

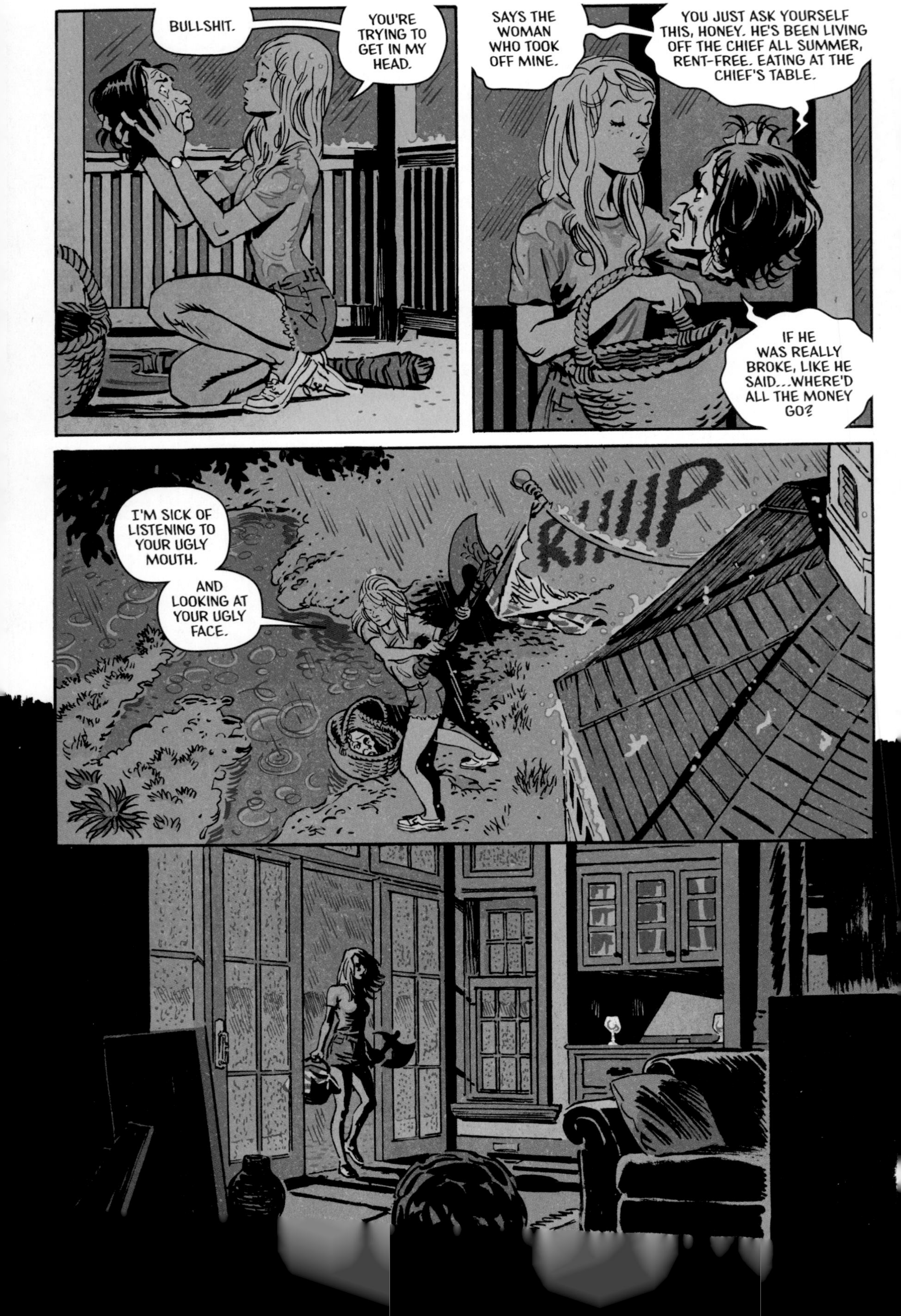
BULLSHIT.
YOU'RE TRYING TO GET IN MY HEAD.
SAYS THE WOMAN WHO TOOK OFF MINE.
YOU JUST ASK YOURSELF THIS, HONEY. HE'S BEEN LIVING OFF THE CHIEF ALL SUMMER, RENT-FREE. EATING AT THE CHIEF'S TABLE.
IF HE WAS REALLY BROKE, LIKE HE SAID...WHERE'D ALL THE MONEY GO?
I'M SICK OF LISTENING TO YOUR UGLY MOUTH.
AND LOOKING AT YOUR UGLY FACE.
RIIIIP

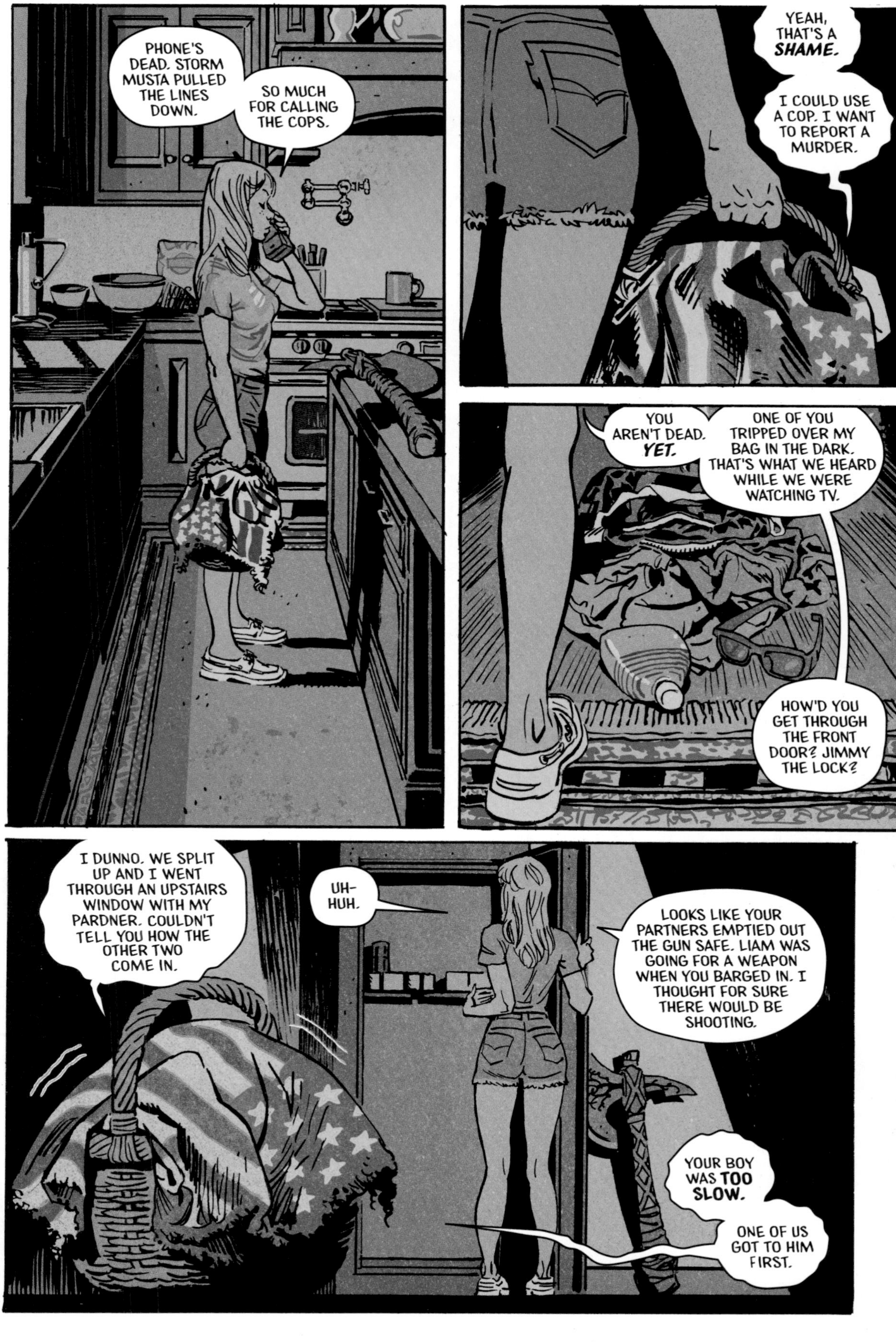
PHONE'S DEAD. STORM MUSTA PULLED THE LINES DOWN.
SO MUCH FOR CALLING THE COPS.
YEAH, THAT'S A SHAME.
I COULD USE A COP. I WANT TO REPORT A MURDER.
YOU AREN'T DEAD. YET.
ONE OF YOU TRIPPED OVER MY BAG IN THE DARK. THAT'S WHAT WE HEARD WHILE WE WERE WATCHING TV.
HOW'D YOU GET THROUGH THE FRONT DOOR? JIMMY THE LOCK?
I DUNNO. WE SPLIT UP AND I WENT THROUGH AN UPSTAIRS WINDOW WITH MY PARDNER. COULDN'T TELL YOU HOW THE OTHER TWO COME IN.
UH-HUH.
LOOKS LIKE YOUR PARTNERS EMPTIED OUT THE GUN SAFE. LIAM WAS GOING FOR A WEAPON WHEN YOU BARGED IN. I THOUGHT FOR SURE THERE WOULD BE SHOOTING.
YOUR BOY WAS TOO SLOW.
ONE OF US GOT TO HIM FIRST.

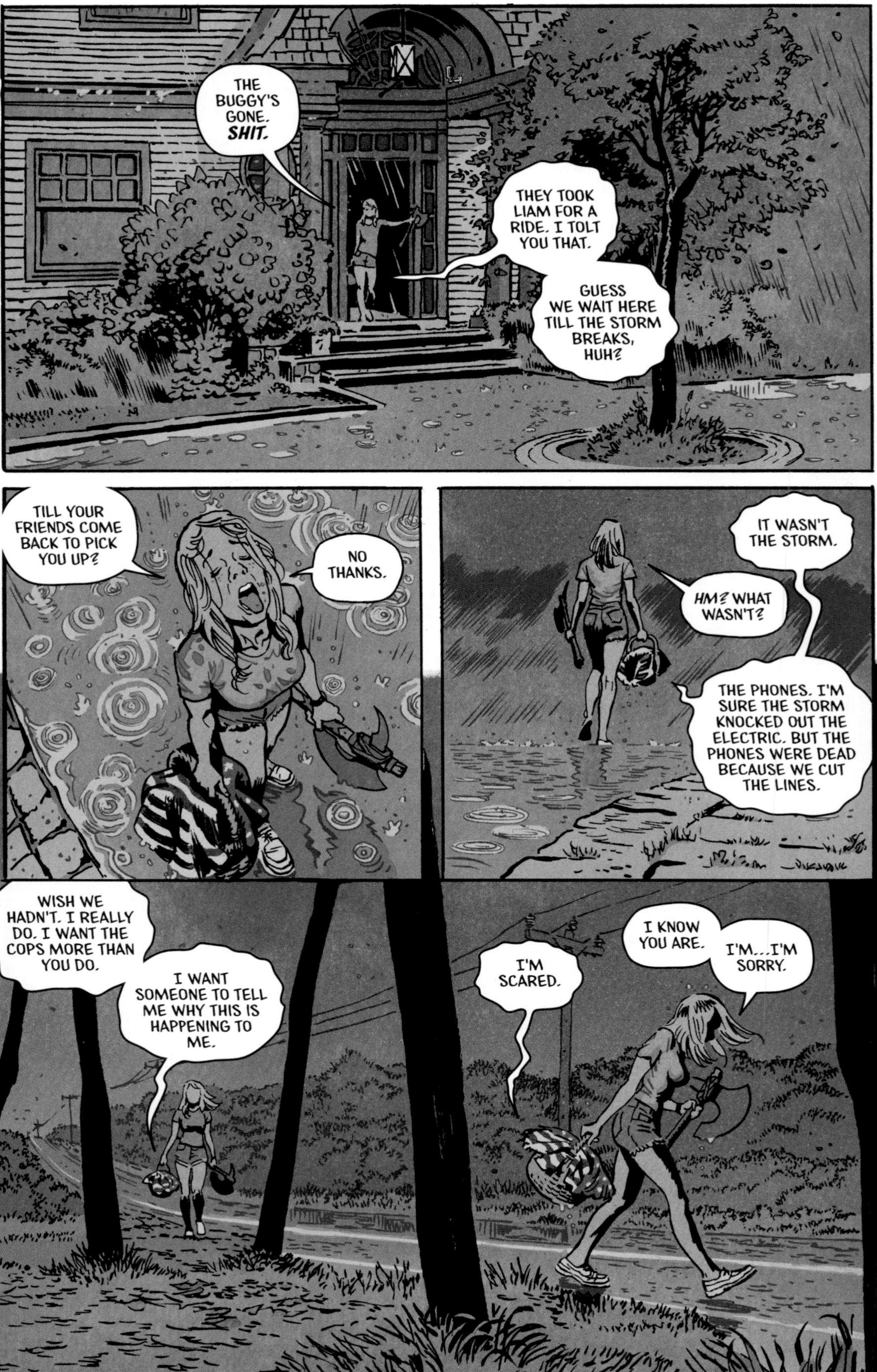
THE BUGGY'S GONE. SHIT.
THEY TOOK LIAM FOR A RIDE. I TOLT YOU THAT.
GUESS WE WAIT HERE TILL THE STORM BREAKS, HUH?
TILL YOUR FRIENDS COME BACK TO PICK YOU UP?
NO THANKS.
IT WASN'T THE STORM.
HM? WHAT WASN'T?
THE PHONES. I'M SURE THE STORM KNOCKED OUT THE ELECTRIC. BUT THE PHONES WERE DEAD BECAUSE WE CUT THE LINES.
WISH WE HADN'T. I REALLY DO. I WANT THE COPS MORE THAN YOU DO.
I WANT SOMEONE TO TELL ME WHY THIS IS HAPPENING TO ME.
I'M SCARED.
I KNOW YOU ARE.
I'M...I'M SORRY.

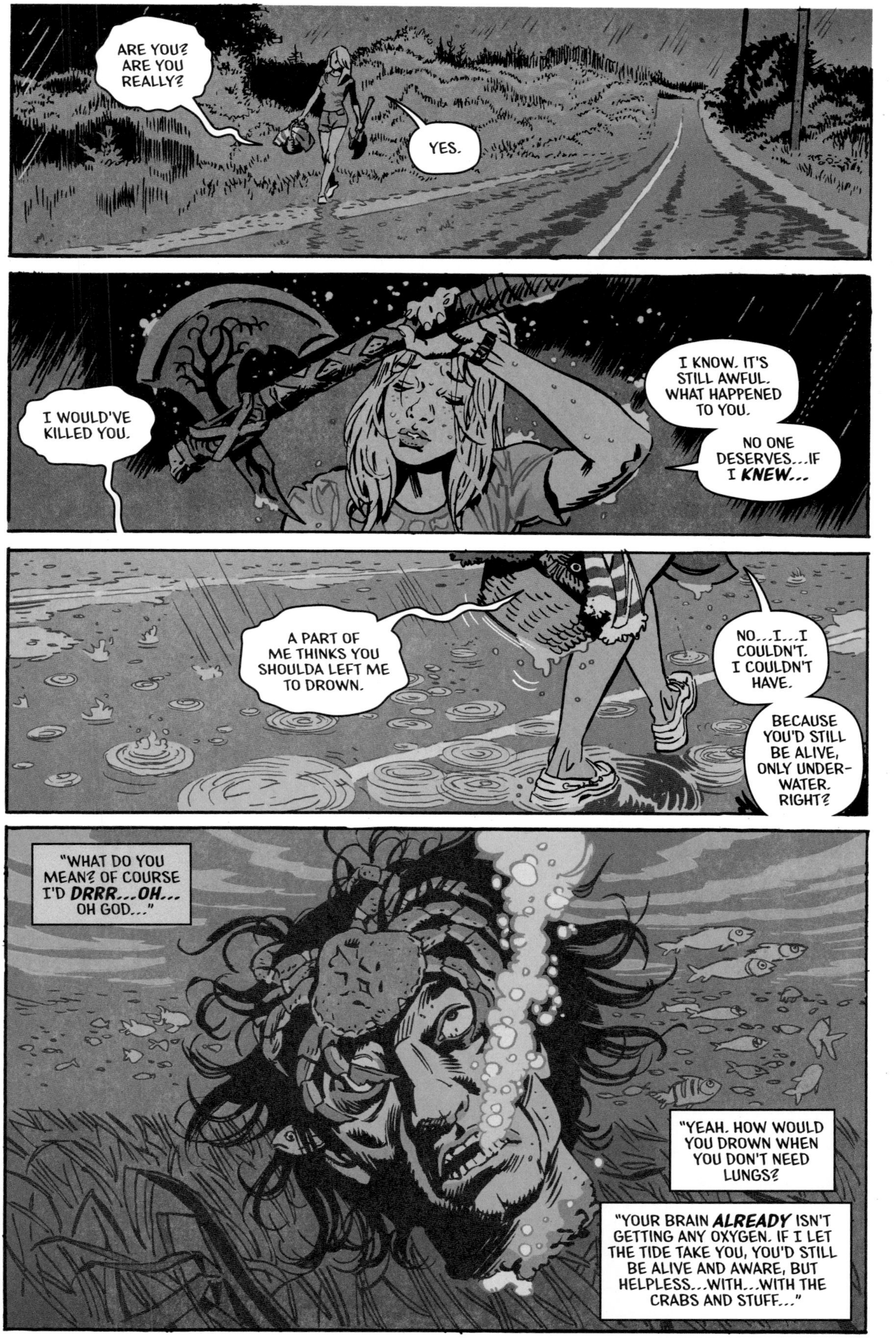
ARE YOU? ARE YOU REALLY?
YES.
I WOULD'VE KILLED YOU.
I KNOW. IT'S STILL AWFUL. WHAT HAPPENED TO YOU.
NO ONE DESERVES...IF I ***KNEW...***
A PART OF ME THINKS YOU SHOULDA LEFT ME TO DROWN.
NO...I...I COULDN'T. I COULDN'T HAVE.
BECAUSE YOU'D STILL BE ALIVE, ONLY UNDER-WATER. RIGHT?
"WHAT DO YOU MEAN? OF COURSE I'D ***DRRR...OH...*** OH GOD..."
"YEAH. HOW WOULD YOU DROWN WHEN YOU DON'T NEED LUNGS?
"YOUR BRAIN ***ALREADY*** ISN'T GETTING ANY OXYGEN. IF I LET THE TIDE TAKE YOU, YOU'D STILL BE ALIVE AND AWARE, BUT HELPLESS...WITH...WITH THE CRABS AND STUFF..."

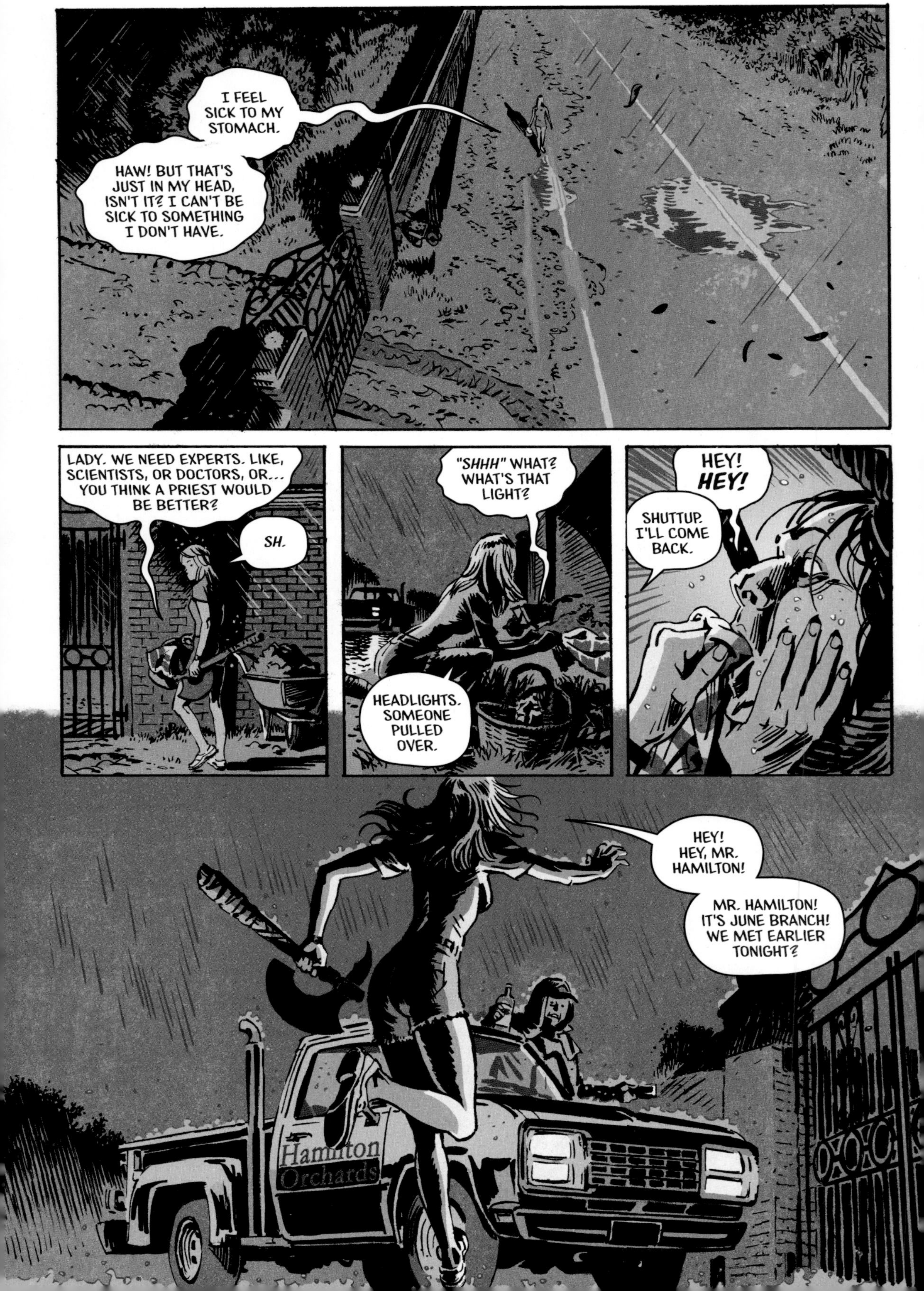
I FEEL SICK TO MY STOMACH.
HAW! BUT THAT'S JUST IN MY HEAD, ISN'T IT? I CAN'T BE SICK TO SOMETHING I DON'T HAVE.
LADY. WE NEED EXPERTS. LIKE, SCIENTISTS, OR DOCTORS, OR... YOU THINK A PRIEST WOULD BE BETTER?
SH.
"SHHH" WHAT? WHAT'S THAT LIGHT?
HEADLIGHTS. SOMEONE PULLED OVER.
HEY! HEY!
SHUTTUP. I'LL COME BACK.
HEY! HEY, MR. HAMILTON!
MR. HAMILTON! IT'S JUNE BRANCH! WE MET EARLIER TONIGHT?
Hamilton Orchards

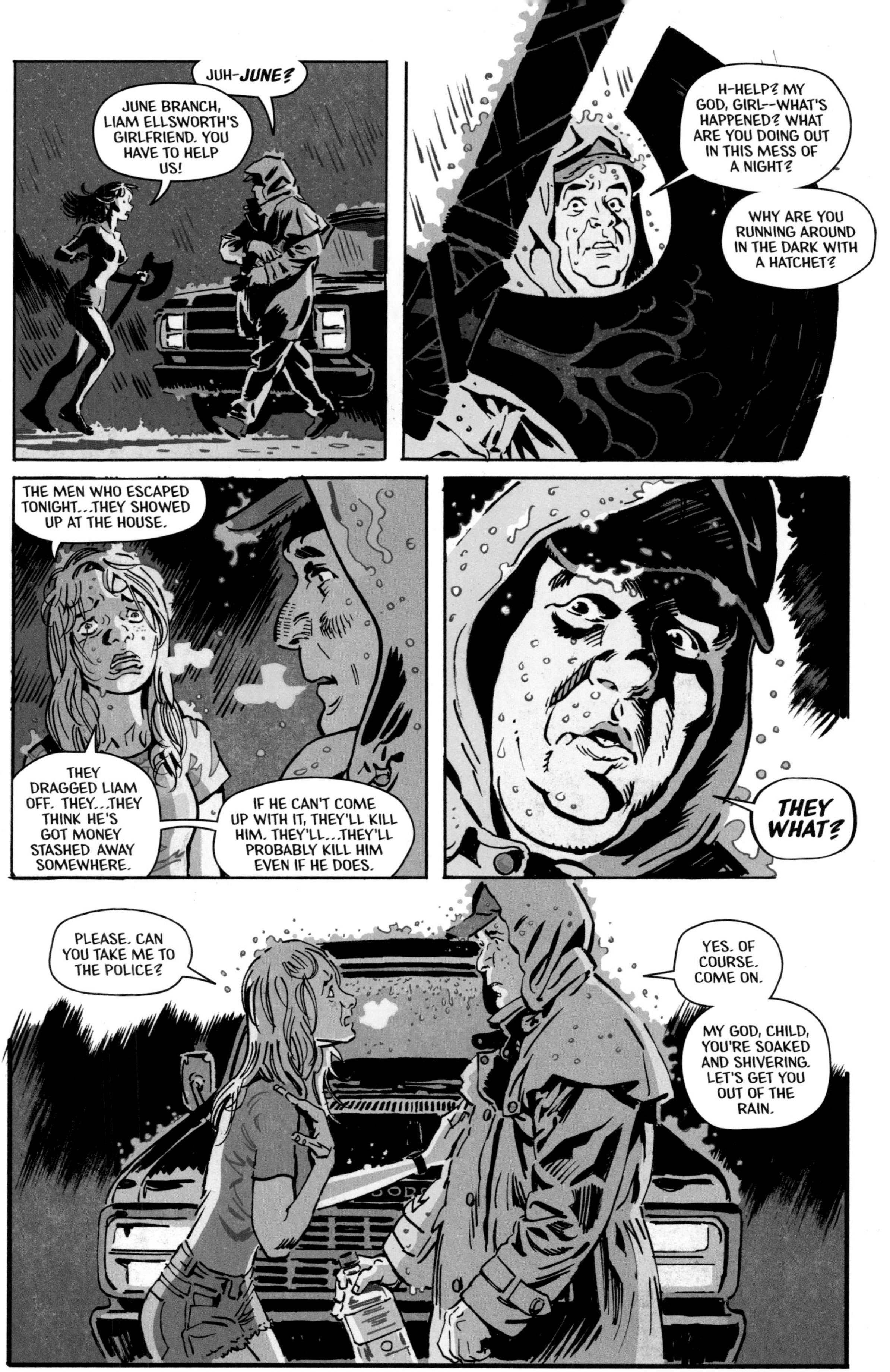
JUH-JUNE?
JUNE BRANCH, LIAM ELLSWORTH'S GIRLFRIEND. YOU HAVE TO HELP US!
H-HELP? MY GOD, GIRL--WHAT'S HAPPENED? WHAT ARE YOU DOING OUT IN THIS MESS OF A NIGHT?
WHY ARE YOU RUNNING AROUND IN THE DARK WITH A HATCHET?
THE MEN WHO ESCAPED TONIGHT...THEY SHOWED UP AT THE HOUSE.
THEY DRAGGED LIAM OFF. THEY...THEY THINK HE'S GOT MONEY STASHED AWAY SOMEWHERE.
IF HE CAN'T COME UP WITH IT, THEY'LL KILL HIM. THEY'LL...THEY'LL PROBABLY KILL HIM EVEN IF HE DOES.
THEY WHAT?
PLEASE. CAN YOU TAKE ME TO THE POLICE?
YES. OF COURSE. COME ON.
MY GOD, CHILD, YOU'RE SOAKED AND SHIVERING. LET'S GET YOU OUT OF THE RAIN.

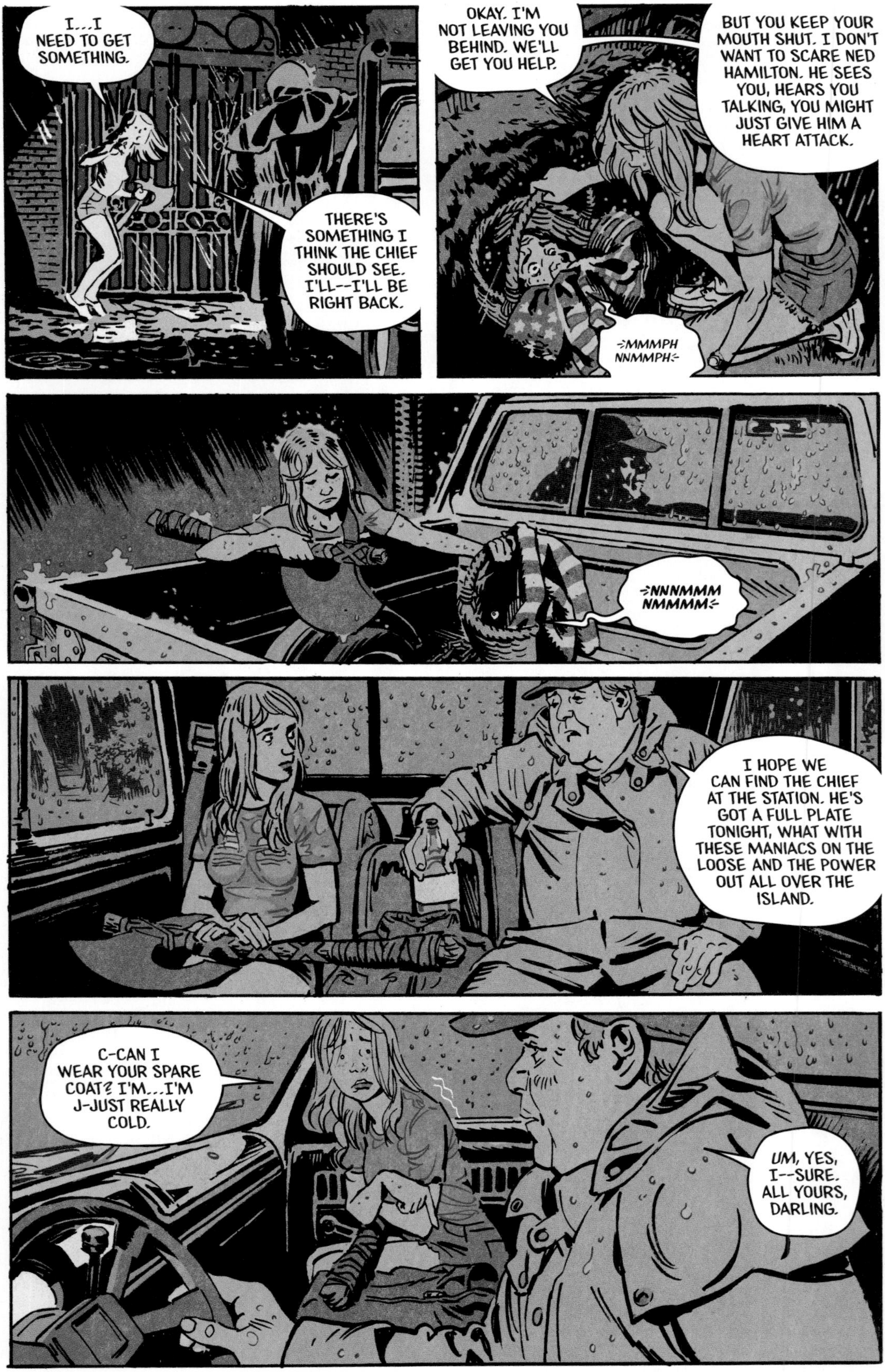
I...I NEED TO GET SOMETHING.
THERE'S SOMETHING I THINK THE CHIEF SHOULD SEE. I'LL--I'LL BE RIGHT BACK.
OKAY. I'M NOT LEAVING YOU BEHIND. WE'LL GET YOU HELP.
BUT YOU KEEP YOUR MOUTH SHUT. I DON'T WANT TO SCARE NED HAMILTON. HE SEES YOU, HEARS YOU TALKING, YOU MIGHT JUST GIVE HIM A HEART ATTACK.
=MMMPH NNMMPH=
=NNNMMM NMMMM=
I HOPE WE CAN FIND THE CHIEF AT THE STATION. HE'S GOT A FULL PLATE TONIGHT, WHAT WITH THESE MANIACS ON THE LOOSE AND THE POWER OUT ALL OVER THE ISLAND.
C-CAN I WEAR YOUR SPARE COAT? I'M...I'M J-JUST REALLY COLD.
UM, YES, I--SURE. ALL YOURS, DARLING.

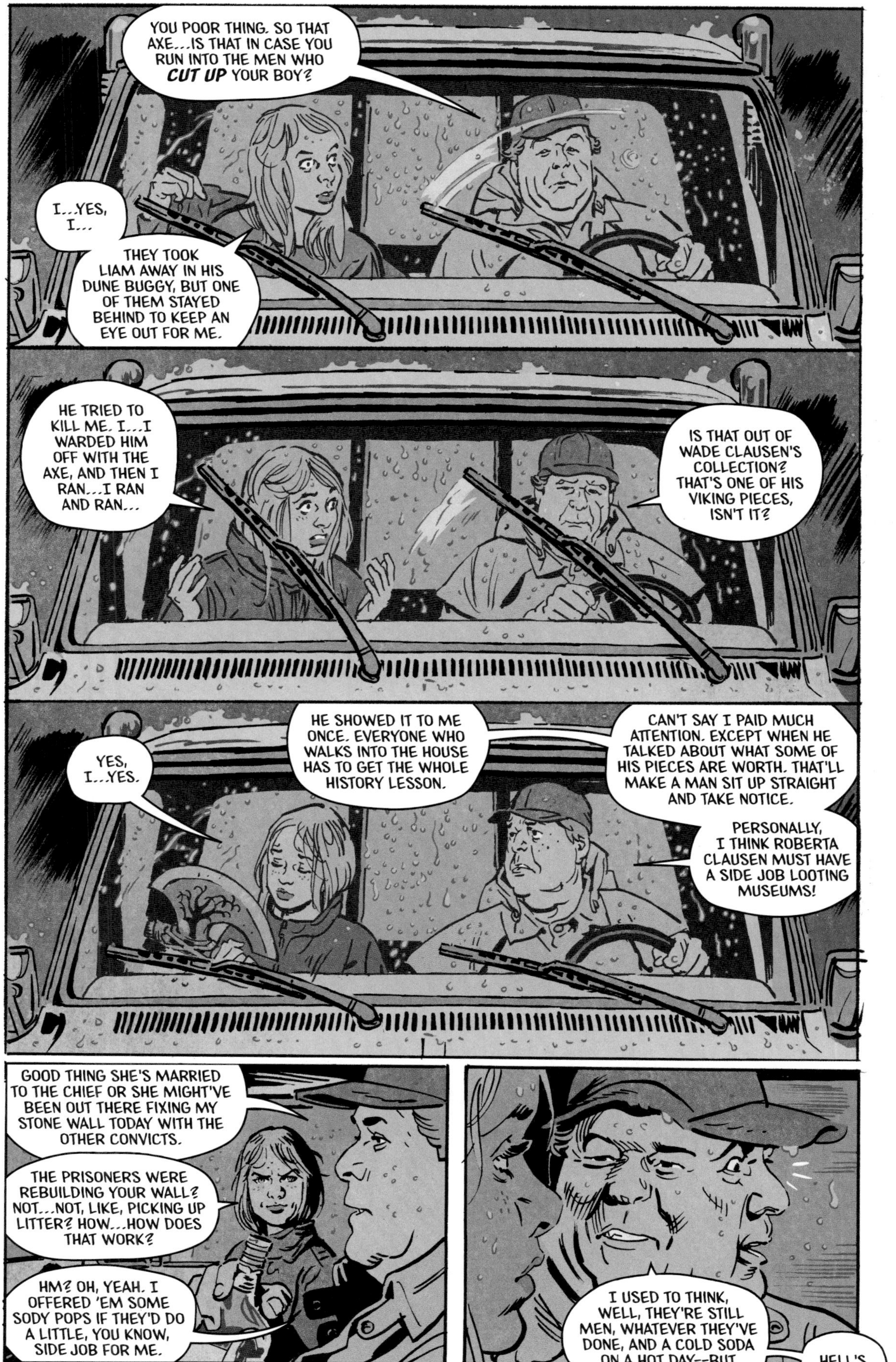
YOU POOR THING. SO THAT AXE...IS THAT IN CASE YOU RUN INTO THE MEN WHO CUT UP YOUR BOY?
I...YES, I...
THEY TOOK LIAM AWAY IN HIS DUNE BUGGY, BUT ONE OF THEM STAYED BEHIND TO KEEP AN EYE OUT FOR ME.
HE TRIED TO KILL ME. I...I WARDED HIM OFF WITH THE AXE, AND THEN I RAN...I RAN AND RAN...
IS THAT OUT OF WADE CLAUSEN'S COLLECTION? THAT'S ONE OF HIS VIKING PIECES, ISN'T IT?
YES, I...YES.
HE SHOWED IT TO ME ONCE. EVERYONE WHO WALKS INTO THE HOUSE HAS TO GET THE WHOLE HISTORY LESSON.
CAN'T SAY I PAID MUCH ATTENTION. EXCEPT WHEN HE TALKED ABOUT WHAT SOME OF HIS PIECES ARE WORTH. THAT'LL MAKE A MAN SIT UP STRAIGHT AND TAKE NOTICE.
PERSONALLY, I THINK ROBERTA CLAUSEN MUST HAVE A SIDE JOB LOOTING MUSEUMS!
GOOD THING SHE'S MARRIED TO THE CHIEF OR SHE MIGHT'VE BEEN OUT THERE FIXING MY STONE WALL TODAY WITH THE OTHER CONVICTS.
THE PRISONERS WERE REBUILDING YOUR WALL? NOT...NOT, LIKE, PICKING UP LITTER? HOW...HOW DOES THAT WORK?
HM? OH, YEAH. I OFFERED 'EM SOME SODY POPS IF THEY'D DO A LITTLE, YOU KNOW, SIDE JOB FOR ME.
I USED TO THINK, WELL, THEY'RE STILL MEN, WHATEVER THEY'VE DONE, AND A COLD SODA ON A HOT DAY--BUT AFTER TONIGHT--
HELL'S THAT?

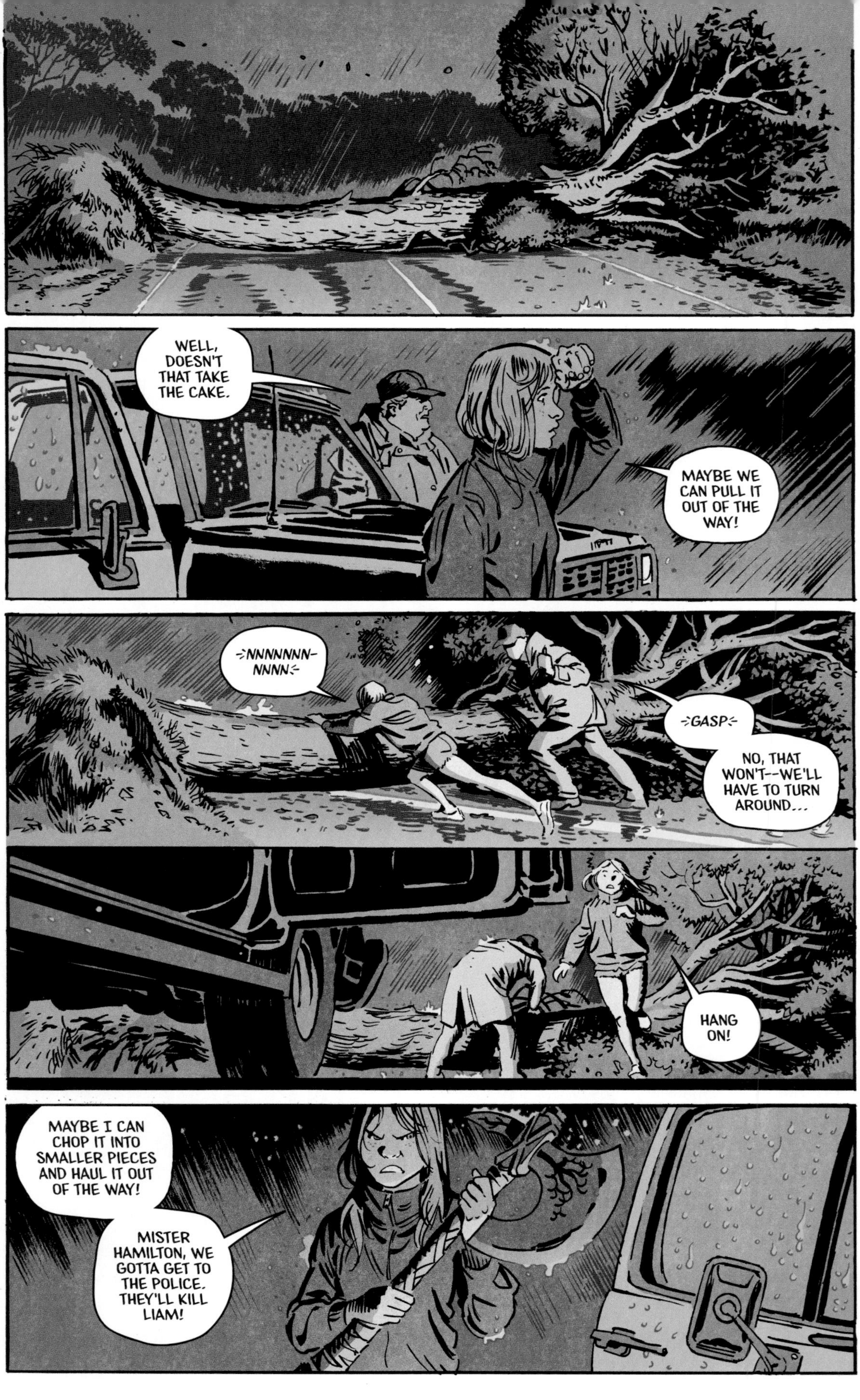
WELL, DOESN'T THAT TAKE THE CAKE.
MAYBE WE CAN PULL IT OUT OF THE WAY!
NNNNNNN-NNNN
GASP
NO, THAT WON'T--WE'LL HAVE TO TURN AROUND...
HANG ON!
MAYBE I CAN CHOP IT INTO SMALLER PIECES AND HAUL IT OUT OF THE WAY!
MISTER HAMILTON, WE GOTTA GET TO THE POLICE. THEY'LL KILL LIAM!

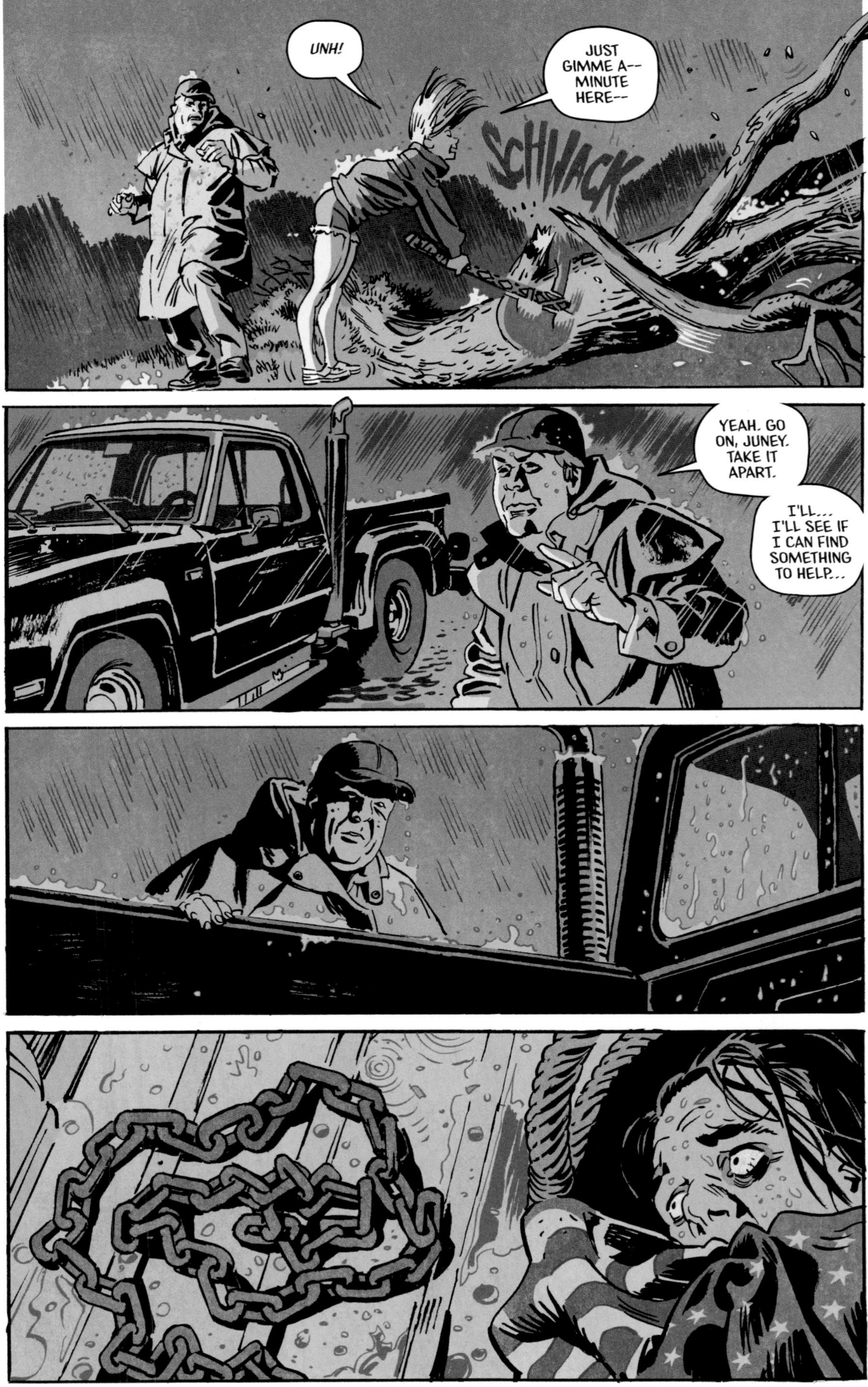
UNH!
JUST GIMME A-- MINUTE HERE--
SCHWACK
YEAH. GO ON, JUNEY. TAKE IT APART.
I'LL... I'LL SEE IF I CAN FIND SOMETHING TO HELP...

THERE. THAT'S PART OF IT, MR. HAMILTON.

UGH. CRAMP.

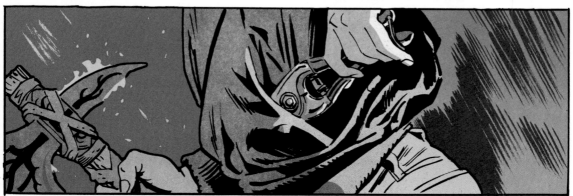

HNH.

TAKE A PAIR OF GARDEN SHEARS TO HIS SKINNY LITTLE *PRICK*, HE WOULDA TOLD US WHAT WE WANTED TO KNOW--

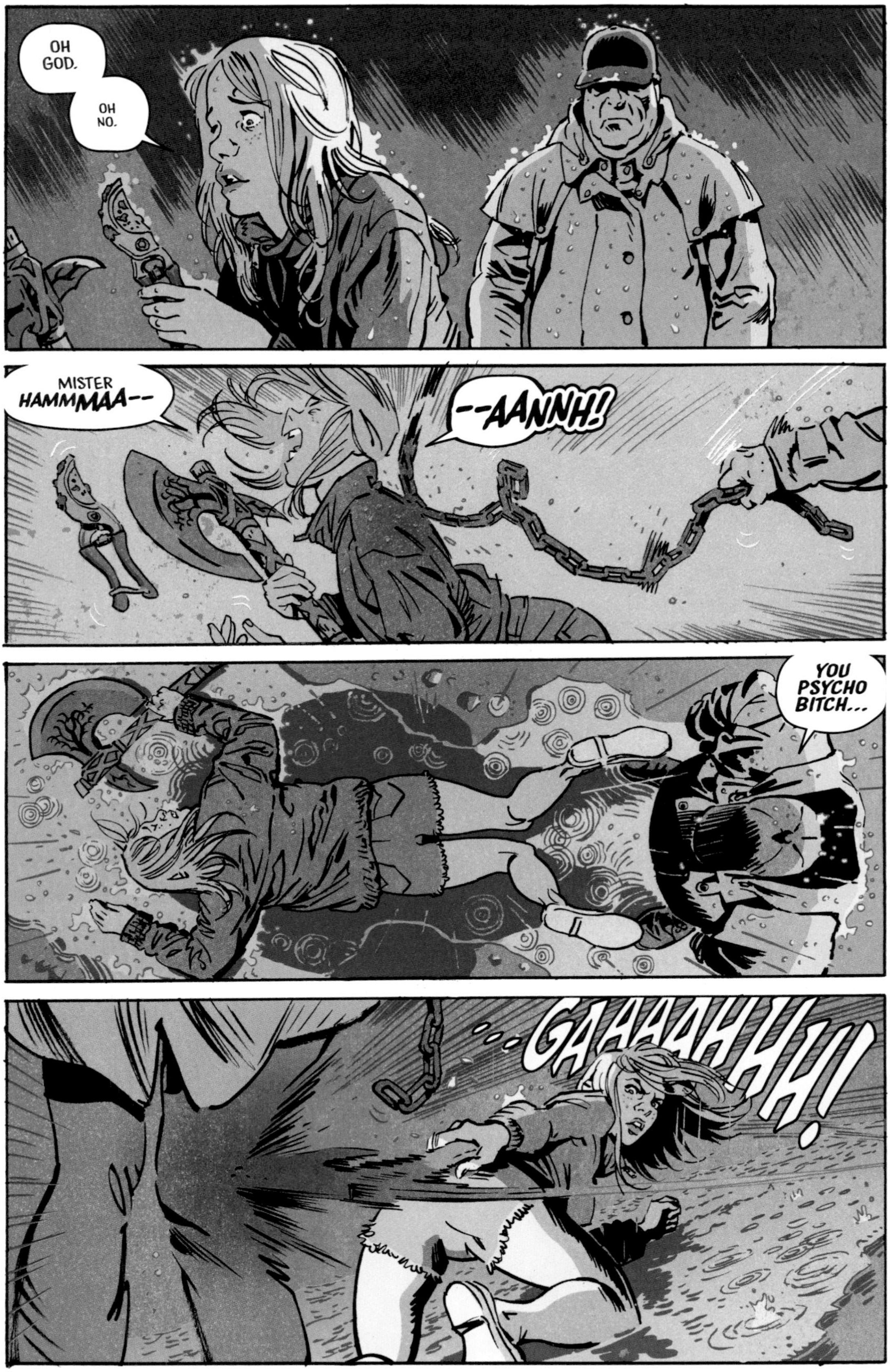
OH GOD.
OH NO.
MISTER HAMMMAA--
--AANNH!
YOU PSYCHO BITCH...
--GAAAAHHH!

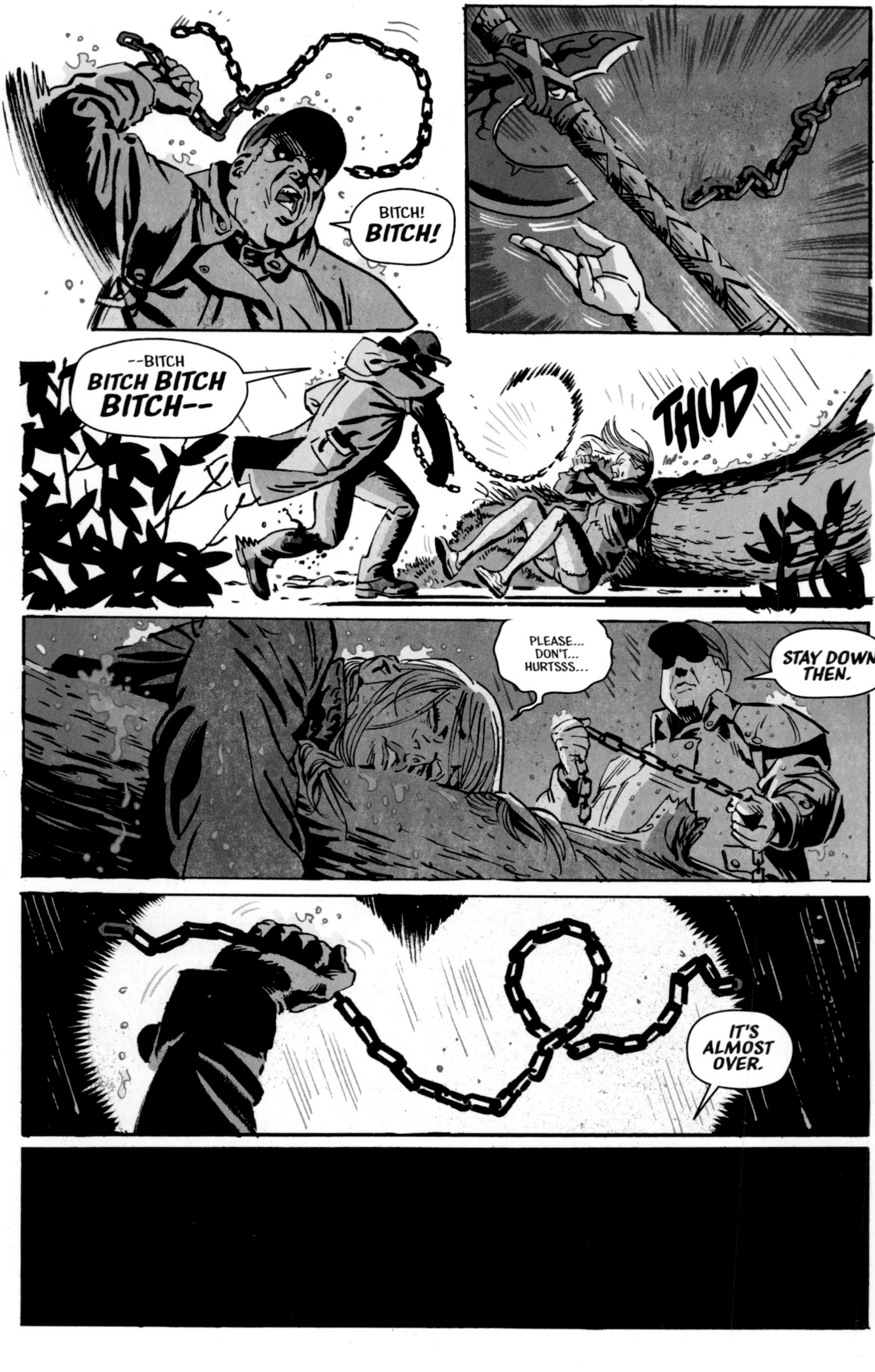
BITCH!
BITCH!
--BITCH
BITCH BITCH
BITCH--
THUD
PLEASE...
DON'T...
HURTSSS...
STAY DOWN
THEN.
IT'S
ALMOST
OVER.

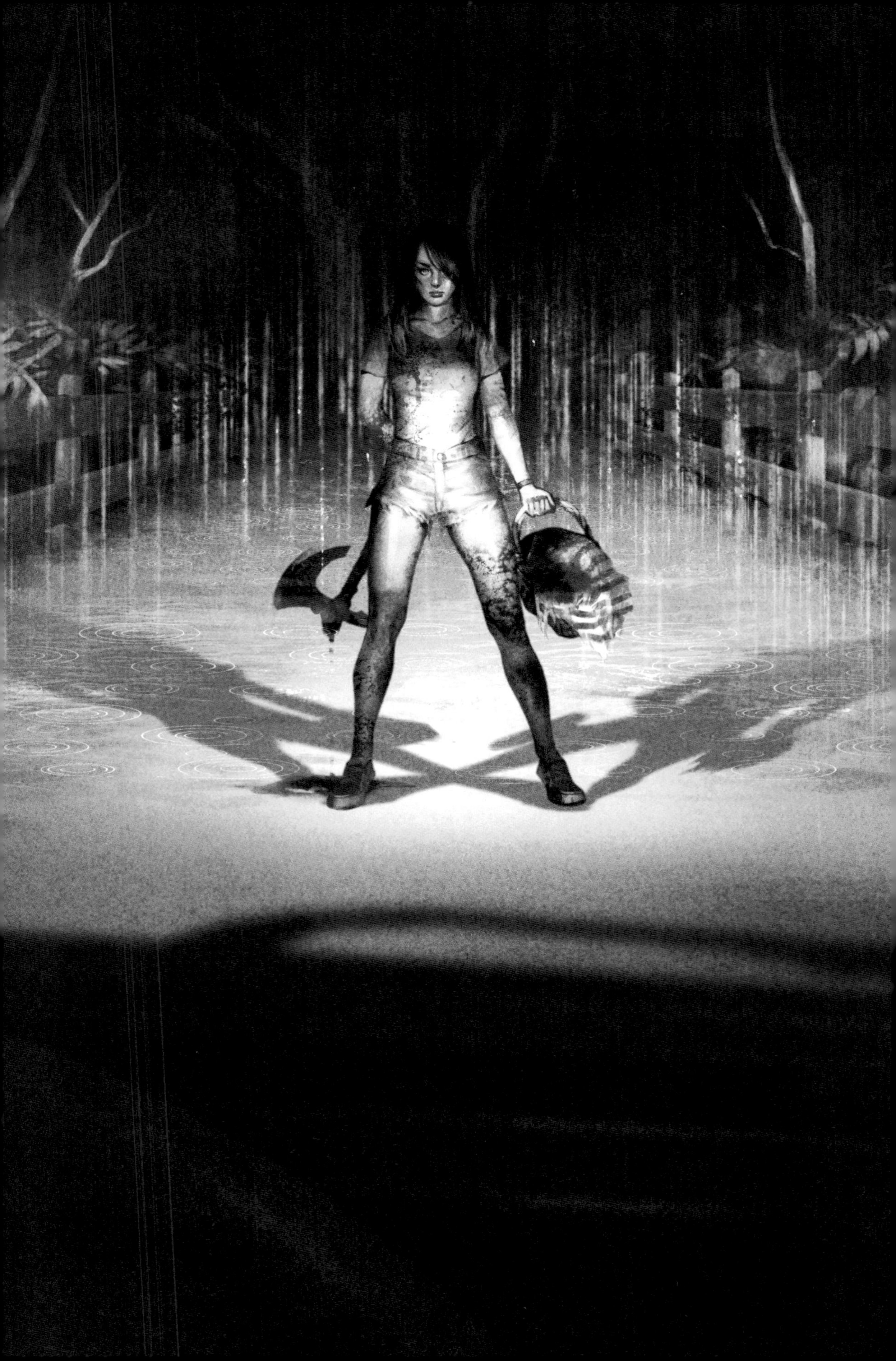

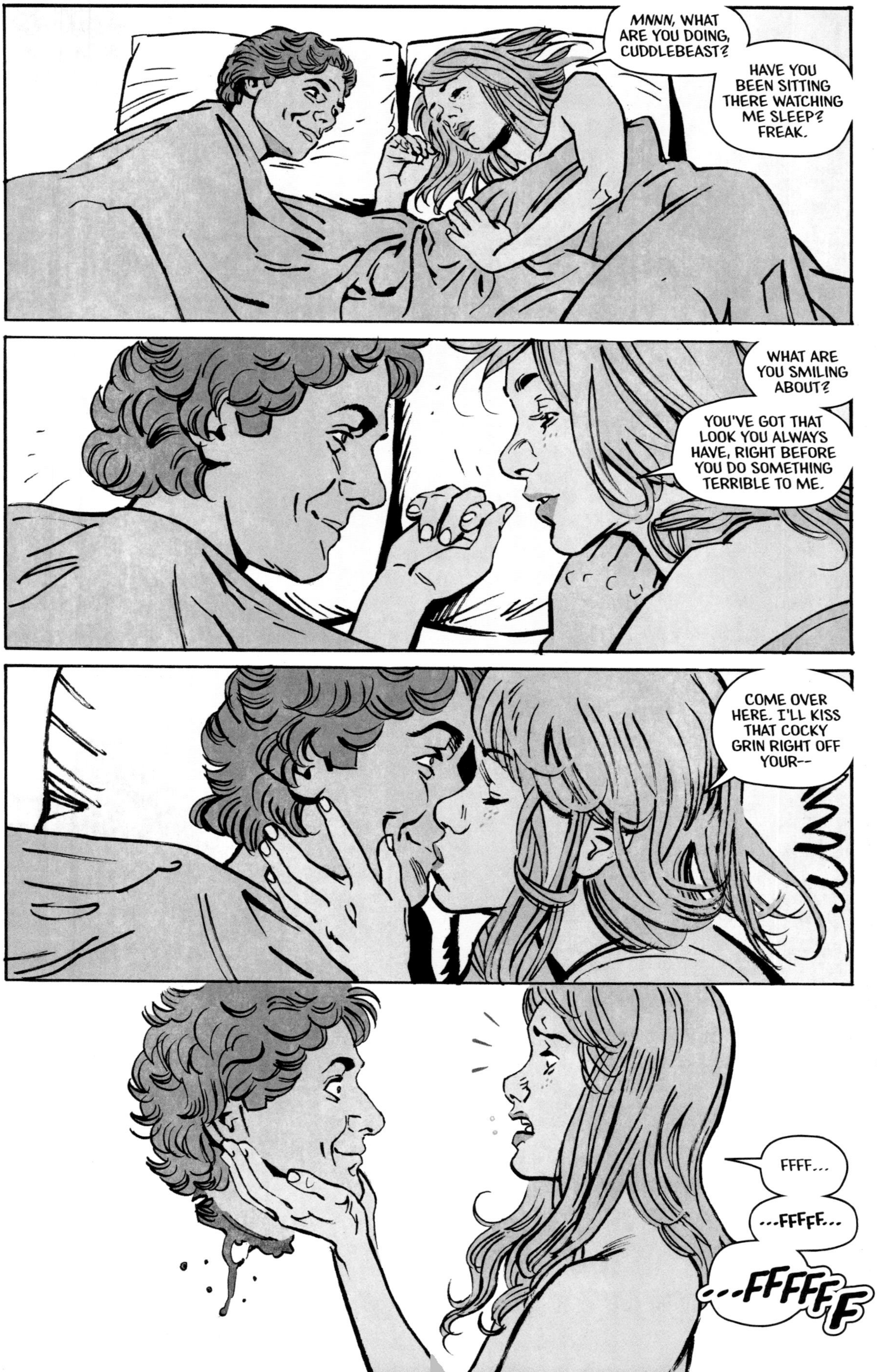
MNNN, WHAT ARE YOU DOING, CUDDLEBEAST?
HAVE YOU BEEN SITTING THERE WATCHING ME SLEEP? FREAK.
WHAT ARE YOU SMILING ABOUT?
YOU'VE GOT THAT LOOK YOU ALWAYS HAVE, RIGHT BEFORE YOU DO SOMETHING TERRIBLE TO ME.
COME OVER HERE. I'LL KISS THAT COCKY GRIN RIGHT OFF YOUR--
FFFF...
...FFFFF...
...FFFFFF

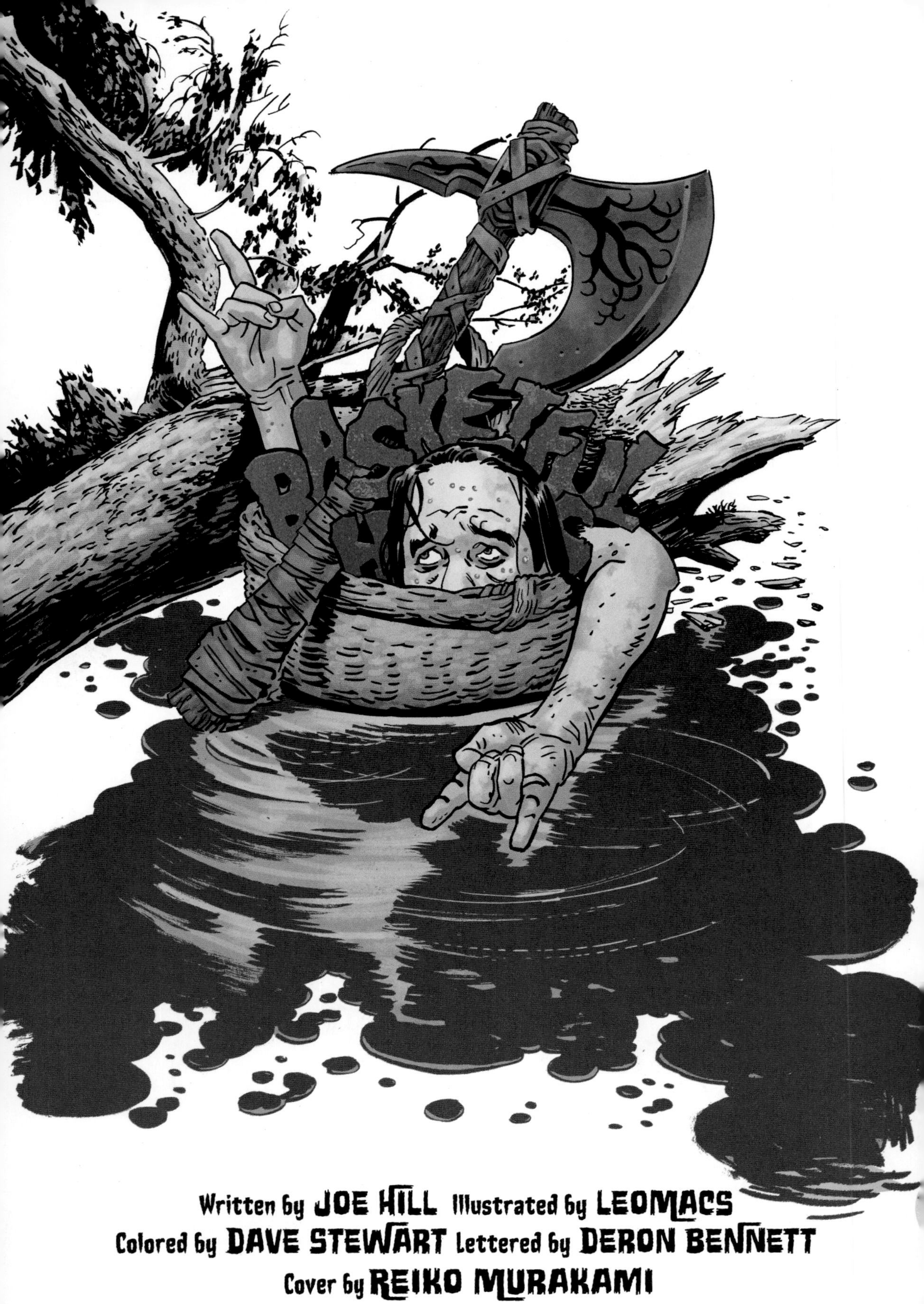
BASKETFUL

Written by JOE HILL Illustrated by LEOMACS
Colored by DAVE STEWART Lettered by DERON BENNETT
Cover by REIKO MURAKAMI
Edited by MARK DOYLE & AMEDEO TURTURRO

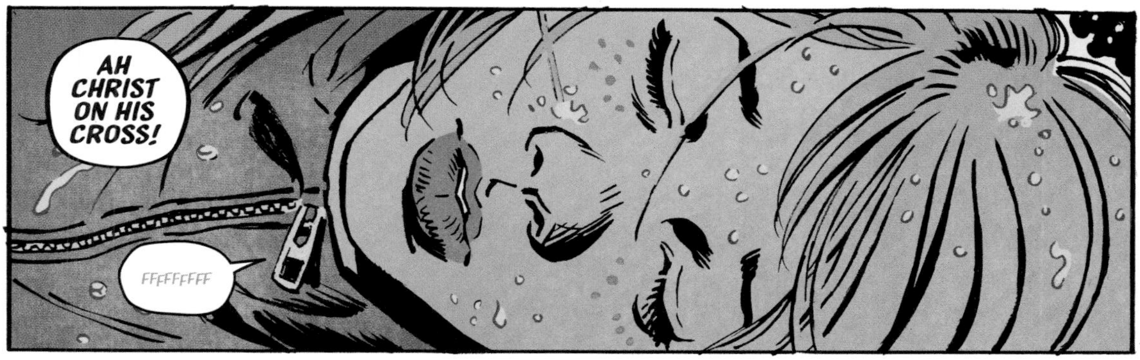
AH CHRIST ON HIS CROSS!
FFFFFFFFF

BRODY ISLAND

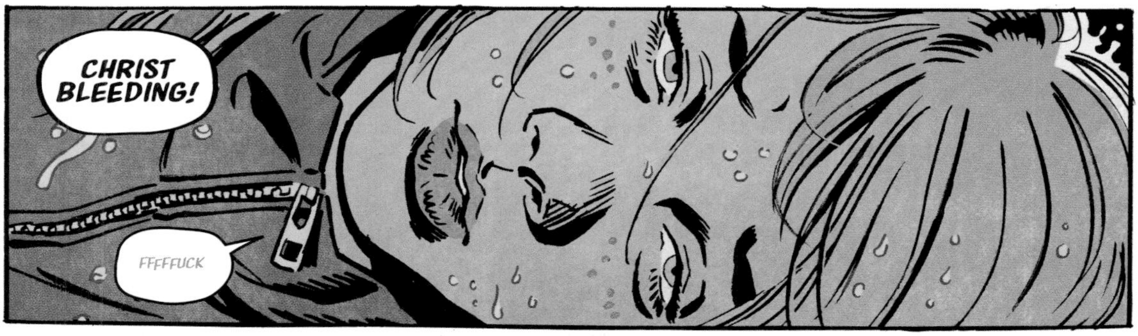
CHRIST BLEEDING!
FFFFFUCK

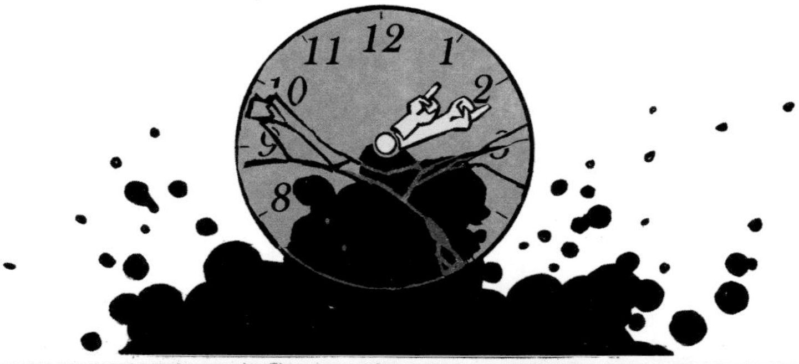

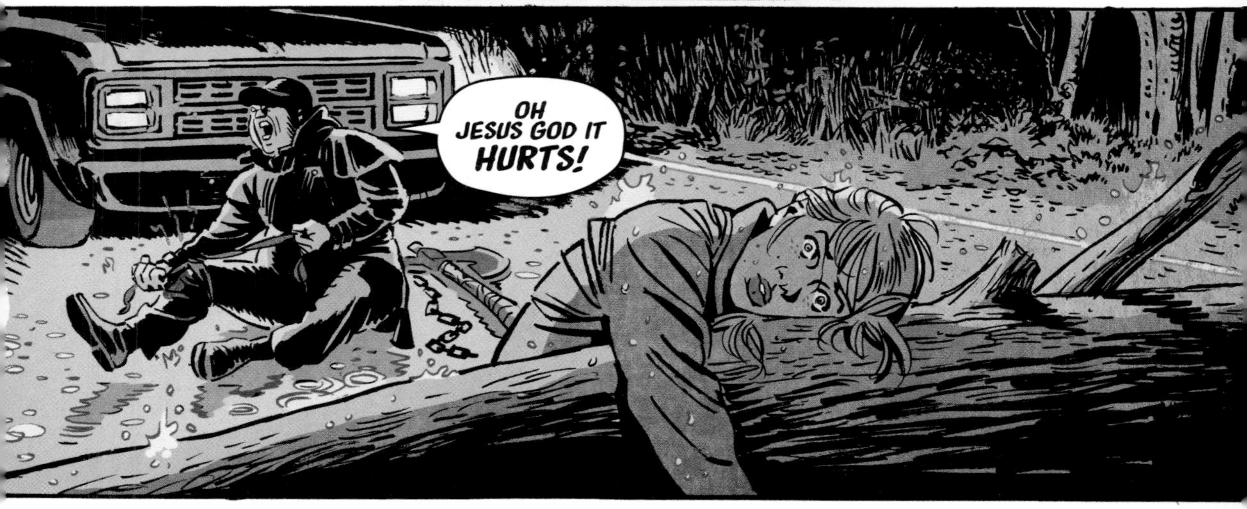
OH JESUS GOD IT HURTS!

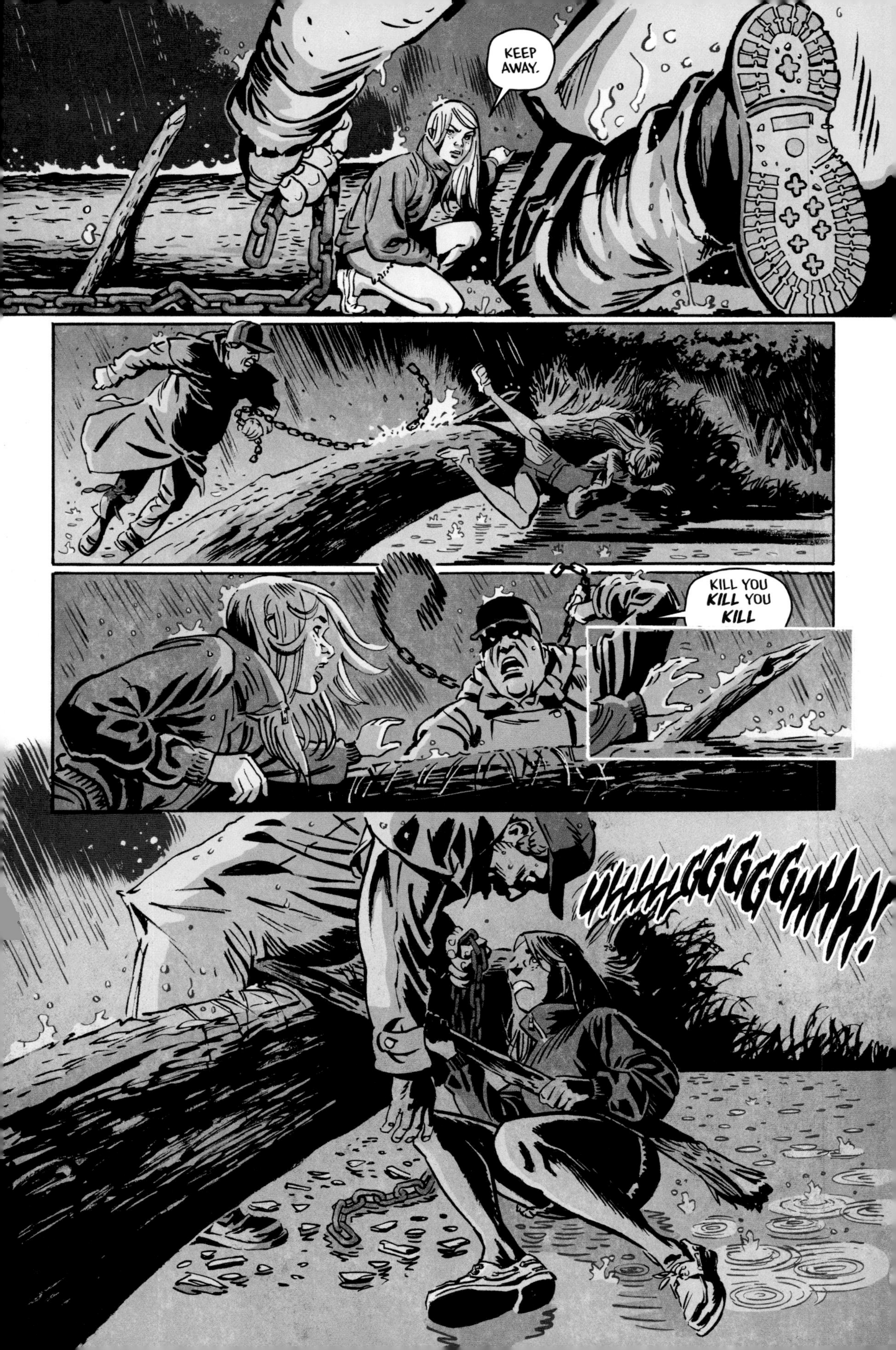
KEEP AWAY.
KILL YOU KILL YOU KILL
UHHHGGGGHHH!

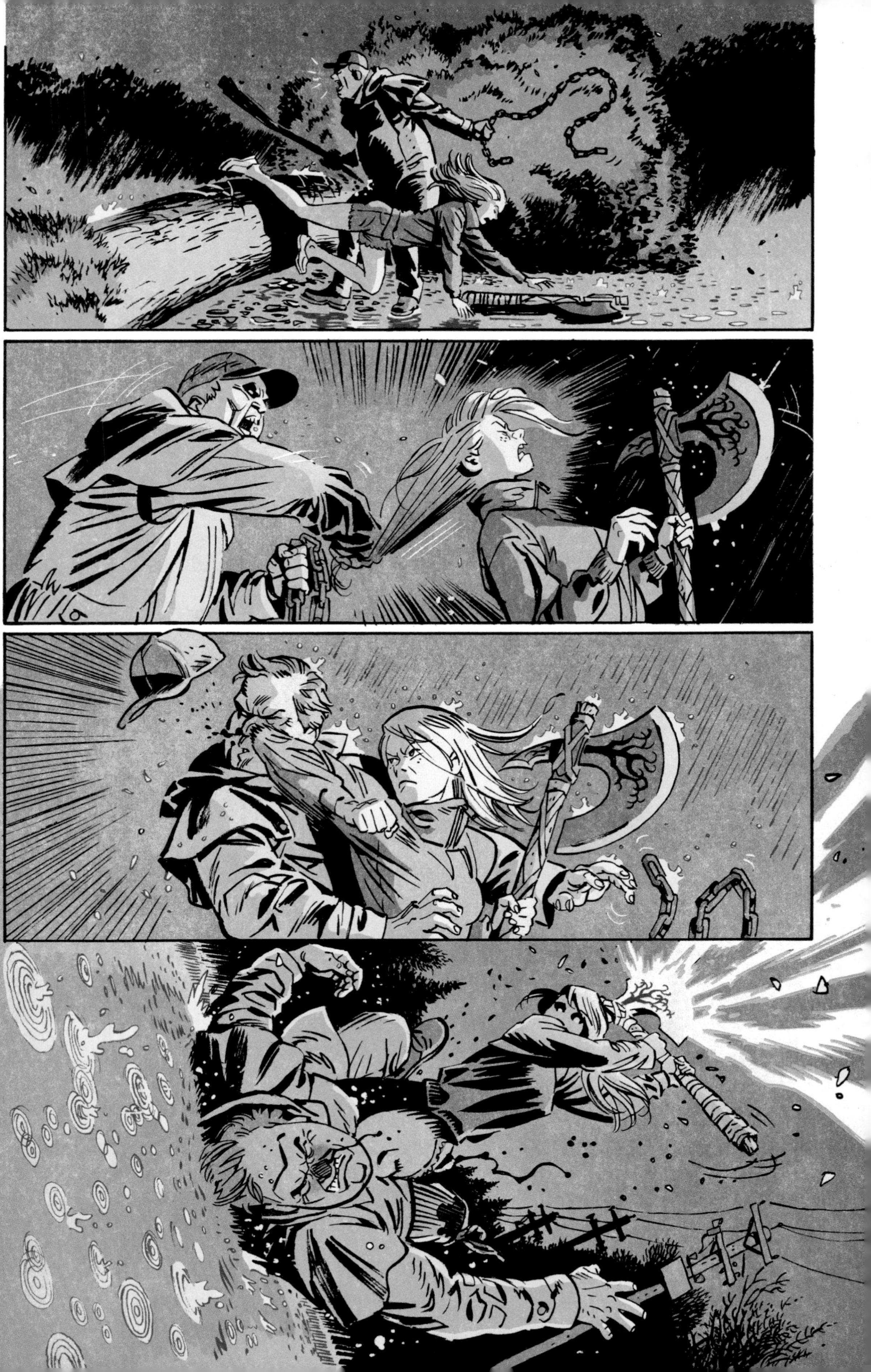

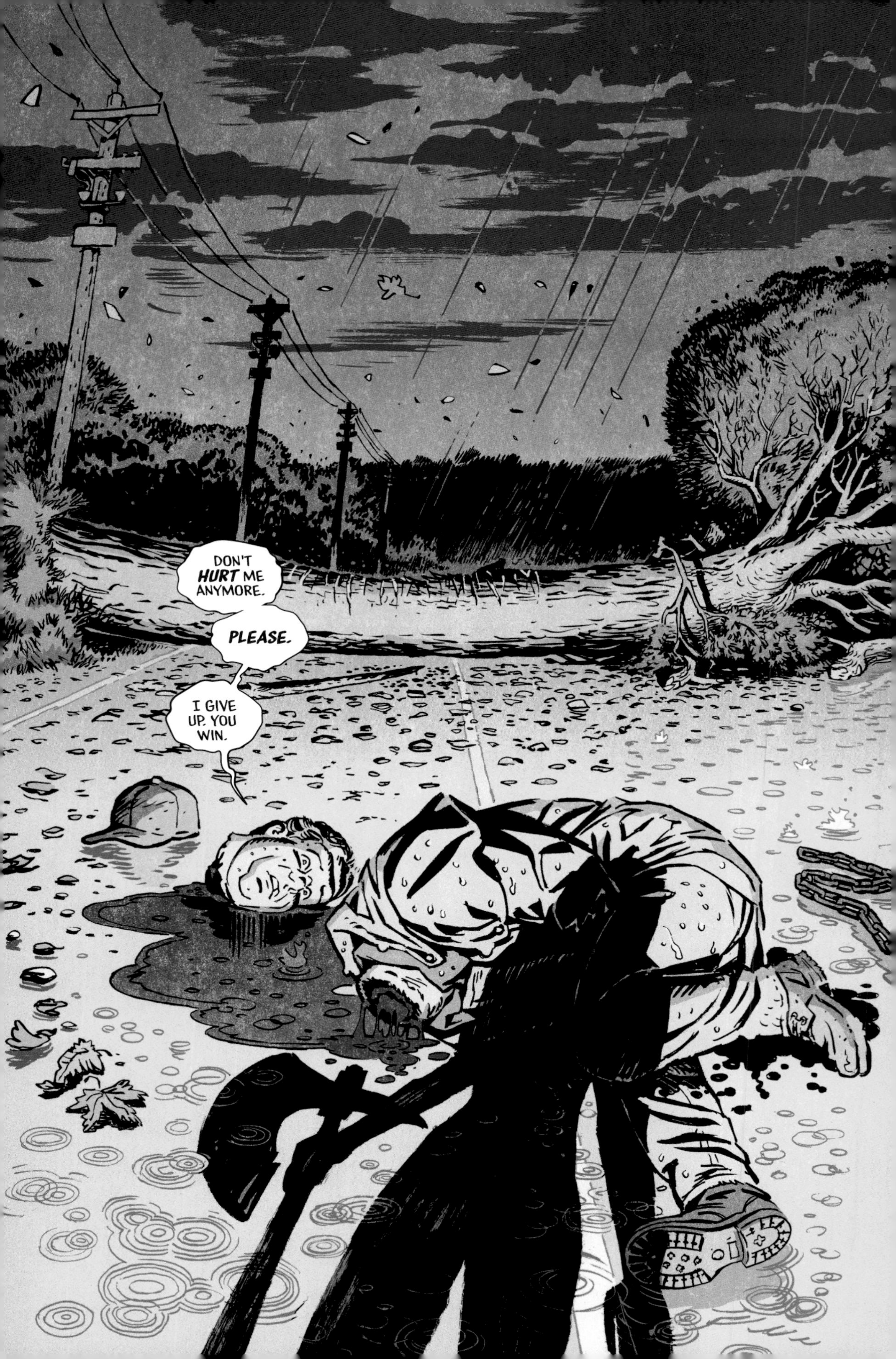
DON'T HURT ME ANYMORE.
PLEASE.
I GIVE UP. YOU WIN.

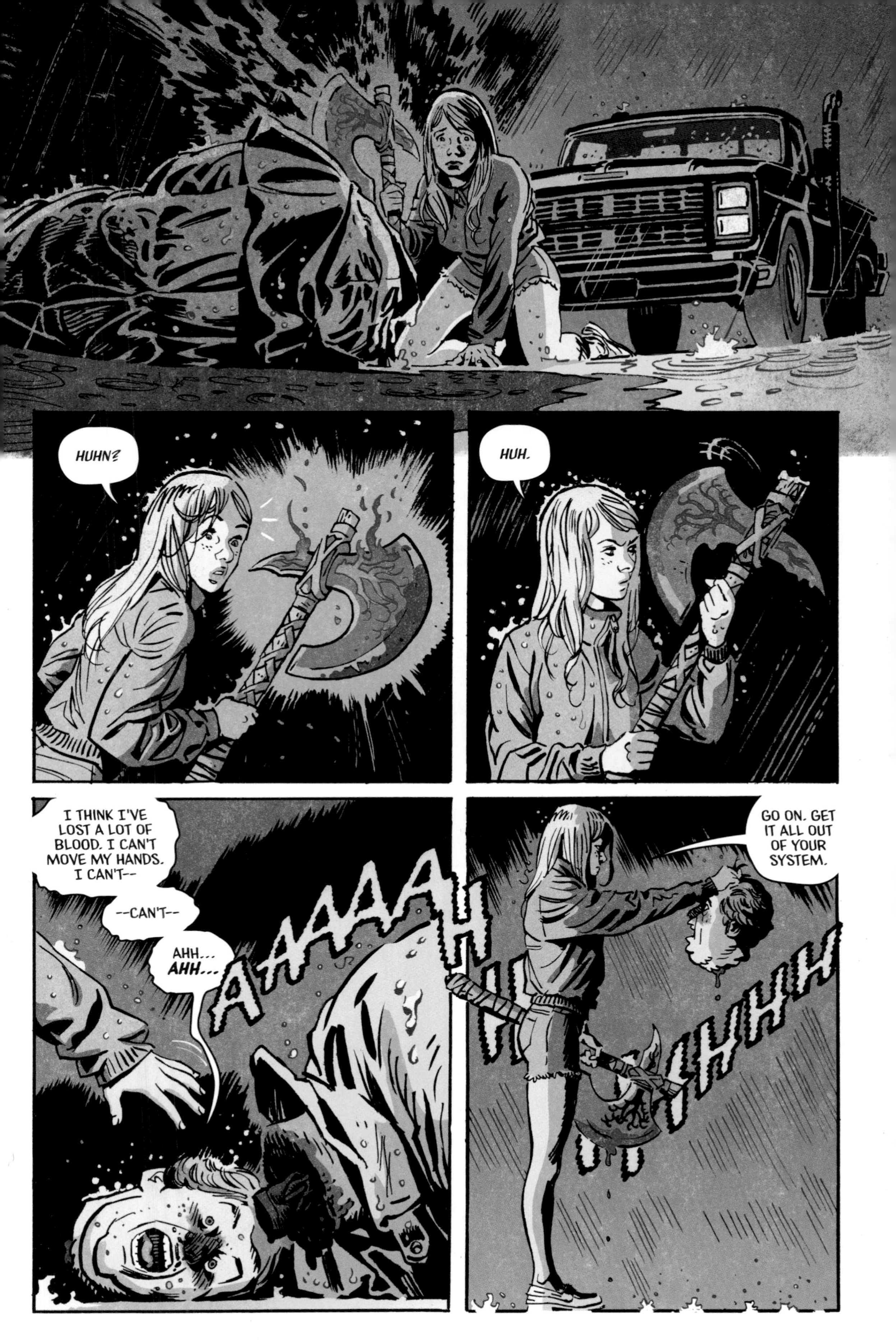
HUHN?
HUH.
I THINK I'VE LOST A LOT OF BLOOD. I CAN'T MOVE MY HANDS. I CAN'T--
--CAN'T--
AHH... **AHH...**
GO ON. GET IT ALL OUT OF YOUR SYSTEM.
AAAAAHHHHHHHHH

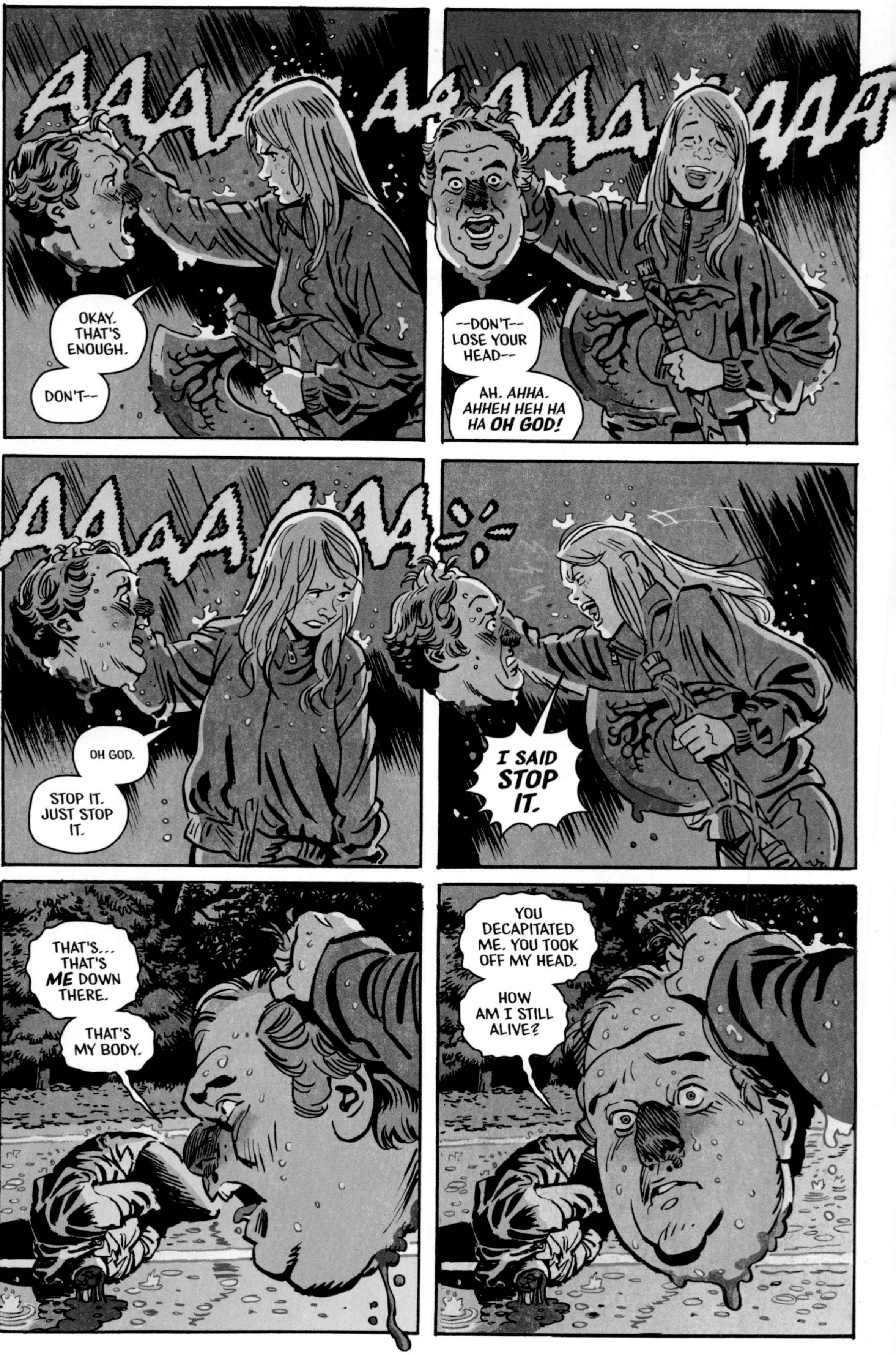
OKAY. THAT'S ENOUGH.
DON'T--
--DON'T-- LOSE YOUR HEAD--
AH. AHHA. AHHEH HEH HA HA OH GOD!
OH GOD.
STOP IT. JUST STOP IT.
I SAID STOP IT.
THAT'S... THAT'S ME DOWN THERE.
THAT'S MY BODY.
YOU DECAPITATED ME. YOU TOOK OFF MY HEAD.
HOW AM I STILL ALIVE?

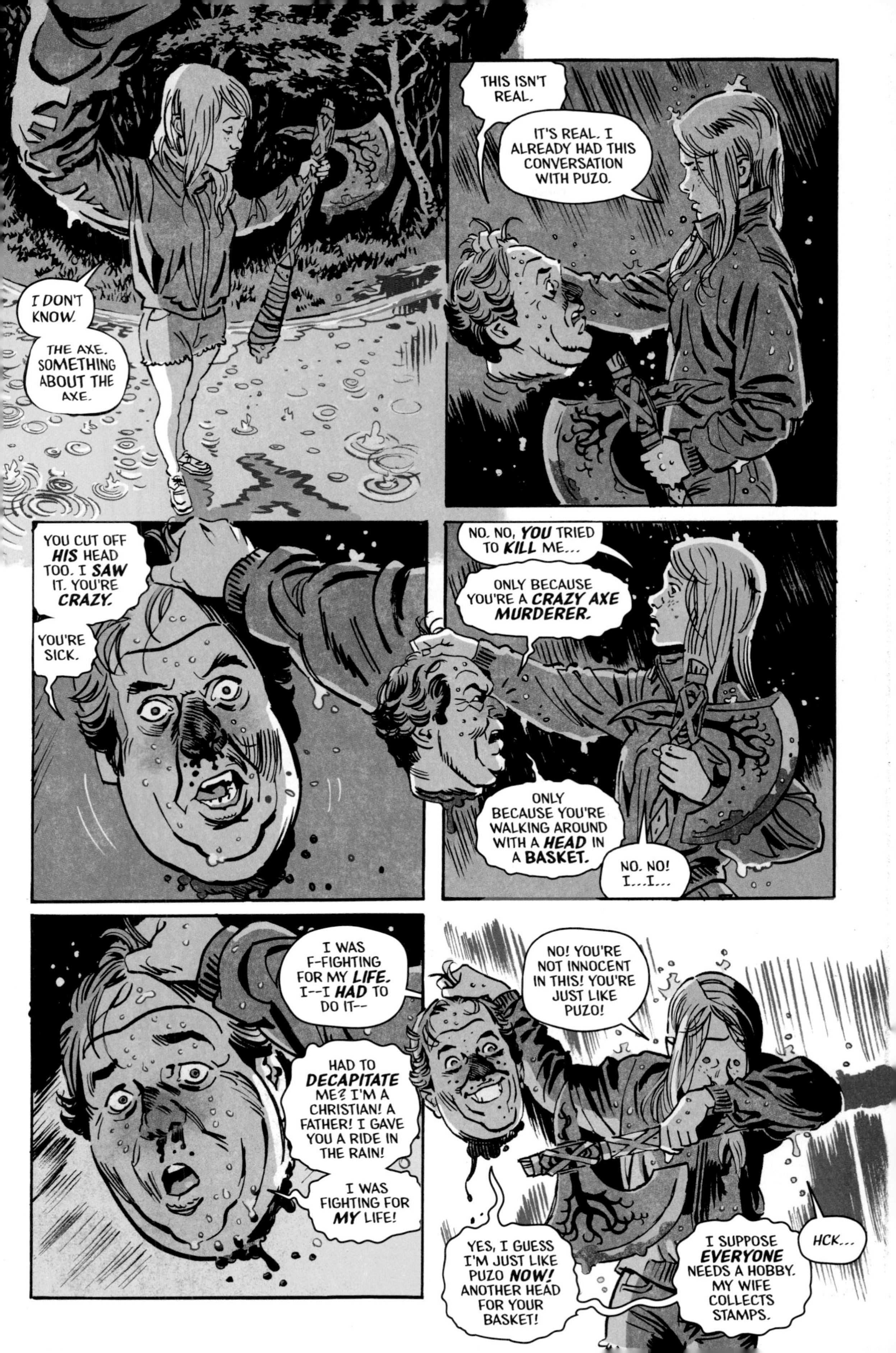
THIS ISN'T REAL.
I DON'T KNOW.
THE AXE. SOMETHING ABOUT THE AXE.
IT'S REAL. I ALREADY HAD THIS CONVERSATION WITH PUZO.
YOU CUT OFF **HIS** HEAD TOO. I **SAW** IT. YOU'RE **CRAZY.**
YOU'RE SICK.
NO. NO, **YOU** TRIED TO **KILL** ME...
ONLY BECAUSE YOU'RE A **CRAZY AXE MURDERER.**
ONLY BECAUSE YOU'RE WALKING AROUND WITH A **HEAD** IN A **BASKET.**
NO. NO! I...I...
I WAS F--FIGHTING FOR MY **LIFE.** I--I **HAD** TO DO IT--
HAD TO **DECAPITATE** ME? I'M A CHRISTIAN! A FATHER! I GAVE YOU A RIDE IN THE RAIN!
I WAS FIGHTING FOR **MY** LIFE!
NO! YOU'RE NOT INNOCENT IN THIS! YOU'RE JUST LIKE PUZO!
YES, I GUESS I'M JUST LIKE PUZO **NOW!** ANOTHER HEAD FOR YOUR BASKET!
I SUPPOSE **EVERYONE** NEEDS A HOBBY. MY WIFE COLLECTS STAMPS.
HCK...

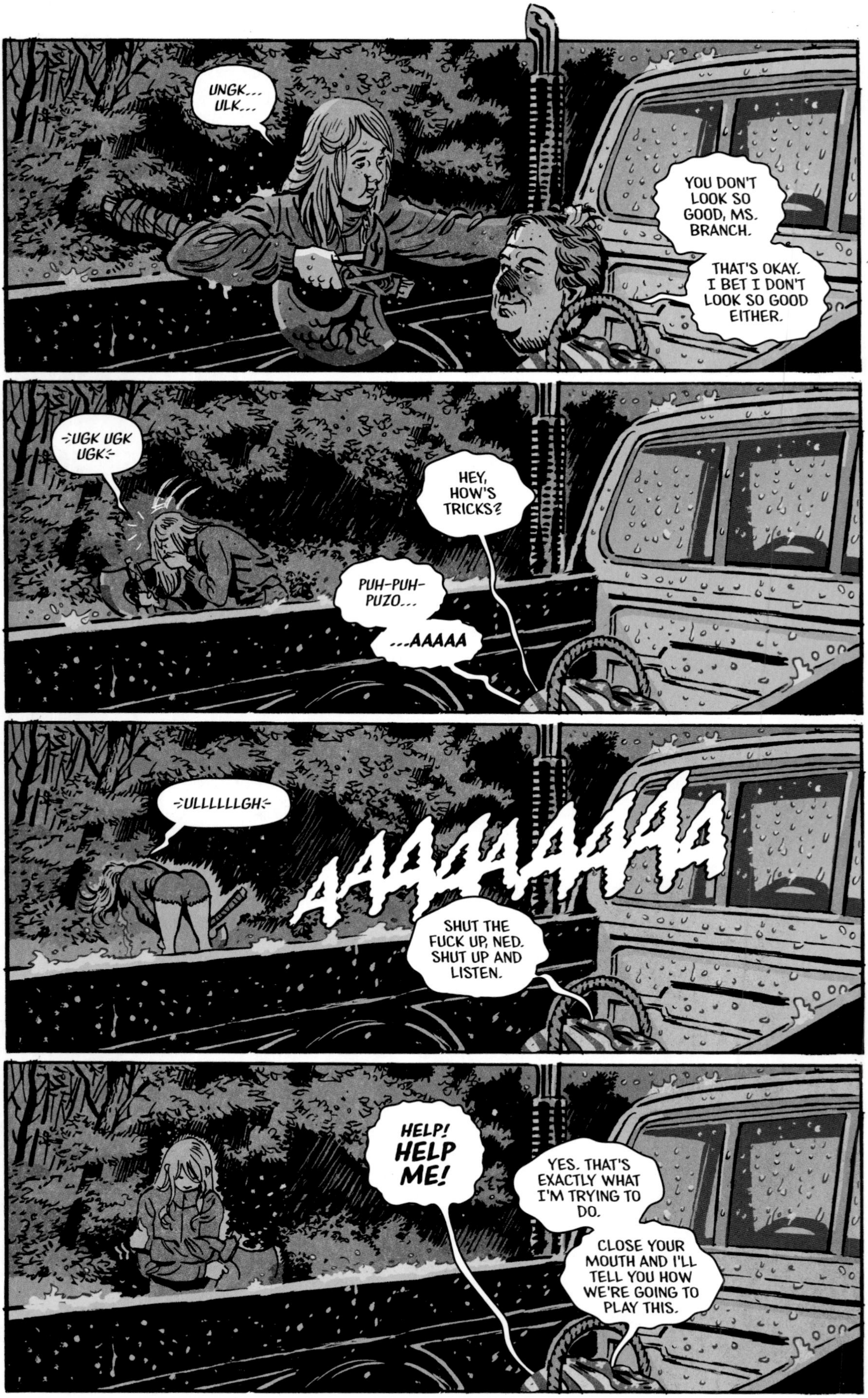
UNGK... ULK...
YOU DON'T LOOK SO GOOD, MS. BRANCH.
THAT'S OKAY. I BET I DON'T LOOK SO GOOD EITHER.
UGK UGK UGK
HEY, HOW'S TRICKS?
PUH-PUH-PUZO...
...AAAAA
ULLLLLLGH
AAAAAAAA
SHUT THE FUCK UP, NED. SHUT UP AND LISTEN.
HELP! HELP ME!
YES. THAT'S EXACTLY WHAT I'M TRYING TO DO.
CLOSE YOUR MOUTH AND I'LL TELL YOU HOW WE'RE GOING TO PLAY THIS.

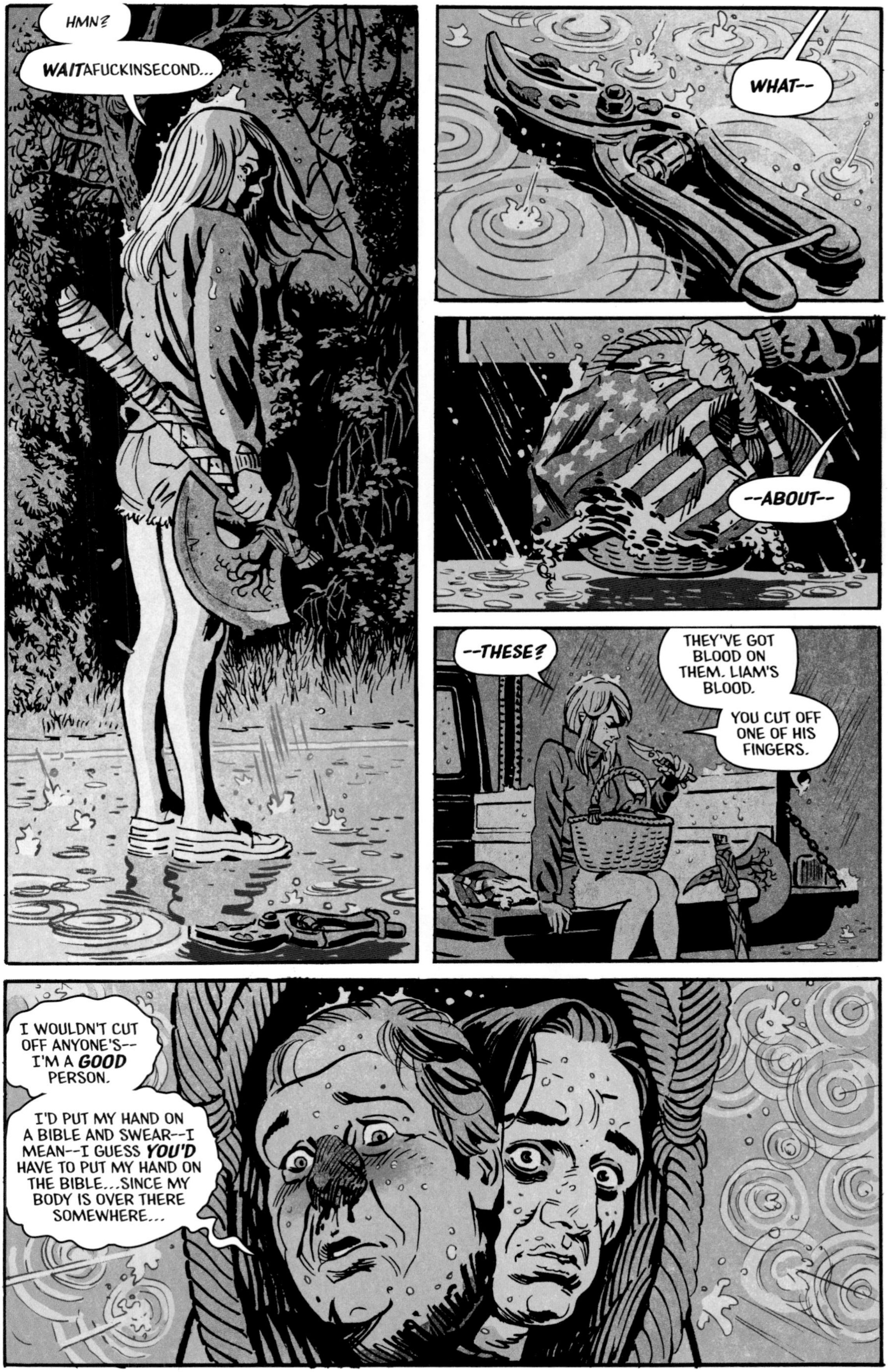
HMN?
WAITAFUCKINSECOND...
WHAT--
--ABOUT--
--THESE?
THEY'VE GOT BLOOD ON THEM. LIAM'S BLOOD.
YOU CUT OFF ONE OF HIS FINGERS.
I WOULDN'T CUT OFF ANYONE'S-- I'M A GOOD PERSON.
I'D PUT MY HAND ON A BIBLE AND SWEAR--I MEAN--I GUESS YOU'D HAVE TO PUT MY HAND ON THE BIBLE...SINCE MY BODY IS OVER THERE SOMEWHERE...

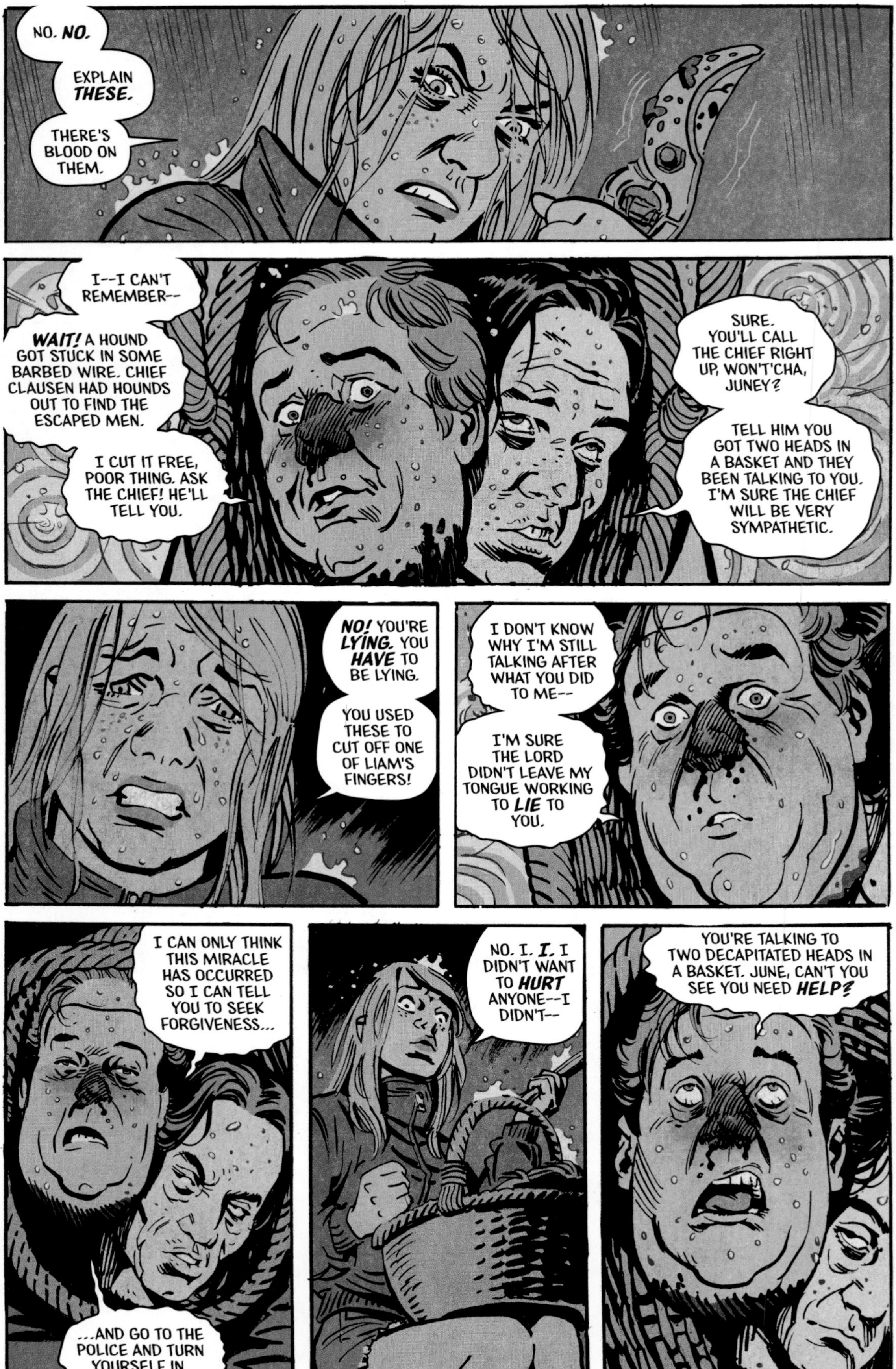
NO. NO.
EXPLAIN THESE.
THERE'S BLOOD ON THEM.
I--I CAN'T REMEMBER--
WAIT! A HOUND GOT STUCK IN SOME BARBED WIRE. CHIEF CLAUSEN HAD HOUNDS OUT TO FIND THE ESCAPED MEN.
I CUT IT FREE, POOR THING. ASK THE CHIEF! HE'LL TELL YOU.
SURE. YOU'LL CALL THE CHIEF RIGHT UP, WON'T'CHA, JUNEY?
TELL HIM YOU GOT TWO HEADS IN A BASKET AND THEY BEEN TALKING TO YOU. I'M SURE THE CHIEF WILL BE VERY SYMPATHETIC.
NO! YOU'RE LYING. YOU HAVE TO BE LYING.
YOU USED THESE TO CUT OFF ONE OF LIAM'S FINGERS!
I DON'T KNOW WHY I'M STILL TALKING AFTER WHAT YOU DID TO ME--
I'M SURE THE LORD DIDN'T LEAVE MY TONGUE WORKING TO LIE TO YOU.
I CAN ONLY THINK THIS MIRACLE HAS OCCURRED SO I CAN TELL YOU TO SEEK FORGIVENESS...
...AND GO TO THE POLICE AND TURN YOURSELF IN.
NO. I. I. I DIDN'T WANT TO HURT ANYONE--I DIDN'T--
YOU'RE TALKING TO TWO DECAPITATED HEADS IN A BASKET. JUNE, CAN'T YOU SEE YOU NEED HELP?

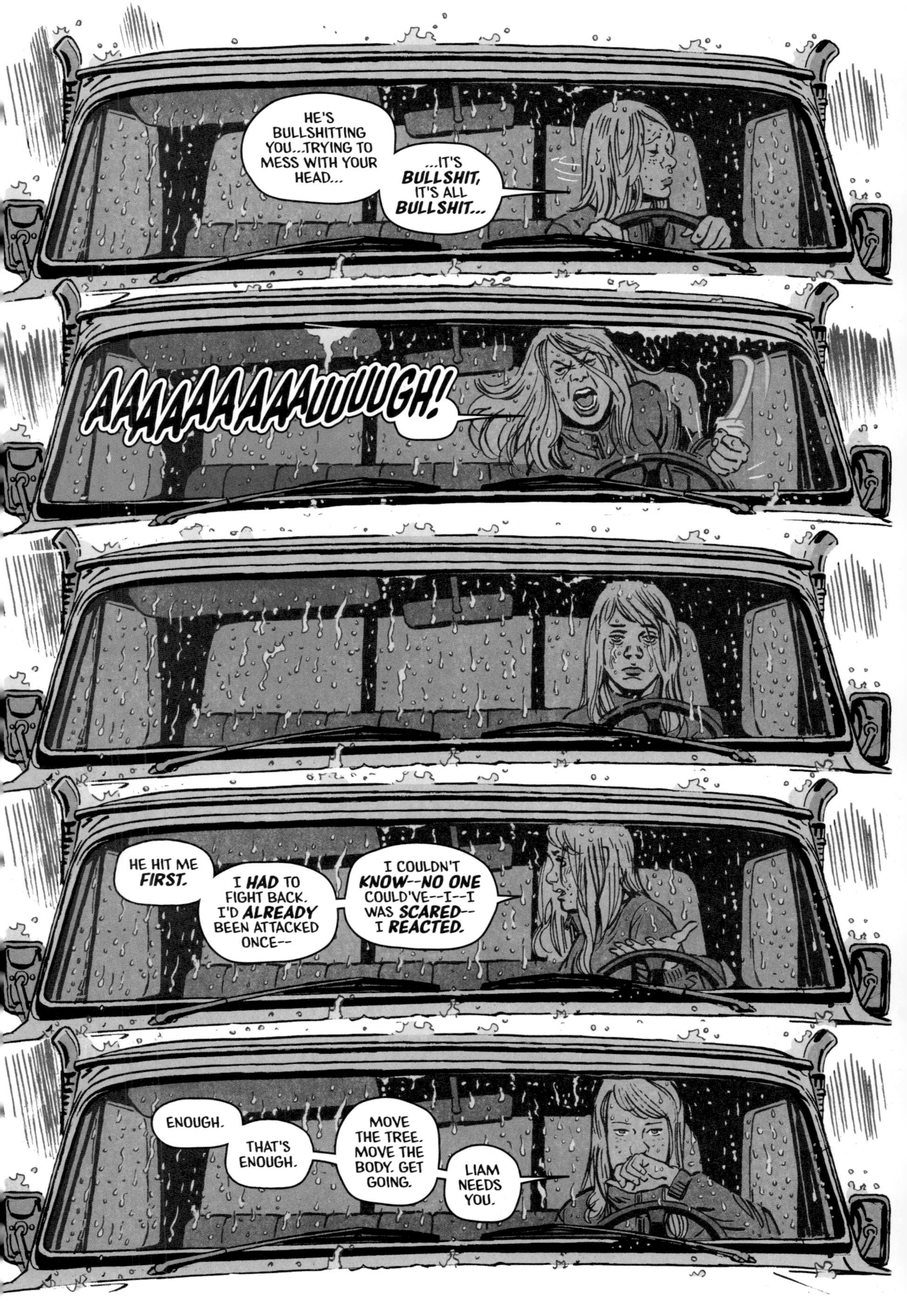
HE'S BULLSHITTING YOU...TRYING TO MESS WITH YOUR HEAD...
...IT'S BULLSHIT, IT'S ALL BULLSHIT...
AAAAAAAAAUUUUGH!
HE HIT ME FIRST.
I HAD TO FIGHT BACK. I'D ALREADY BEEN ATTACKED ONCE--
I COULDN'T KNOW--NO ONE COULD'VE--I--I WAS SCARED-- I REACTED.
ENOUGH.
THAT'S ENOUGH.
MOVE THE TREE. MOVE THE BODY. GET GOING.
LIAM NEEDS YOU.

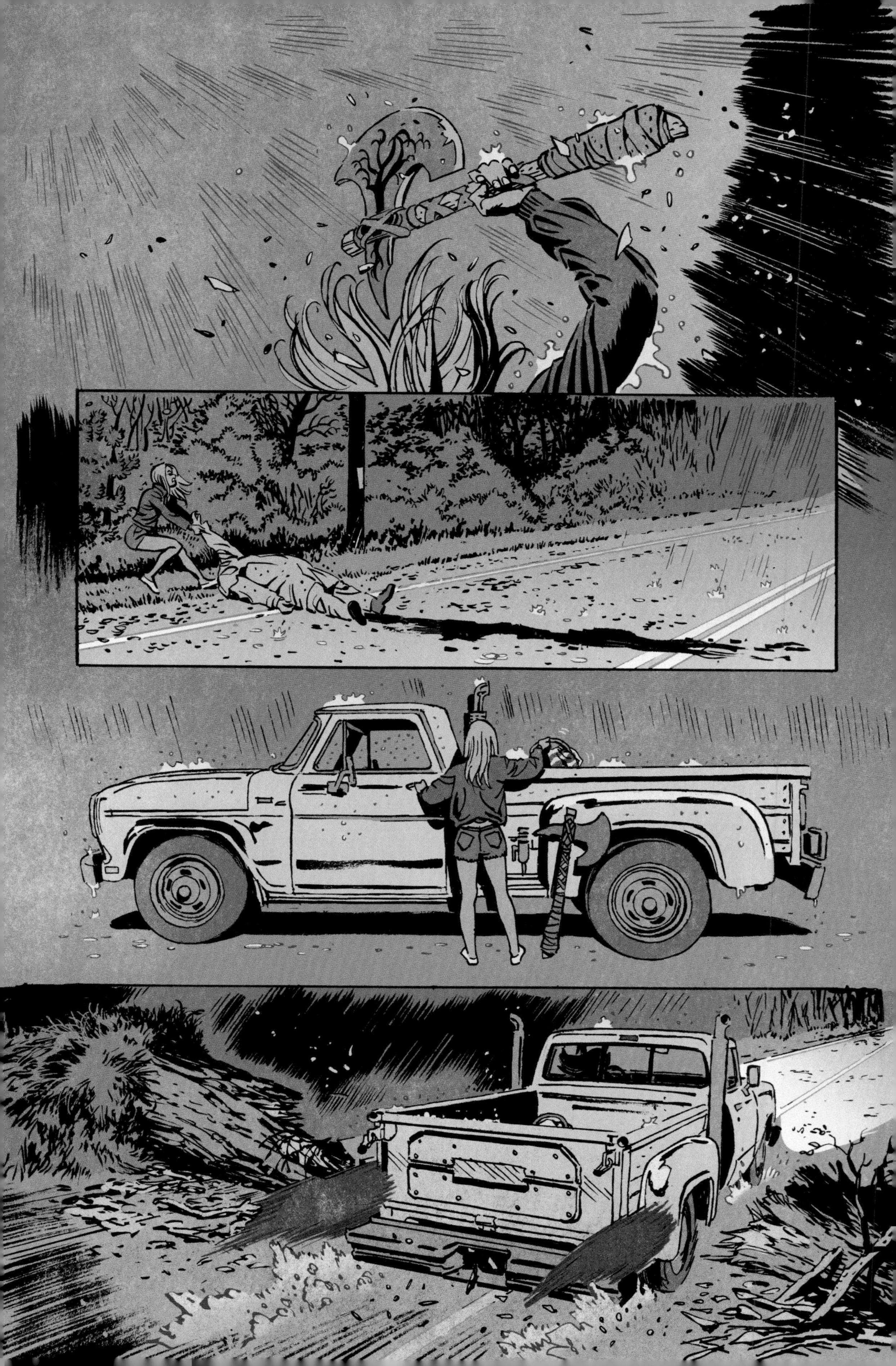

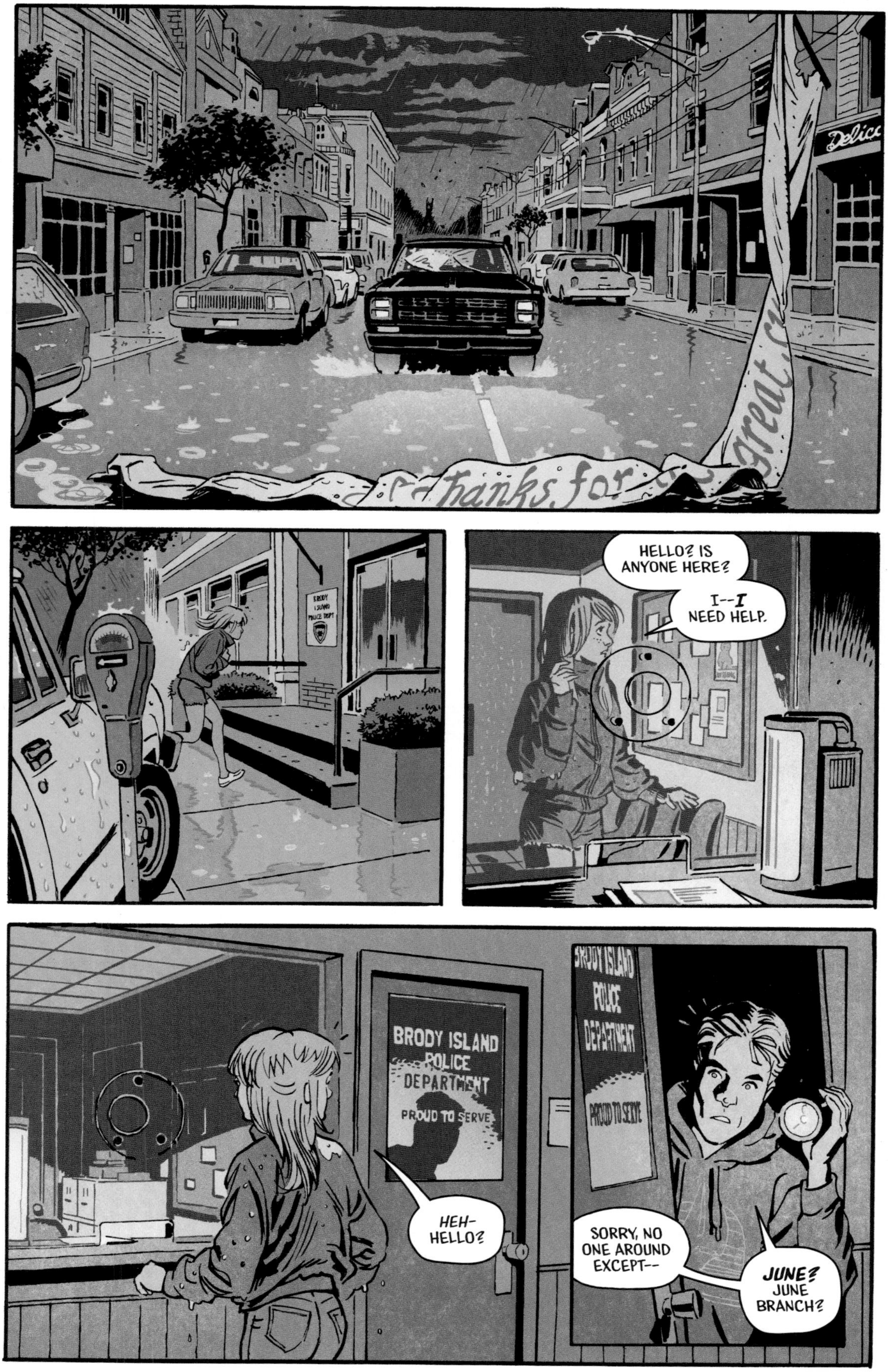
HELLO? IS ANYONE HERE?
I--I NEED HELP.
BRODY ISLAND POLICE DEPARTMENT
PROUD TO SERVE
HEH- HELLO?
SORRY, NO ONE AROUND EXCEPT--
JUNE? JUNE BRANCH?

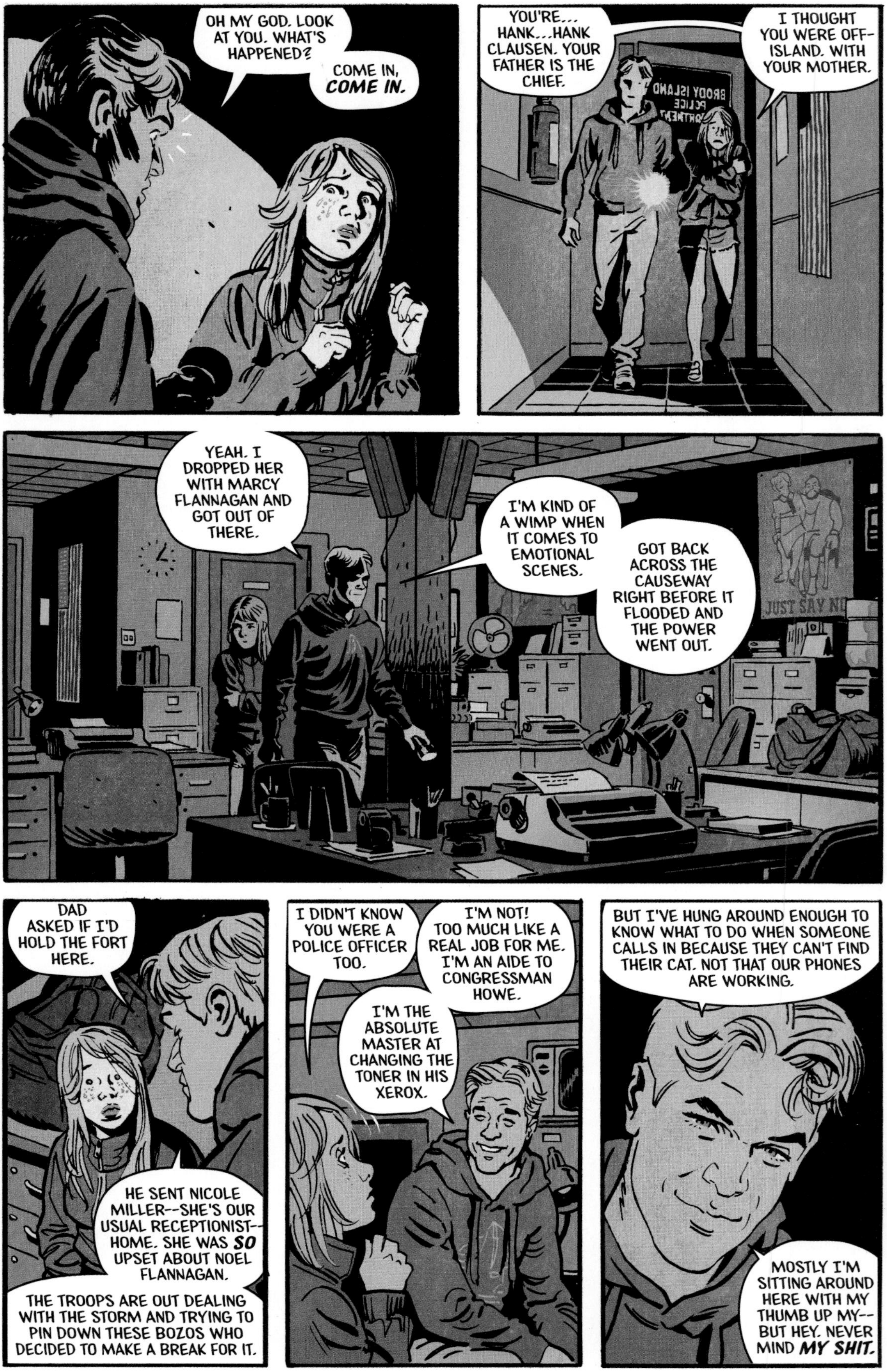
OH MY GOD. LOOK AT YOU. WHAT'S HAPPENED?
COME IN, *COME IN.*
YOU'RE... HANK... HANK CLAUSEN. YOUR FATHER IS THE CHIEF.
I THOUGHT YOU WERE OFF-ISLAND. WITH YOUR MOTHER.
YEAH. I DROPPED HER WITH MARCY FLANNAGAN AND GOT OUT OF THERE.
I'M KIND OF A WIMP WHEN IT COMES TO EMOTIONAL SCENES.
GOT BACK ACROSS THE CAUSEWAY RIGHT BEFORE IT FLOODED AND THE POWER WENT OUT.
DAD ASKED IF I'D HOLD THE FORT HERE.
HE SENT NICOLE MILLER--SHE'S OUR USUAL RECEPTIONIST--HOME. SHE WAS *SO* UPSET ABOUT NOEL FLANNAGAN.
THE TROOPS ARE OUT DEALING WITH THE STORM AND TRYING TO PIN DOWN THESE BOZOS WHO DECIDED TO MAKE A BREAK FOR IT.
I DIDN'T KNOW YOU WERE A POLICE OFFICER TOO.
I'M NOT! TOO MUCH LIKE A REAL JOB FOR ME. I'M AN AIDE TO CONGRESSMAN HOWE.
I'M THE ABSOLUTE MASTER AT CHANGING THE TONER IN HIS XEROX.
BUT I'VE HUNG AROUND ENOUGH TO KNOW WHAT TO DO WHEN SOMEONE CALLS IN BECAUSE THEY CAN'T FIND THEIR CAT. NOT THAT OUR PHONES ARE WORKING.
MOSTLY I'M SITTING AROUND HERE WITH MY THUMB UP MY--BUT HEY. NEVER MIND *MY SHIT.*

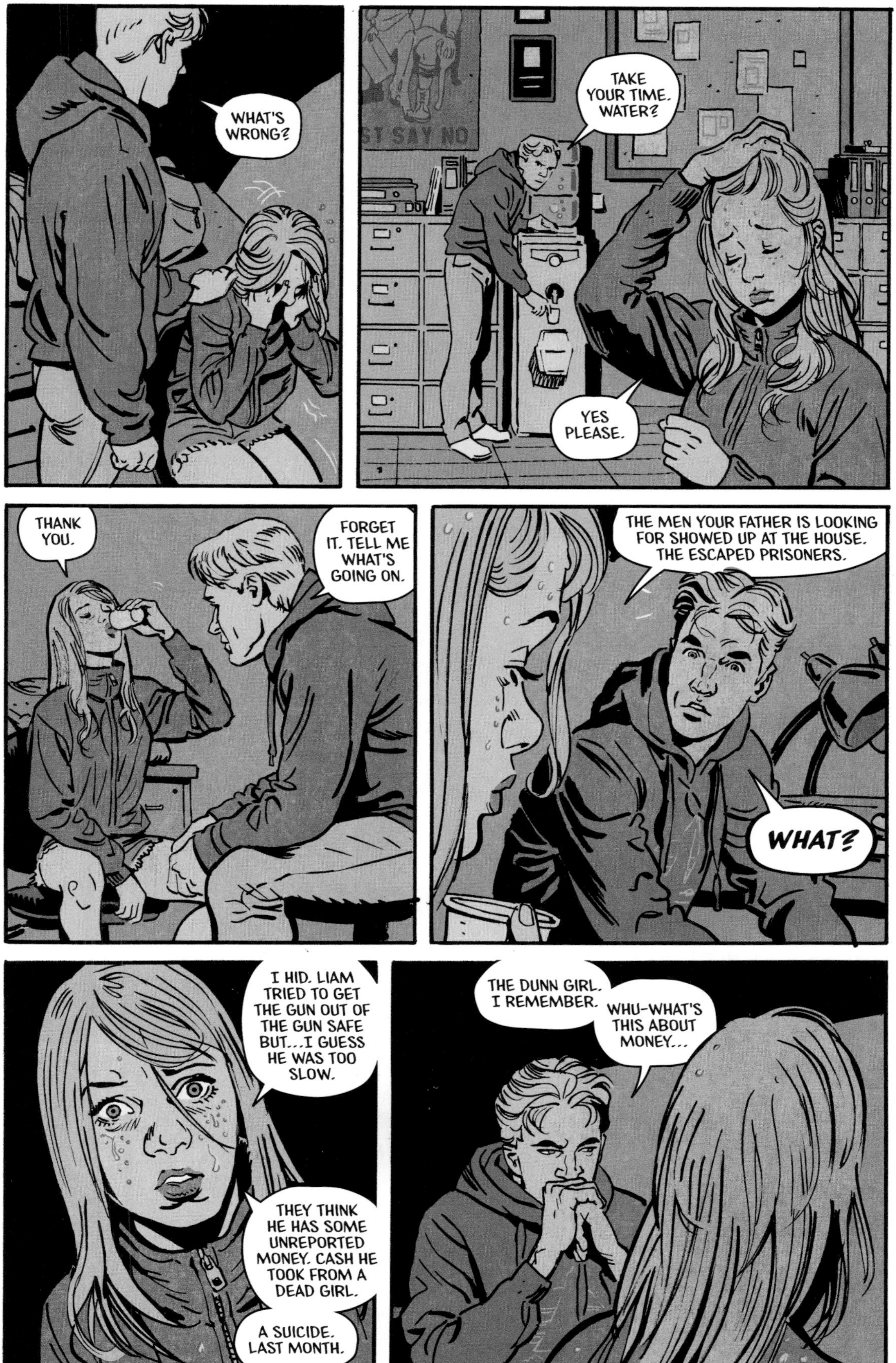
WHAT'S WRONG?
TAKE YOUR TIME. WATER?
YES PLEASE.
THANK YOU.
FORGET IT. TELL ME WHAT'S GOING ON.
THE MEN YOUR FATHER IS LOOKING FOR SHOWED UP AT THE HOUSE. THE ESCAPED PRISONERS.
WHAT?
I HID. LIAM TRIED TO GET THE GUN OUT OF THE GUN SAFE BUT...I GUESS HE WAS TOO SLOW.
THEY THINK HE HAS SOME UNREPORTED MONEY. CASH HE TOOK FROM A DEAD GIRL.
A SUICIDE. LAST MONTH.
THE DUNN GIRL. I REMEMBER.
WHU-WHAT'S THIS ABOUT MONEY...

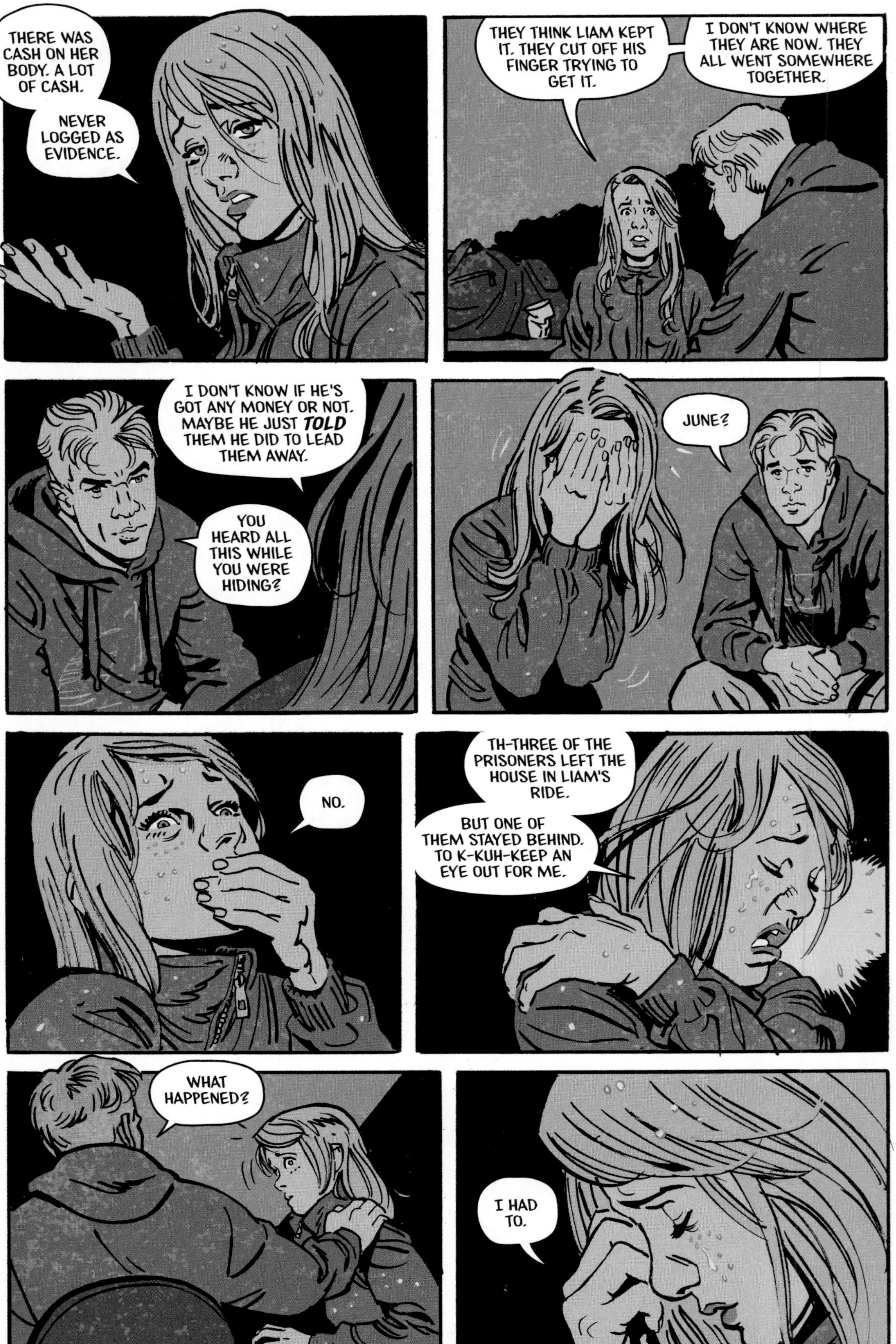
THERE WAS CASH ON HER BODY. A LOT OF CASH.
NEVER LOGGED AS EVIDENCE.
THEY THINK LIAM KEPT IT. THEY CUT OFF HIS FINGER TRYING TO GET IT.
I DON'T KNOW WHERE THEY ARE NOW. THEY ALL WENT SOMEWHERE TOGETHER.
I DON'T KNOW IF HE'S GOT ANY MONEY OR NOT. MAYBE HE JUST TOLD THEM HE DID TO LEAD THEM AWAY.
YOU HEARD ALL THIS WHILE YOU WERE HIDING?
JUNE?
NO.
TH-THREE OF THE PRISONERS LEFT THE HOUSE IN LIAM'S RIDE.
BUT ONE OF THEM STAYED BEHIND. TO K-KUH-KEEP AN EYE OUT FOR ME.
WHAT HAPPENED?
I HAD TO.

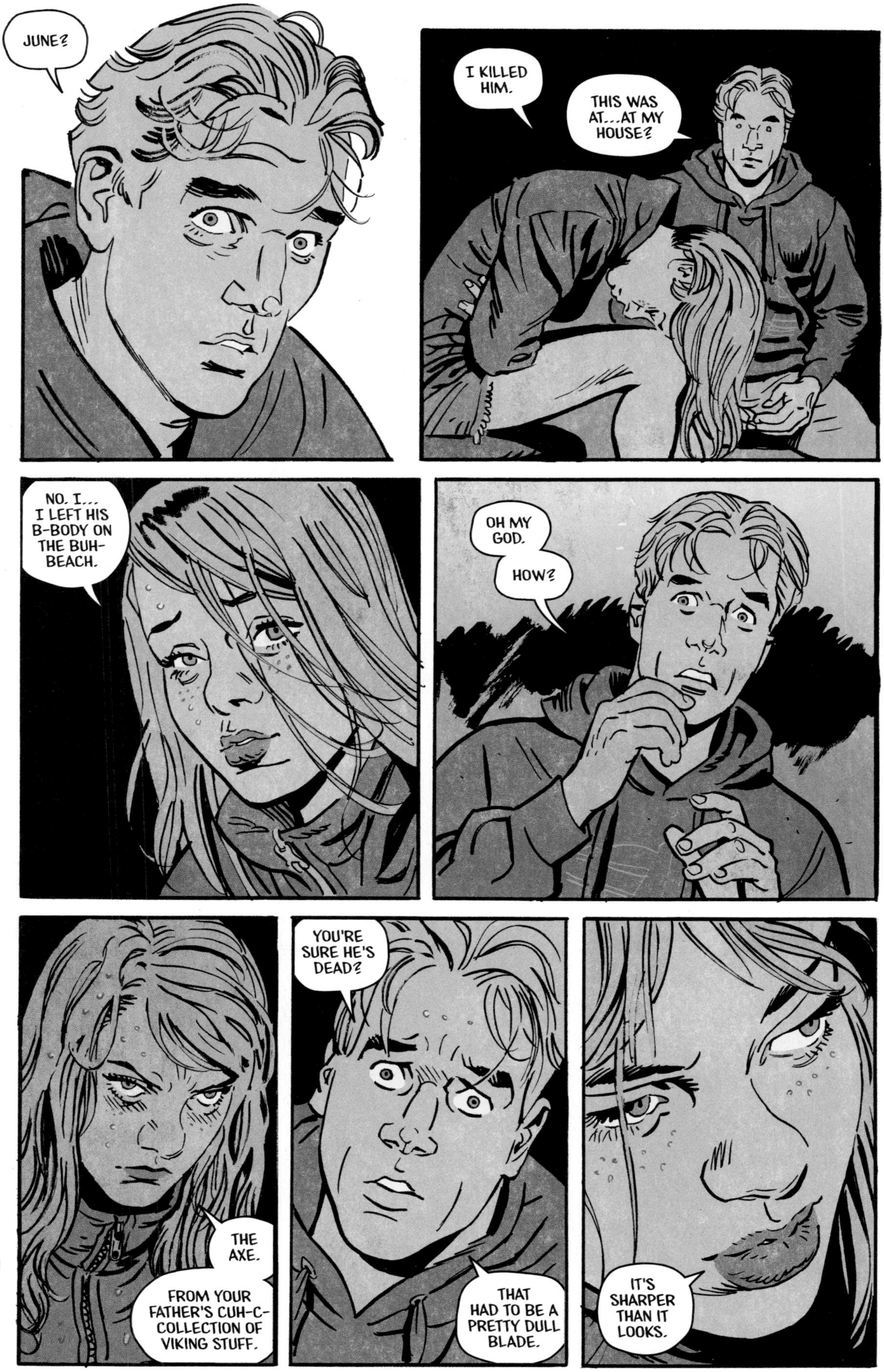
JUNE?
I KILLED HIM.
THIS WAS AT...AT MY HOUSE?
NO. I... I LEFT HIS B-BODY ON THE BUH-BEACH.
OH MY GOD.
HOW?
THE AXE.
FROM YOUR FATHER'S CUH-C-COLLECTION OF VIKING STUFF.
YOU'RE SURE HE'S DEAD?
THAT HAD TO BE A PRETTY DULL BLADE.
IT'S SHARPER THAN IT LOOKS.

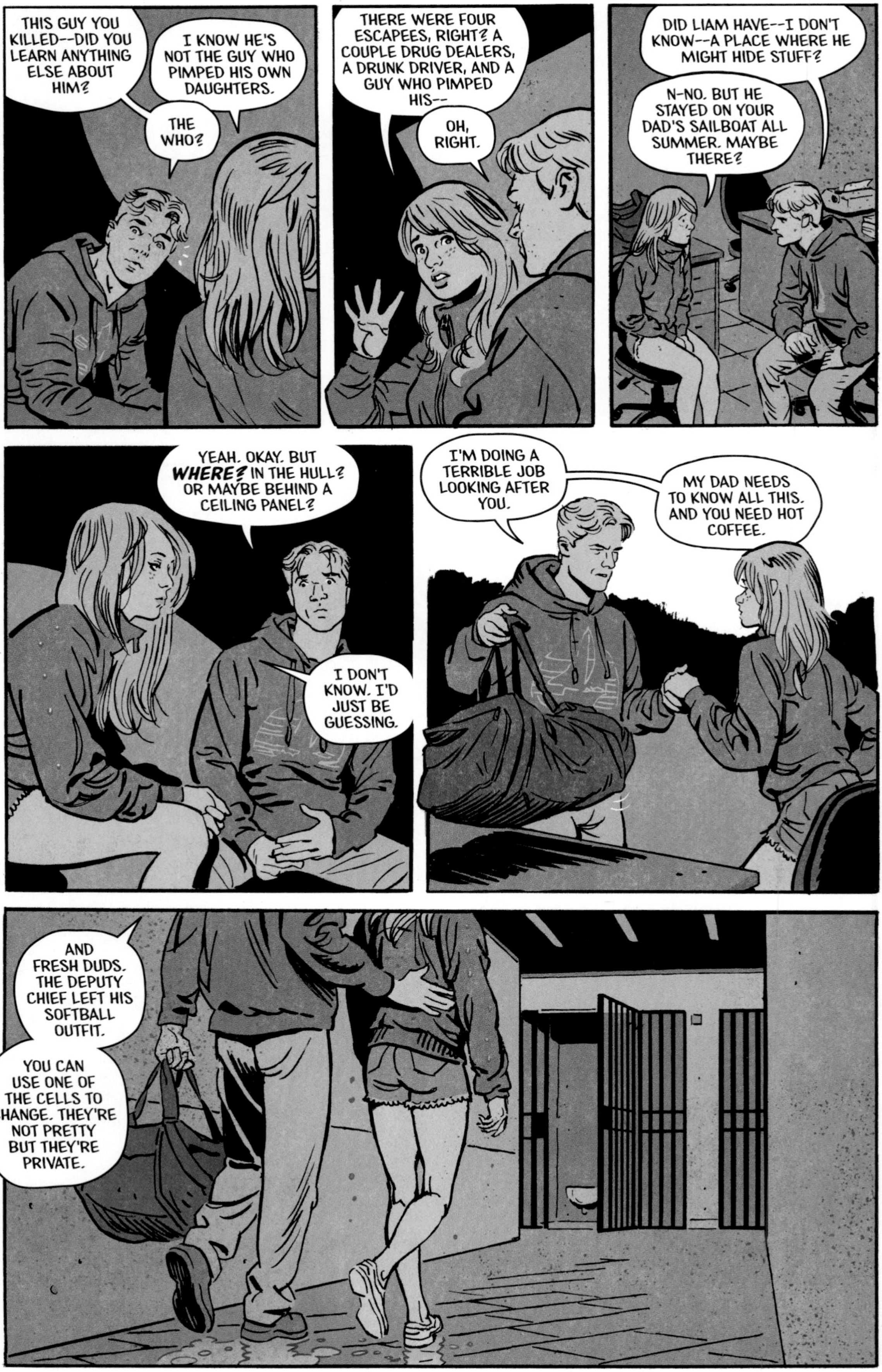
THIS GUY YOU KILLED--DID YOU LEARN ANYTHING ELSE ABOUT HIM?
I KNOW HE'S NOT THE GUY WHO PIMPED HIS OWN DAUGHTERS.
THE WHO?
THERE WERE FOUR ESCAPEES, RIGHT? A COUPLE DRUG DEALERS, A DRUNK DRIVER, AND A GUY WHO PIMPED HIS--
OH, RIGHT.
DID LIAM HAVE--I DON'T KNOW--A PLACE WHERE HE MIGHT HIDE STUFF?
N-NO. BUT HE STAYED ON YOUR DAD'S SAILBOAT ALL SUMMER. MAYBE THERE?
YEAH. OKAY. BUT WHERE? IN THE HULL? OR MAYBE BEHIND A CEILING PANEL?
I DON'T KNOW. I'D JUST BE GUESSING.
I'M DOING A TERRIBLE JOB LOOKING AFTER YOU.
MY DAD NEEDS TO KNOW ALL THIS. AND YOU NEED HOT COFFEE.
AND FRESH DUDS. THE DEPUTY CHIEF LEFT HIS SOFTBALL OUTFIT.
YOU CAN USE ONE OF THE CELLS TO CHANGE. THEY'RE NOT PRETTY BUT THEY'RE PRIVATE.

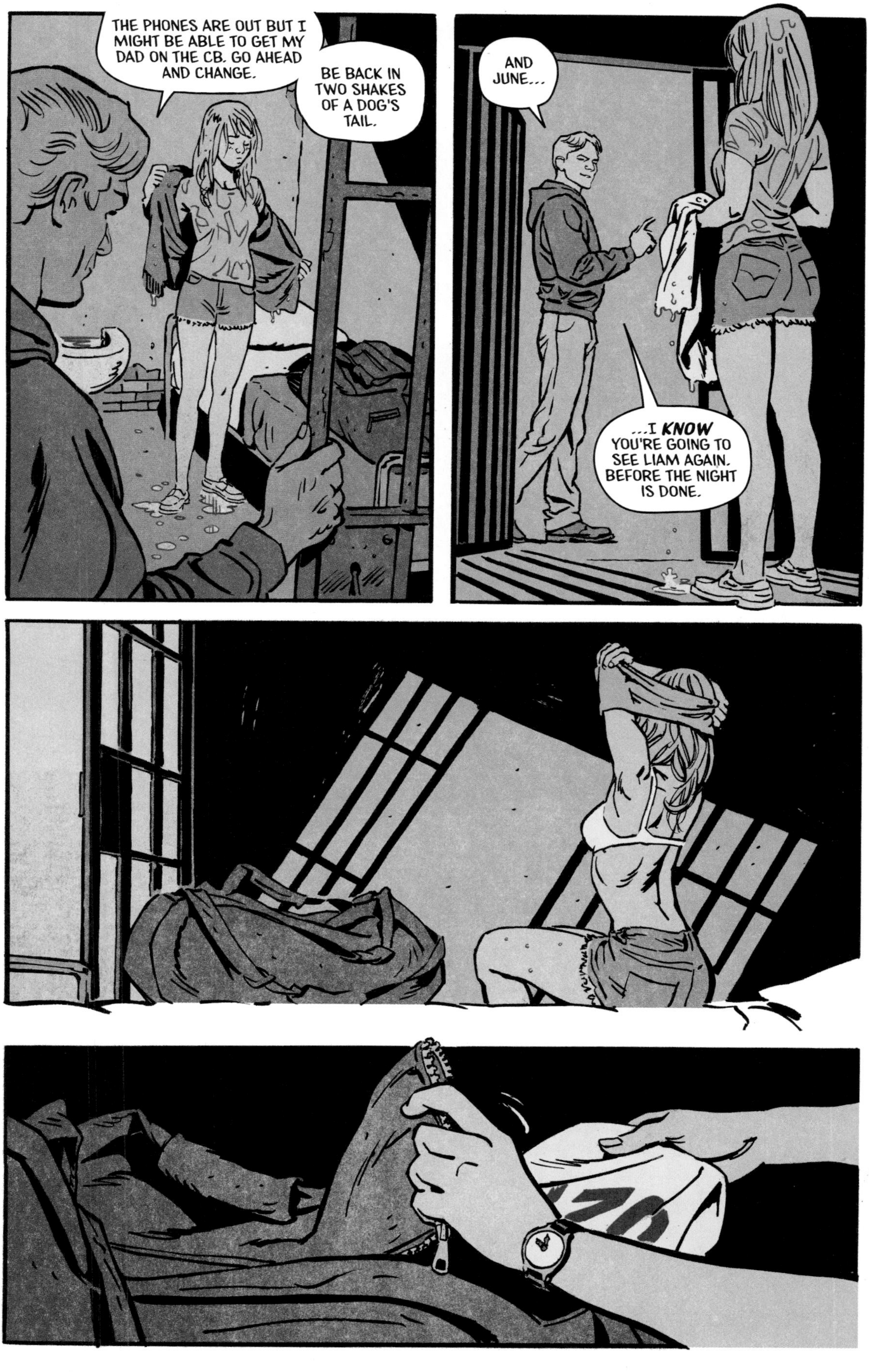
THE PHONES ARE OUT BUT I MIGHT BE ABLE TO GET MY DAD ON THE CB. GO AHEAD AND CHANGE.
BE BACK IN TWO SHAKES OF A DOG'S TAIL.
AND JUNE...
...I KNOW YOU'RE GOING TO SEE LIAM AGAIN. BEFORE THE NIGHT IS DONE.

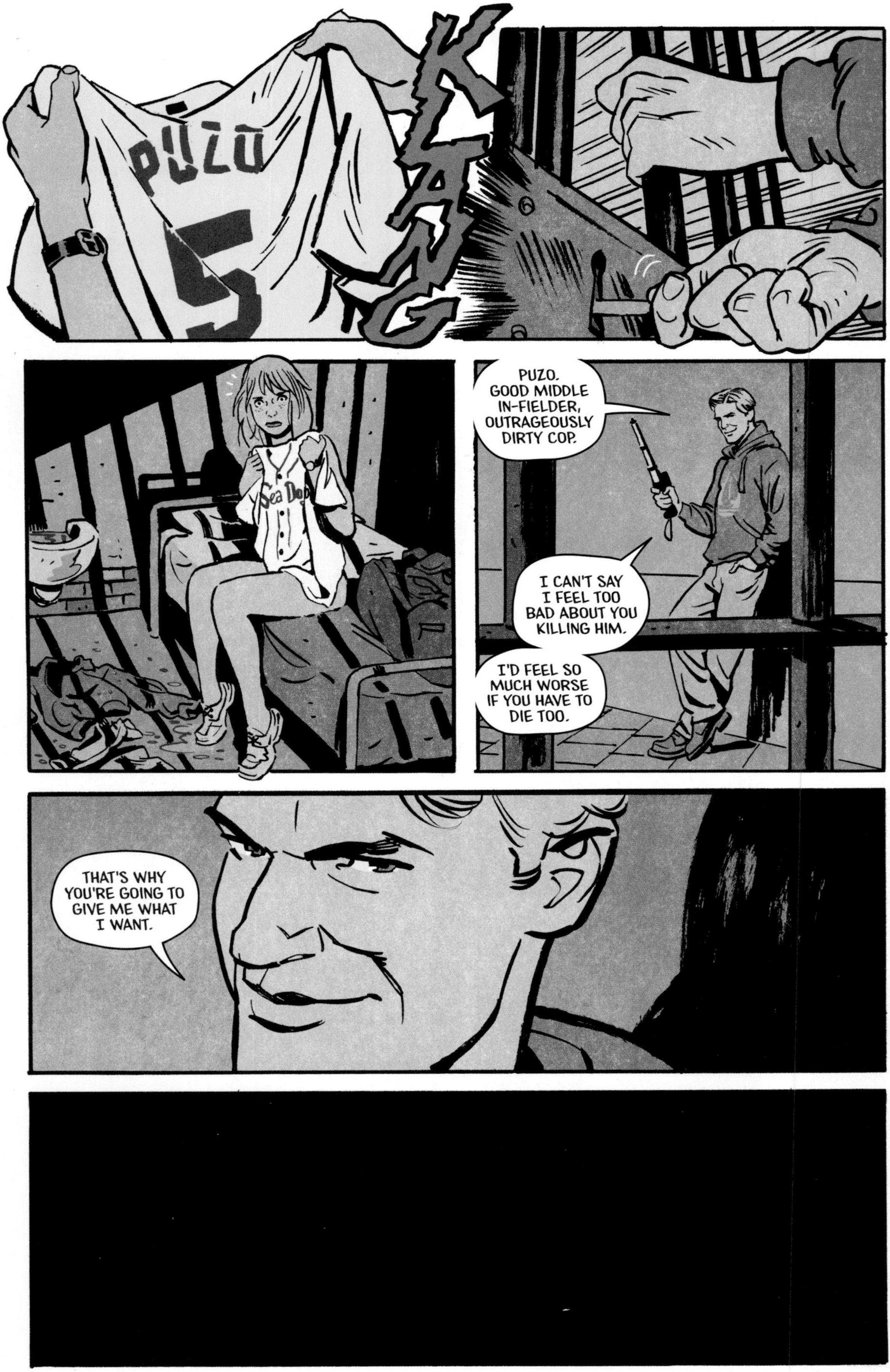
PUZO
5
KLANG
Sea Dogs
PUZO. GOOD MIDDLE IN-FIELDER, OUTRAGEOUSLY DIRTY COP.
I CAN'T SAY I FEEL TOO BAD ABOUT YOU KILLING HIM.
I'D FEEL SO MUCH WORSE IF YOU HAVE TO DIE TOO.
THAT'S WHY YOU'RE GOING TO GIVE ME WHAT I WANT.

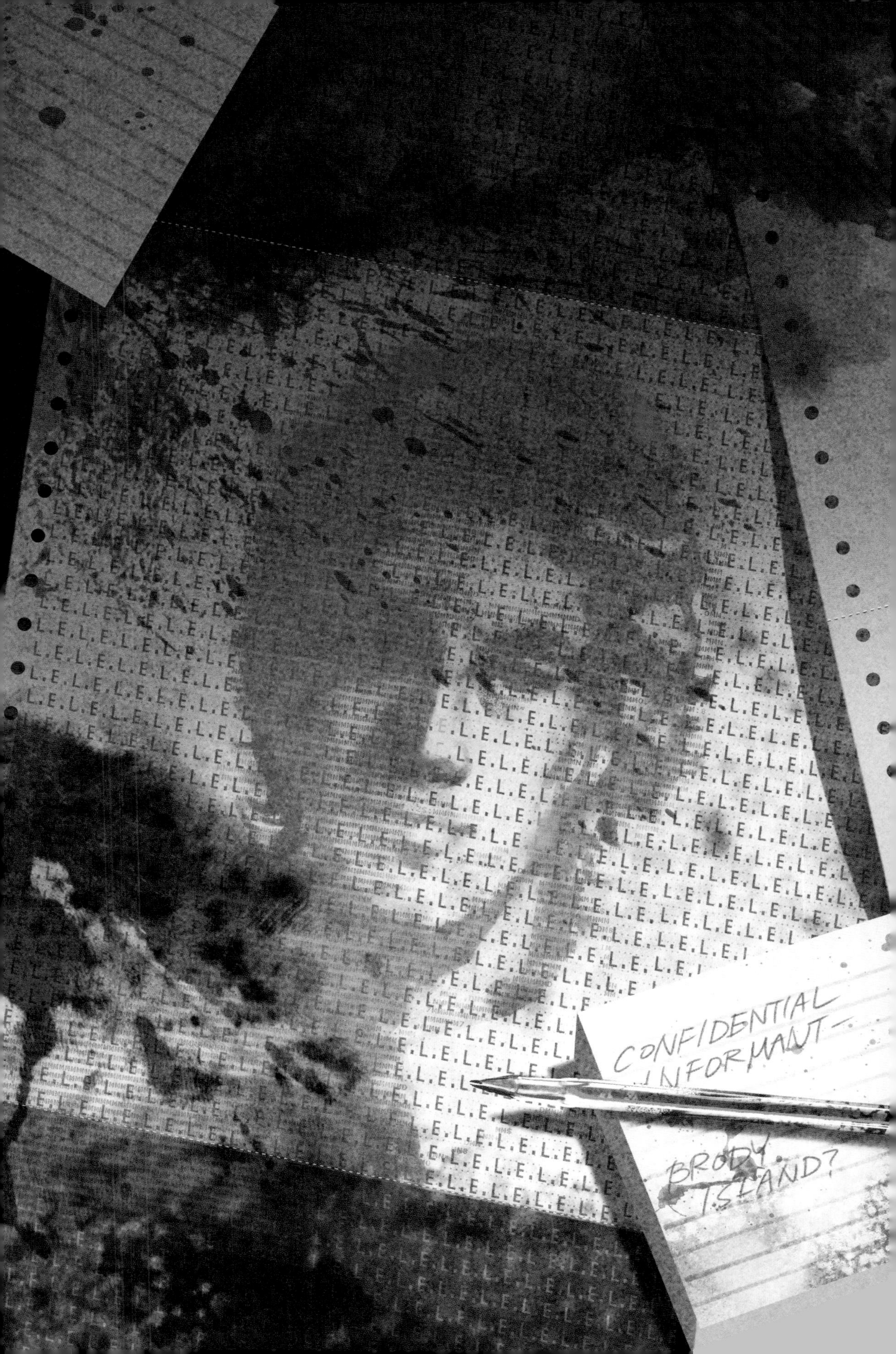
CONFIDENTIAL INFORMANT—
BRODY.
ISLAND?

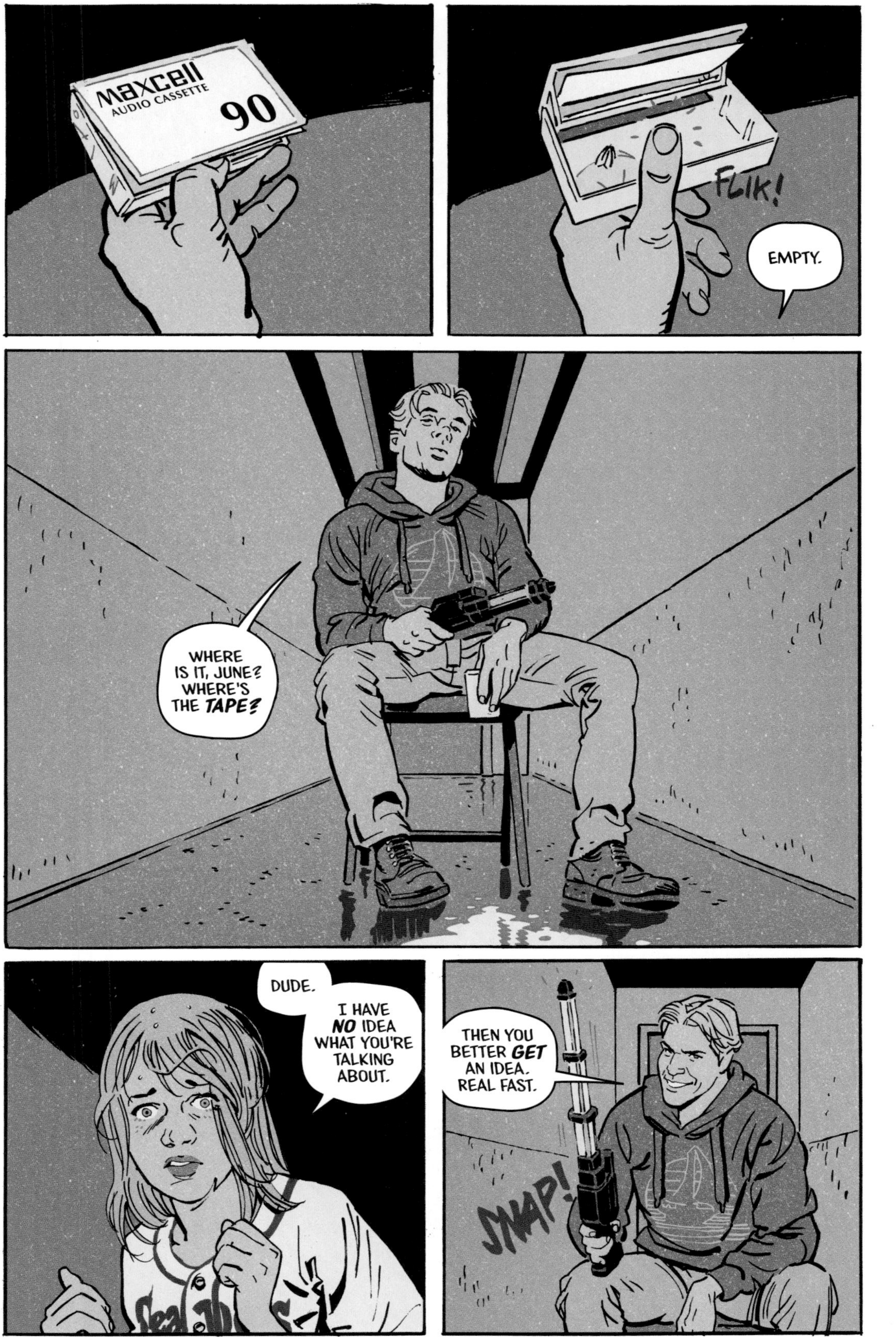
maxell
AUDIO CASSETTE
90
FLIK!
EMPTY.
WHERE IS IT, JUNE? WHERE'S THE TAPE?
DUDE.
I HAVE NO IDEA WHAT YOU'RE TALKING ABOUT.
THEN YOU BETTER GET AN IDEA. REAL FAST.
SNAP!

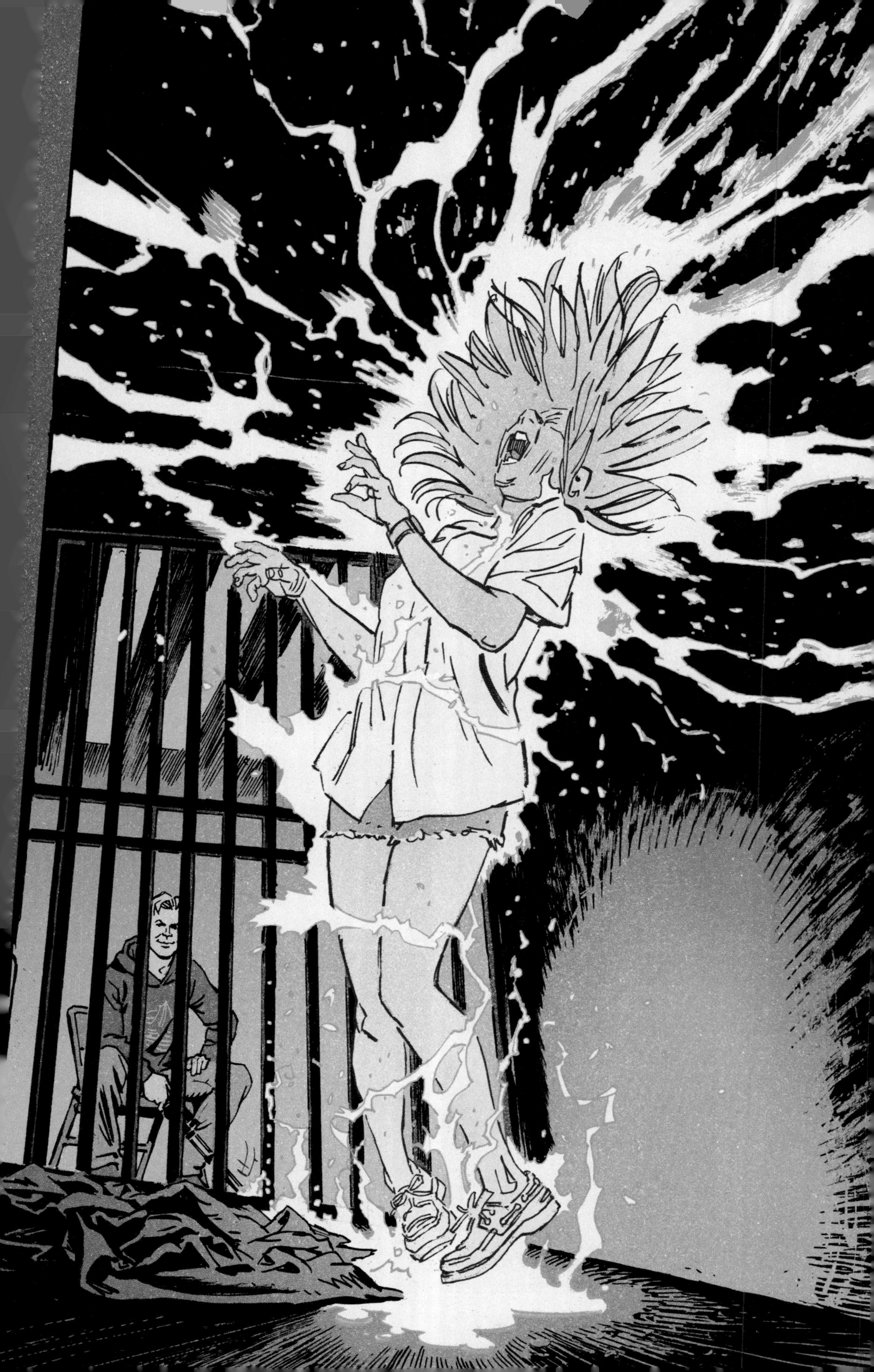

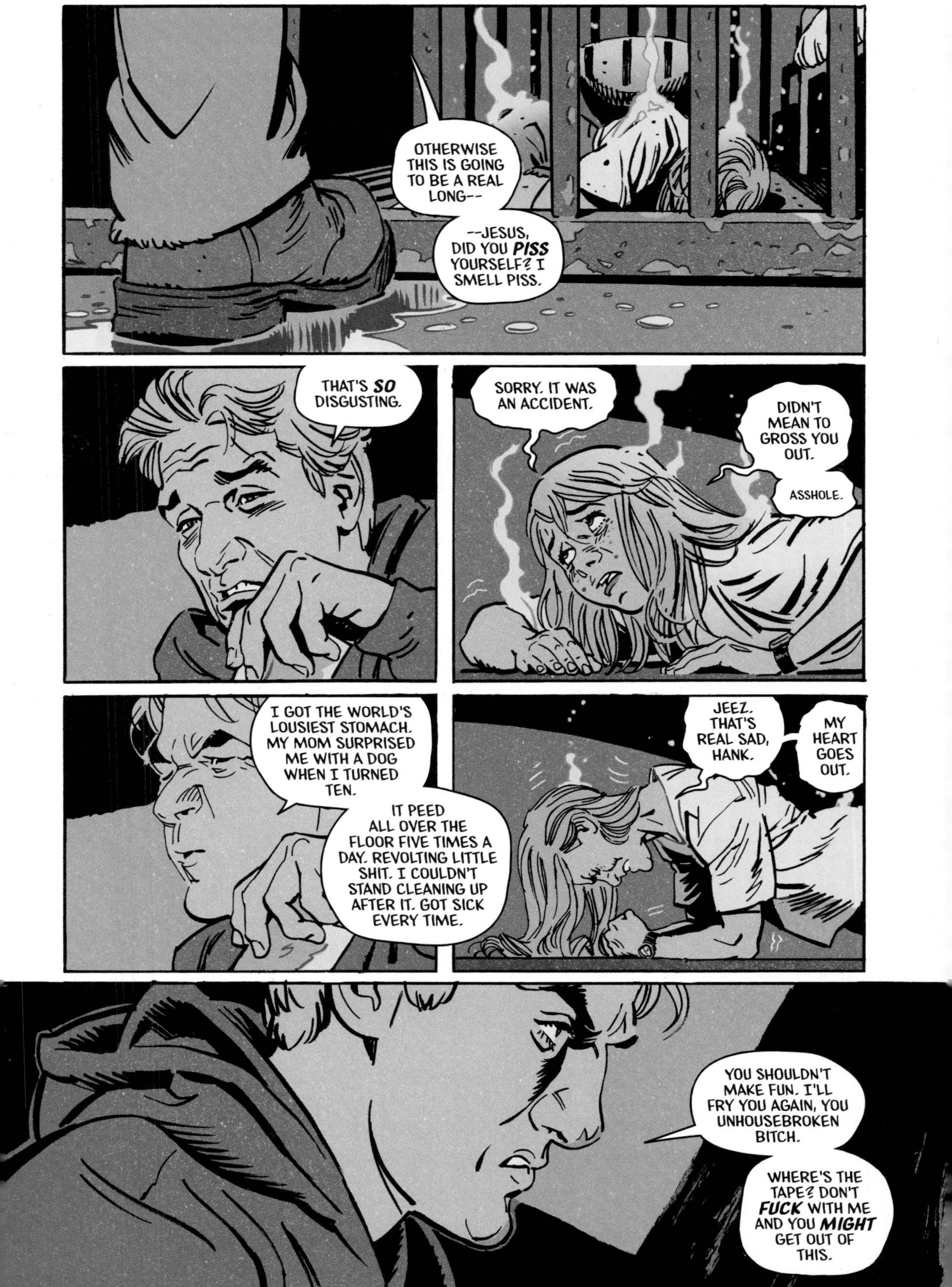
OTHERWISE THIS IS GOING TO BE A REAL LONG--
--JESUS, DID YOU PISS YOURSELF? I SMELL PISS.
THAT'S SO DISGUSTING.
SORRY. IT WAS AN ACCIDENT.
DIDN'T MEAN TO GROSS YOU OUT.
ASSHOLE.
I GOT THE WORLD'S LOUSIEST STOMACH. MY MOM SURPRISED ME WITH A DOG WHEN I TURNED TEN.
IT PEED ALL OVER THE FLOOR FIVE TIMES A DAY. REVOLTING LITTLE SHIT. I COULDN'T STAND CLEANING UP AFTER IT. GOT SICK EVERY TIME.
JEEZ. THAT'S REAL SAD, HANK.
MY HEART GOES OUT.
YOU SHOULDN'T MAKE FUN. I'LL FRY YOU AGAIN, YOU UNHOUSEBROKEN BITCH.
WHERE'S THE TAPE? DON'T FUCK WITH ME AND YOU MIGHT GET OUT OF THIS.

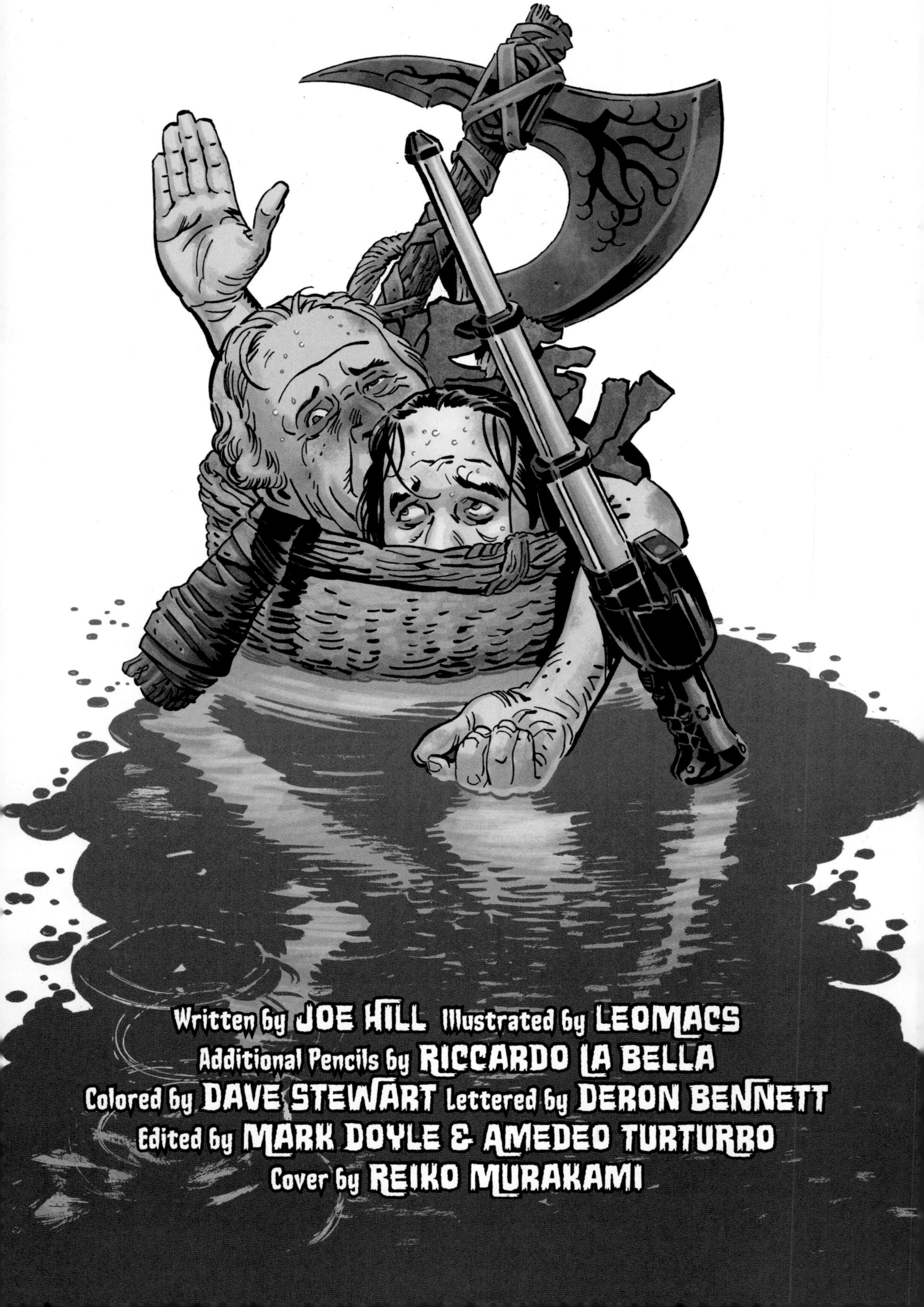

Written by JOE HILL Illustrated by LEOMACS
Additional Pencils by RICCARDO LA BELLA
Colored by DAVE STEWART Lettered by DERON BENNETT
Edited by MARK DOYLE & AMEDEO TURTURRO
Cover by REIKO MURAKAMI

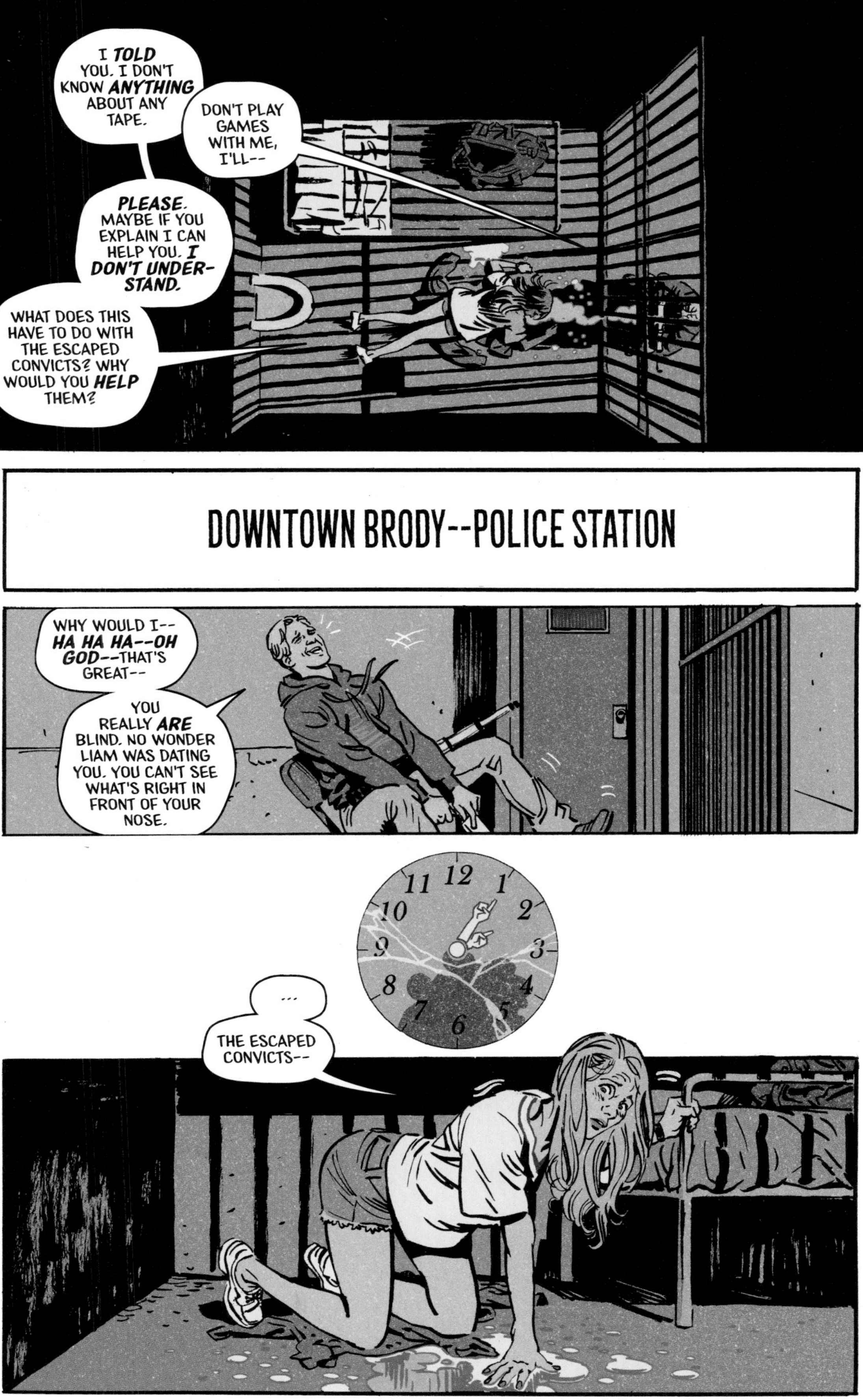
I TOLD YOU. I DON'T KNOW ANYTHING ABOUT ANY TAPE.
DON'T PLAY GAMES WITH ME, I'LL--
PLEASE. MAYBE IF YOU EXPLAIN I CAN HELP YOU. I DON'T UNDER-STAND.
WHAT DOES THIS HAVE TO DO WITH THE ESCAPED CONVICTS? WHY WOULD YOU HELP THEM?
DOWNTOWN BRODY--POLICE STATION
WHY WOULD I-- HA HA HA--OH GOD--THAT'S GREAT--
YOU REALLY ARE BLIND. NO WONDER LIAM WAS DATING YOU. YOU CAN'T SEE WHAT'S RIGHT IN FRONT OF YOUR NOSE.
12 1 2 3 4 5 6 7 8 9 10 11
...
THE ESCAPED CONVICTS--

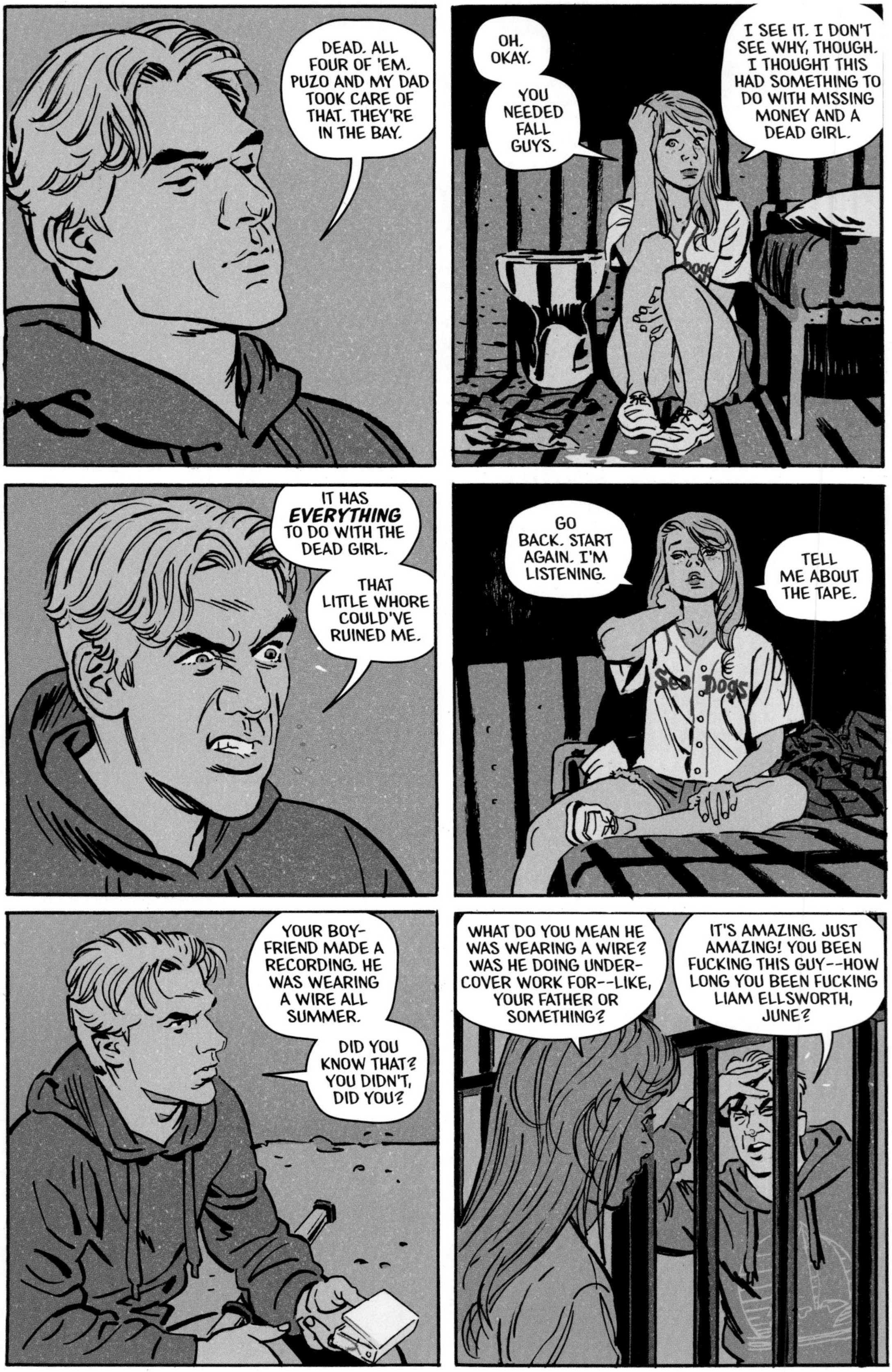
DEAD. ALL FOUR OF 'EM. PUZO AND MY DAD TOOK CARE OF THAT. THEY'RE IN THE BAY.
OH. OKAY.
YOU NEEDED FALL GUYS.
I SEE IT. I DON'T SEE WHY, THOUGH. I THOUGHT THIS HAD SOMETHING TO DO WITH MISSING MONEY AND A DEAD GIRL.
IT HAS ***EVERYTHING*** TO DO WITH THE DEAD GIRL.
THAT LITTLE WHORE COULD'VE RUINED ME.
GO BACK. START AGAIN. I'M LISTENING.
TELL ME ABOUT THE TAPE.
Sea Dogs
YOUR BOY-FRIEND MADE A RECORDING. HE WAS WEARING A WIRE ALL SUMMER.
DID YOU KNOW THAT? YOU DIDN'T, DID YOU?
WHAT DO YOU MEAN HE WAS WEARING A WIRE? WAS HE DOING UNDER-COVER WORK FOR--LIKE, YOUR FATHER OR SOMETHING?
IT'S AMAZING. JUST AMAZING! YOU BEEN FUCKING THIS GUY--HOW LONG YOU BEEN FUCKING LIAM ELLSWORTH, JUNE?

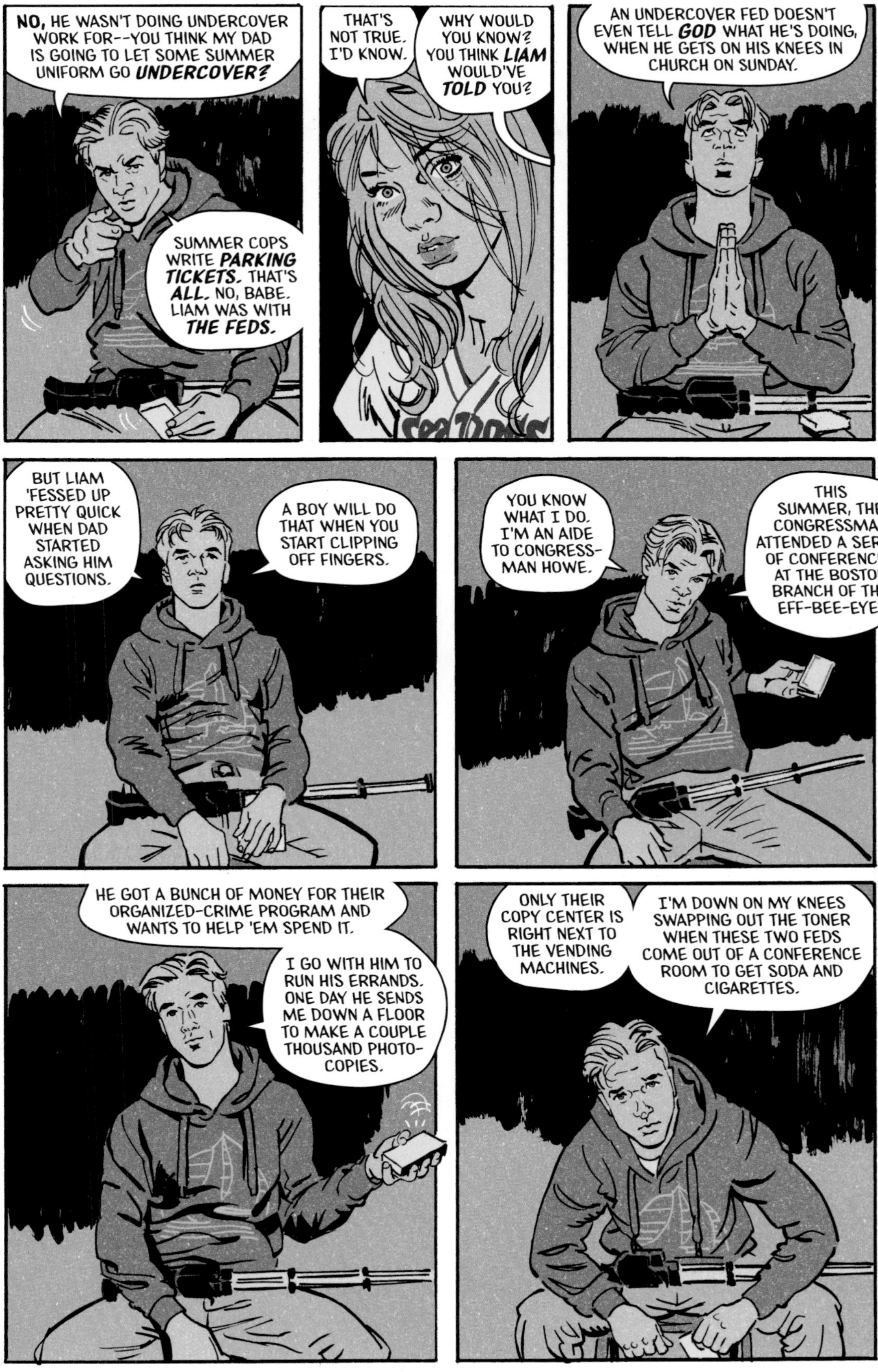
NO, HE WASN'T DOING UNDERCOVER WORK FOR--YOU THINK MY DAD IS GOING TO LET SOME SUMMER UNIFORM GO UNDERCOVER?
SUMMER COPS WRITE PARKING TICKETS. THAT'S ALL. NO, BABE. LIAM WAS WITH THE FEDS.
THAT'S NOT TRUE. I'D KNOW.
WHY WOULD YOU KNOW? YOU THINK LIAM WOULD'VE TOLD YOU?
AN UNDERCOVER FED DOESN'T EVEN TELL GOD WHAT HE'S DOING, WHEN HE GETS ON HIS KNEES IN CHURCH ON SUNDAY.
BUT LIAM 'FESSED UP PRETTY QUICK WHEN DAD STARTED ASKING HIM QUESTIONS.
A BOY WILL DO THAT WHEN YOU START CLIPPING OFF FINGERS.
YOU KNOW WHAT I DO. I'M AN AIDE TO CONGRESSMAN HOWE.
THIS SUMMER, THE CONGRESSMAN ATTENDED A SERIES OF CONFERENCES AT THE BOSTON BRANCH OF THE EFF-BEE-EYE.
HE GOT A BUNCH OF MONEY FOR THEIR ORGANIZED-CRIME PROGRAM AND WANTS TO HELP 'EM SPEND IT.
I GO WITH HIM TO RUN HIS ERRANDS. ONE DAY HE SENDS ME DOWN A FLOOR TO MAKE A COUPLE THOUSAND PHOTOCOPIES.
ONLY THEIR COPY CENTER IS RIGHT NEXT TO THE VENDING MACHINES.
I'M DOWN ON MY KNEES SWAPPING OUT THE TONER WHEN THESE TWO FEDS COME OUT OF A CONFERENCE ROOM TO GET SODA AND CIGARETTES.

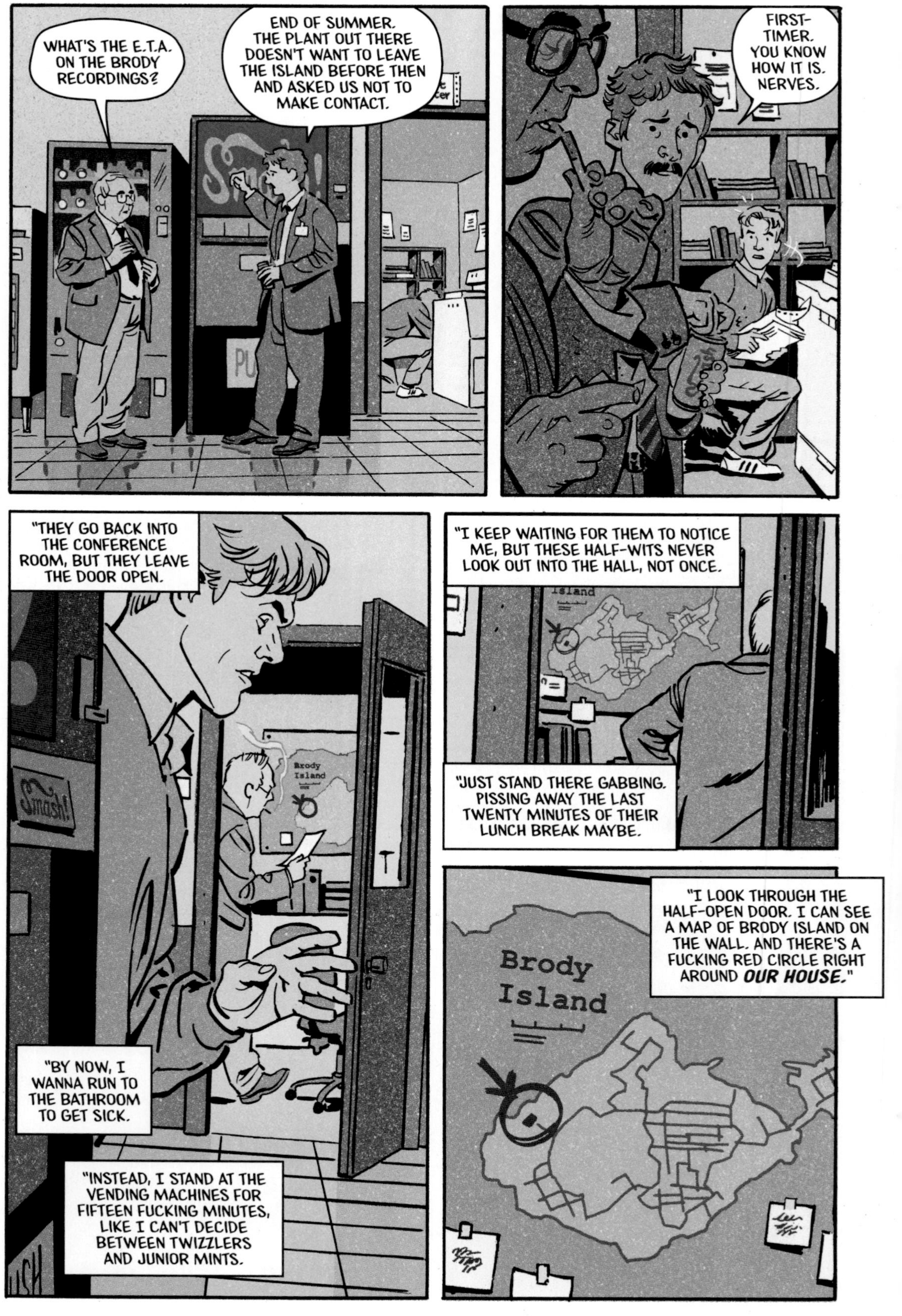
WHAT'S THE E.T.A. ON THE BRODY RECORDINGS?
END OF SUMMER. THE PLANT OUT THERE DOESN'T WANT TO LEAVE THE ISLAND BEFORE THEN AND ASKED US NOT TO MAKE CONTACT.
FIRST-TIMER. YOU KNOW HOW IT IS. NERVES.
"THEY GO BACK INTO THE CONFERENCE ROOM, BUT THEY LEAVE THE DOOR OPEN.
Smash!
Brody Island
"BY NOW, I WANNA RUN TO THE BATHROOM TO GET SICK.
"INSTEAD, I STAND AT THE VENDING MACHINES FOR FIFTEEN FUCKING MINUTES, LIKE I CAN'T DECIDE BETWEEN TWIZZLERS AND JUNIOR MINTS.
"I KEEP WAITING FOR THEM TO NOTICE ME, BUT THESE HALF-WITS NEVER LOOK OUT INTO THE HALL, NOT ONCE.
"JUST STAND THERE GABBING. PISSING AWAY THE LAST TWENTY MINUTES OF THEIR LUNCH BREAK MAYBE.
"I LOOK THROUGH THE HALF-OPEN DOOR. I CAN SEE A MAP OF BRODY ISLAND ON THE WALL. AND THERE'S A FUCKING RED CIRCLE RIGHT AROUND ***OUR HOUSE.***"
Brody Island

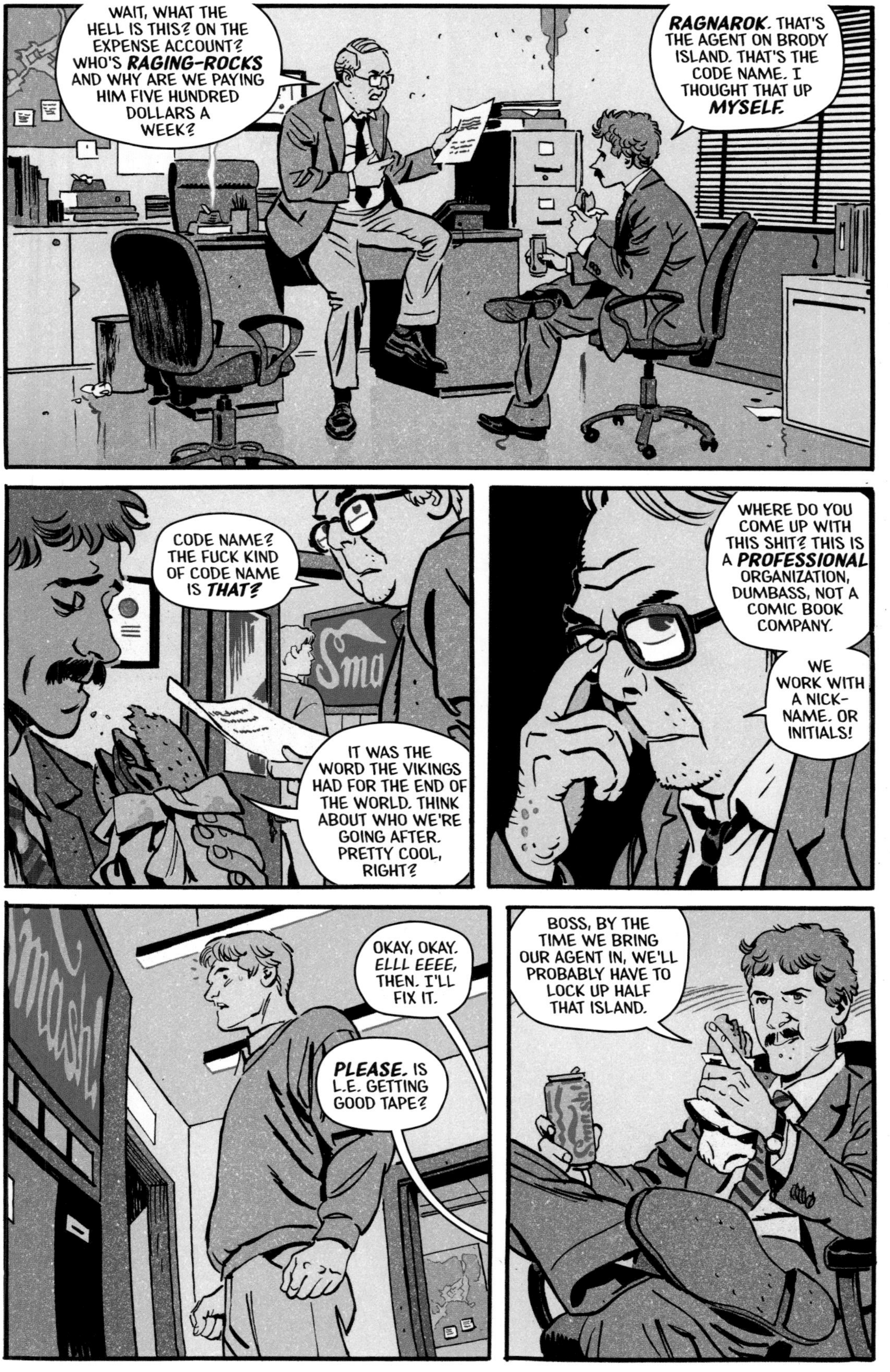
WAIT, WHAT THE HELL IS THIS? ON THE EXPENSE ACCOUNT? WHO'S **RAGING-ROCKS** AND WHY ARE WE PAYING HIM FIVE HUNDRED DOLLARS A WEEK?
RAGNAROK. THAT'S THE AGENT ON BRODY ISLAND. THAT'S THE CODE NAME. I THOUGHT THAT UP **MYSELF.**
CODE NAME? THE FUCK KIND OF CODE NAME IS **THAT?**
IT WAS THE WORD THE VIKINGS HAD FOR THE END OF THE WORLD. THINK ABOUT WHO WE'RE GOING AFTER. PRETTY COOL, RIGHT?
WHERE DO YOU COME UP WITH THIS SHIT? THIS IS A **PROFESSIONAL** ORGANIZATION, DUMBASS, NOT A COMIC BOOK COMPANY.
WE WORK WITH A NICK-NAME. OR INITIALS!
OKAY, OKAY. ELLL EEEE, THEN. I'LL FIX IT.
PLEASE. IS L.E. GETTING GOOD TAPE?
BOSS, BY THE TIME WE BRING OUR AGENT IN, WE'LL PROBABLY HAVE TO LOCK UP HALF THAT ISLAND.

LIAM.

L.E. LIAM ELLSWORTH.

YOUR BOYFRIEND'S BEEN STAYING RENT-FREE ON MY PARENTS' BOAT ALL SUMMER.

ONE DAY WHEN HE WAS ON THE JOB I WENT IN FOR A POKE AROUND AND FOUND THIS.

POLICE—EVIDENCE

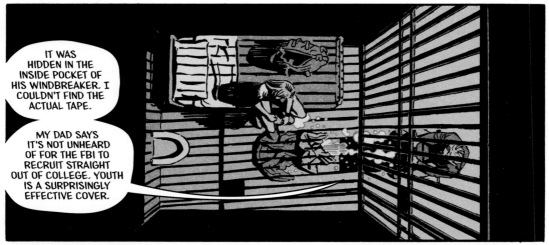

IT WAS HIDDEN IN THE INSIDE POCKET OF HIS WINDBREAKER. I COULDN'T FIND THE ACTUAL TAPE.

MY DAD SAYS IT'S NOT UNHEARD OF FOR THE FBI TO RECRUIT STRAIGHT OUT OF COLLEGE. YOUTH IS A SURPRISINGLY EFFECTIVE COVER.

MY DAD'S OUT ON THE BOAT WITH HIM RIGHT NOW. LIAM'S BEING A LITTLE BITCH.

HE SAYS SOMEONE'S HOLDING THE TAPE, AND IF HE DISAPPEARS, IT'LL BE DELIVERED TO HIS MAN AT THE FBI.

WHAT I'VE BEEN WONDERING IS IF THE PERSON HOLDING THE TAPE FOR HIM IS YOU.

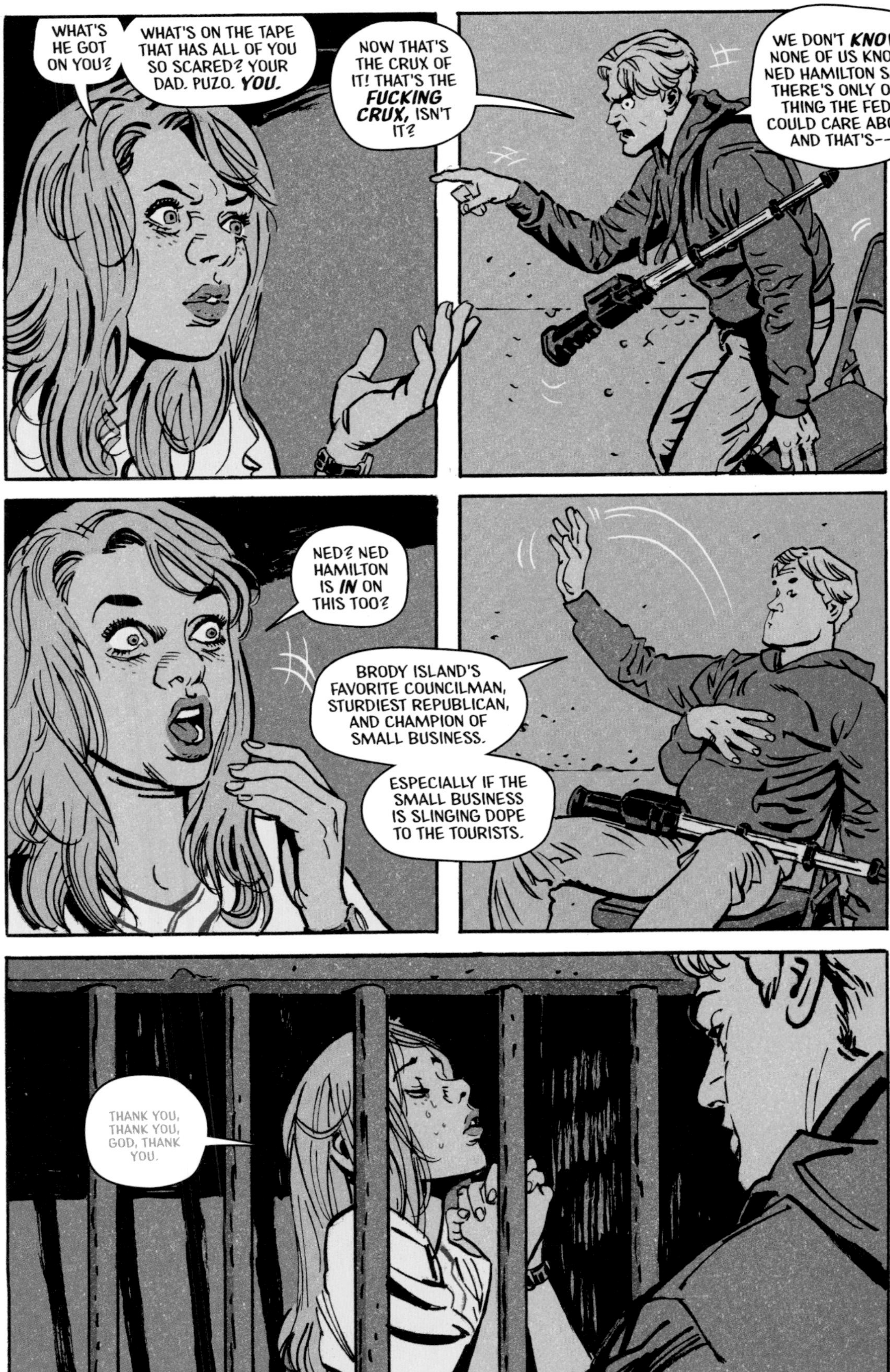
WHAT'S HE GOT ON YOU?
WHAT'S ON THE TAPE THAT HAS ALL OF YOU SO SCARED? YOUR DAD. PUZO. *YOU.*
NOW THAT'S THE CRUX OF IT! THAT'S THE *FUCKING CRUX,* ISN'T IT?
WE DON'T *KNOW.* NONE OF US KNOW. NED HAMILTON SAYS THERE'S ONLY ONE THING THE FEDS COULD CARE ABOUT AND THAT'S--
NED? NED HAMILTON IS *IN* ON THIS TOO?
BRODY ISLAND'S FAVORITE COUNCILMAN, STURDIEST REPUBLICAN, AND CHAMPION OF SMALL BUSINESS.
ESPECIALLY IF THE SMALL BUSINESS IS SLINGING DOPE TO THE TOURISTS.
THANK YOU, THANK YOU, GOD, THANK YOU.

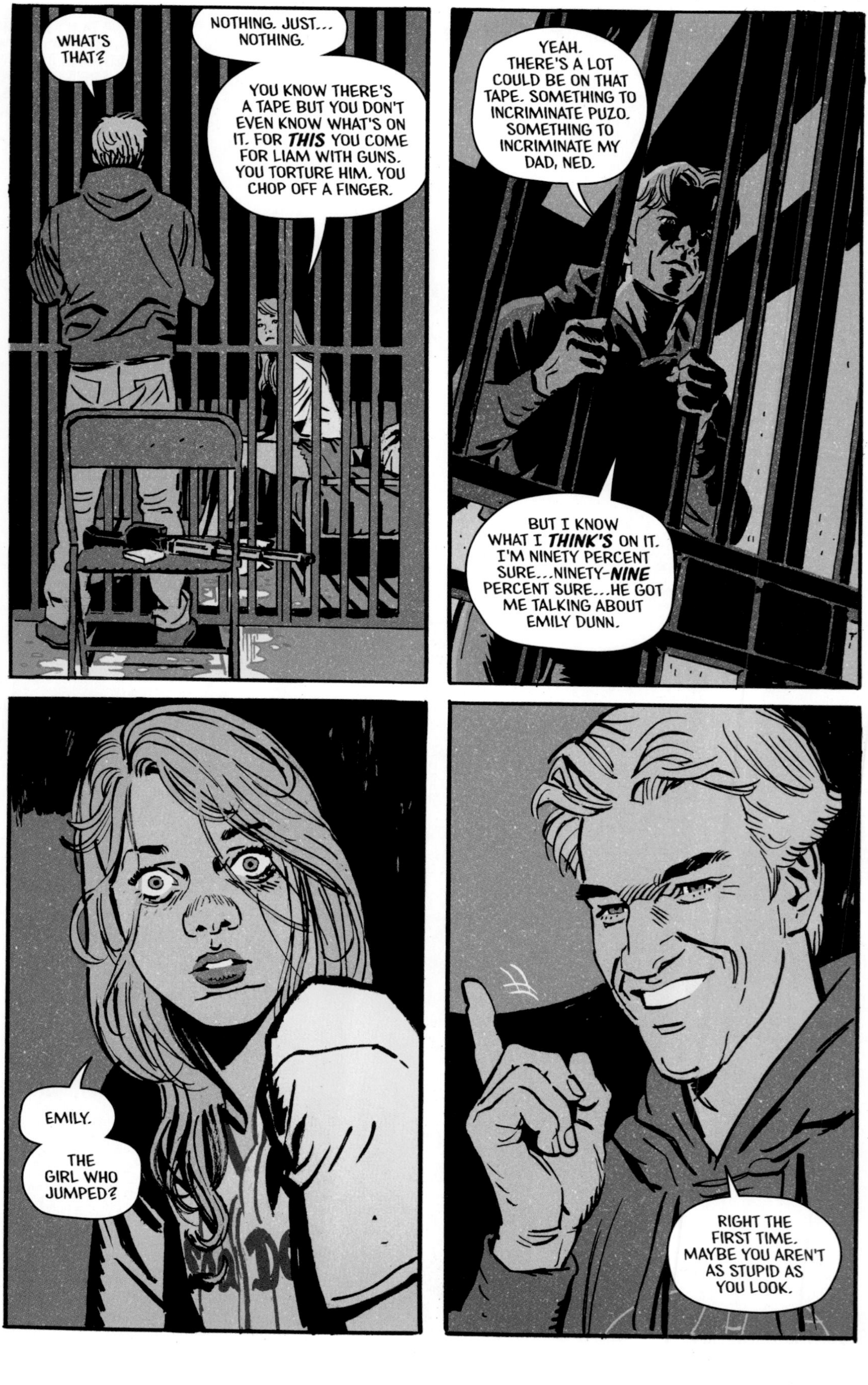
WHAT'S THAT?
NOTHING. JUST... NOTHING.
YOU KNOW THERE'S A TAPE BUT YOU DON'T EVEN KNOW WHAT'S ON IT. FOR *THIS* YOU COME FOR LIAM WITH GUNS. YOU TORTURE HIM. YOU CHOP OFF A FINGER.
YEAH. THERE'S A LOT COULD BE ON THAT TAPE. SOMETHING TO INCRIMINATE PUZO. SOMETHING TO INCRIMINATE MY DAD, NED.
BUT I KNOW WHAT I *THINK'S* ON IT. I'M NINETY PERCENT SURE...NINETY-*NINE* PERCENT SURE...HE GOT ME TALKING ABOUT EMILY DUNN.
EMILY.
THE GIRL WHO JUMPED?
RIGHT THE FIRST TIME. MAYBE YOU AREN'T AS STUPID AS YOU LOOK.

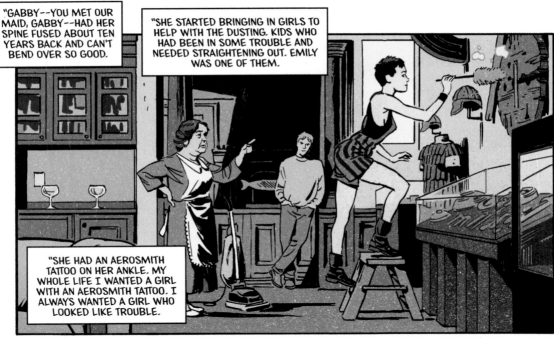

"GABBY--YOU MET OUR MAID, GABBY--HAD HER SPINE FUSED ABOUT TEN YEARS BACK AND CAN'T BEND OVER SO GOOD.

"SHE STARTED BRINGING IN GIRLS TO HELP WITH THE DUSTING. KIDS WHO HAD BEEN IN SOME TROUBLE AND NEEDED STRAIGHTENING OUT. EMILY WAS ONE OF THEM.

"SHE HAD AN AEROSMITH TATTOO ON HER ANKLE. MY WHOLE LIFE I WANTED A GIRL WITH AN AEROSMITH TATTOO. I ALWAYS WANTED A GIRL WHO LOOKED LIKE TROUBLE.

"MORAL OF THIS STORY IS BE CAREFUL WHAT YOU WISH FOR. YOU MIGHT GET IT.

"SHE FOUND MY OLD SKIN MAGAZINES ONE DAY, WHILE SHE WAS REORGANIZING MY CLOSET. STUFF I'VE HAD SINCE I WAS TWELVE.

"I FOUND HER LOOKING AT THEM. BUT SHE WASN'T UPSET. SHE WAS REAL COOL. REAL FUNNY. WE SAT AND TALKED ABOUT THEM. THAT'S HOW IT STARTED.

"MY MOM WOULD'VE LOST HER MIND IF SHE KNEW WE WERE A THING, SO WE HAD TO GET OFF-ISLAND TO HAVE FUN.

"BOSTON, NEW YORK. SHE'D BLOW ME RIGHT IN A TOWN CAR, DRIVER LOOKING AT BOTH OF US, DIDN'T EVEN CARE. SHE'D LAUGH ABOUT IT.

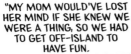

"EMILY KNEW HOW TO HAVE FUN AND SHE WASN'T A REPRESSED, *SAVING-IT-FOR-MARRIAGE* CUNT, LIKE MOST OF THE TRUST-FUND BITCHES I MET AT HARVARD. GIRLS WHO WERE ALWAYS TOO GOOD FOR A SMALL-TOWN POLICEMAN'S SON."

I CAN'T IMAGINE WHY THE HARVARD GIRLS WEREN'T SWAYED BY YOUR CHARMS, HANK.

A ROMANTIC LIKE YOU.

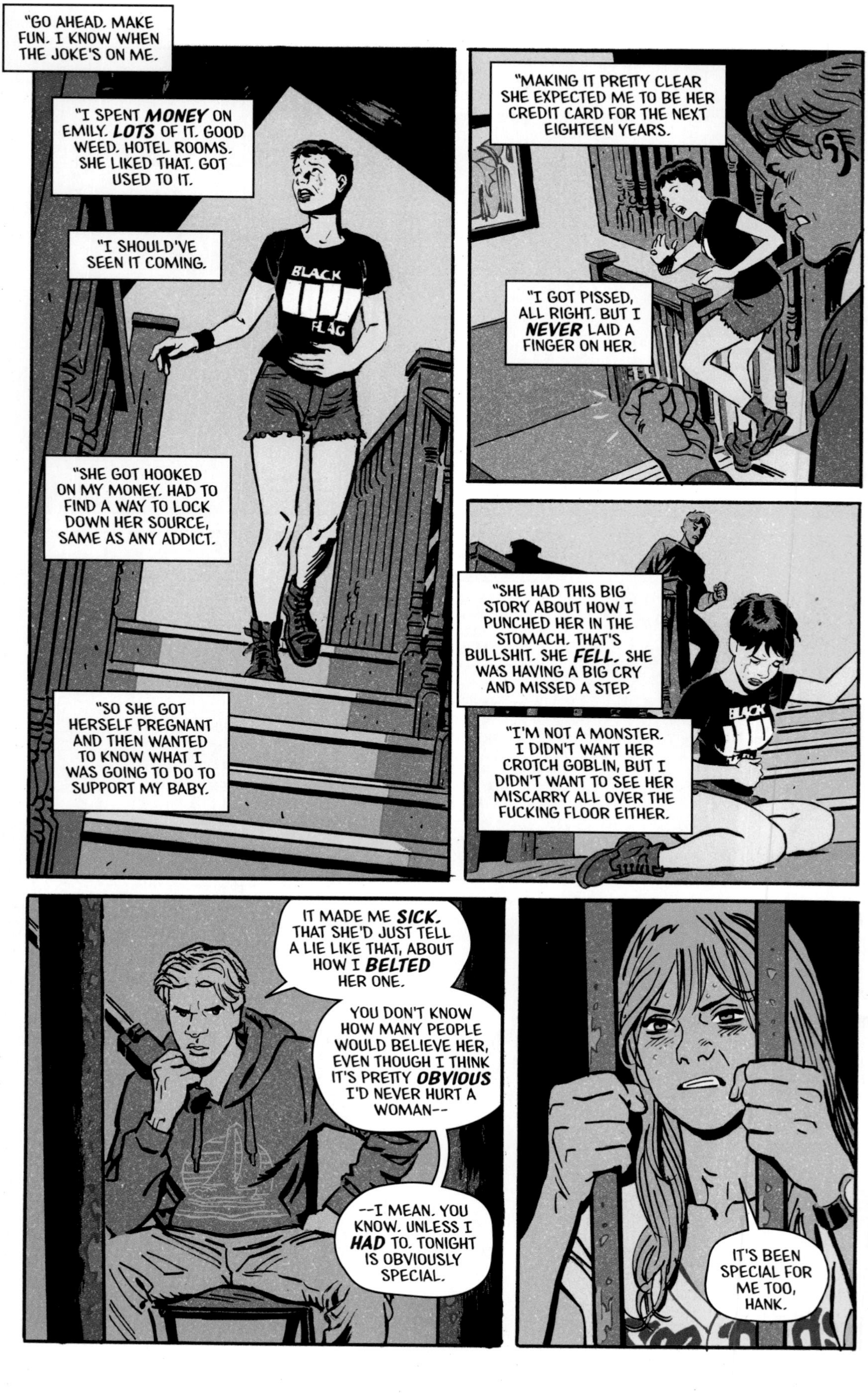
"GO AHEAD. MAKE FUN. I KNOW WHEN THE JOKE'S ON ME.
"I SPENT MONEY ON EMILY. LOTS OF IT. GOOD WEED. HOTEL ROOMS. SHE LIKED THAT. GOT USED TO IT.
"I SHOULD'VE SEEN IT COMING.
BLACK FLAG
"SHE GOT HOOKED ON MY MONEY. HAD TO FIND A WAY TO LOCK DOWN HER SOURCE, SAME AS ANY ADDICT.
"SO SHE GOT HERSELF PREGNANT AND THEN WANTED TO KNOW WHAT I WAS GOING TO DO TO SUPPORT MY BABY.
"MAKING IT PRETTY CLEAR SHE EXPECTED ME TO BE HER CREDIT CARD FOR THE NEXT EIGHTEEN YEARS.
"I GOT PISSED, ALL RIGHT. BUT I NEVER LAID A FINGER ON HER.
"SHE HAD THIS BIG STORY ABOUT HOW I PUNCHED HER IN THE STOMACH. THAT'S BULLSHIT. SHE FELL. SHE WAS HAVING A BIG CRY AND MISSED A STEP.
"I'M NOT A MONSTER. I DIDN'T WANT HER CROTCH GOBLIN, BUT I DIDN'T WANT TO SEE HER MISCARRY ALL OVER THE FUCKING FLOOR EITHER.
IT MADE ME SICK. THAT SHE'D JUST TELL A LIE LIKE THAT, ABOUT HOW I BELTED HER ONE.
YOU DON'T KNOW HOW MANY PEOPLE WOULD BELIEVE HER, EVEN THOUGH I THINK IT'S PRETTY OBVIOUS I'D NEVER HURT A WOMAN--
--I MEAN. YOU KNOW. UNLESS I HAD TO. TONIGHT IS OBVIOUSLY SPECIAL.
IT'S BEEN SPECIAL FOR ME TOO, HANK.

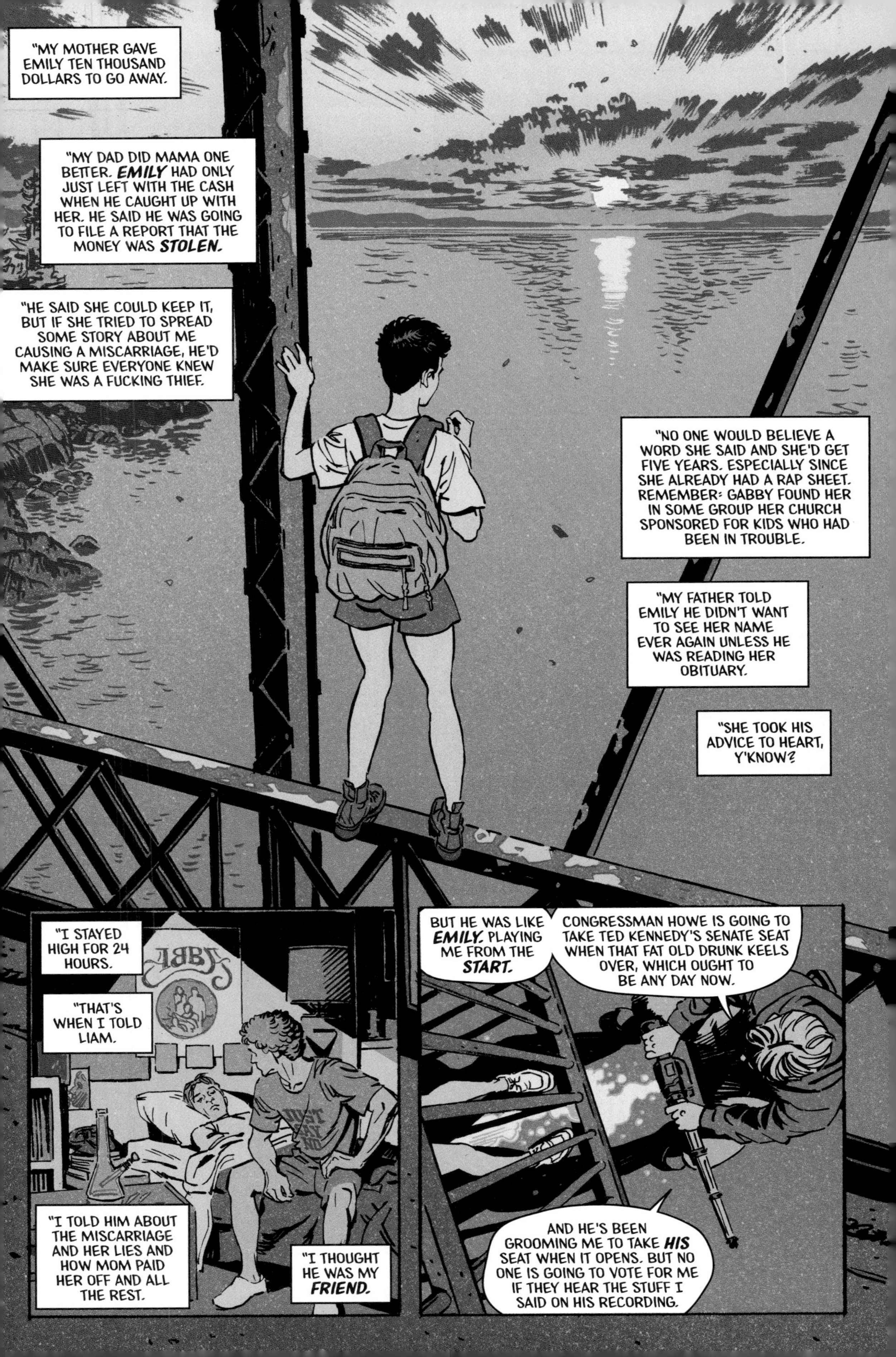
"MY MOTHER GAVE EMILY TEN THOUSAND DOLLARS TO GO AWAY.
"MY DAD DID MAMA ONE BETTER. EMILY HAD ONLY JUST LEFT WITH THE CASH WHEN HE CAUGHT UP WITH HER. HE SAID HE WAS GOING TO FILE A REPORT THAT THE MONEY WAS STOLEN.
"HE SAID SHE COULD KEEP IT, BUT IF SHE TRIED TO SPREAD SOME STORY ABOUT ME CAUSING A MISCARRIAGE, HE'D MAKE SURE EVERYONE KNEW SHE WAS A FUCKING THIEF.
"NO ONE WOULD BELIEVE A WORD SHE SAID AND SHE'D GET FIVE YEARS. ESPECIALLY SINCE SHE ALREADY HAD A RAP SHEET. REMEMBER: GABBY FOUND HER IN SOME GROUP HER CHURCH SPONSORED FOR KIDS WHO HAD BEEN IN TROUBLE.
"MY FATHER TOLD EMILY HE DIDN'T WANT TO SEE HER NAME EVER AGAIN UNLESS HE WAS READING HER OBITUARY.
"SHE TOOK HIS ADVICE TO HEART, Y'KNOW?
"I STAYED HIGH FOR 24 HOURS.
"THAT'S WHEN I TOLD LIAM.
"I TOLD HIM ABOUT THE MISCARRIAGE AND HER LIES AND HOW MOM PAID HER OFF AND ALL THE REST.
"I THOUGHT HE WAS MY FRIEND.
BUT HE WAS LIKE EMILY. PLAYING ME FROM THE START.
CONGRESSMAN HOWE IS GOING TO TAKE TED KENNEDY'S SENATE SEAT WHEN THAT FAT OLD DRUNK KEELS OVER, WHICH OUGHT TO BE ANY DAY NOW.
AND HE'S BEEN GROOMING ME TO TAKE HIS SEAT WHEN IT OPENS. BUT NO ONE IS GOING TO VOTE FOR ME IF THEY HEAR THE STUFF I SAID ON HIS RECORDING.

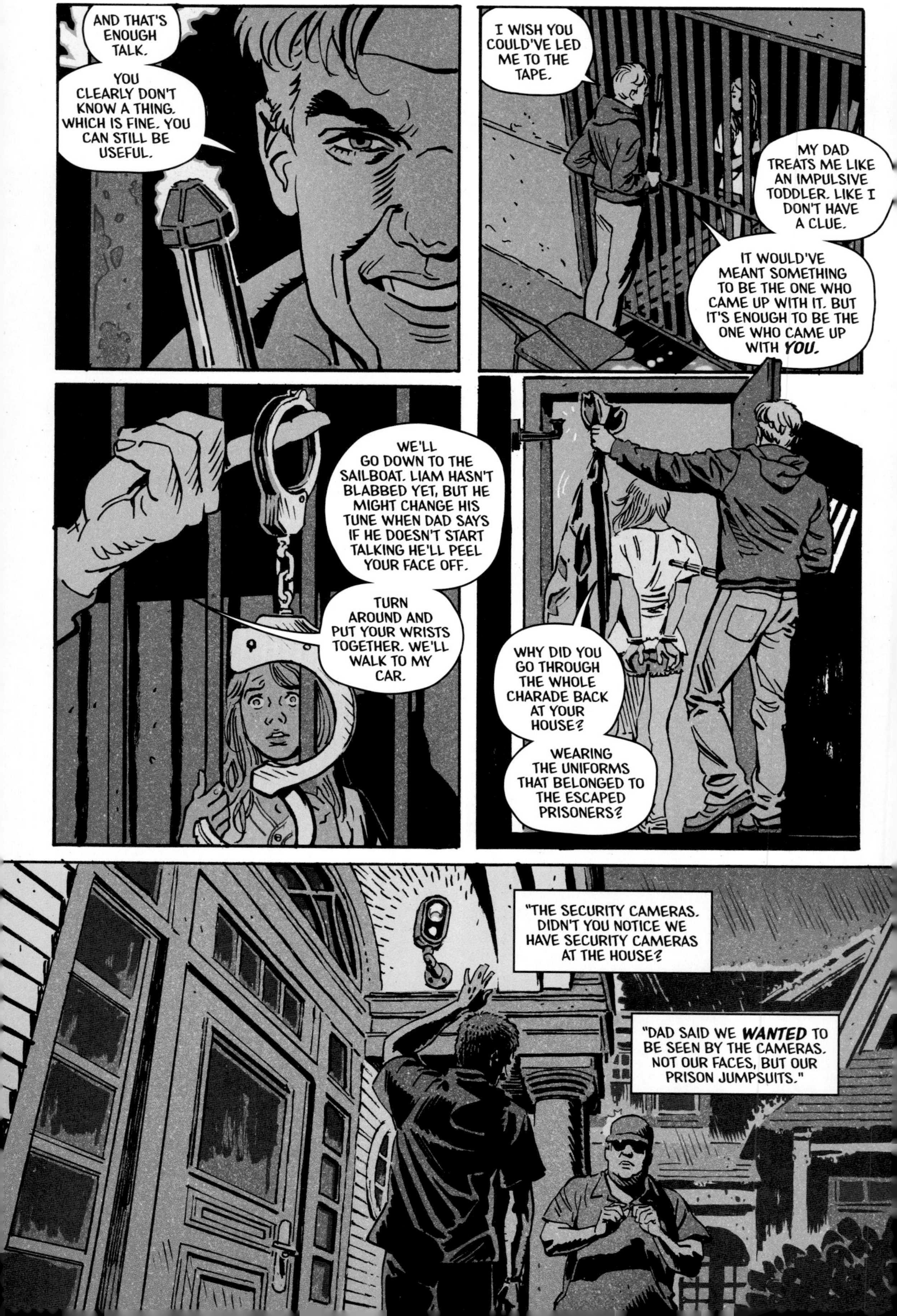
AND THAT'S ENOUGH TALK.
YOU CLEARLY DON'T KNOW A THING. WHICH IS FINE. YOU CAN STILL BE USEFUL.
I WISH YOU COULD'VE LED ME TO THE TAPE.
MY DAD TREATS ME LIKE AN IMPULSIVE TODDLER. LIKE I DON'T HAVE A CLUE.
IT WOULD'VE MEANT SOMETHING TO BE THE ONE WHO CAME UP WITH IT. BUT IT'S ENOUGH TO BE THE ONE WHO CAME UP WITH *YOU.*
WE'LL GO DOWN TO THE SAILBOAT. LIAM HASN'T BLABBED YET, BUT HE MIGHT CHANGE HIS TUNE WHEN DAD SAYS IF HE DOESN'T START TALKING HE'LL PEEL YOUR FACE OFF.
TURN AROUND AND PUT YOUR WRISTS TOGETHER. WE'LL WALK TO MY CAR.
WHY DID YOU GO THROUGH THE WHOLE CHARADE BACK AT YOUR HOUSE?
WEARING THE UNIFORMS THAT BELONGED TO THE ESCAPED PRISONERS?
"THE SECURITY CAMERAS. DIDN'T YOU NOTICE WE HAVE SECURITY CAMERAS AT THE HOUSE?
"DAD SAID WE *WANTED* TO BE SEEN BY THE CAMERAS. NOT OUR FACES, BUT OUR PRISON JUMPSUITS."

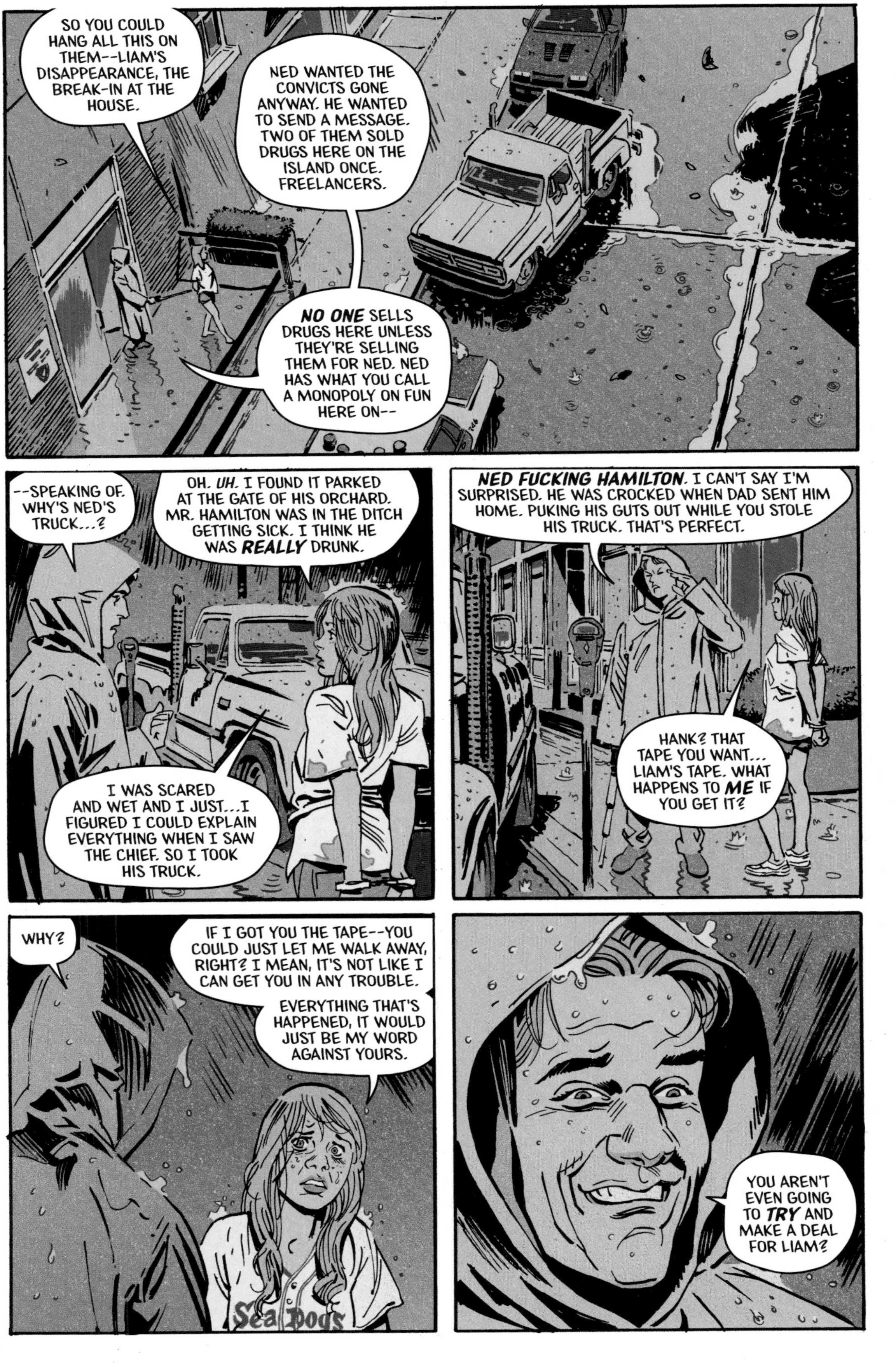
SO YOU COULD HANG ALL THIS ON THEM--LIAM'S DISAPPEARANCE, THE BREAK-IN AT THE HOUSE.
NED WANTED THE CONVICTS GONE ANYWAY. HE WANTED TO SEND A MESSAGE. TWO OF THEM SOLD DRUGS HERE ON THE ISLAND ONCE. FREELANCERS.
NO ONE SELLS DRUGS HERE UNLESS THEY'RE SELLING THEM FOR NED. NED HAS WHAT YOU CALL A MONOPOLY ON FUN HERE ON--
--SPEAKING OF. WHY'S NED'S TRUCK...?
OH. UH. I FOUND IT PARKED AT THE GATE OF HIS ORCHARD. MR. HAMILTON WAS IN THE DITCH GETTING SICK. I THINK HE WAS REALLY DRUNK.
I WAS SCARED AND WET AND I JUST...I FIGURED I COULD EXPLAIN EVERYTHING WHEN I SAW THE CHIEF. SO I TOOK HIS TRUCK.
NED FUCKING HAMILTON. I CAN'T SAY I'M SURPRISED. HE WAS CROCKED WHEN DAD SENT HIM HOME. PUKING HIS GUTS OUT WHILE YOU STOLE HIS TRUCK. THAT'S PERFECT.
HANK? THAT TAPE YOU WANT... LIAM'S TAPE. WHAT HAPPENS TO ME IF YOU GET IT?
WHY?
IF I GOT YOU THE TAPE--YOU COULD JUST LET ME WALK AWAY, RIGHT? I MEAN, IT'S NOT LIKE I CAN GET YOU IN ANY TROUBLE.
EVERYTHING THAT'S HAPPENED, IT WOULD JUST BE MY WORD AGAINST YOURS.
Sea Dogs
YOU AREN'T EVEN GOING TO TRY AND MAKE A DEAL FOR LIAM?

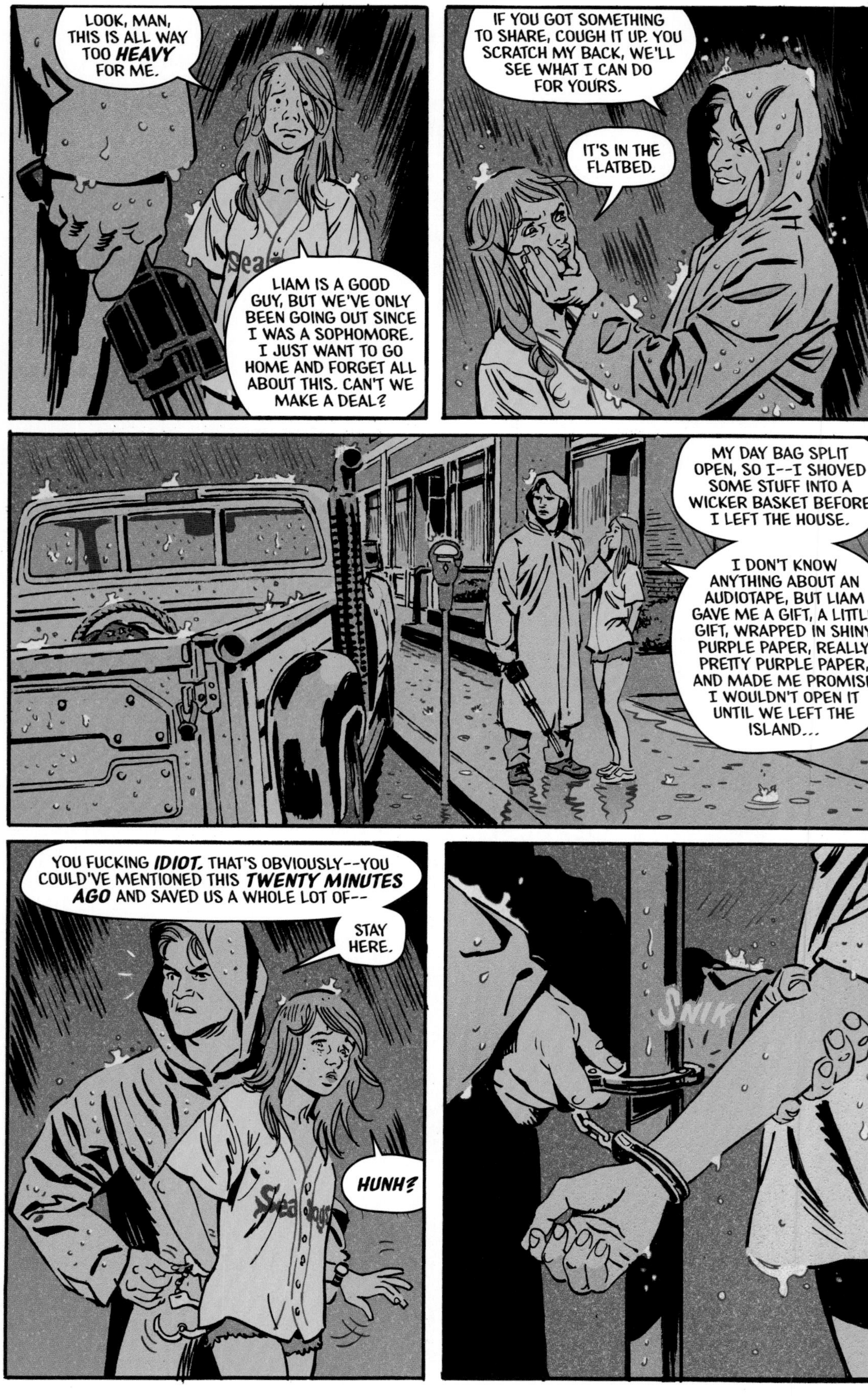
LOOK, MAN, THIS IS ALL WAY TOO HEAVY FOR ME.
LIAM IS A GOOD GUY, BUT WE'VE ONLY BEEN GOING OUT SINCE I WAS A SOPHOMORE. I JUST WANT TO GO HOME AND FORGET ALL ABOUT THIS. CAN'T WE MAKE A DEAL?
IF YOU GOT SOMETHING TO SHARE, COUGH IT UP. YOU SCRATCH MY BACK, WE'LL SEE WHAT I CAN DO FOR YOURS.
IT'S IN THE FLATBED.
MY DAY BAG SPLIT OPEN, SO I--I SHOVED SOME STUFF INTO A WICKER BASKET BEFORE I LEFT THE HOUSE.
I DON'T KNOW ANYTHING ABOUT AN AUDIOTAPE, BUT LIAM GAVE ME A GIFT, A LITTLE GIFT, WRAPPED IN SHINY PURPLE PAPER, REALLY PRETTY PURPLE PAPER, AND MADE ME PROMISE I WOULDN'T OPEN IT UNTIL WE LEFT THE ISLAND...
YOU FUCKING IDIOT. THAT'S OBVIOUSLY--YOU COULD'VE MENTIONED THIS TWENTY MINUTES AGO AND SAVED US A WHOLE LOT OF--
STAY HERE.
HUNH?
SNIK

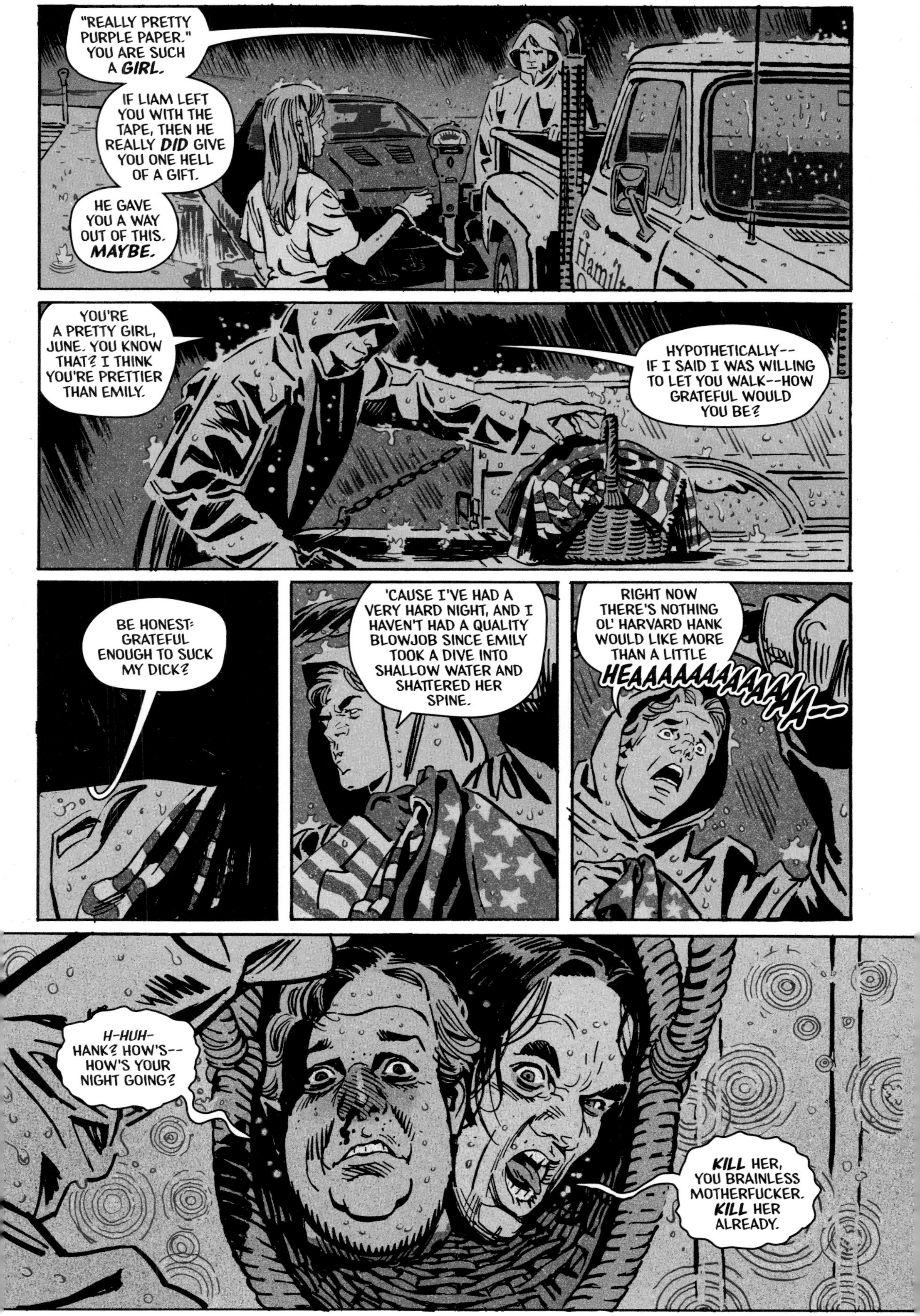
"REALLY PRETTY PURPLE PAPER." YOU ARE SUCH A GIRL.
IF LIAM LEFT YOU WITH THE TAPE, THEN HE REALLY DID GIVE YOU ONE HELL OF A GIFT.
HE GAVE YOU A WAY OUT OF THIS. MAYBE.
Hamilt
YOU'RE A PRETTY GIRL, JUNE. YOU KNOW THAT? I THINK YOU'RE PRETTIER THAN EMILY.
HYPOTHETICALLY-- IF I SAID I WAS WILLING TO LET YOU WALK--HOW GRATEFUL WOULD YOU BE?
BE HONEST: GRATEFUL ENOUGH TO SUCK MY DICK?
'CAUSE I'VE HAD A VERY HARD NIGHT, AND I HAVEN'T HAD A QUALITY BLOWJOB SINCE EMILY TOOK A DIVE INTO SHALLOW WATER AND SHATTERED HER SPINE.
RIGHT NOW THERE'S NOTHING OL' HARVARD HANK WOULD LIKE MORE THAN A LITTLE
HEAAAAAAAAAAAAAA--
H-HUH-HANK? HOW'S-- HOW'S YOUR NIGHT GOING?
KILL HER, YOU BRAINLESS MOTHERFUCKER. KILL HER ALREADY.

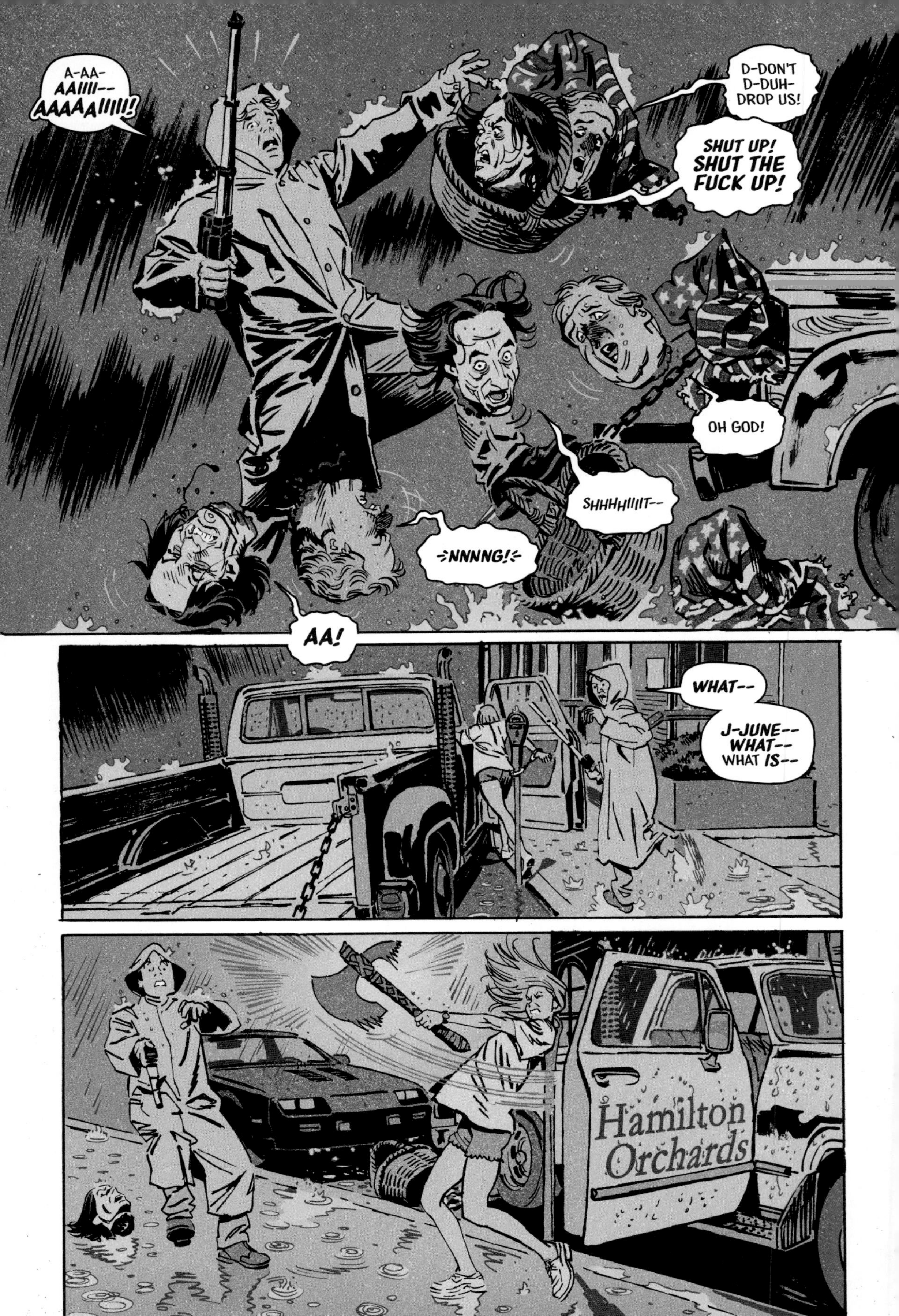
A-AA-
AAIIII--
AAAAAIIIII!
D-DON'T
D-DUH-
DROP US!
SHUT UP!
SHUT THE
FUCK UP!
OH GOD!
SHHHHIIIIT--
-NNNNG!-
AA!
WHAT--
J-JUNE--
WHAT--
WHAT IS--
Hamilton
Orchards

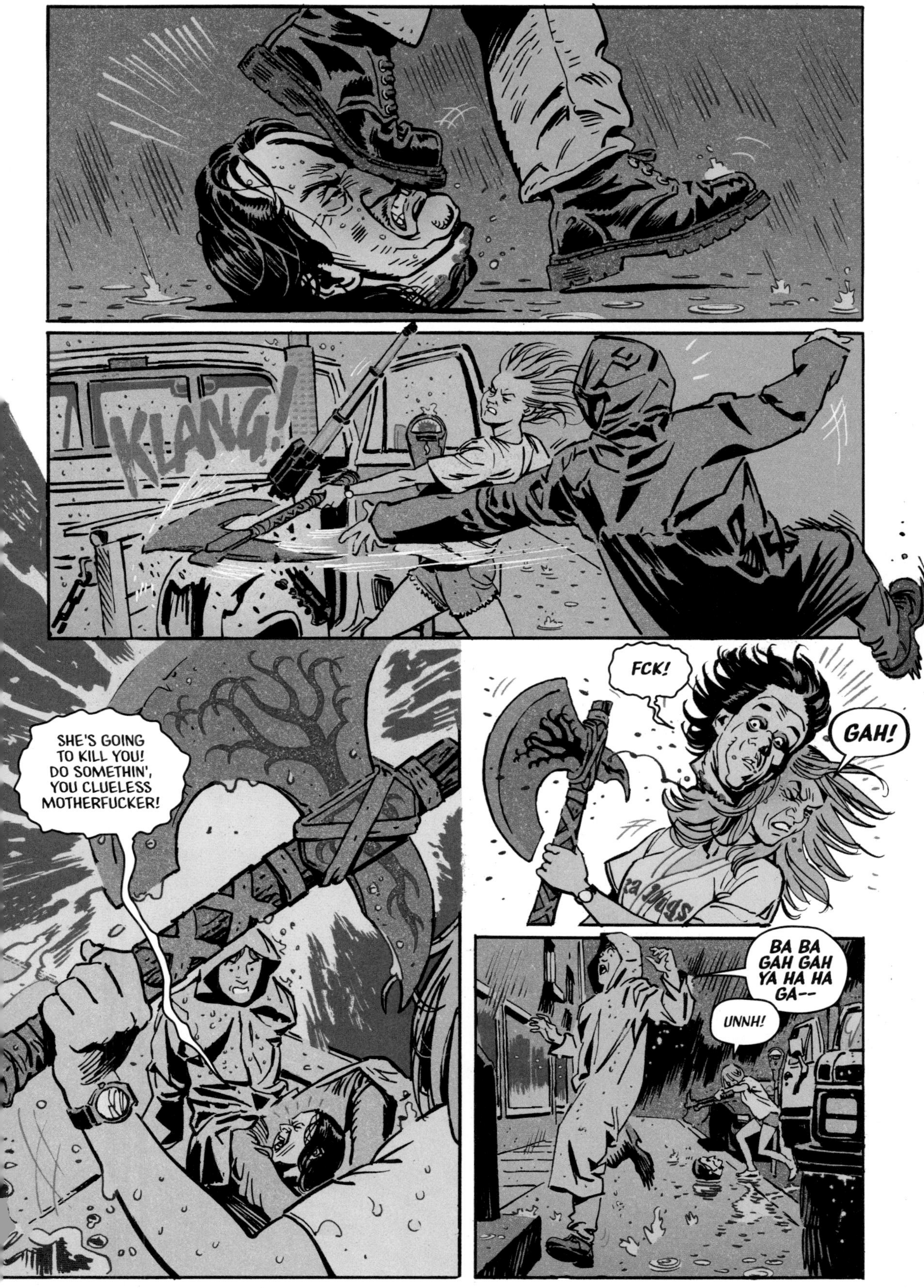
KLANG!
SHE'S GOING TO KILL YOU! DO SOMETHIN', YOU CLUELESS MOTHERFUCKER!
FCK!
GAH!
BA BA GAH GAH YA HA HA GA--
UNNH!

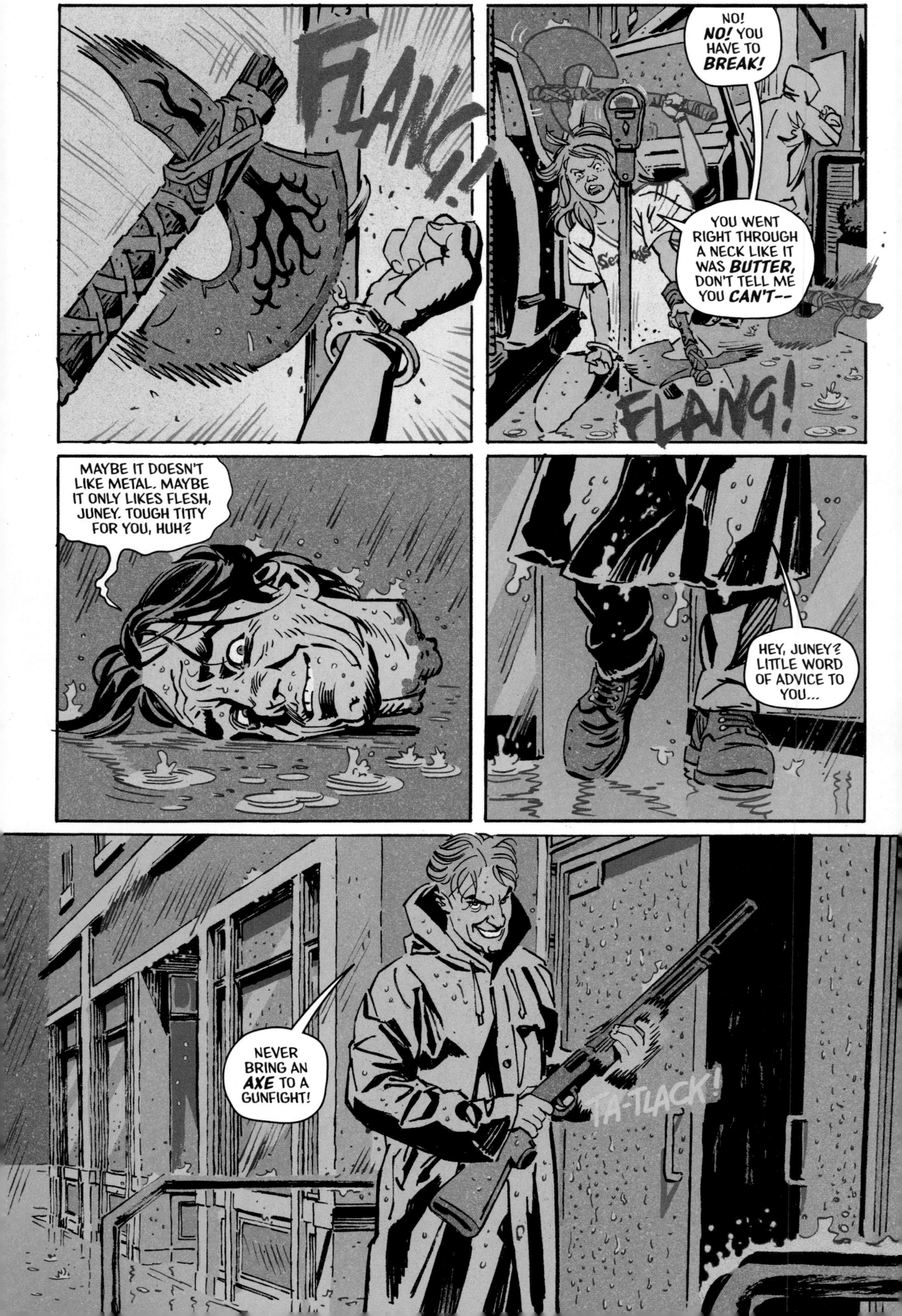
FLANG!!
NO! NO! YOU HAVE TO BREAK!
YOU WENT RIGHT THROUGH A NECK LIKE IT WAS BUTTER, DON'T TELL ME YOU CAN'T--
FLANG!
MAYBE IT DOESN'T LIKE METAL. MAYBE IT ONLY LIKES FLESH, JUNEY. TOUGH TITTY FOR YOU, HUH?
HEY, JUNEY? LITTLE WORD OF ADVICE TO YOU...
NEVER BRING AN AXE TO A GUNFIGHT!
TA-TLACK!

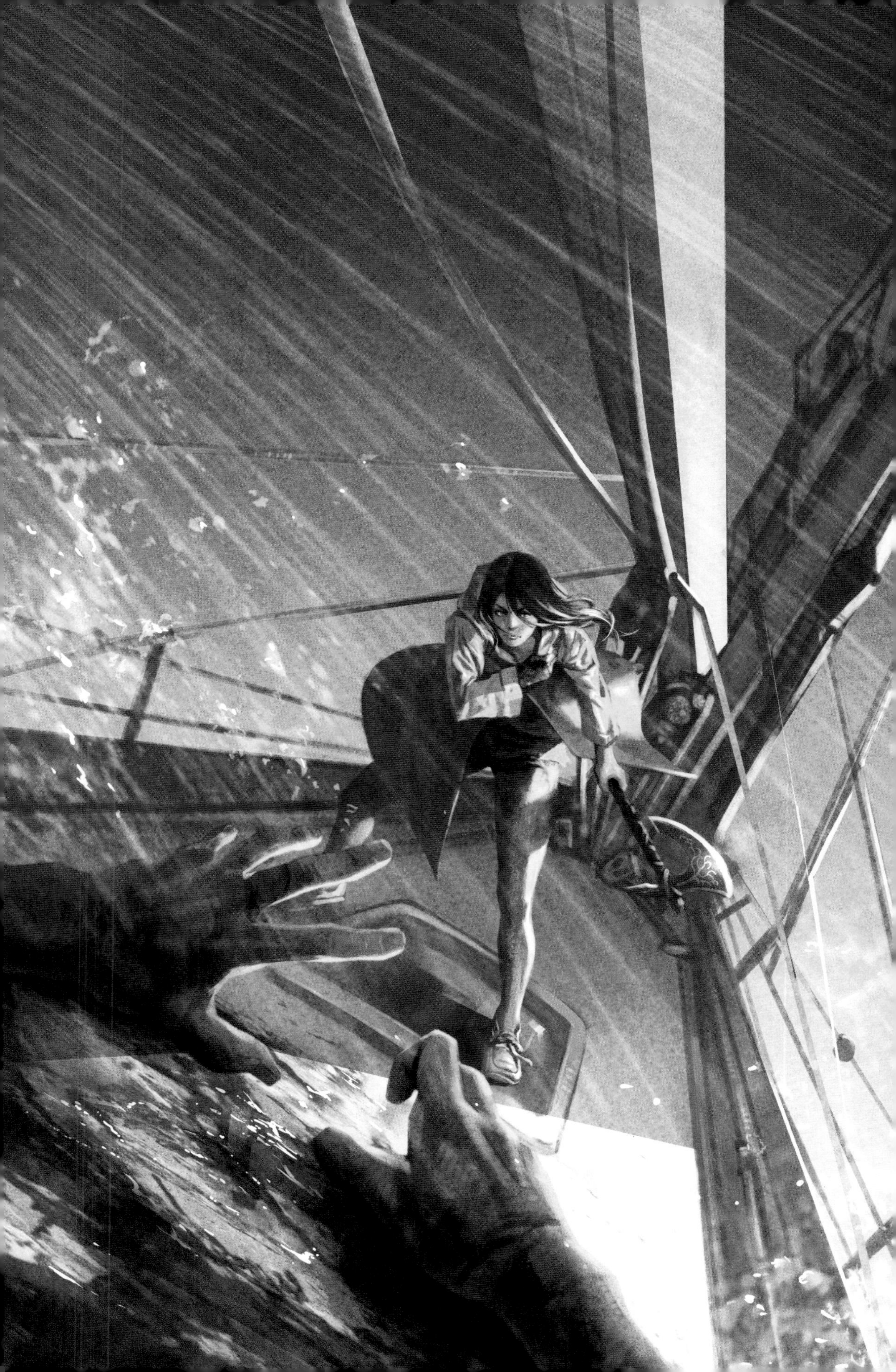

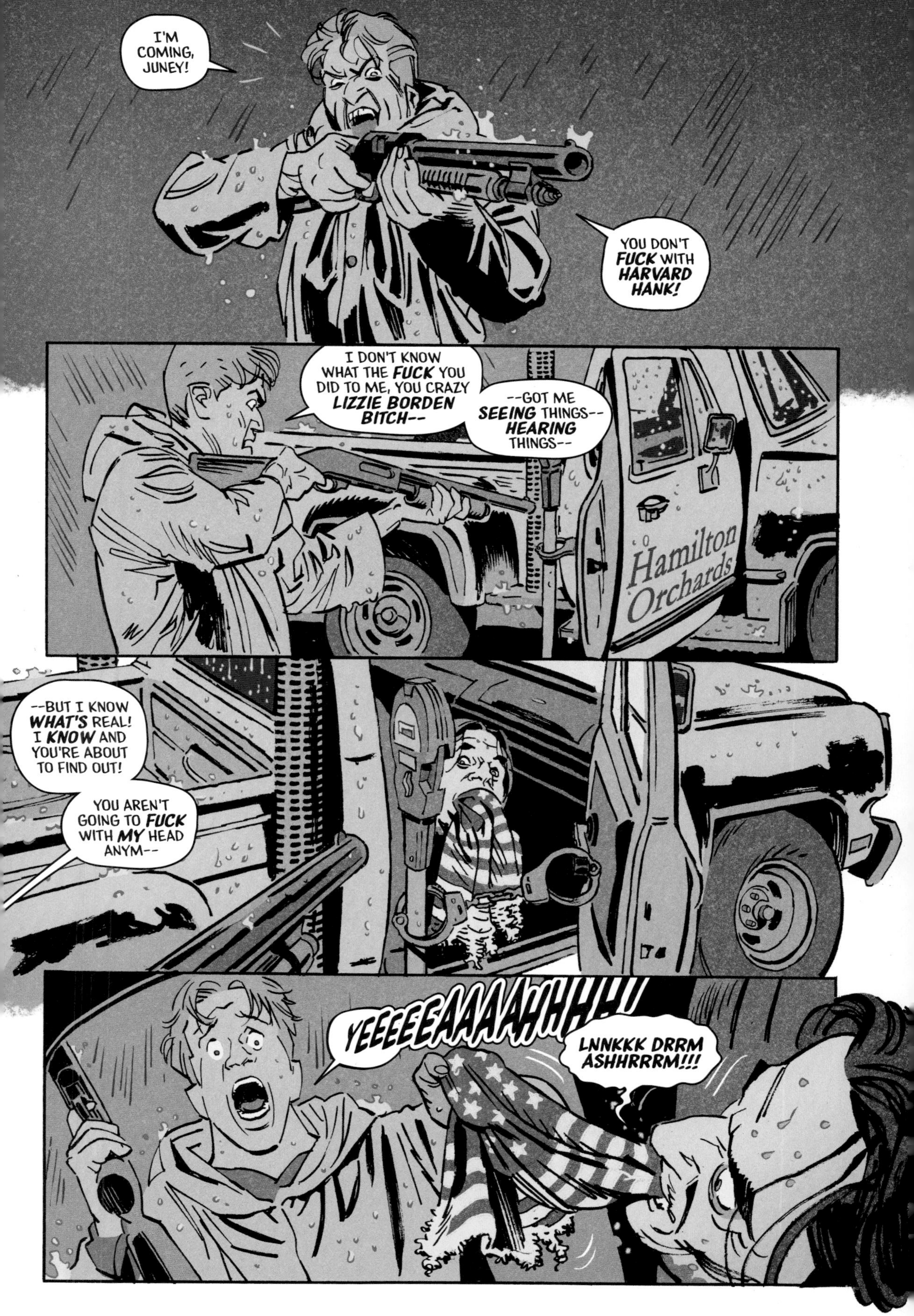

I'M COMING, JUNEY!
YOU DON'T FUCK WITH HARVARD HANK!
I DON'T KNOW WHAT THE FUCK YOU DID TO ME, YOU CRAZY LIZZIE BORDEN BITCH--
--GOT ME SEEING THINGS-- HEARING THINGS--
Hamilton Orchards
--BUT I KNOW WHAT'S REAL! I KNOW AND YOU'RE ABOUT TO FIND OUT!
YOU AREN'T GOING TO FUCK WITH MY HEAD ANYM--
YEEEEEAAAAHHHH!
LNNKKK DRRM ASHHRRRM!!!

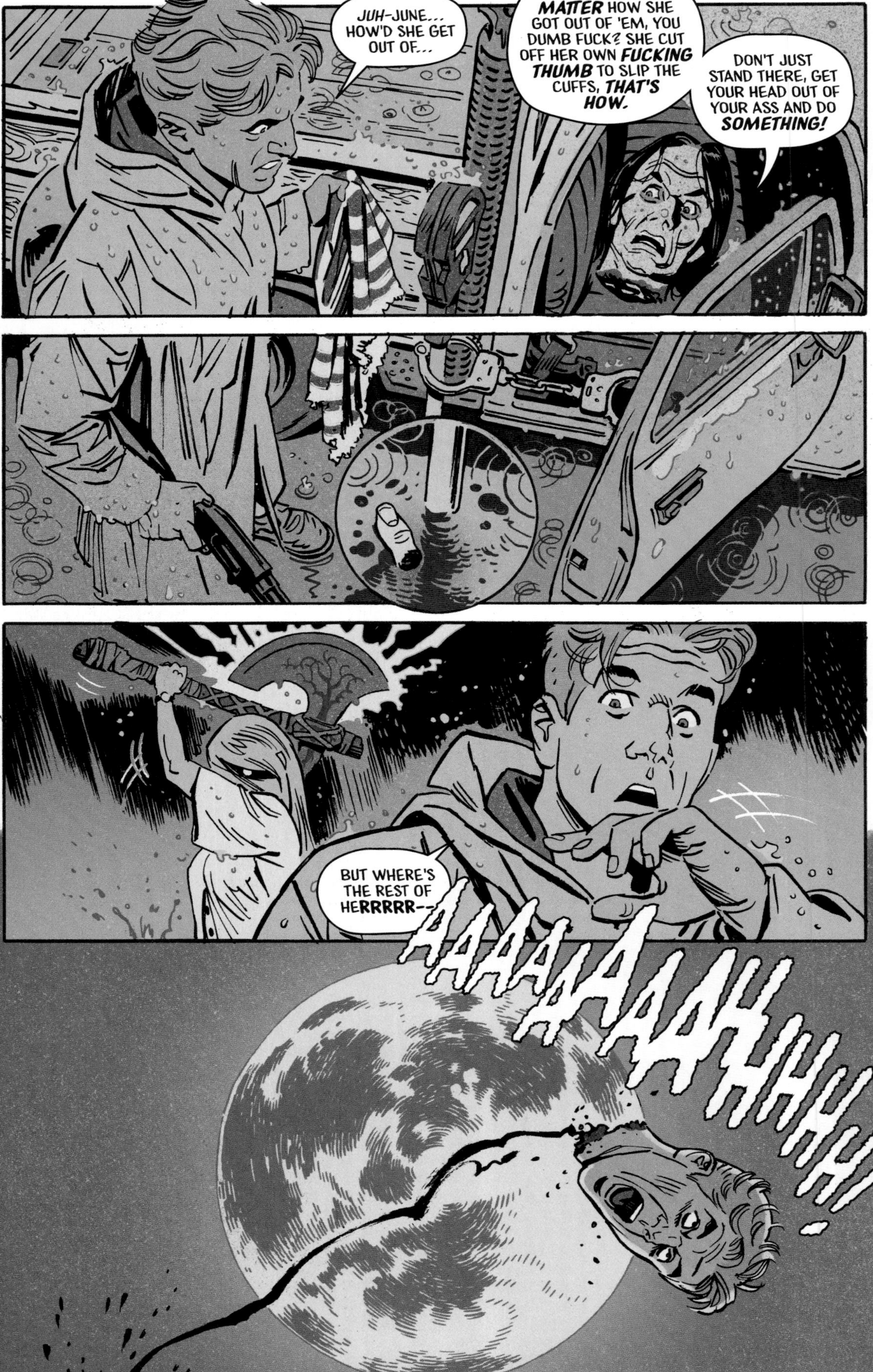
JUH-JUNE... HOW'D SHE GET OUT OF...
WHAT'S IT **MATTER** HOW SHE GOT OUT OF 'EM, YOU DUMB FUCK? SHE CUT OFF HER OWN **FUCKING THUMB** TO SLIP THE CUFFS, **THAT'S HOW.**
DON'T JUST STAND THERE, GET YOUR HEAD OUT OF YOUR ASS AND DO **SOMETHING!**
BUT WHERE'S THE REST OF HE**RRRRR**--
AAAAAAAAAHHHHH!!

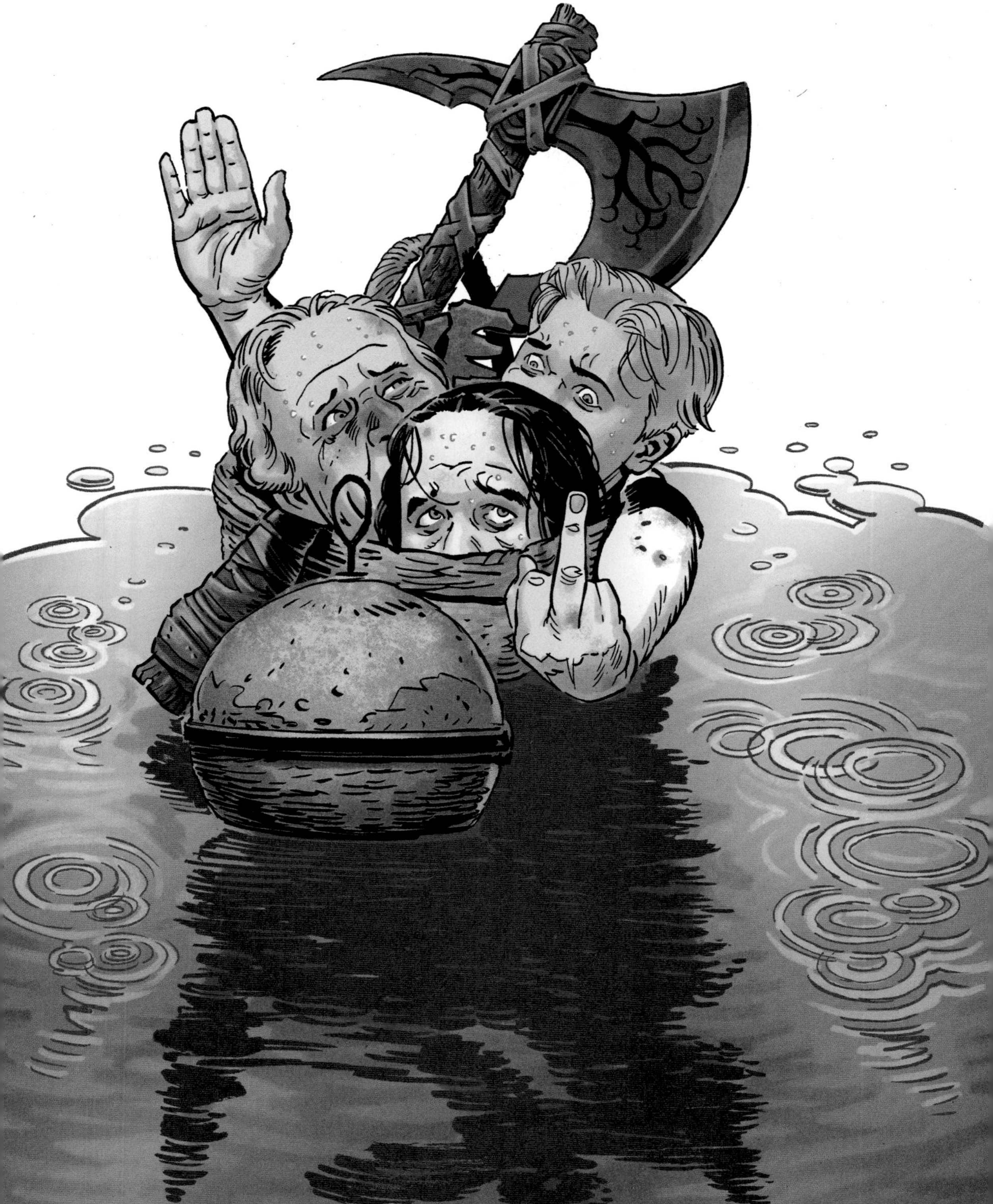

Written by JOE HILL Illustrated by LEOMACS
Colored by DAVE STEWART Lettered by DERON BENNETT
Edited by MARK DOYLE & AMEDEO TURTURRO
Cover by REIKO MURAKAMI

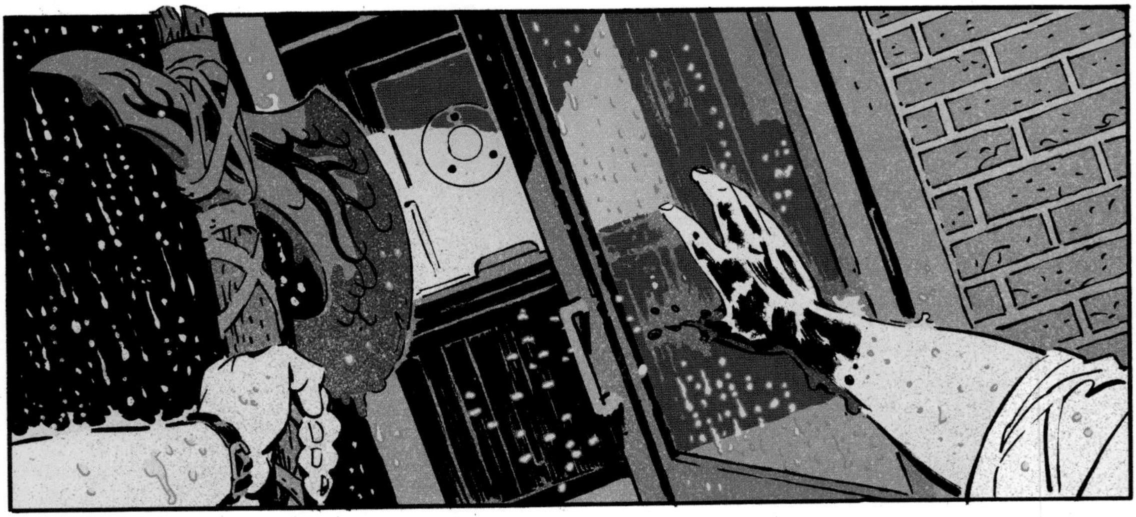

DOWNTOWN BRODY -- POLICE STATION.

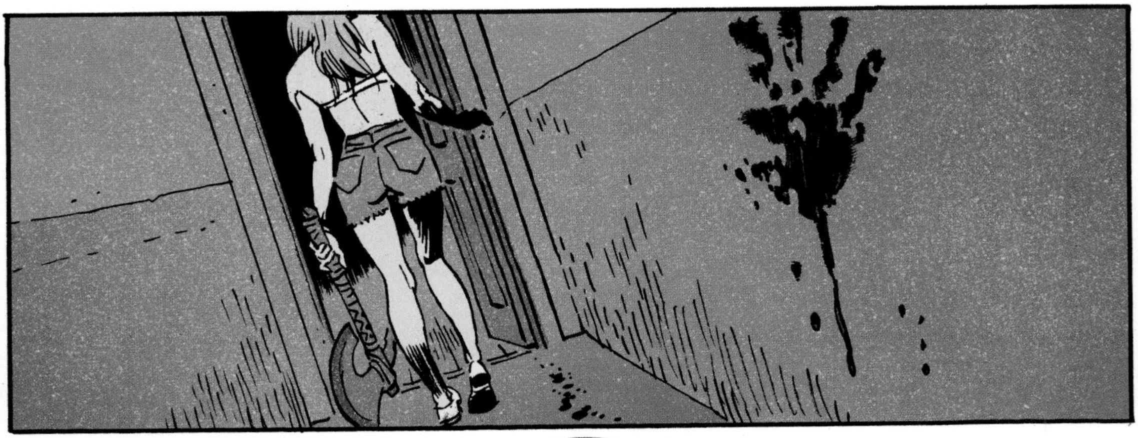

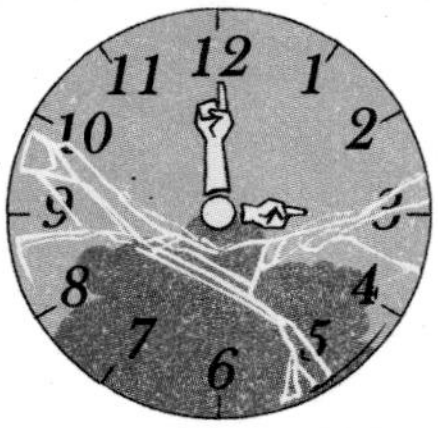

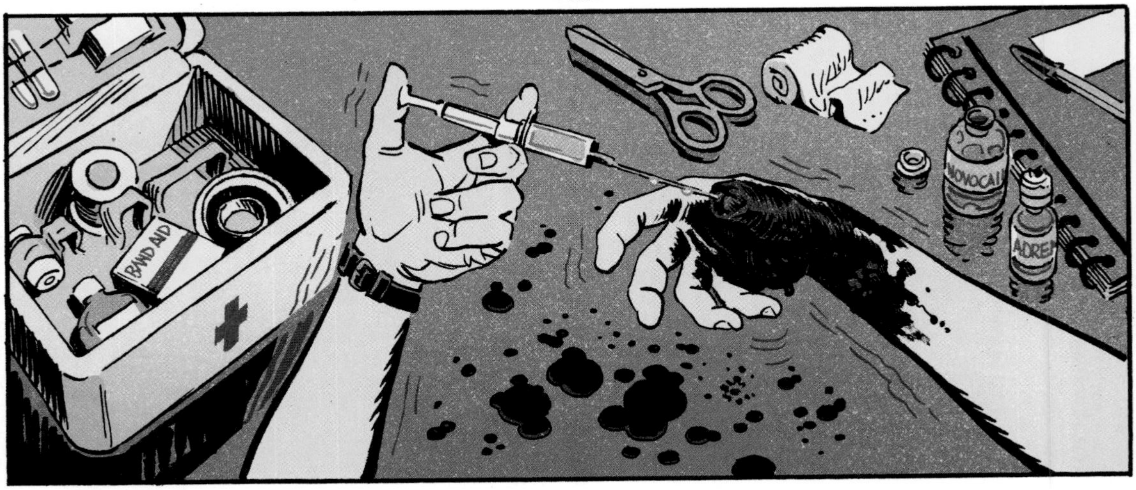
BAND AID

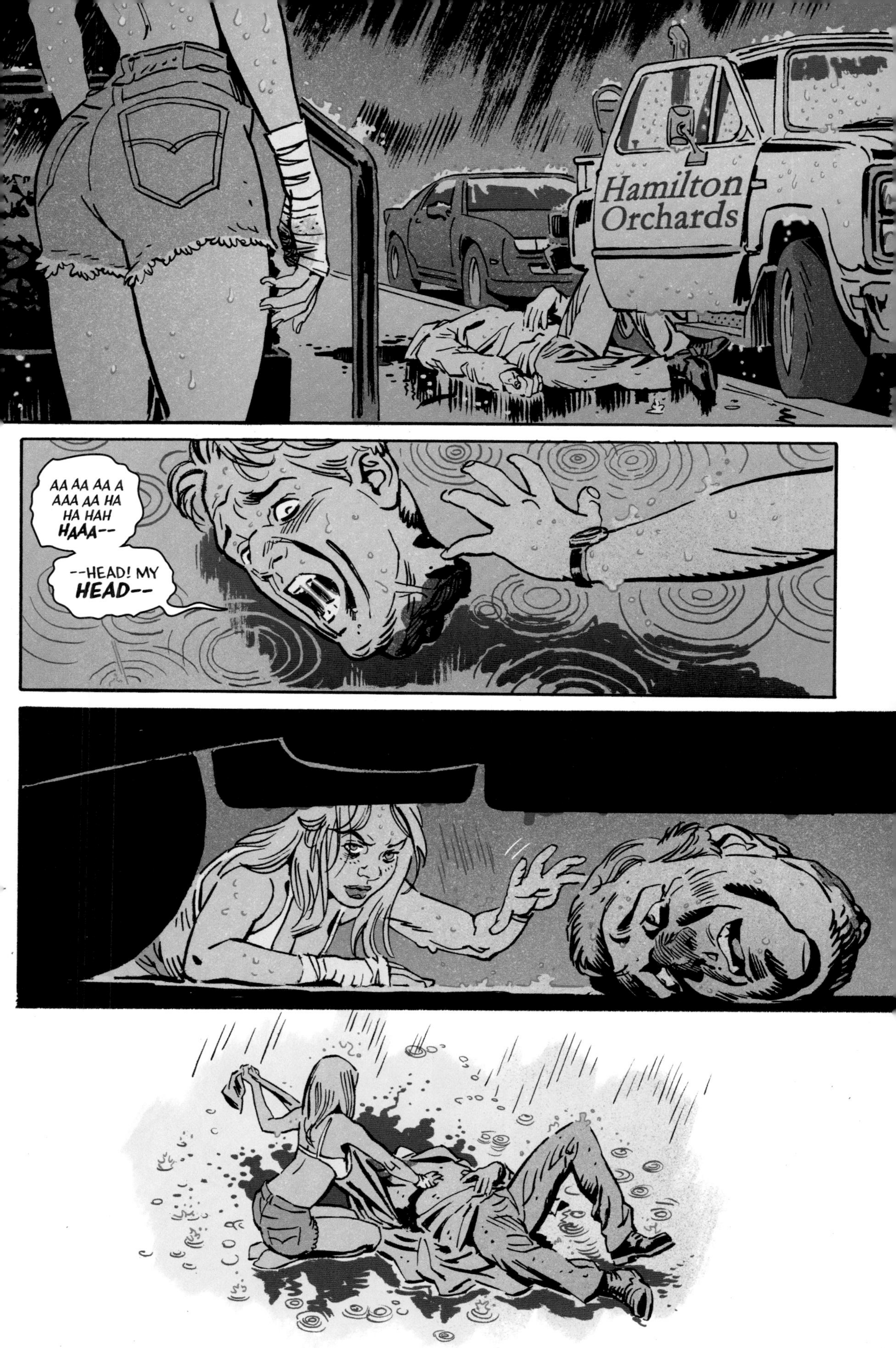
Hamilton Orchards
AA AA AA A AAA AA HA HA HAH HAAA--
--HEAD! MY HEAD--

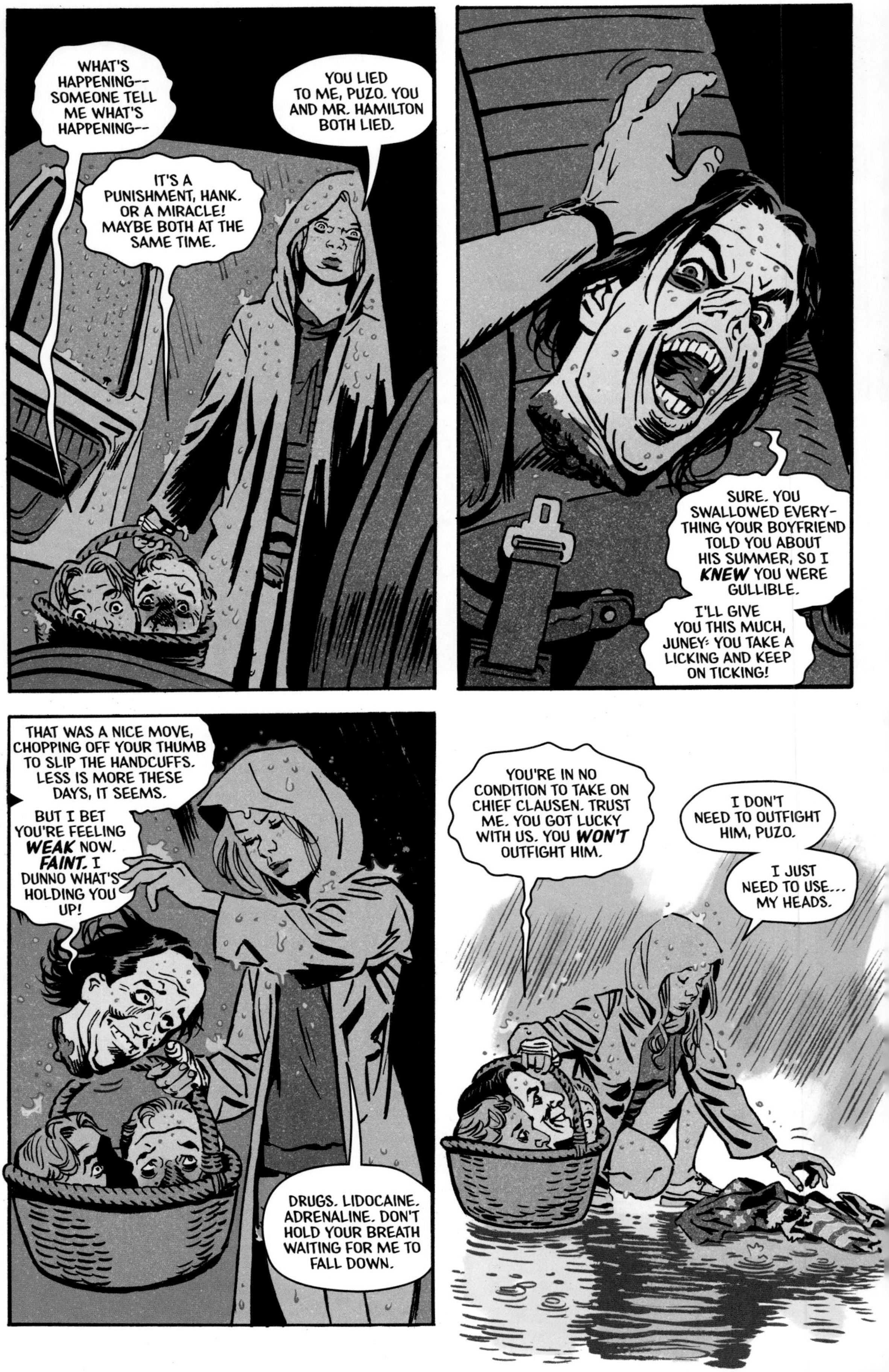
WHAT'S HAPPENING-- SOMEONE TELL ME WHAT'S HAPPENING--
IT'S A PUNISHMENT, HANK. OR A MIRACLE! MAYBE BOTH AT THE SAME TIME.
YOU LIED TO ME, PUZO. YOU AND MR. HAMILTON BOTH LIED.
SURE. YOU SWALLOWED EVERY-THING YOUR BOYFRIEND TOLD YOU ABOUT HIS SUMMER, SO I KNEW YOU WERE GULLIBLE.
I'LL GIVE YOU THIS MUCH, JUNEY: YOU TAKE A LICKING AND KEEP ON TICKING!
THAT WAS A NICE MOVE, CHOPPING OFF YOUR THUMB TO SLIP THE HANDCUFFS. LESS IS MORE THESE DAYS, IT SEEMS.
BUT I BET YOU'RE FEELING WEAK NOW. FAINT. I DUNNO WHAT'S HOLDING YOU UP!
DRUGS. LIDOCAINE. ADRENALINE. DON'T HOLD YOUR BREATH WAITING FOR ME TO FALL DOWN.
YOU'RE IN NO CONDITION TO TAKE ON CHIEF CLAUSEN. TRUST ME. YOU GOT LUCKY WITH US. YOU WON'T OUTFIGHT HIM.
I DON'T NEED TO OUTFIGHT HIM, PUZO.
I JUST NEED TO USE... MY HEADS.

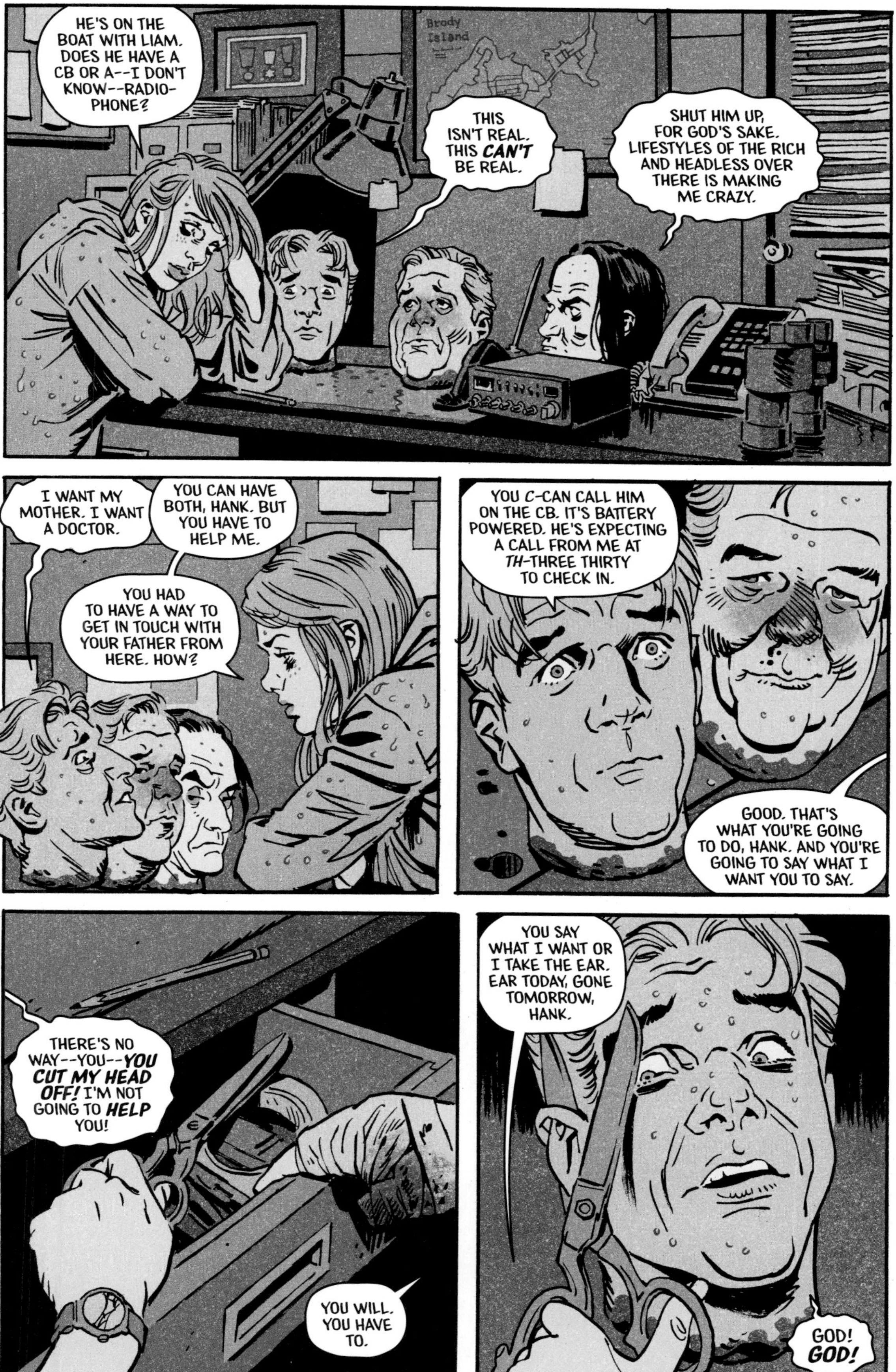
HE'S ON THE BOAT WITH LIAM. DOES HE HAVE A CB OR A--I DON'T KNOW--RADIO-PHONE?
Brody Island
THIS ISN'T REAL. THIS CAN'T BE REAL.
SHUT HIM UP, FOR GOD'S SAKE. LIFESTYLES OF THE RICH AND HEADLESS OVER THERE IS MAKING ME CRAZY.
I WANT MY MOTHER. I WANT A DOCTOR.
YOU CAN HAVE BOTH, HANK. BUT YOU HAVE TO HELP ME.
YOU HAD TO HAVE A WAY TO GET IN TOUCH WITH YOUR FATHER FROM HERE. HOW?
YOU C-CAN CALL HIM ON THE CB. IT'S BATTERY POWERED. HE'S EXPECTING A CALL FROM ME AT TH-THREE THIRTY TO CHECK IN.
GOOD. THAT'S WHAT YOU'RE GOING TO DO, HANK. AND YOU'RE GOING TO SAY WHAT I WANT YOU TO SAY.
THERE'S NO WAY--YOU--YOU CUT MY HEAD OFF! I'M NOT GOING TO HELP YOU!
YOU WILL. YOU HAVE TO.
YOU SAY WHAT I WANT OR I TAKE THE EAR. EAR TODAY, GONE TOMORROW, HANK.
GOD! GOD!

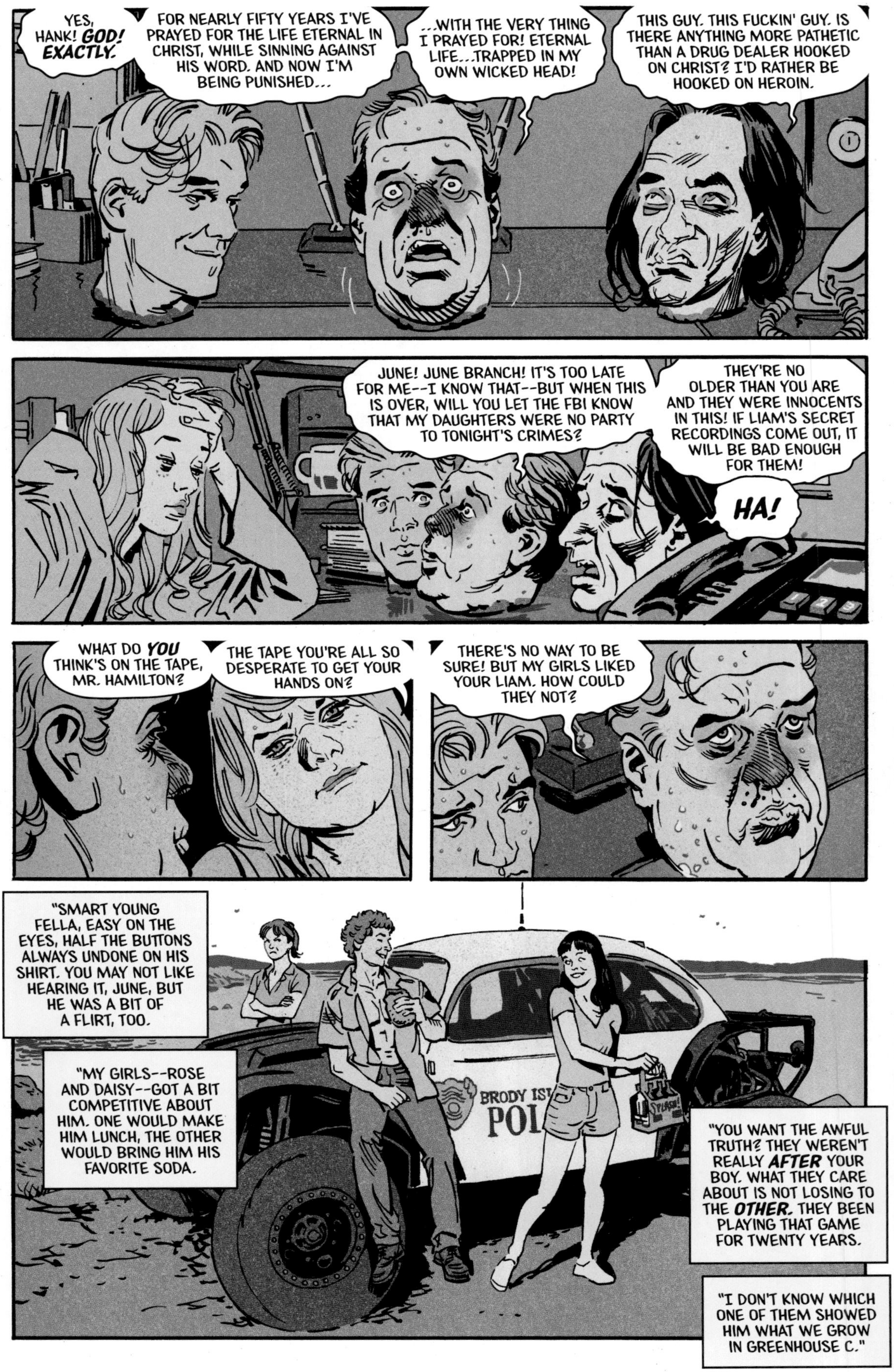

YES, HANK! GOD! EXACTLY.
FOR NEARLY FIFTY YEARS I'VE PRAYED FOR THE LIFE ETERNAL IN CHRIST, WHILE SINNING AGAINST HIS WORD. AND NOW I'M BEING PUNISHED...
...WITH THE VERY THING I PRAYED FOR! ETERNAL LIFE...TRAPPED IN MY OWN WICKED HEAD!
THIS GUY. THIS FUCKIN' GUY. IS THERE ANYTHING MORE PATHETIC THAN A DRUG DEALER HOOKED ON CHRIST? I'D RATHER BE HOOKED ON HEROIN.
JUNE! JUNE BRANCH! IT'S TOO LATE FOR ME--I KNOW THAT--BUT WHEN THIS IS OVER, WILL YOU LET THE FBI KNOW THAT MY DAUGHTERS WERE NO PARTY TO TONIGHT'S CRIMES?
THEY'RE NO OLDER THAN YOU ARE AND THEY WERE INNOCENTS IN THIS! IF LIAM'S SECRET RECORDINGS COME OUT, IT WILL BE BAD ENOUGH FOR THEM!
HA!
WHAT DO YOU THINK'S ON THE TAPE, MR. HAMILTON?
THE TAPE YOU'RE ALL SO DESPERATE TO GET YOUR HANDS ON?
THERE'S NO WAY TO BE SURE! BUT MY GIRLS LIKED YOUR LIAM. HOW COULD THEY NOT?
"SMART YOUNG FELLA, EASY ON THE EYES, HALF THE BUTTONS ALWAYS UNDONE ON HIS SHIRT. YOU MAY NOT LIKE HEARING IT, JUNE, BUT HE WAS A BIT OF A FLIRT, TOO.
"MY GIRLS--ROSE AND DAISY--GOT A BIT COMPETITIVE ABOUT HIM. ONE WOULD MAKE HIM LUNCH, THE OTHER WOULD BRING HIM HIS FAVORITE SODA.
BRODY ISL
POL
"YOU WANT THE AWFUL TRUTH? THEY WEREN'T REALLY AFTER YOUR BOY. WHAT THEY CARE ABOUT IS NOT LOSING TO THE OTHER. THEY BEEN PLAYING THAT GAME FOR TWENTY YEARS.
"I DON'T KNOW WHICH ONE OF THEM SHOWED HIM WHAT WE GROW IN GREENHOUSE C."

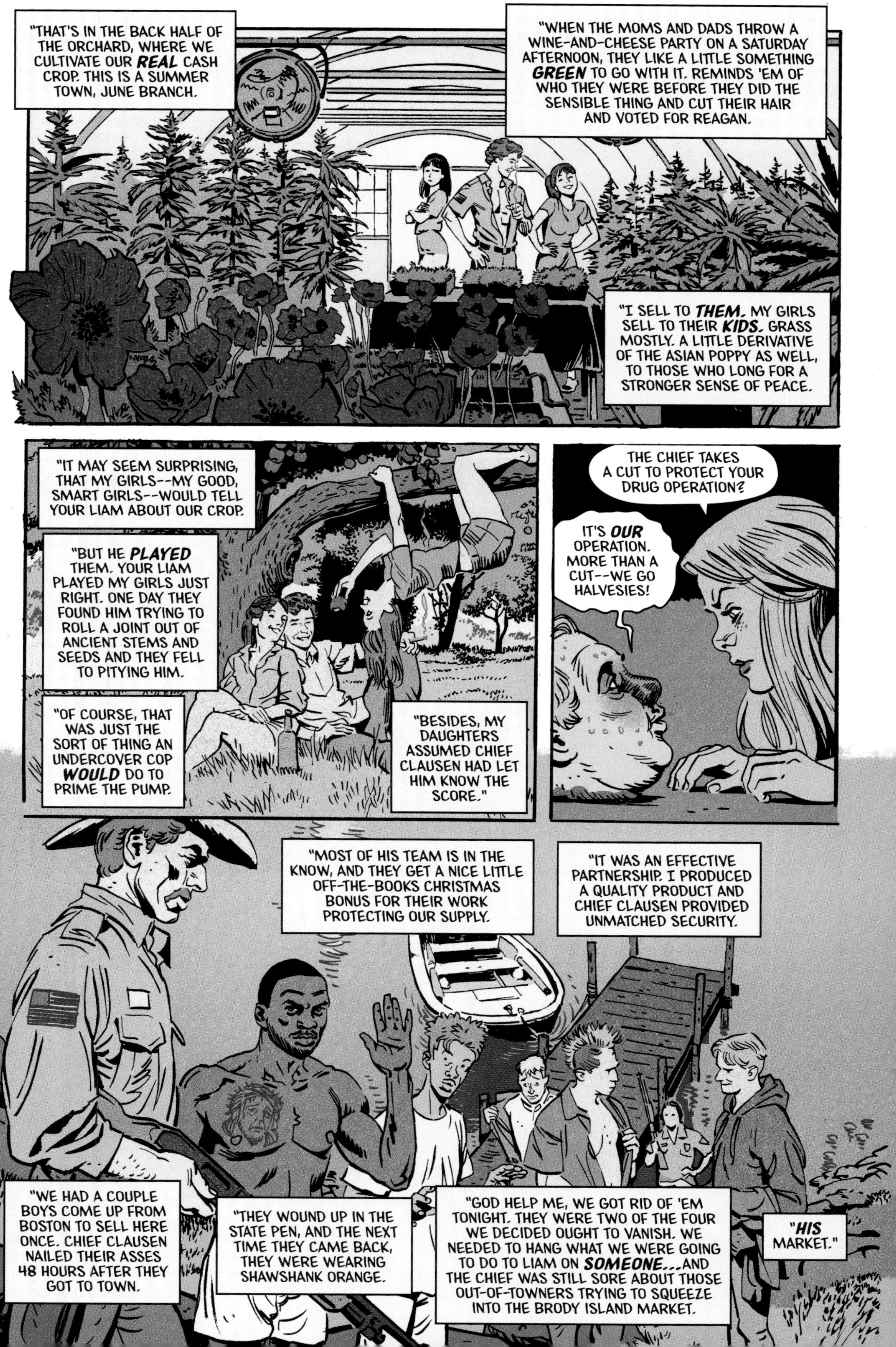

"THAT'S IN THE BACK HALF OF THE ORCHARD, WHERE WE CULTIVATE OUR *REAL* CASH CROP. THIS IS A SUMMER TOWN, JUNE BRANCH.
"WHEN THE MOMS AND DADS THROW A WINE-AND-CHEESE PARTY ON A SATURDAY AFTERNOON, THEY LIKE A LITTLE SOMETHING *GREEN* TO GO WITH IT. REMINDS 'EM OF WHO THEY WERE BEFORE THEY DID THE SENSIBLE THING AND CUT THEIR HAIR AND VOTED FOR REAGAN.
"I SELL TO *THEM.* MY GIRLS SELL TO THEIR *KIDS.* GRASS MOSTLY. A LITTLE DERIVATIVE OF THE ASIAN POPPY AS WELL, TO THOSE WHO LONG FOR A STRONGER SENSE OF PEACE.
"IT MAY SEEM SURPRISING, THAT MY GIRLS--MY GOOD, SMART GIRLS--WOULD TELL YOUR LIAM ABOUT OUR CROP.
"BUT HE *PLAYED* THEM. YOUR LIAM PLAYED MY GIRLS JUST RIGHT. ONE DAY THEY FOUND HIM TRYING TO ROLL A JOINT OUT OF ANCIENT STEMS AND SEEDS AND THEY FELL TO PITYING HIM.
"OF COURSE, THAT WAS JUST THE SORT OF THING AN UNDERCOVER COP *WOULD* DO TO PRIME THE PUMP.
"BESIDES, MY DAUGHTERS ASSUMED CHIEF CLAUSEN HAD LET HIM KNOW THE SCORE."
THE CHIEF TAKES A CUT TO PROTECT YOUR DRUG OPERATION?
IT'S *OUR* OPERATION. MORE THAN A CUT--WE GO HALVESIES!
"MOST OF HIS TEAM IS IN THE KNOW, AND THEY GET A NICE LITTLE OFF-THE-BOOKS CHRISTMAS BONUS FOR THEIR WORK PROTECTING OUR SUPPLY.
"IT WAS AN EFFECTIVE PARTNERSHIP. I PRODUCED A QUALITY PRODUCT AND CHIEF CLAUSEN PROVIDED UNMATCHED SECURITY.
"WE HAD A COUPLE BOYS COME UP FROM BOSTON TO SELL HERE ONCE. CHIEF CLAUSEN NAILED THEIR ASSES 48 HOURS AFTER THEY GOT TO TOWN.
"THEY WOUND UP IN THE STATE PEN, AND THE NEXT TIME THEY CAME BACK, THEY WERE WEARING SHAWSHANK ORANGE.
"GOD HELP ME, WE GOT RID OF 'EM TONIGHT. THEY WERE TWO OF THE FOUR WE DECIDED OUGHT TO VANISH. WE NEEDED TO HANG WHAT WE WERE GOING TO DO TO LIAM ON *SOMEONE*...AND THE CHIEF WAS STILL SORE ABOUT THOSE OUT-OF-TOWNERS TRYING TO SQUEEZE INTO THE BRODY ISLAND MARKET.
"*HIS* MARKET."

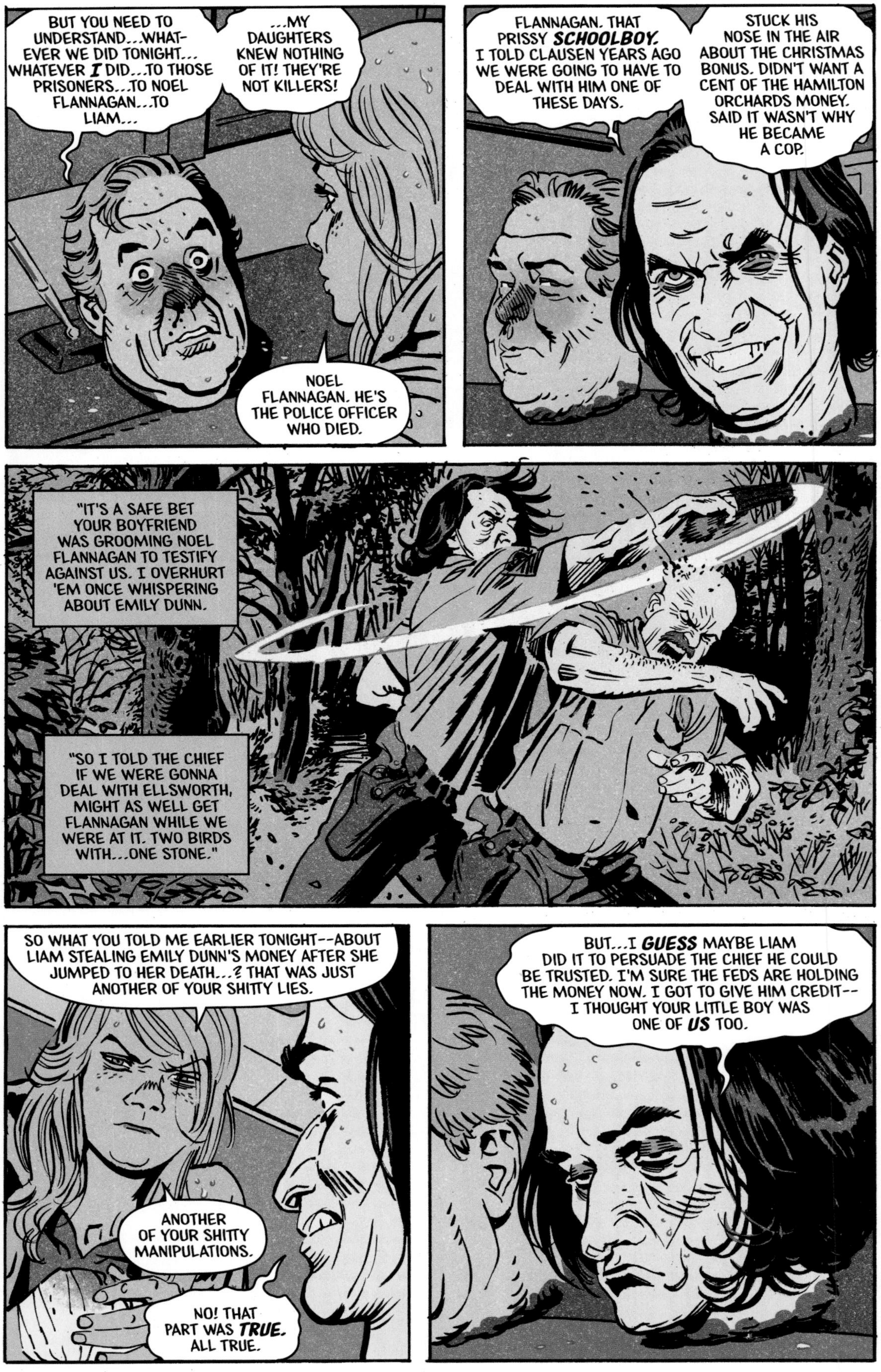
BUT YOU NEED TO UNDERSTAND...WHATEVER WE DID TONIGHT... WHATEVER I DID...TO THOSE PRISONERS...TO NOEL FLANNAGAN...TO LIAM...
...MY DAUGHTERS KNEW NOTHING OF IT! THEY'RE NOT KILLERS!
NOEL FLANNAGAN. HE'S THE POLICE OFFICER WHO DIED.
FLANNAGAN. THAT PRISSY SCHOOLBOY. I TOLD CLAUSEN YEARS AGO WE WERE GOING TO HAVE TO DEAL WITH HIM ONE OF THESE DAYS.
STUCK HIS NOSE IN THE AIR ABOUT THE CHRISTMAS BONUS. DIDN'T WANT A CENT OF THE HAMILTON ORCHARDS MONEY. SAID IT WASN'T WHY HE BECAME A COP.
"IT'S A SAFE BET YOUR BOYFRIEND WAS GROOMING NOEL FLANNAGAN TO TESTIFY AGAINST US. I OVERHURT 'EM ONCE WHISPERING ABOUT EMILY DUNN.
"SO I TOLD THE CHIEF IF WE WERE GONNA DEAL WITH ELLSWORTH, MIGHT AS WELL GET FLANNAGAN WHILE WE WERE AT IT. TWO BIRDS WITH...ONE STONE."
SO WHAT YOU TOLD ME EARLIER TONIGHT--ABOUT LIAM STEALING EMILY DUNN'S MONEY AFTER SHE JUMPED TO HER DEATH...? THAT WAS JUST ANOTHER OF YOUR SHITTY LIES.
ANOTHER OF YOUR SHITTY MANIPULATIONS.
NO! THAT PART WAS TRUE. ALL TRUE.
BUT...I GUESS MAYBE LIAM DID IT TO PERSUADE THE CHIEF HE COULD BE TRUSTED. I'M SURE THE FEDS ARE HOLDING THE MONEY NOW. I GOT TO GIVE HIM CREDIT-- I THOUGHT YOUR LITTLE BOY WAS ONE OF US TOO.

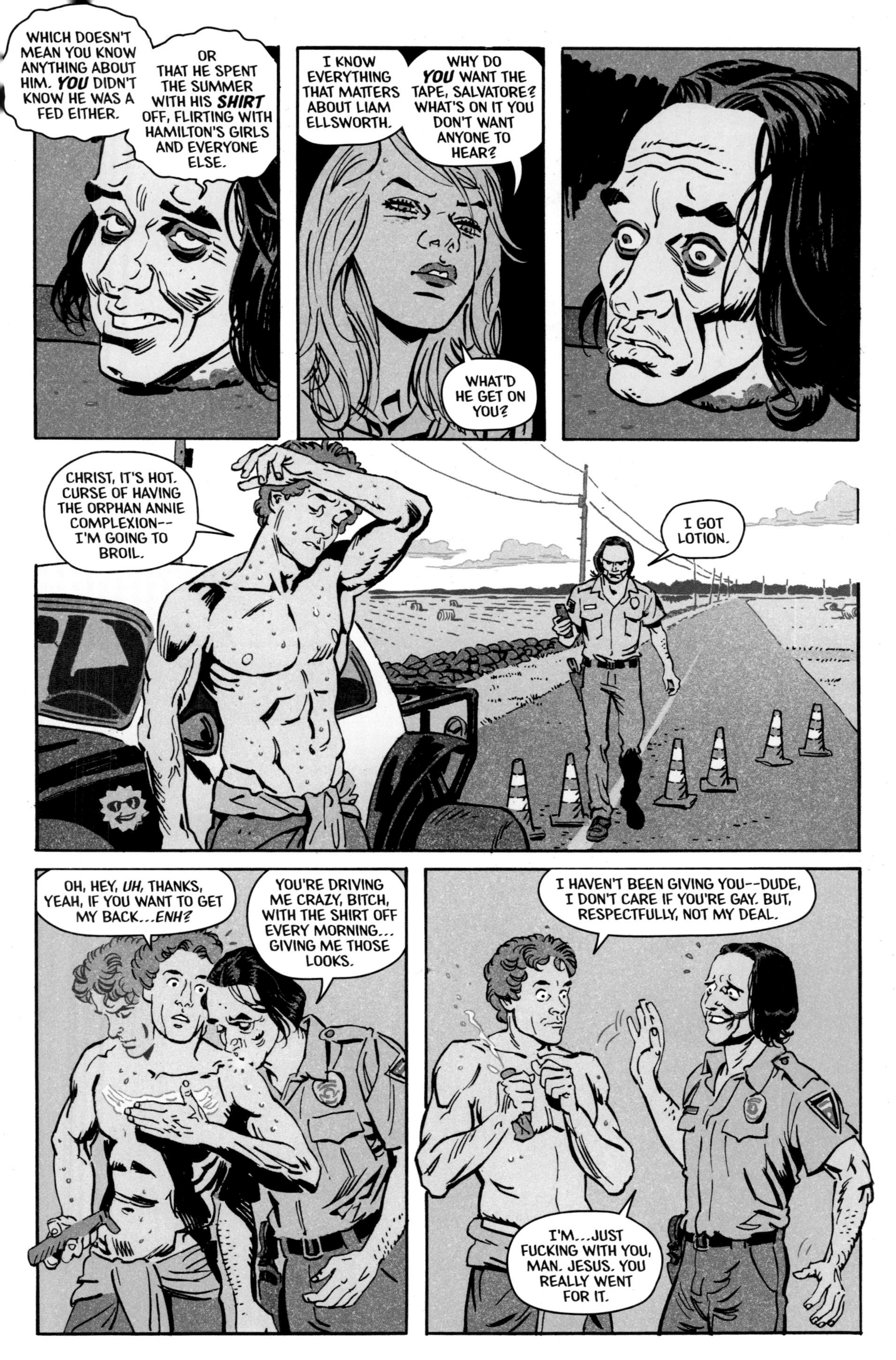
WHICH DOESN'T MEAN YOU KNOW ANYTHING ABOUT HIM. YOU DIDN'T KNOW HE WAS A FED EITHER.
OR THAT HE SPENT THE SUMMER WITH HIS SHIRT OFF, FLIRTING WITH HAMILTON'S GIRLS AND EVERYONE ELSE.
I KNOW EVERYTHING THAT MATTERS ABOUT LIAM ELLSWORTH.
WHY DO YOU WANT THE TAPE, SALVATORE? WHAT'S ON IT YOU DON'T WANT ANYONE TO HEAR?
WHAT'D HE GET ON YOU?
CHRIST, IT'S HOT. CURSE OF HAVING THE ORPHAN ANNIE COMPLEXION-- I'M GOING TO BROIL.
I GOT LOTION.
OH, HEY, UH, THANKS, YEAH, IF YOU WANT TO GET MY BACK... ENH?
YOU'RE DRIVING ME CRAZY, BITCH, WITH THE SHIRT OFF EVERY MORNING... GIVING ME THOSE LOOKS.
I HAVEN'T BEEN GIVING YOU--DUDE, I DON'T CARE IF YOU'RE GAY. BUT, RESPECTFULLY, NOT MY DEAL.
I'M... JUST FUCKING WITH YOU, MAN. JESUS. YOU REALLY WENT FOR IT.

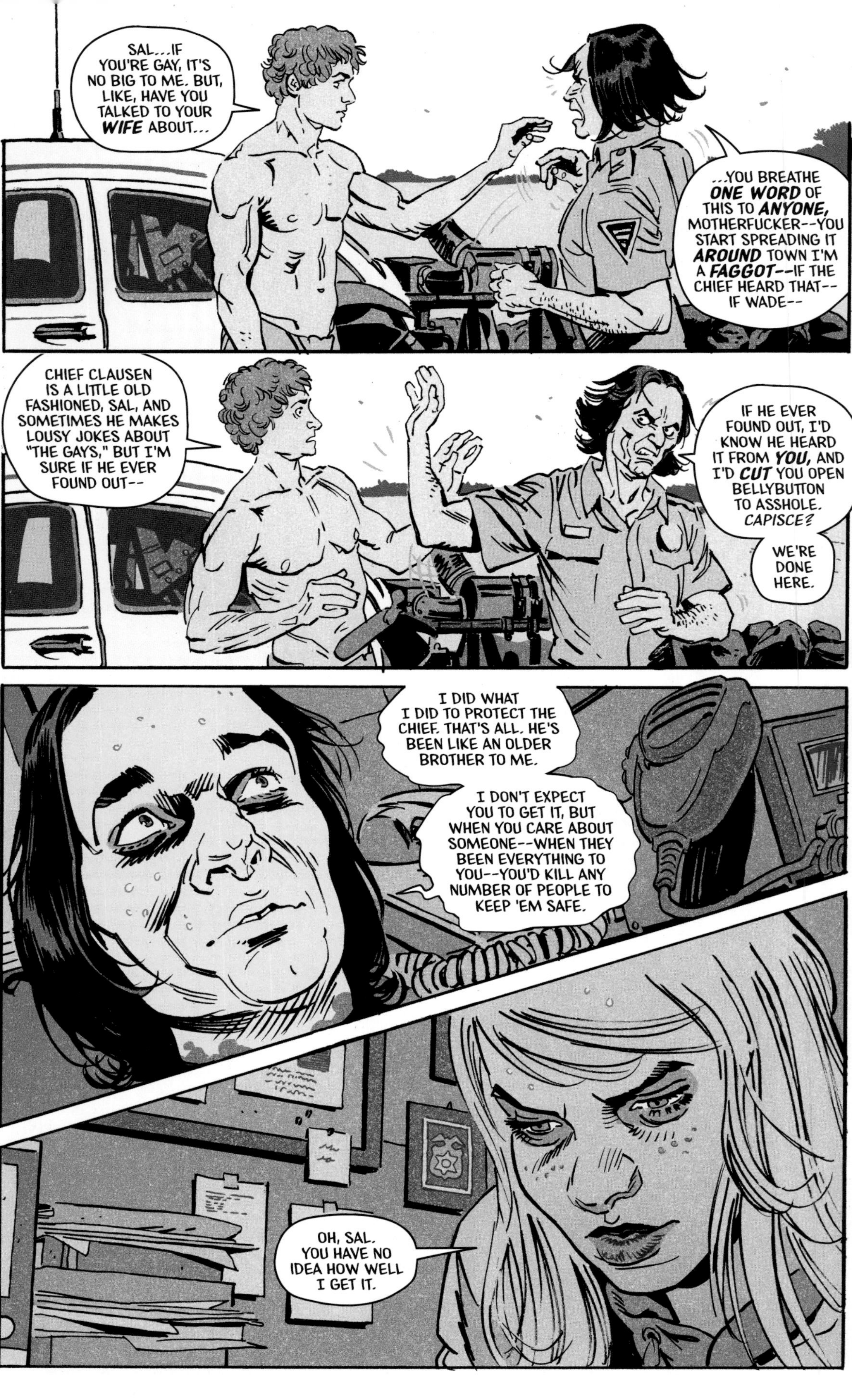
SAL...IF YOU'RE GAY, IT'S NO BIG TO ME. BUT, LIKE, HAVE YOU TALKED TO YOUR WIFE ABOUT...
...YOU BREATHE ONE WORD OF THIS TO ANYONE, MOTHERFUCKER--YOU START SPREADING IT AROUND TOWN I'M A FAGGOT--IF THE CHIEF HEARD THAT--IF WADE--
CHIEF CLAUSEN IS A LITTLE OLD FASHIONED, SAL, AND SOMETIMES HE MAKES LOUSY JOKES ABOUT "THE GAYS," BUT I'M SURE IF HE EVER FOUND OUT--
IF HE EVER FOUND OUT, I'D KNOW HE HEARD IT FROM YOU, AND I'D CUT YOU OPEN BELLYBUTTON TO ASSHOLE. CAPISCE?
WE'RE DONE HERE.
I DID WHAT I DID TO PROTECT THE CHIEF. THAT'S ALL. HE'S BEEN LIKE AN OLDER BROTHER TO ME.
I DON'T EXPECT YOU TO GET IT, BUT WHEN YOU CARE ABOUT SOMEONE--WHEN THEY BEEN EVERYTHING TO YOU--YOU'D KILL ANY NUMBER OF PEOPLE TO KEEP 'EM SAFE.
OH, SAL. YOU HAVE NO IDEA HOW WELL I GET IT.

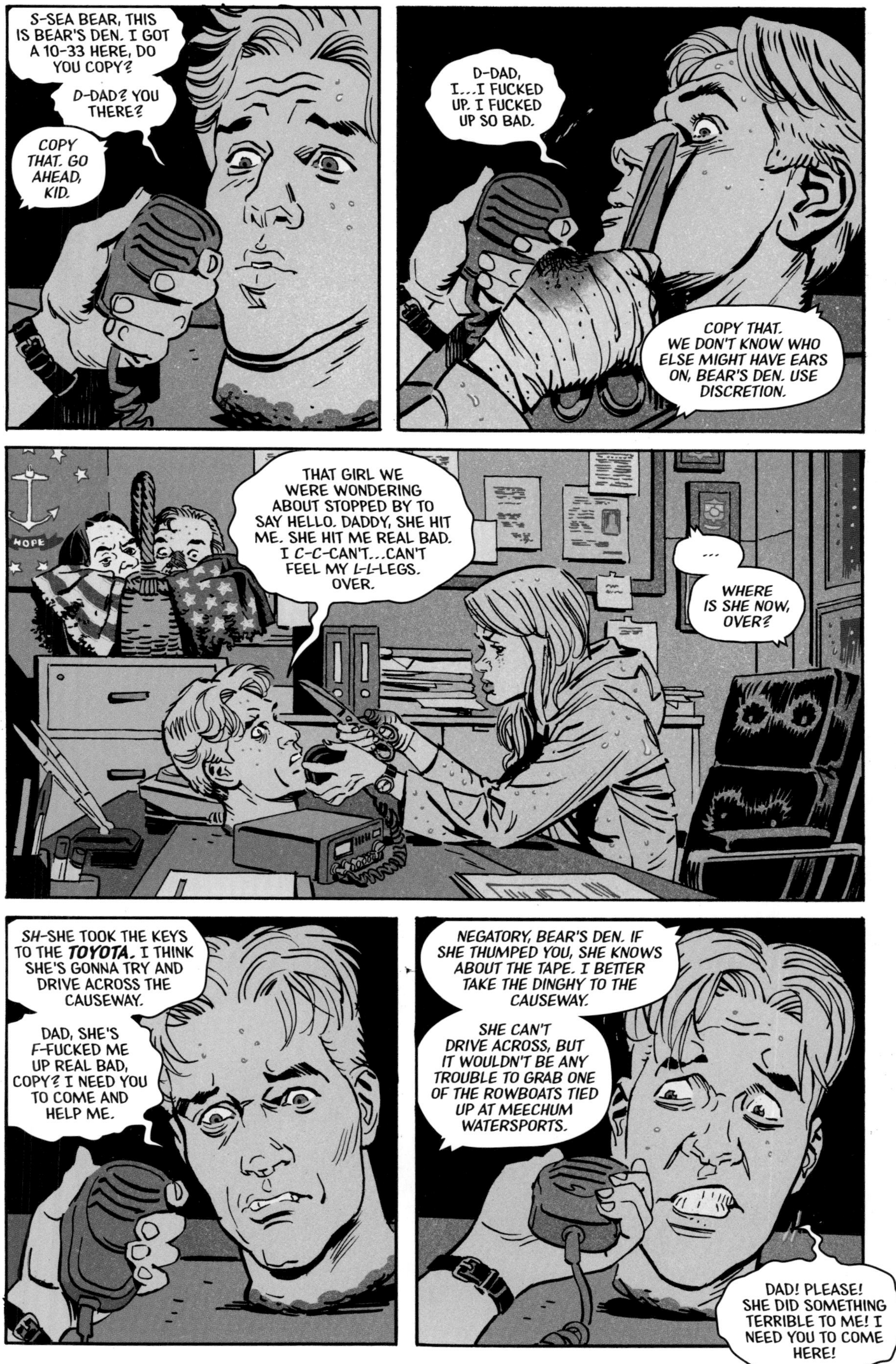
S-SEA BEAR, THIS IS BEAR'S DEN. I GOT A 10-33 HERE, DO YOU COPY?
D-DAD? YOU THERE?
COPY THAT. GO AHEAD, KID.
D-DAD, I...I FUCKED UP. I FUCKED UP SO BAD.
COPY THAT. WE DON'T KNOW WHO ELSE MIGHT HAVE EARS ON, BEAR'S DEN. USE DISCRETION.
THAT GIRL WE WERE WONDERING ABOUT STOPPED BY TO SAY HELLO. DADDY, SHE HIT ME. SHE HIT ME REAL BAD. I C-C-CAN'T...CAN'T FEEL MY L-L-LEGS. OVER.
HOPE
...
WHERE IS SHE NOW, OVER?
SH-SHE TOOK THE KEYS TO THE TOYOTA. I THINK SHE'S GONNA TRY AND DRIVE ACROSS THE CAUSEWAY.
DAD, SHE'S F-FUCKED ME UP REAL BAD, COPY? I NEED YOU TO COME AND HELP ME.
NEGATORY, BEAR'S DEN. IF SHE THUMPED YOU, SHE KNOWS ABOUT THE TAPE. I BETTER TAKE THE DINGHY TO THE CAUSEWAY.
SHE CAN'T DRIVE ACROSS, BUT IT WOULDN'T BE ANY TROUBLE TO GRAB ONE OF THE ROWBOATS TIED UP AT MEECHUM WATERSPORTS.
DAD! PLEASE! SHE DID SOMETHING TERRIBLE TO ME! I NEED YOU TO COME HERE!

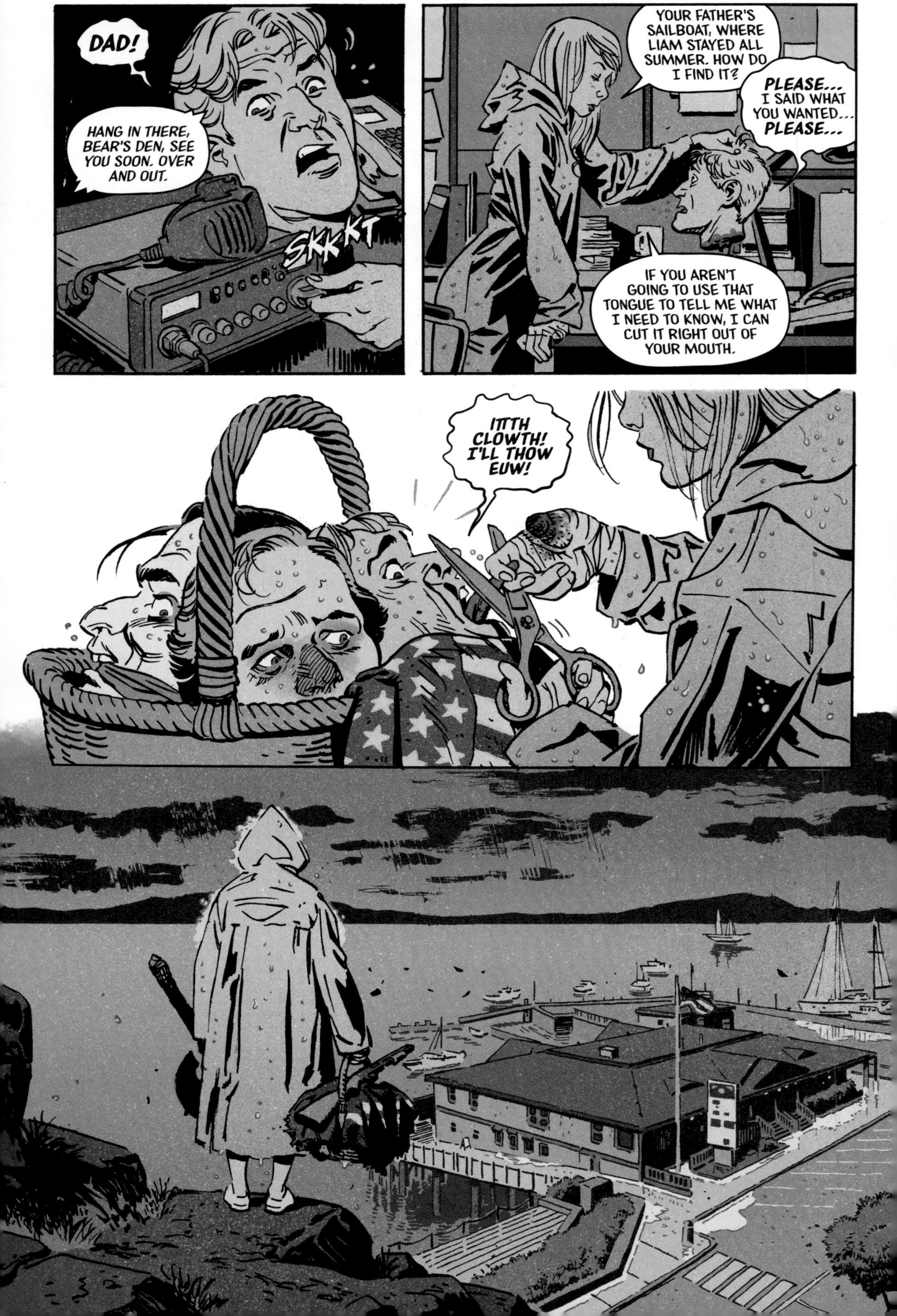
DAD!
HANG IN THERE, BEAR'S DEN, SEE YOU SOON. OVER AND OUT.
SKKKT
YOUR FATHER'S SAILBOAT, WHERE LIAM STAYED ALL SUMMER. HOW DO I FIND IT?
PLEASE... I SAID WHAT YOU WANTED... PLEASE...
IF YOU AREN'T GOING TO USE THAT TONGUE TO TELL ME WHAT I NEED TO KNOW, I CAN CUT IT RIGHT OUT OF YOUR MOUTH.
ITTTH CLOWTH! I'LL THOW EUW!

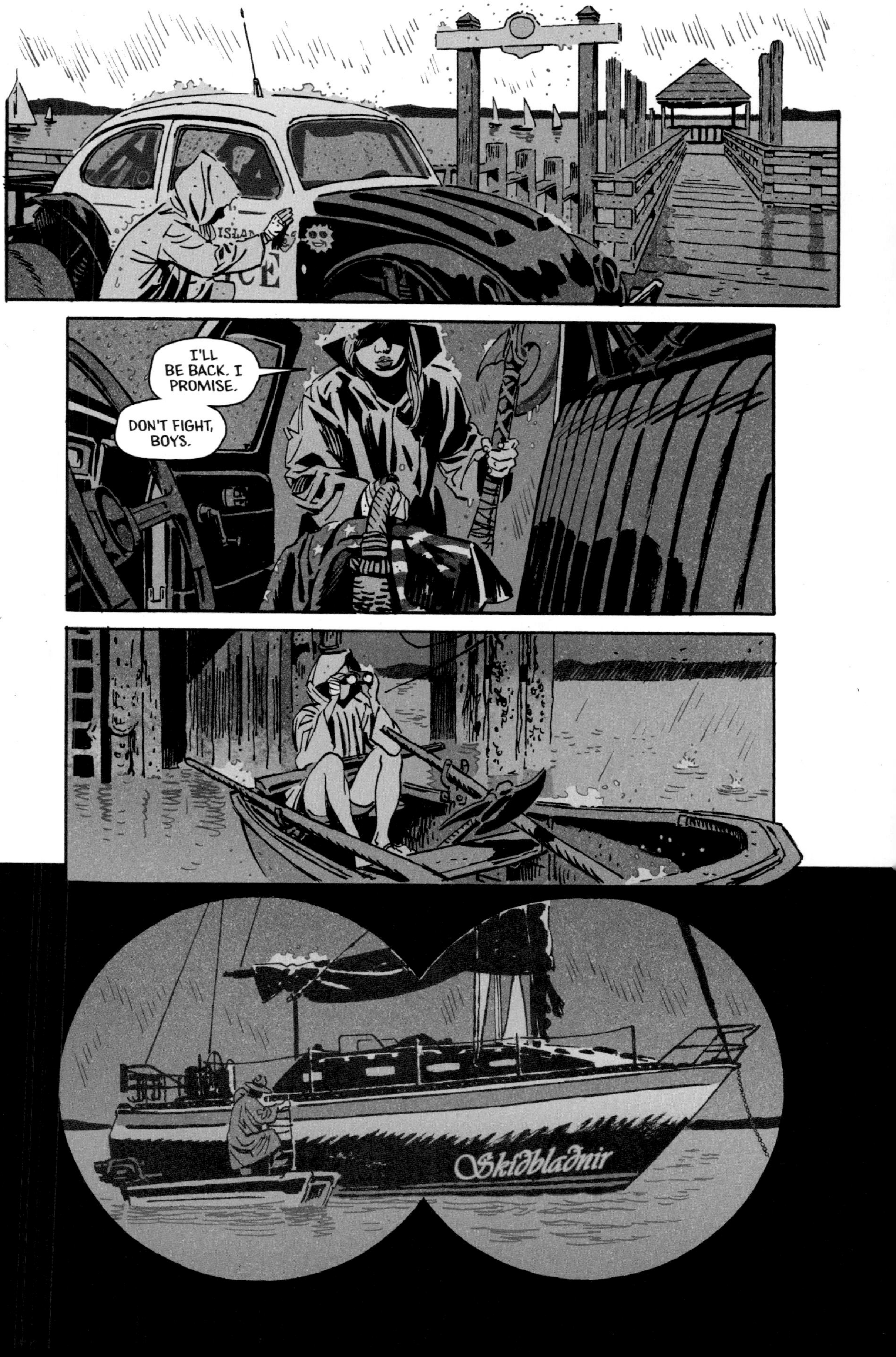

I'LL BE BACK. I PROMISE.
DON'T FIGHT, BOYS.
Skidbladnir

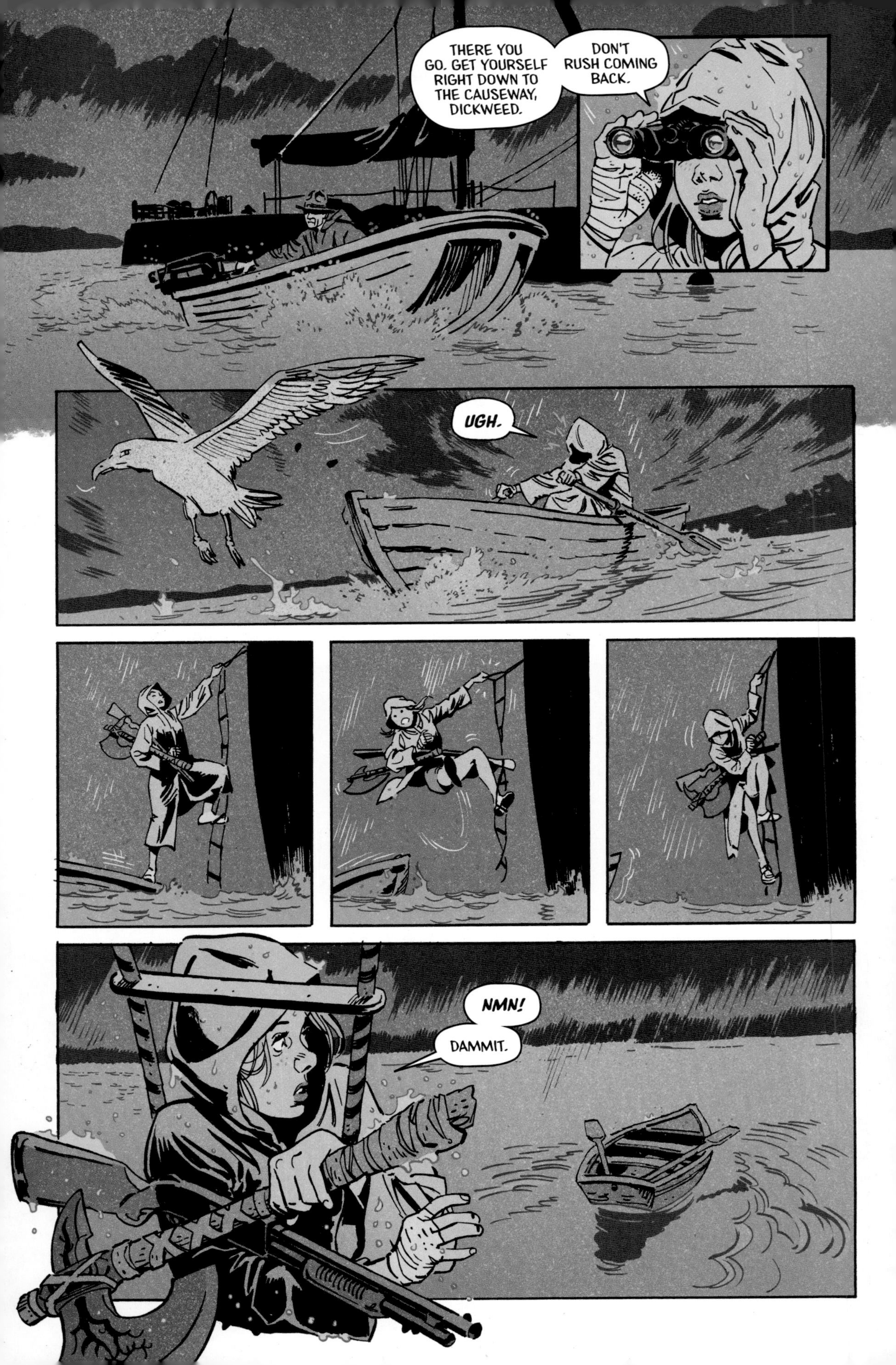
THERE YOU GO. GET YOURSELF RIGHT DOWN TO THE CAUSEWAY, DICKWEED.
DON'T RUSH COMING BACK.
UGH.
NMN!
DAMMIT.

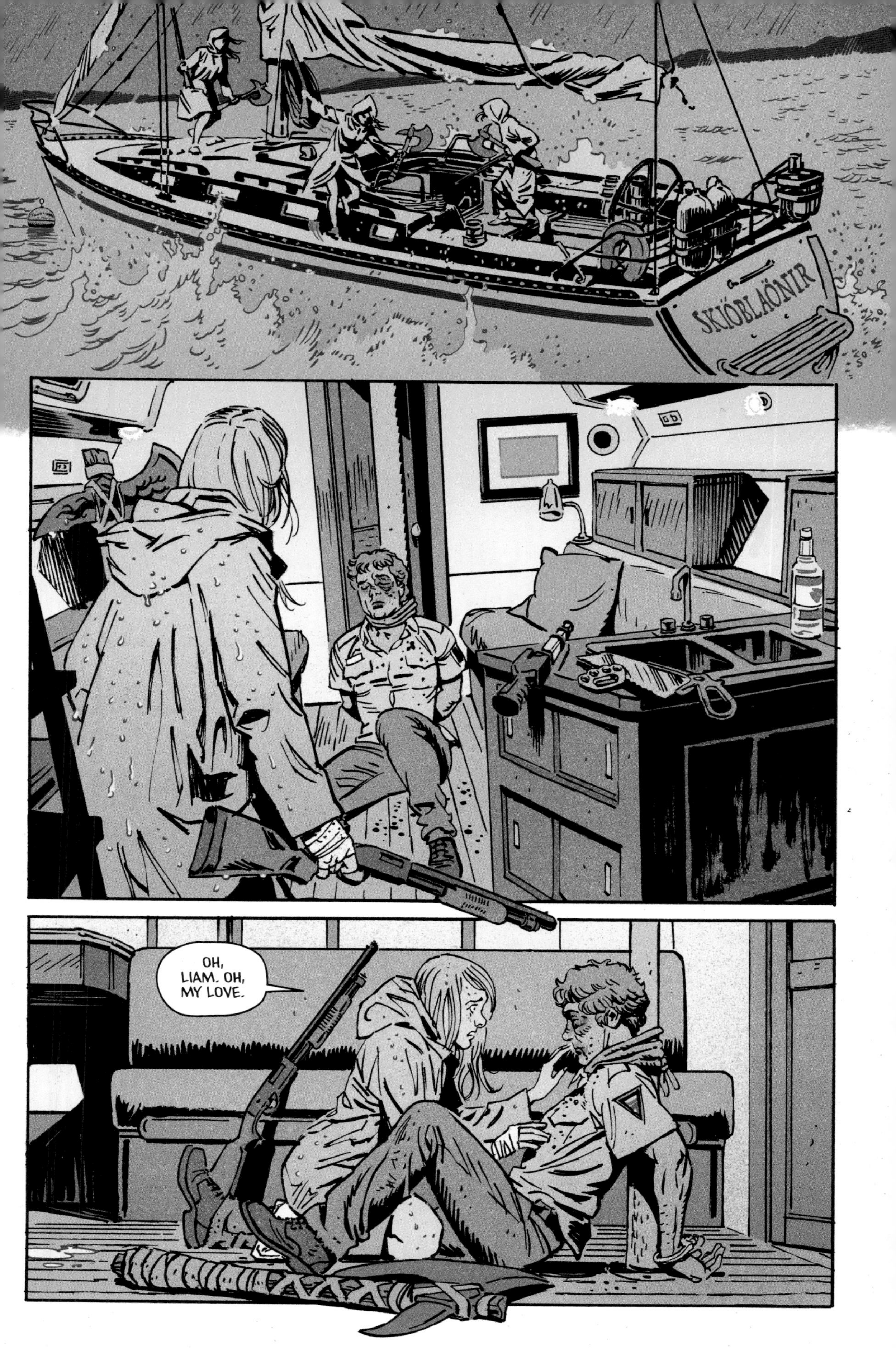
SKIÖBLAÖNIR
OH, LIAM. OH, MY LOVE.

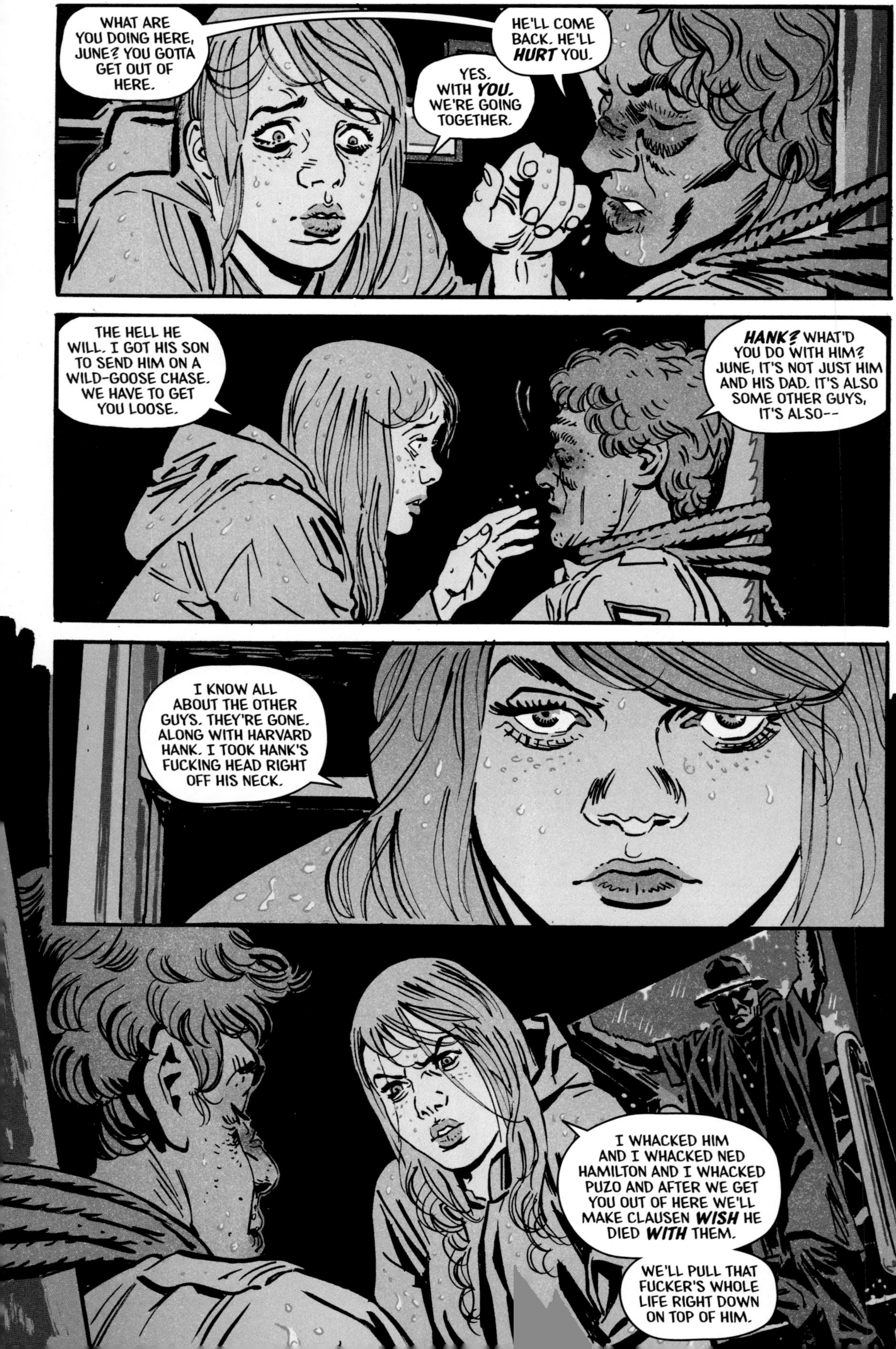
WHAT ARE YOU DOING HERE, JUNE? YOU GOTTA GET OUT OF HERE.
HE'LL COME BACK. HE'LL **HURT** YOU.
YES. WITH **YOU.** WE'RE GOING TOGETHER.
THE HELL HE WILL. I GOT HIS SON TO SEND HIM ON A WILD-GOOSE CHASE. WE HAVE TO GET YOU LOOSE.
HANK? WHAT'D YOU DO WITH HIM? JUNE, IT'S NOT JUST HIM AND HIS DAD. IT'S ALSO SOME OTHER GUYS, IT'S ALSO--
I KNOW ALL ABOUT THE OTHER GUYS. THEY'RE GONE. ALONG WITH HARVARD HANK. I TOOK HANK'S FUCKING HEAD RIGHT OFF HIS NECK.
I WHACKED HIM AND I WHACKED NED HAMILTON AND I WHACKED PUZO AND AFTER WE GET YOU OUT OF HERE WE'LL MAKE CLAUSEN **WISH** HE DIED **WITH** THEM.
WE'LL PULL THAT FUCKER'S WHOLE LIFE RIGHT DOWN ON TOP OF HIM.

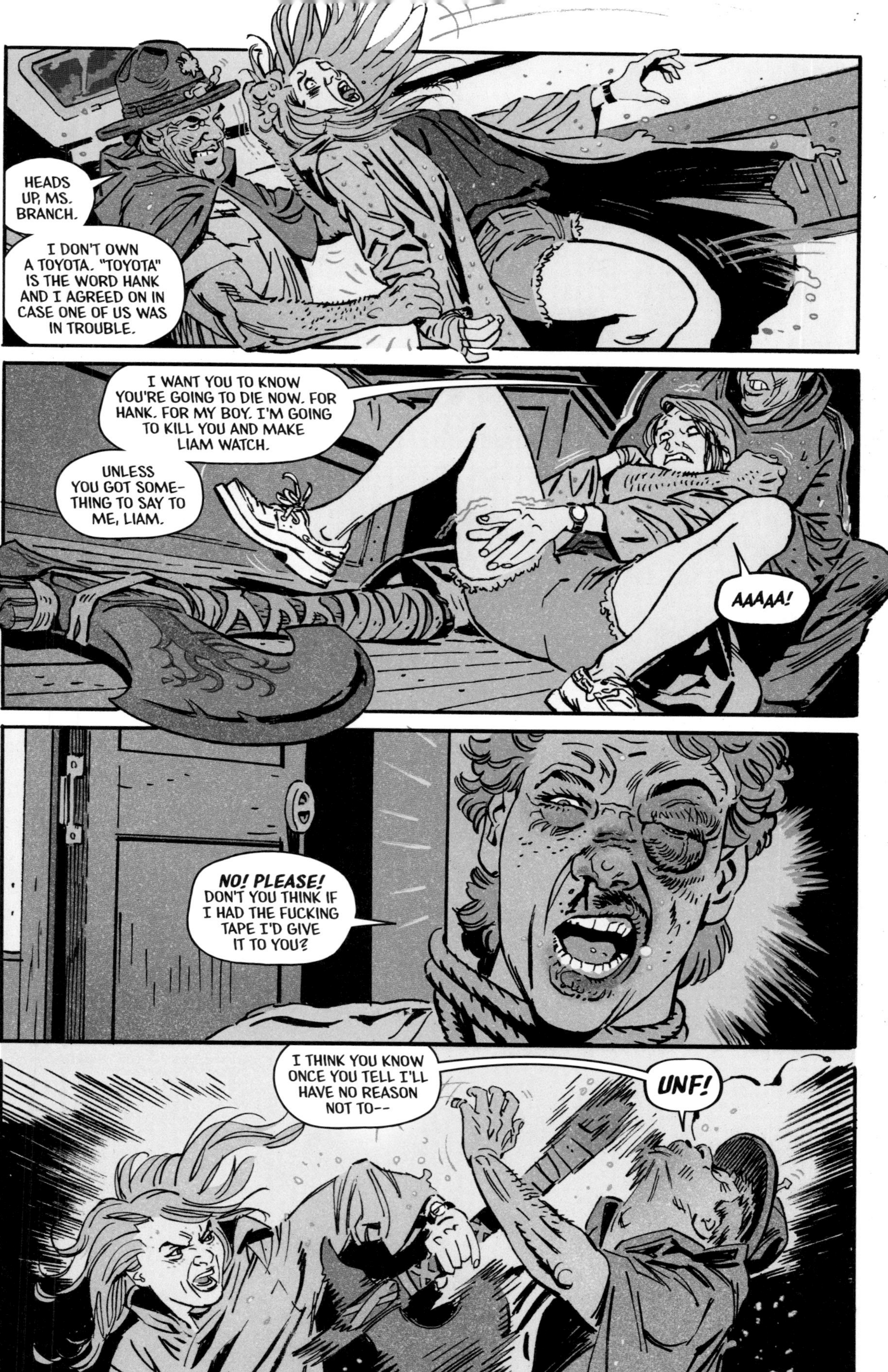
HEADS UP, MS. BRANCH.
I DON'T OWN A TOYOTA. "TOYOTA" IS THE WORD HANK AND I AGREED ON IN CASE ONE OF US WAS IN TROUBLE.
I WANT YOU TO KNOW YOU'RE GOING TO DIE NOW. FOR HANK. FOR MY BOY. I'M GOING TO KILL YOU AND MAKE LIAM WATCH.
UNLESS YOU GOT SOMETHING TO SAY TO ME, LIAM.
AAAAA!
NO! PLEASE! DON'T YOU THINK IF I HAD THE FUCKING TAPE I'D GIVE IT TO YOU?
I THINK YOU KNOW ONCE YOU TELL I'LL HAVE NO REASON NOT TO--
UNF!

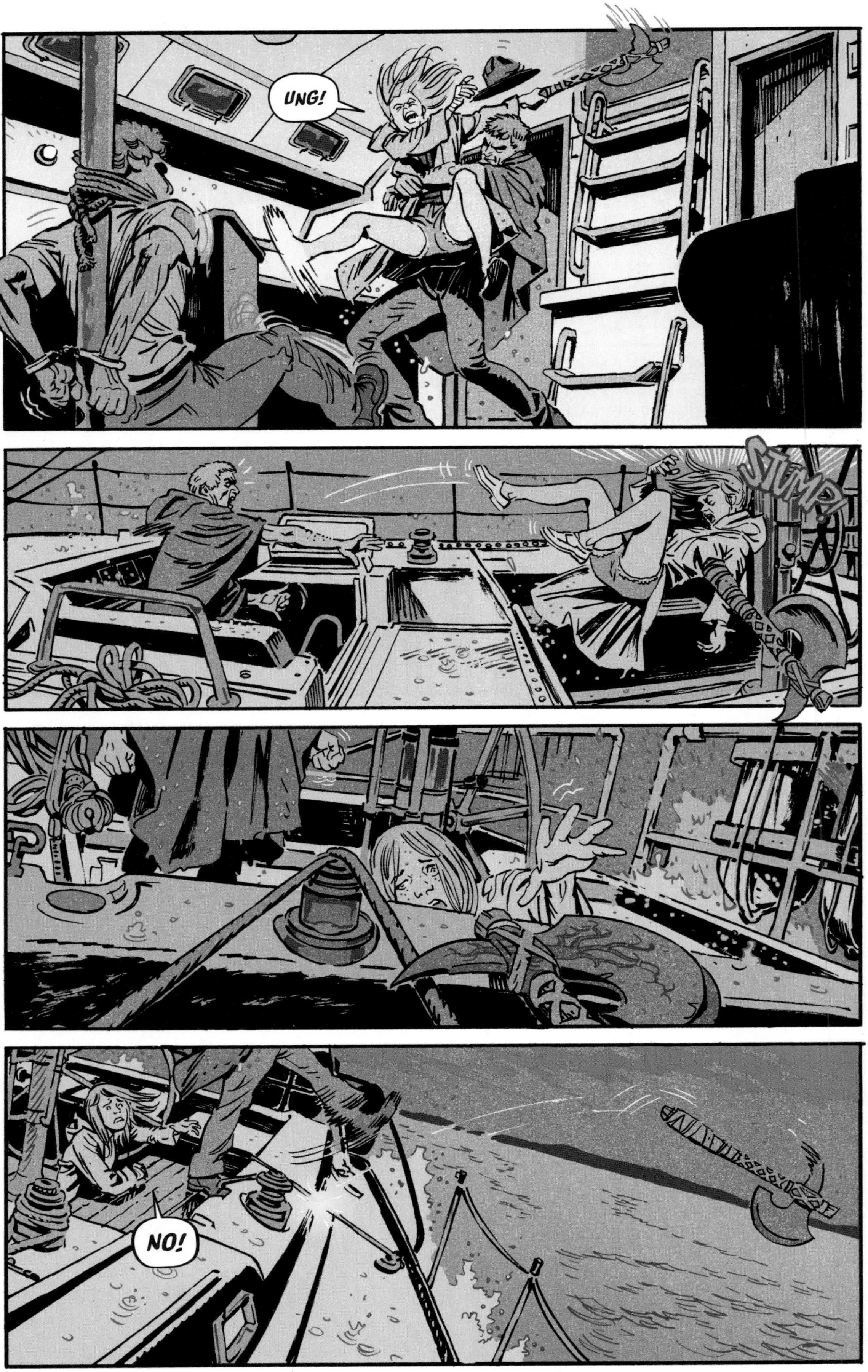
UNG!
STUMP!
NO!

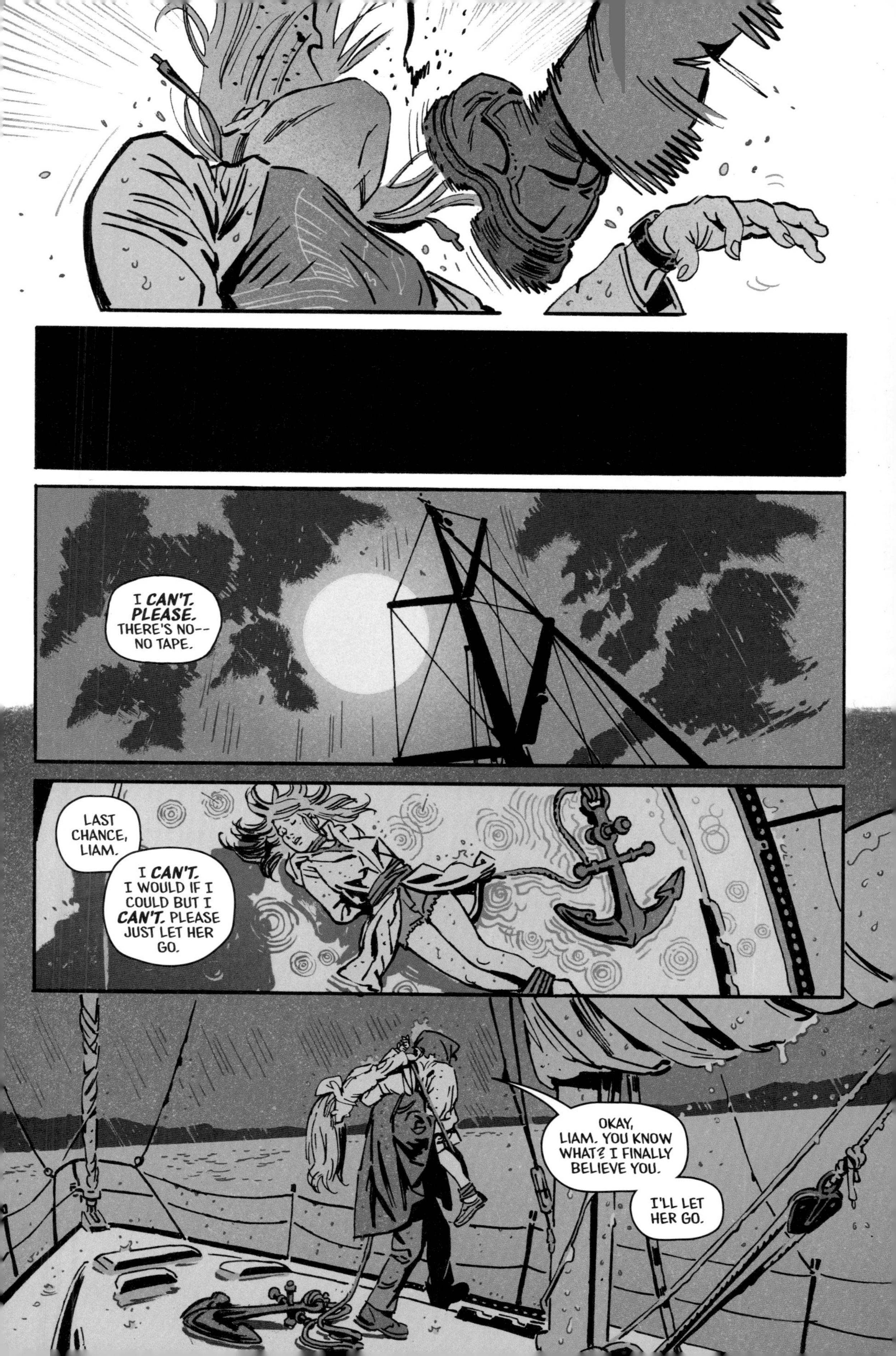
I CAN'T. PLEASE. THERE'S NO-- NO TAPE.
LAST CHANCE, LIAM.
I CAN'T. I WOULD IF I COULD BUT I CAN'T. PLEASE JUST LET HER GO.
OKAY, LIAM. YOU KNOW WHAT? I FINALLY BELIEVE YOU.
I'LL LET HER GO.

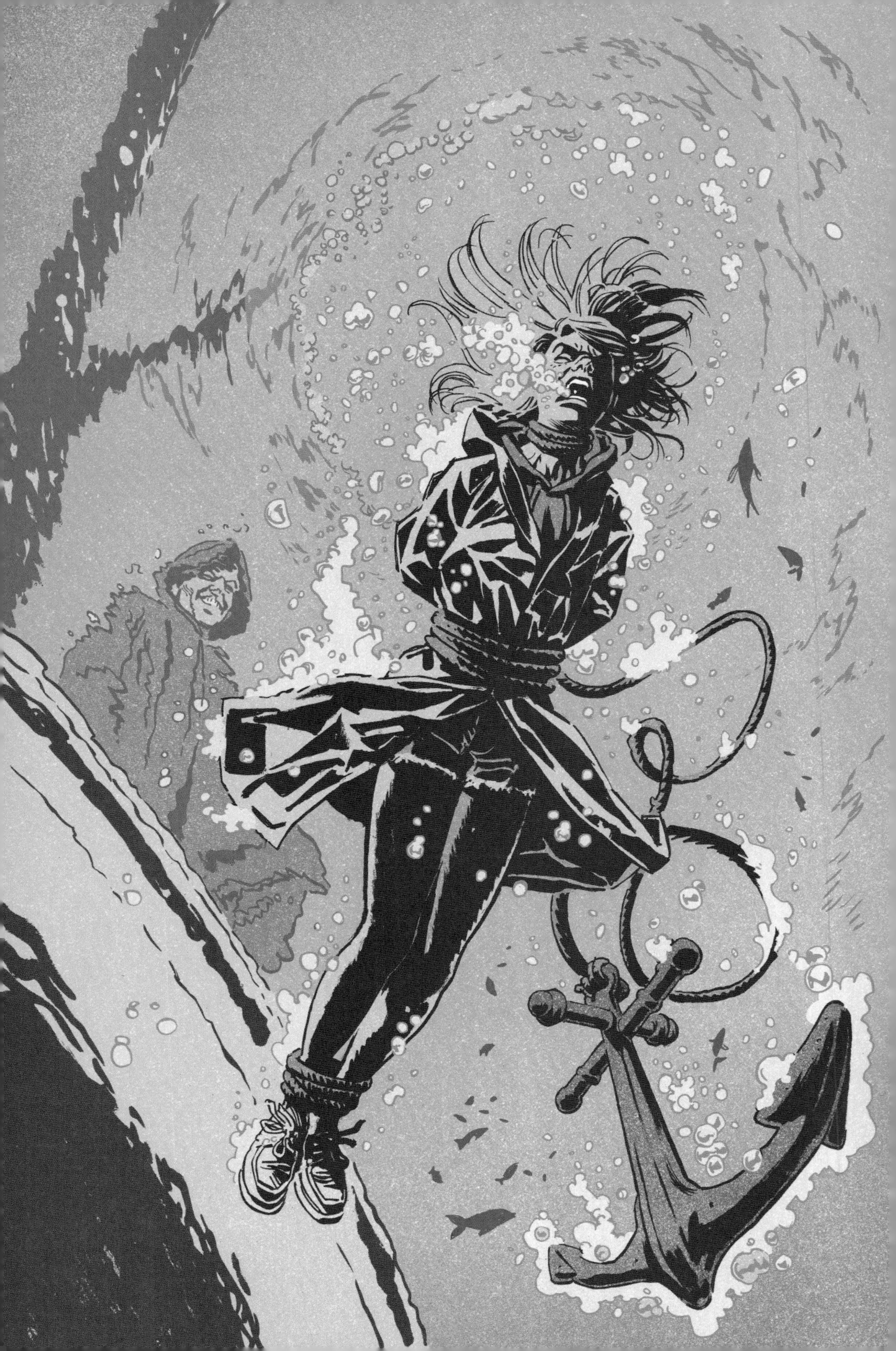

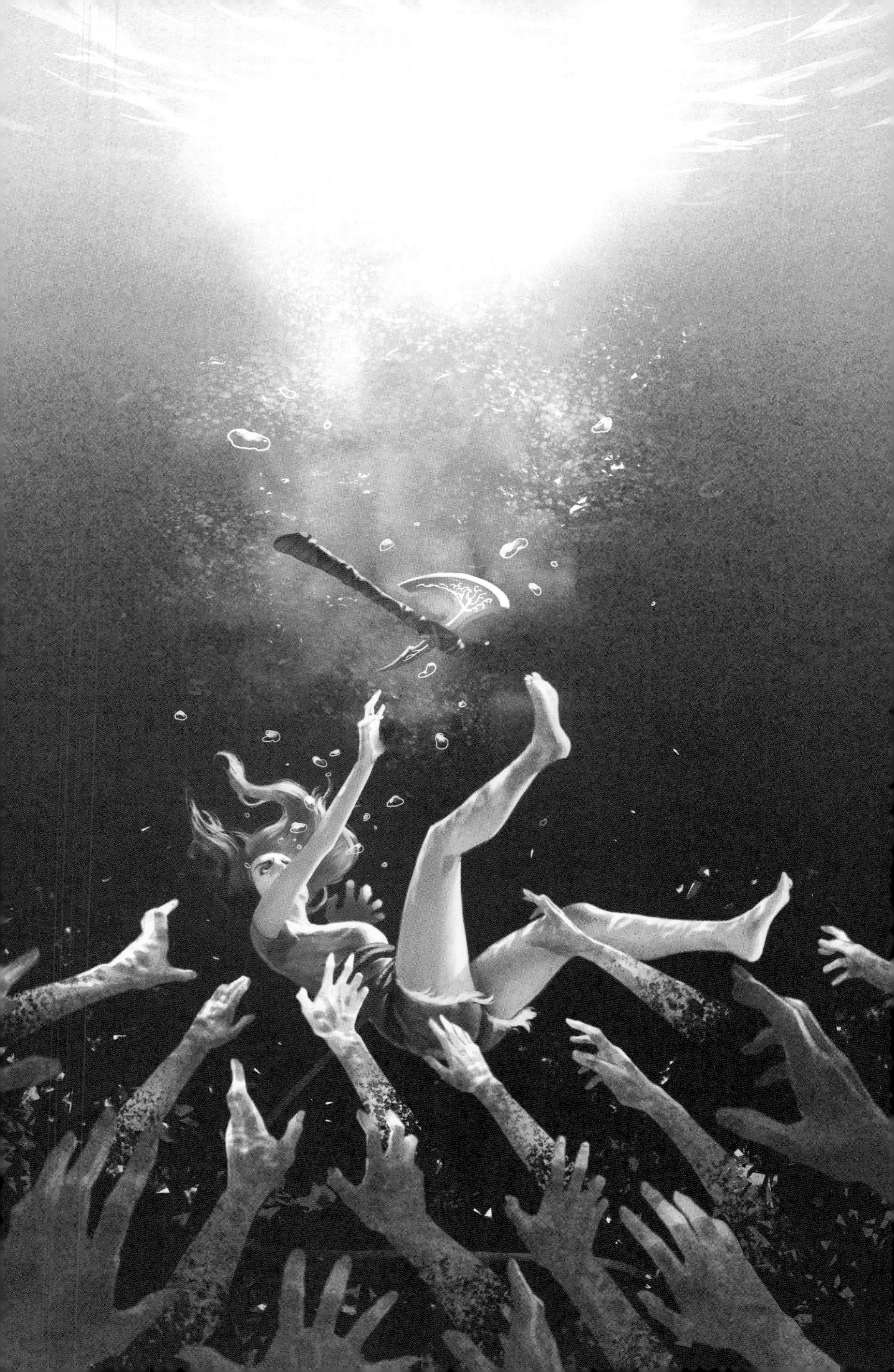

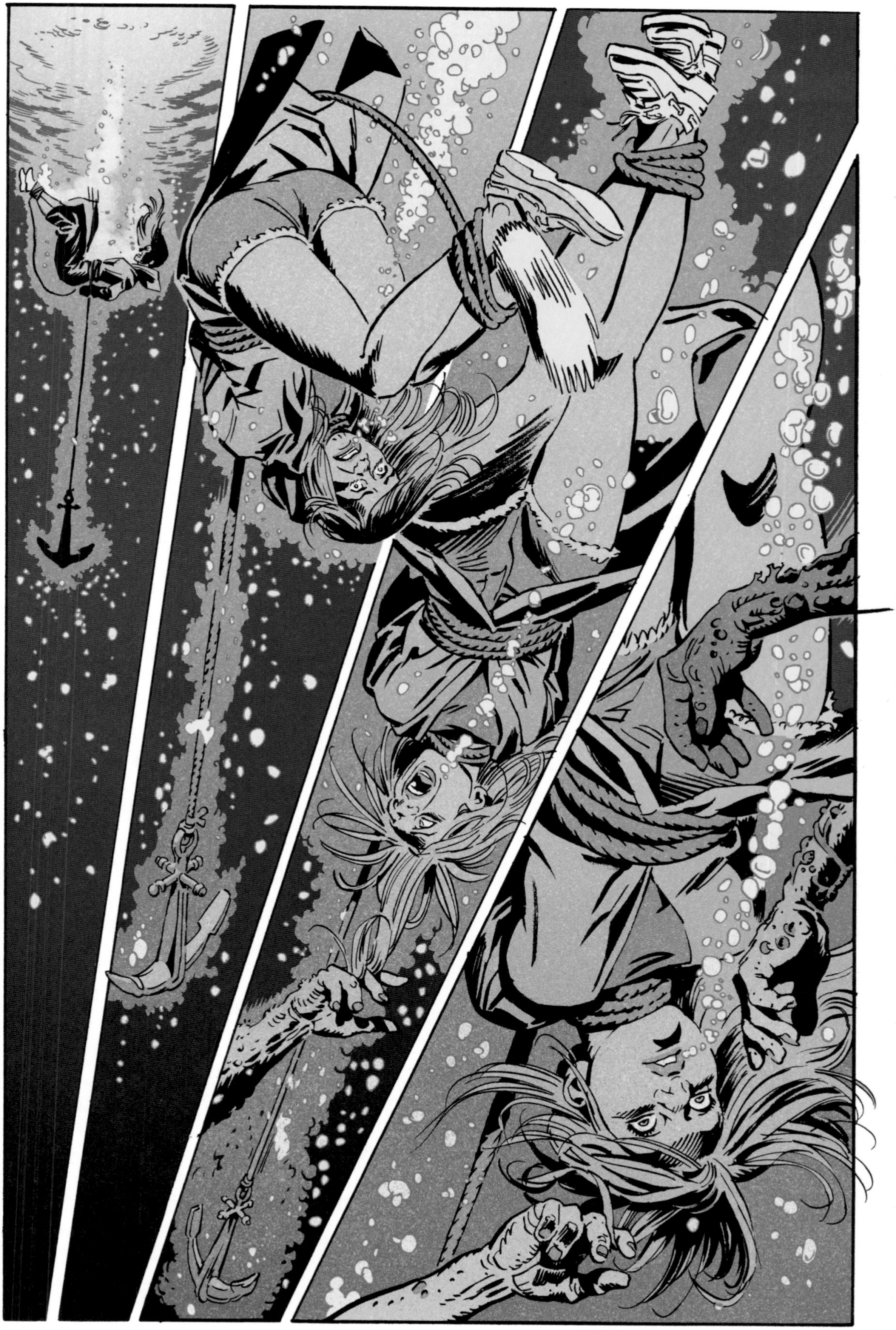

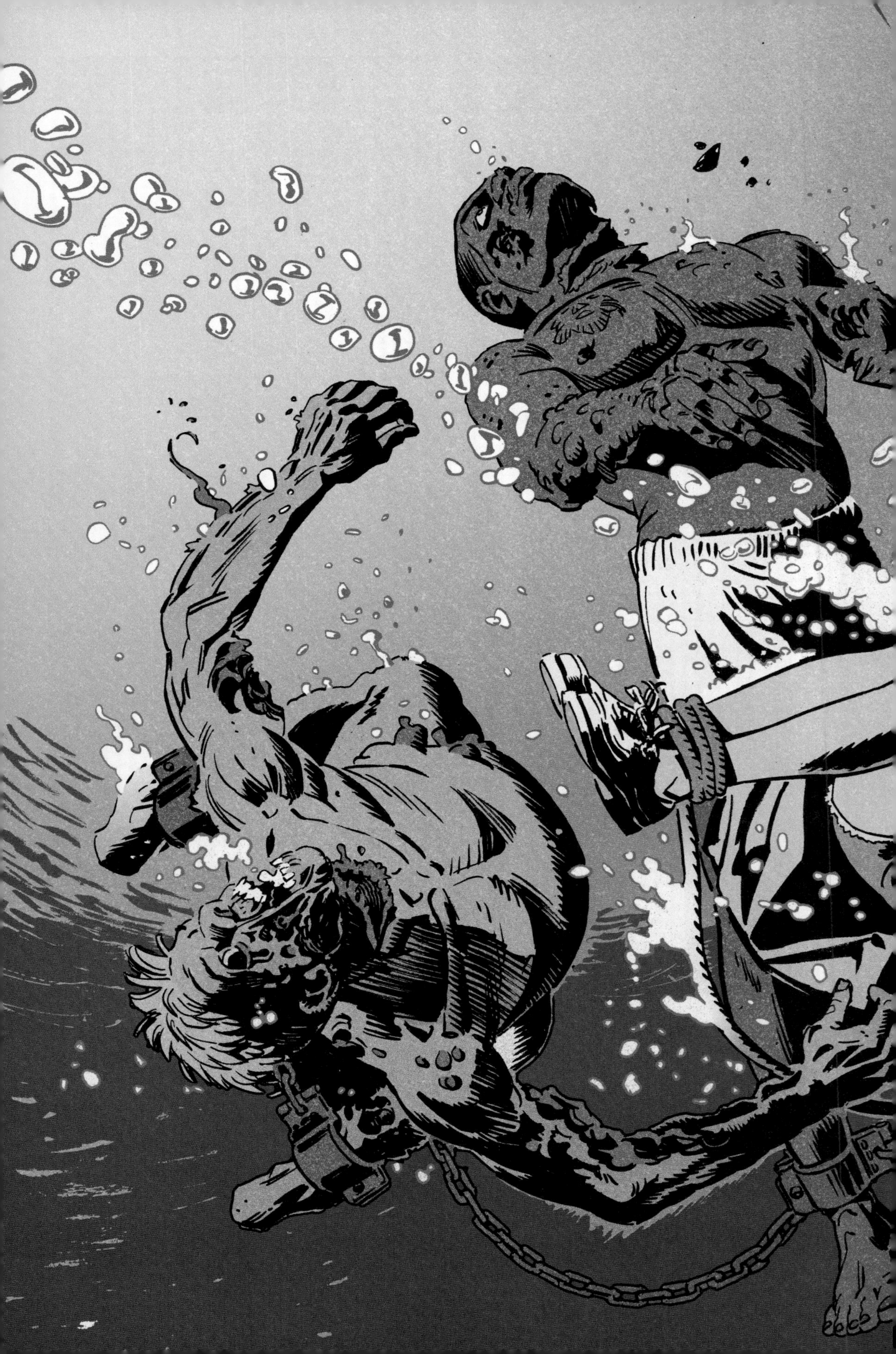

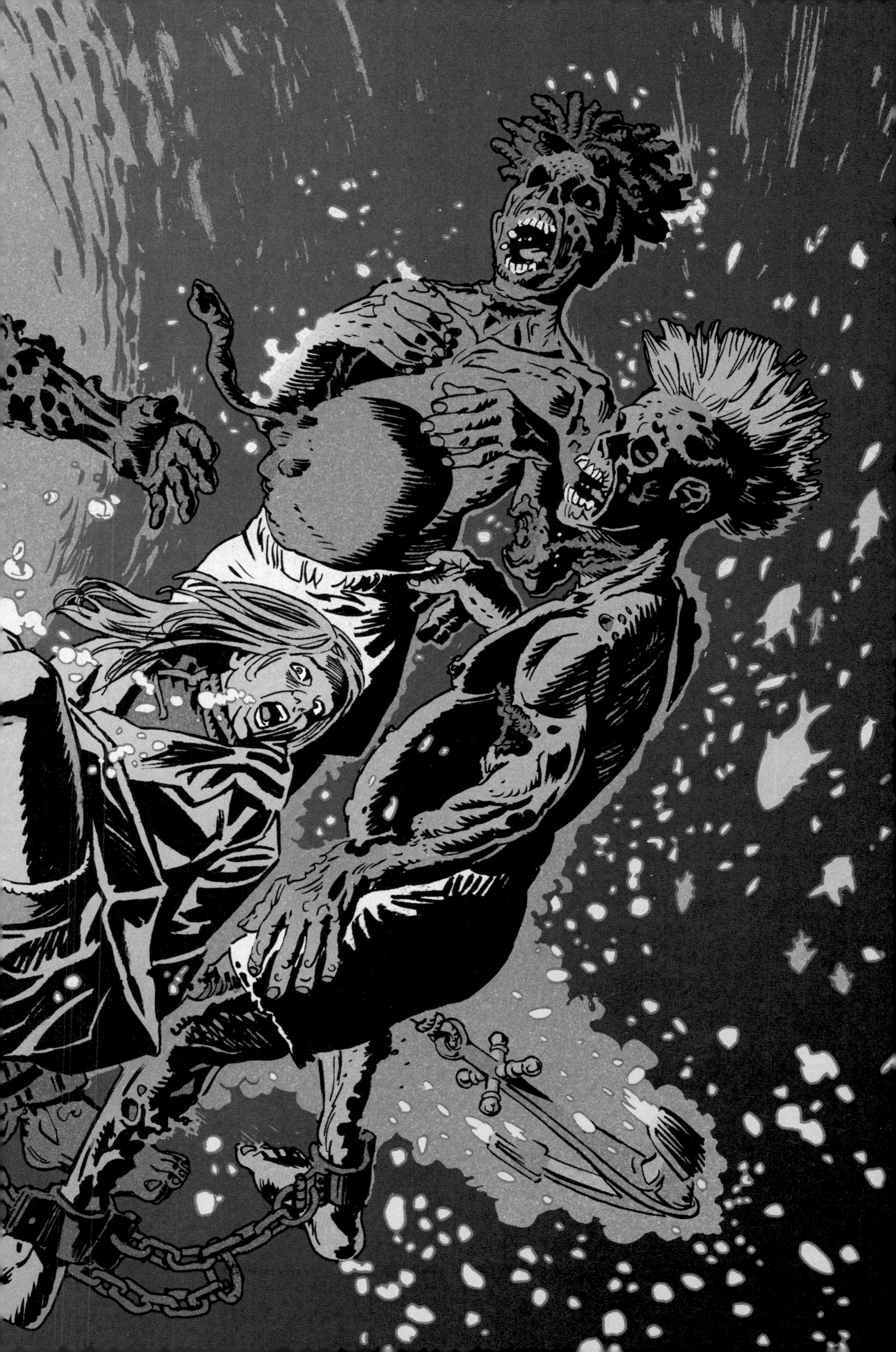

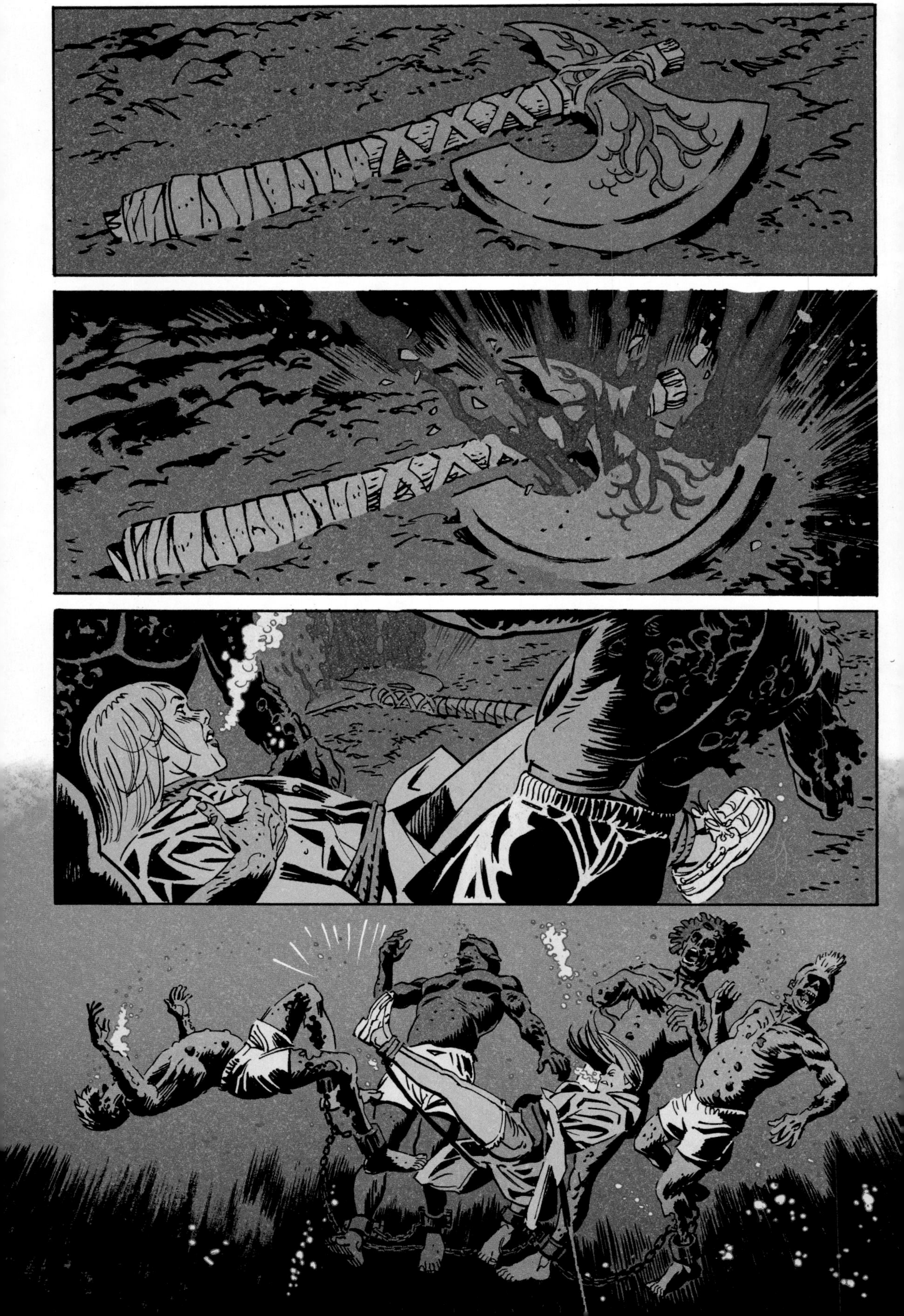

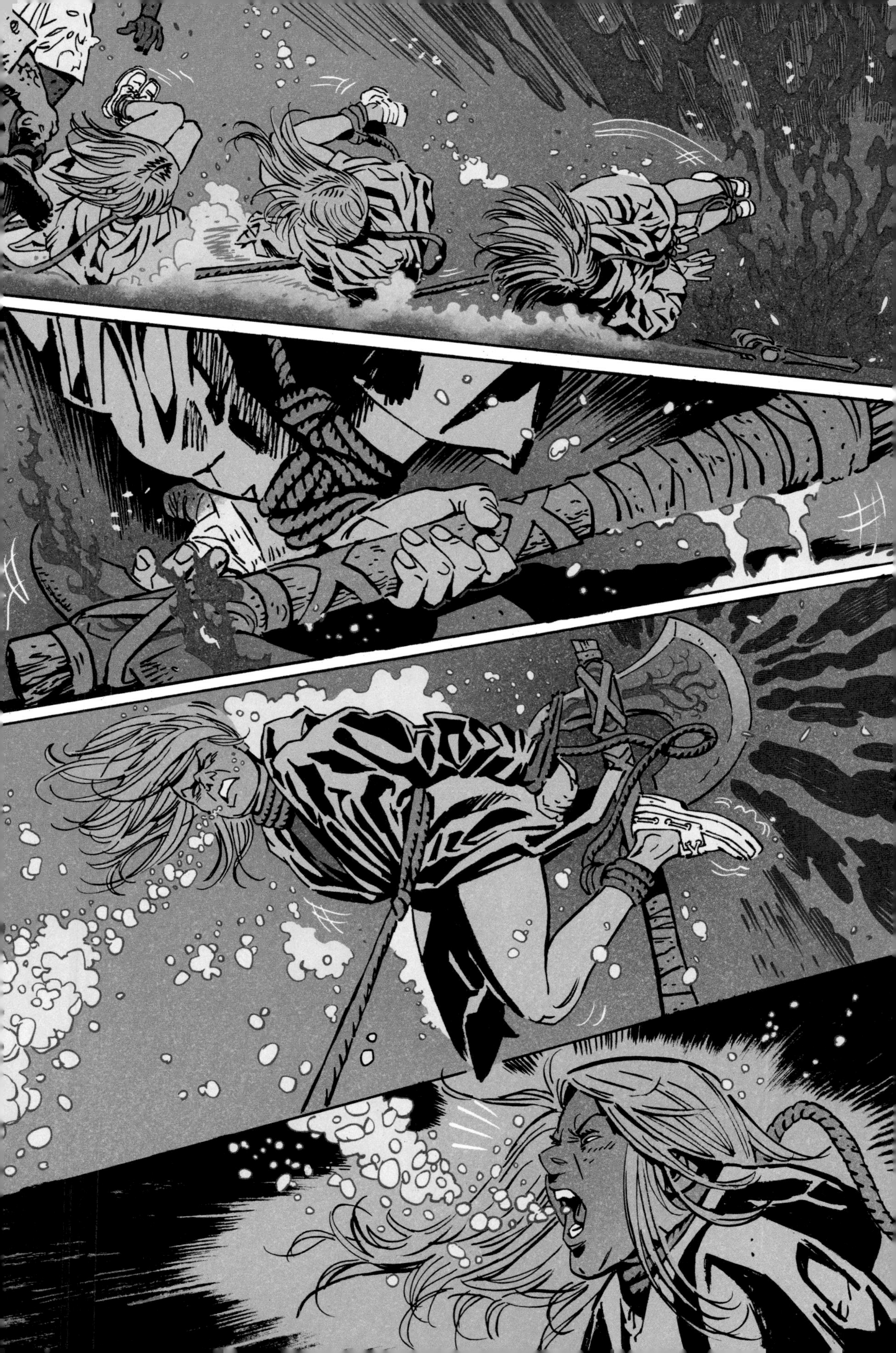

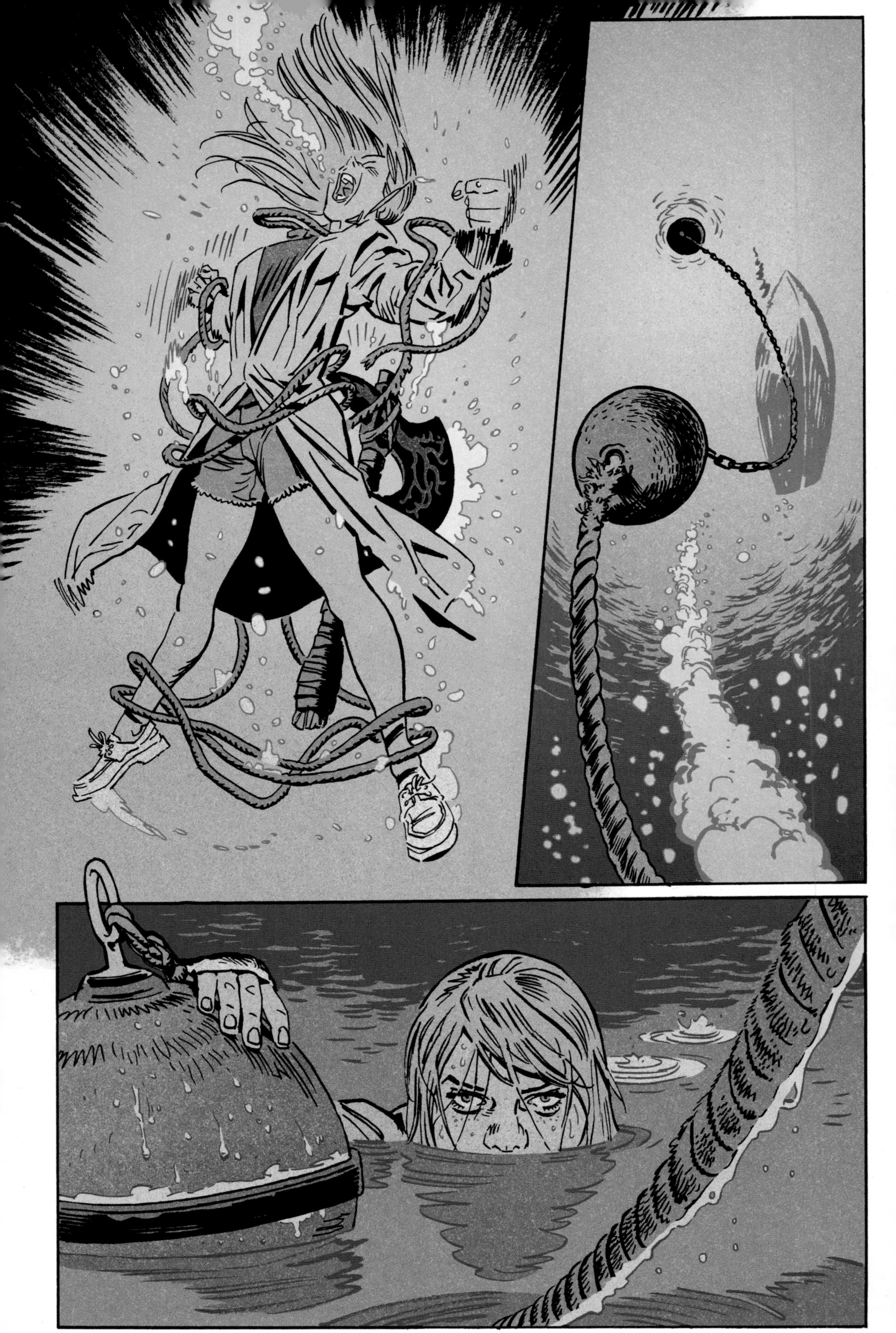

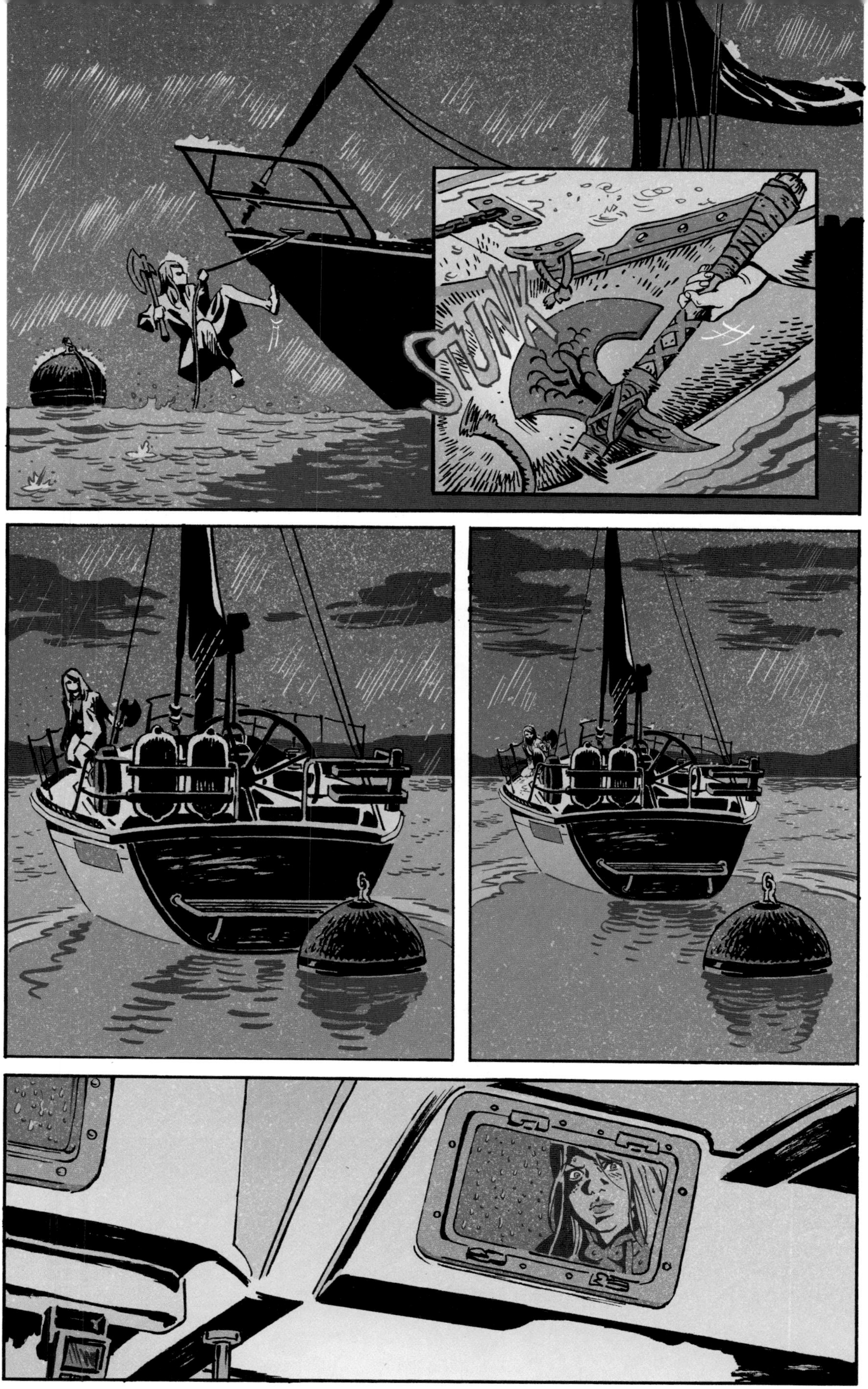
STUNK

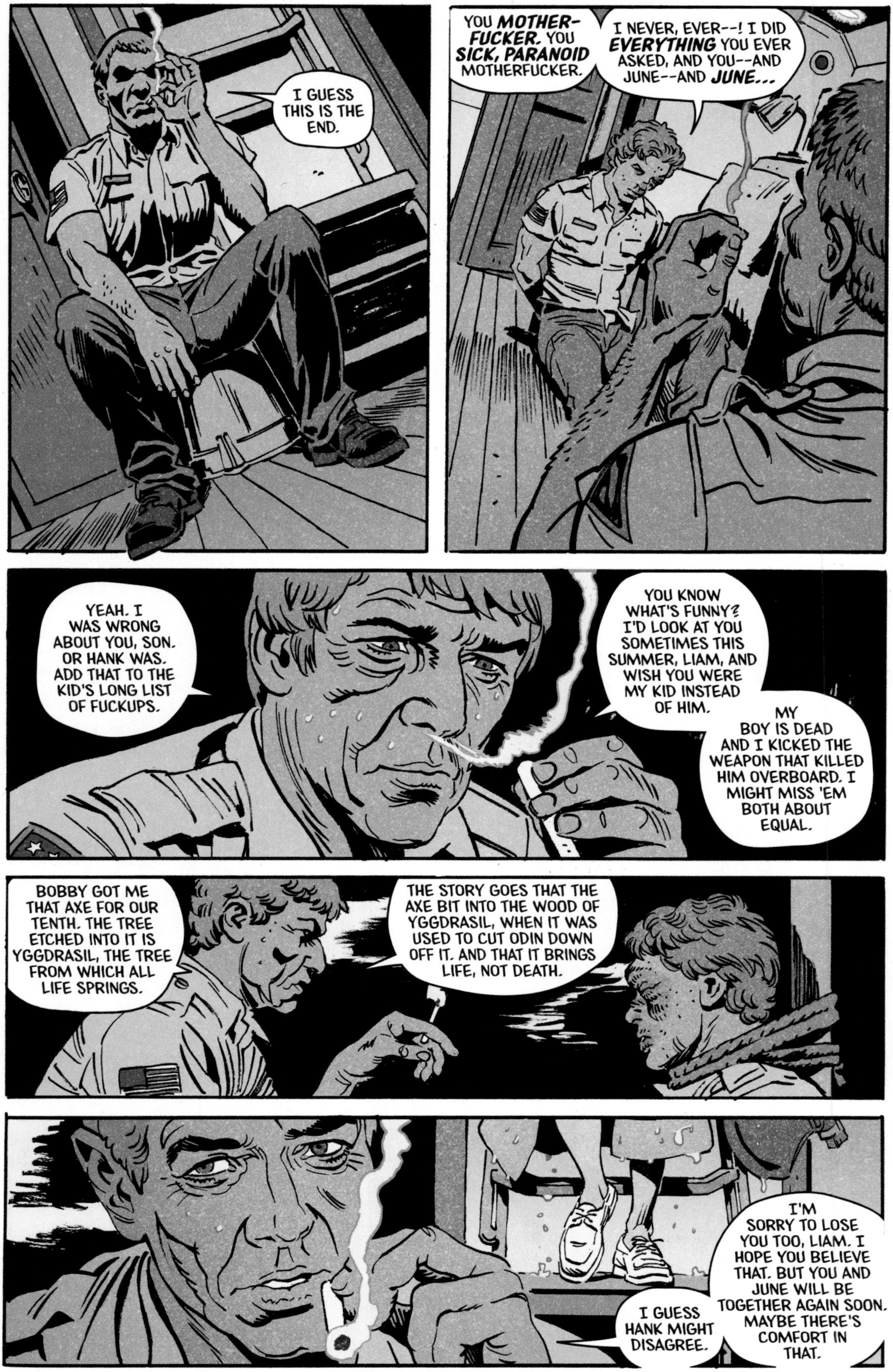
I GUESS THIS IS THE END.
YOU MOTHER-FUCKER. YOU SICK, PARANOID MOTHERFUCKER.
I NEVER, EVER--! I DID EVERYTHING YOU EVER ASKED, AND YOU--AND JUNE--AND JUNE...
YEAH. I WAS WRONG ABOUT YOU, SON. OR HANK WAS. ADD THAT TO THE KID'S LONG LIST OF FUCKUPS.
YOU KNOW WHAT'S FUNNY? I'D LOOK AT YOU SOMETIMES THIS SUMMER, LIAM, AND WISH YOU WERE MY KID INSTEAD OF HIM.
MY BOY IS DEAD AND I KICKED THE WEAPON THAT KILLED HIM OVERBOARD. I MIGHT MISS 'EM BOTH ABOUT EQUAL.
BOBBY GOT ME THAT AXE FOR OUR TENTH. THE TREE ETCHED INTO IT IS YGGDRASIL, THE TREE FROM WHICH ALL LIFE SPRINGS.
THE STORY GOES THAT THE AXE BIT INTO THE WOOD OF YGGDRASIL, WHEN IT WAS USED TO CUT ODIN DOWN OFF IT. AND THAT IT BRINGS LIFE, NOT DEATH.
I'M SORRY TO LOSE YOU TOO, LIAM. I HOPE YOU BELIEVE THAT. BUT YOU AND JUNE WILL BE TOGETHER AGAIN SOON. MAYBE THERE'S COMFORT IN THAT.
I GUESS HANK MIGHT DISAGREE.

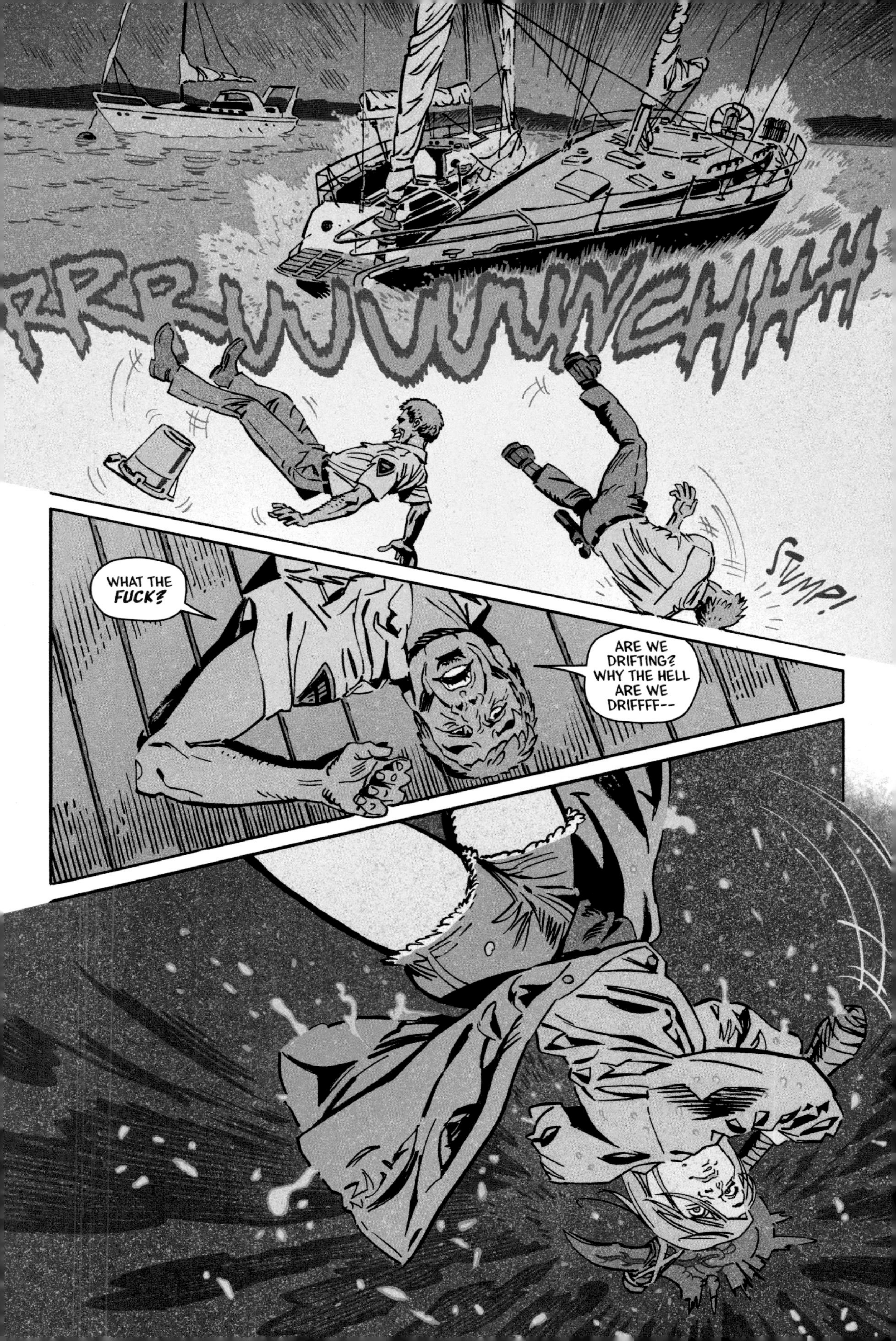
RRRUUUUNCHHH
STUMP!
WHAT THE FUCK?
ARE WE DRIFTING? WHY THE HELL ARE WE DRIFFFF--

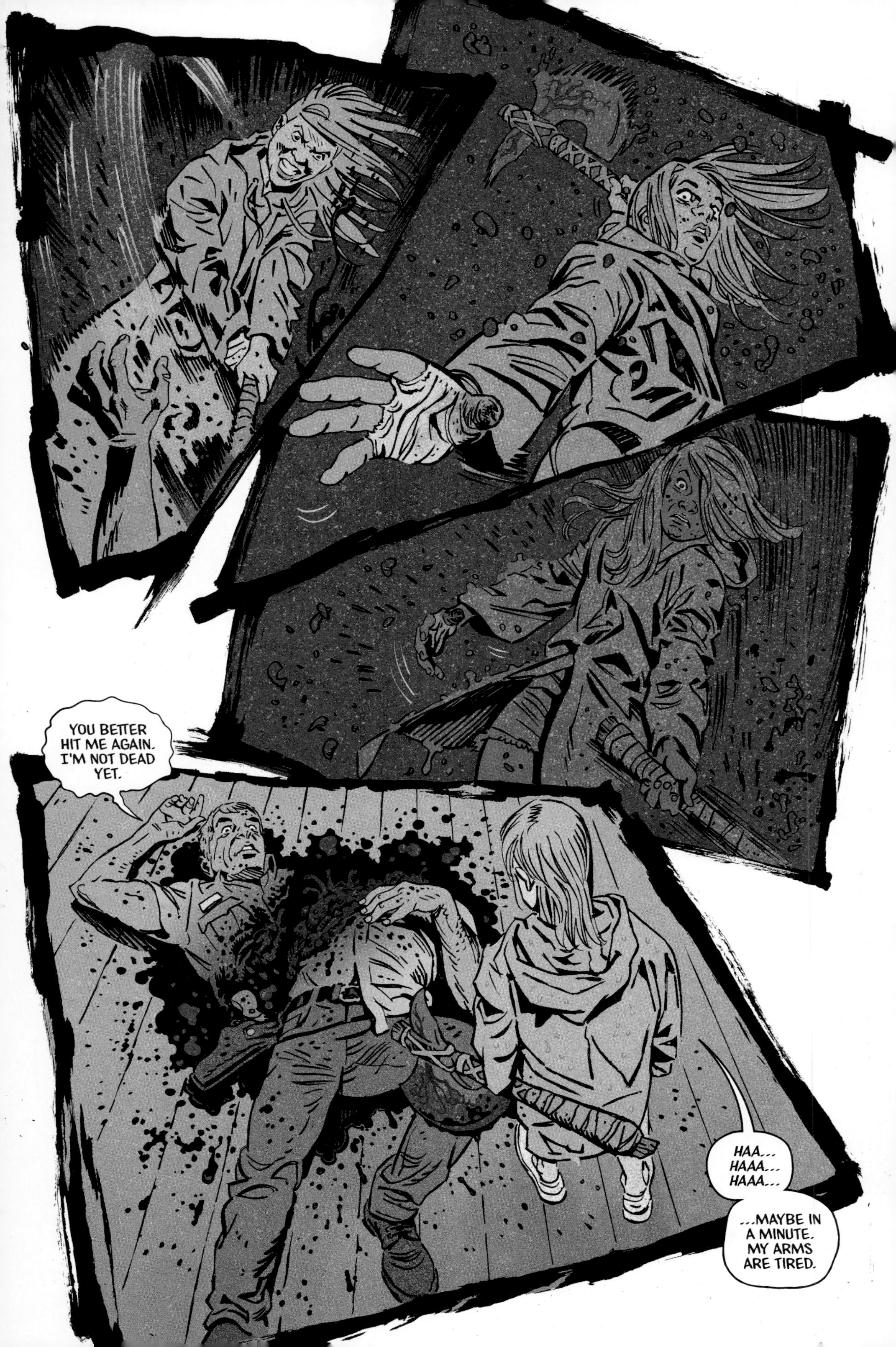
YOU BETTER HIT ME AGAIN. I'M NOT DEAD YET.
HAA... HAAA... HAAA...
...MAYBE IN A MINUTE. MY ARMS ARE TIRED.

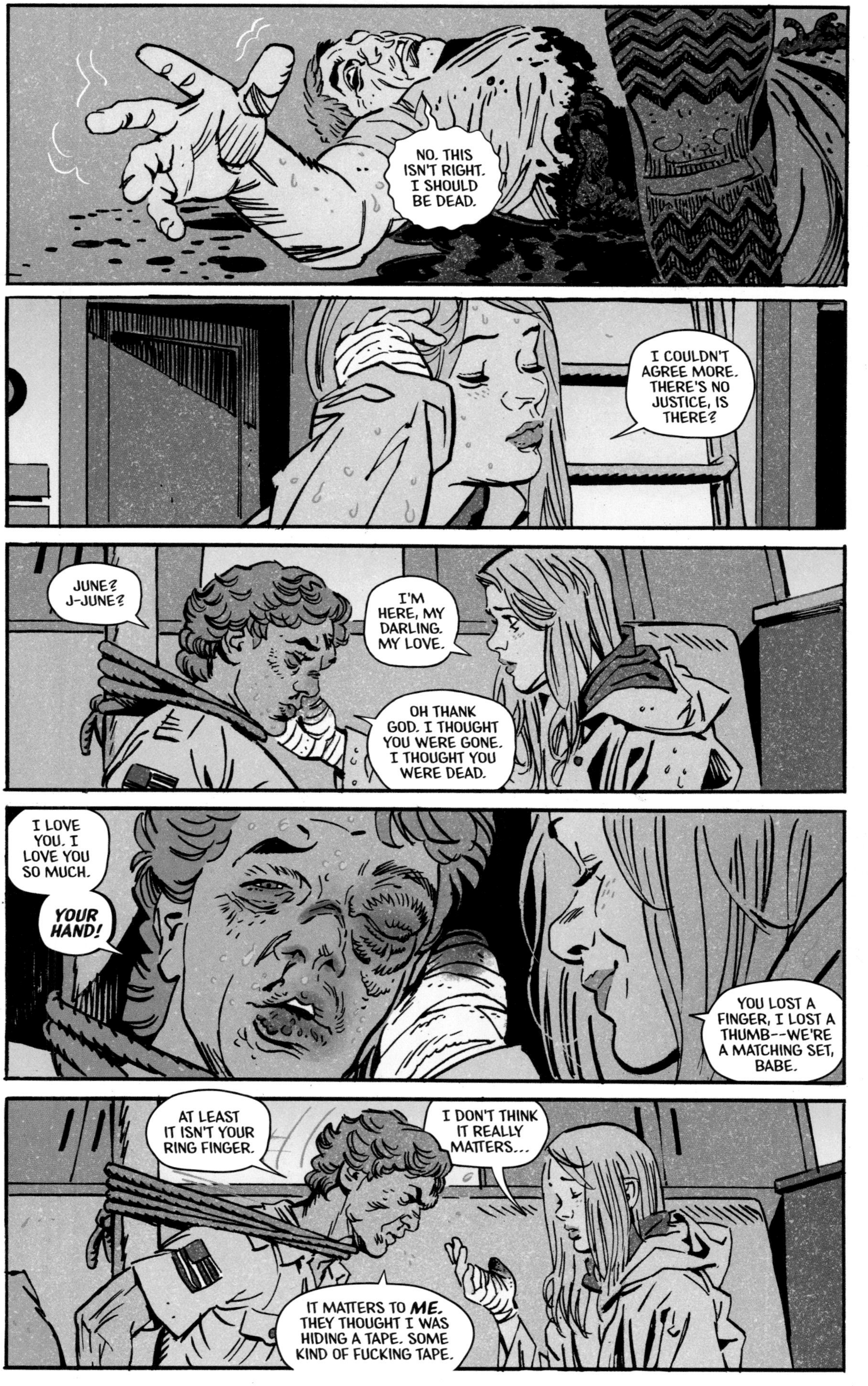
NO. THIS ISN'T RIGHT. I SHOULD BE DEAD.
I COULDN'T AGREE MORE. THERE'S NO JUSTICE, IS THERE?
JUNE? J-JUNE?
I'M HERE, MY DARLING. MY LOVE.
OH THANK GOD. I THOUGHT YOU WERE GONE. I THOUGHT YOU WERE DEAD.
I LOVE YOU. I LOVE YOU SO MUCH.
YOUR HAND!
YOU LOST A FINGER, I LOST A THUMB--WE'RE A MATCHING SET, BABE.
AT LEAST IT ISN'T YOUR RING FINGER.
I DON'T THINK IT REALLY MATTERS...
IT MATTERS TO ME. THEY THOUGHT I WAS HIDING A TAPE. SOME KIND OF FUCKING TAPE.

THEY THOUGHT I WAS SECRETLY RECORDING THEM. I LED THEM AWAY FROM THE HOUSE TO TRY AND KEEP YOU SAFE...TOLD THEM I HAD A HIDING PLACE ON THE BOAT.

BUT THE ONLY THING I WAS KEEPING SECRET OUT HERE...IT'S...IT'S IN CLAUSEN'S SHIRT POCKET NOW.

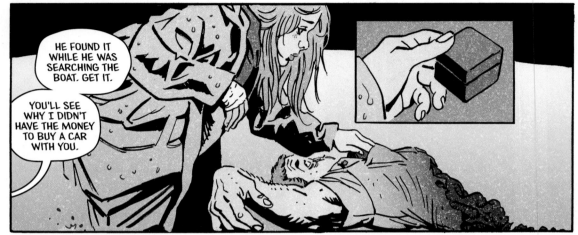

HE FOUND IT WHILE HE WAS SEARCHING THE BOAT. GET IT.

YOU'LL SEE WHY I DIDN'T HAVE THE MONEY TO BUY A CAR WITH YOU.

CRUNK

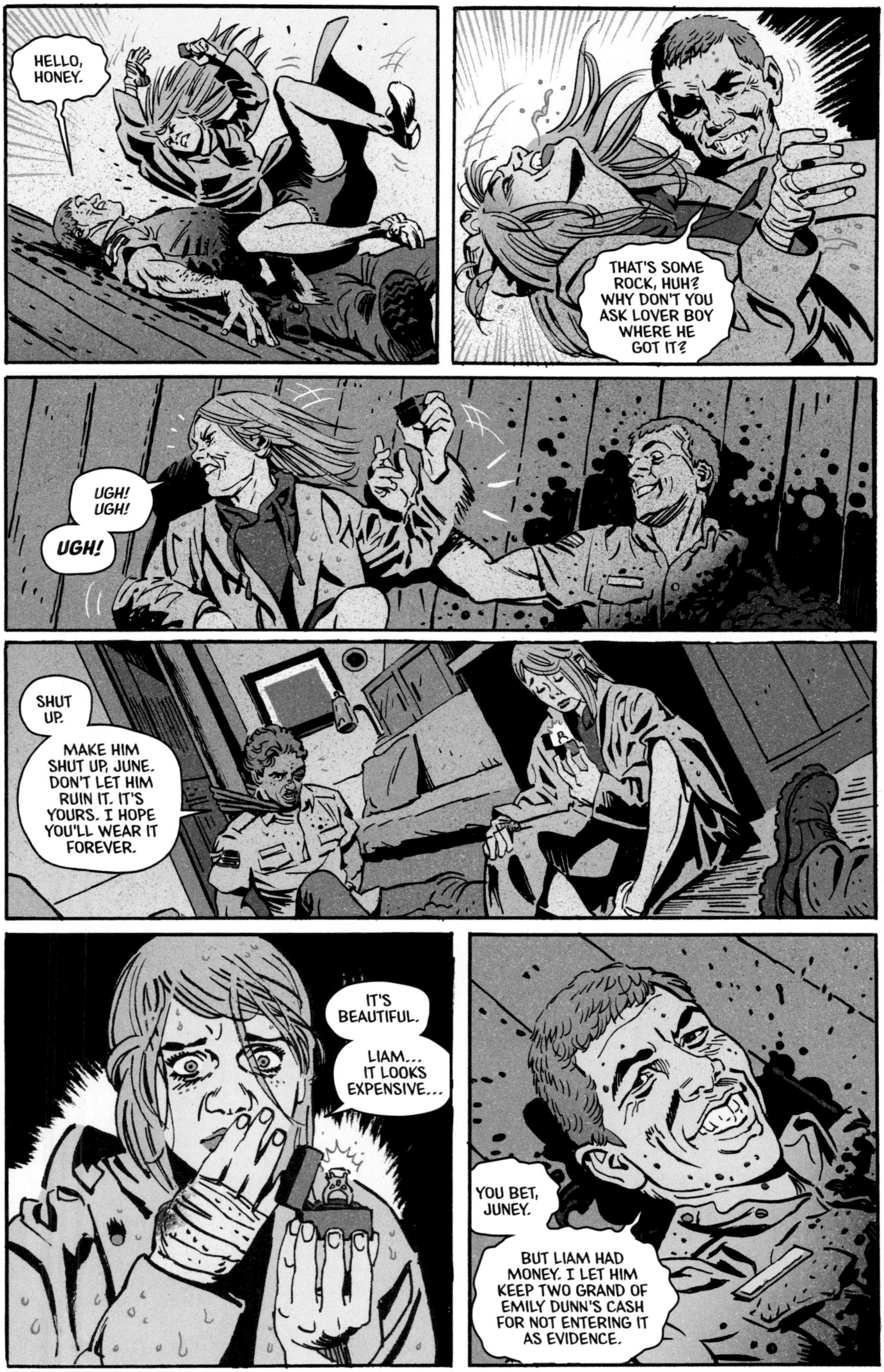
HELLO, HONEY.
THAT'S SOME ROCK, HUH? WHY DON'T YOU ASK LOVER BOY WHERE HE GOT IT?
UGH! UGH!
UGH!
SHUT UP.
MAKE HIM SHUT UP, JUNE. DON'T LET HIM RUIN IT. IT'S YOURS. I HOPE YOU'LL WEAR IT FOREVER.
IT'S BEAUTIFUL.
LIAM... IT LOOKS EXPENSIVE...
YOU BET, JUNEY.
BUT LIAM HAD MONEY. I LET HIM KEEP TWO GRAND OF EMILY DUNN'S CASH FOR NOT ENTERING IT AS EVIDENCE.

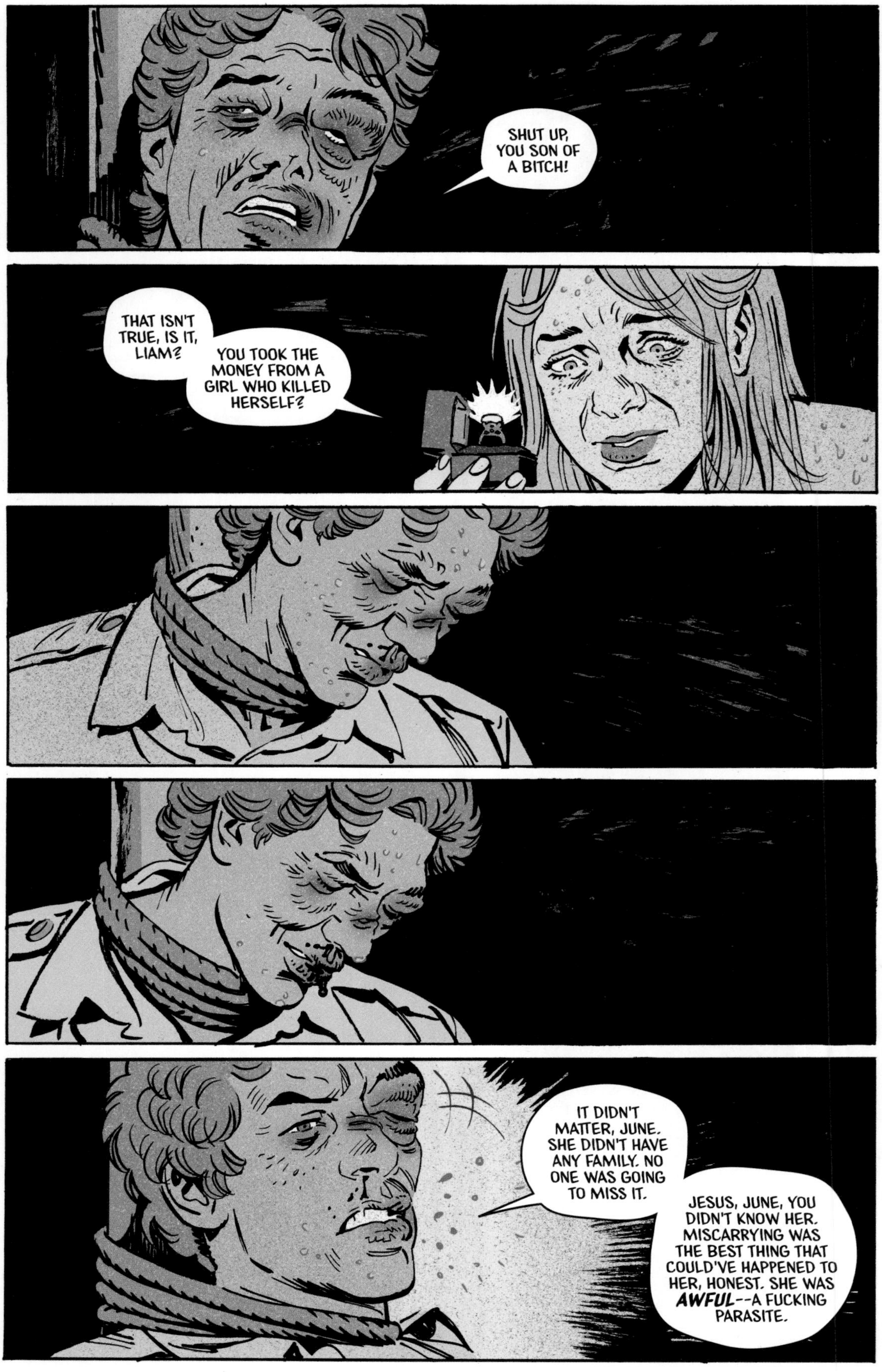
SHUT UP, YOU SON OF A BITCH!
THAT ISN'T TRUE, IS IT, LIAM?
YOU TOOK THE MONEY FROM A GIRL WHO KILLED HERSELF?
IT DIDN'T MATTER, JUNE. SHE DIDN'T HAVE ANY FAMILY. NO ONE WAS GOING TO MISS IT.
JESUS, JUNE, YOU DIDN'T KNOW HER. MISCARRYING WAS THE BEST THING THAT COULD'VE HAPPENED TO HER, HONEST. SHE WAS **AWFUL**--A FUCKING PARASITE.

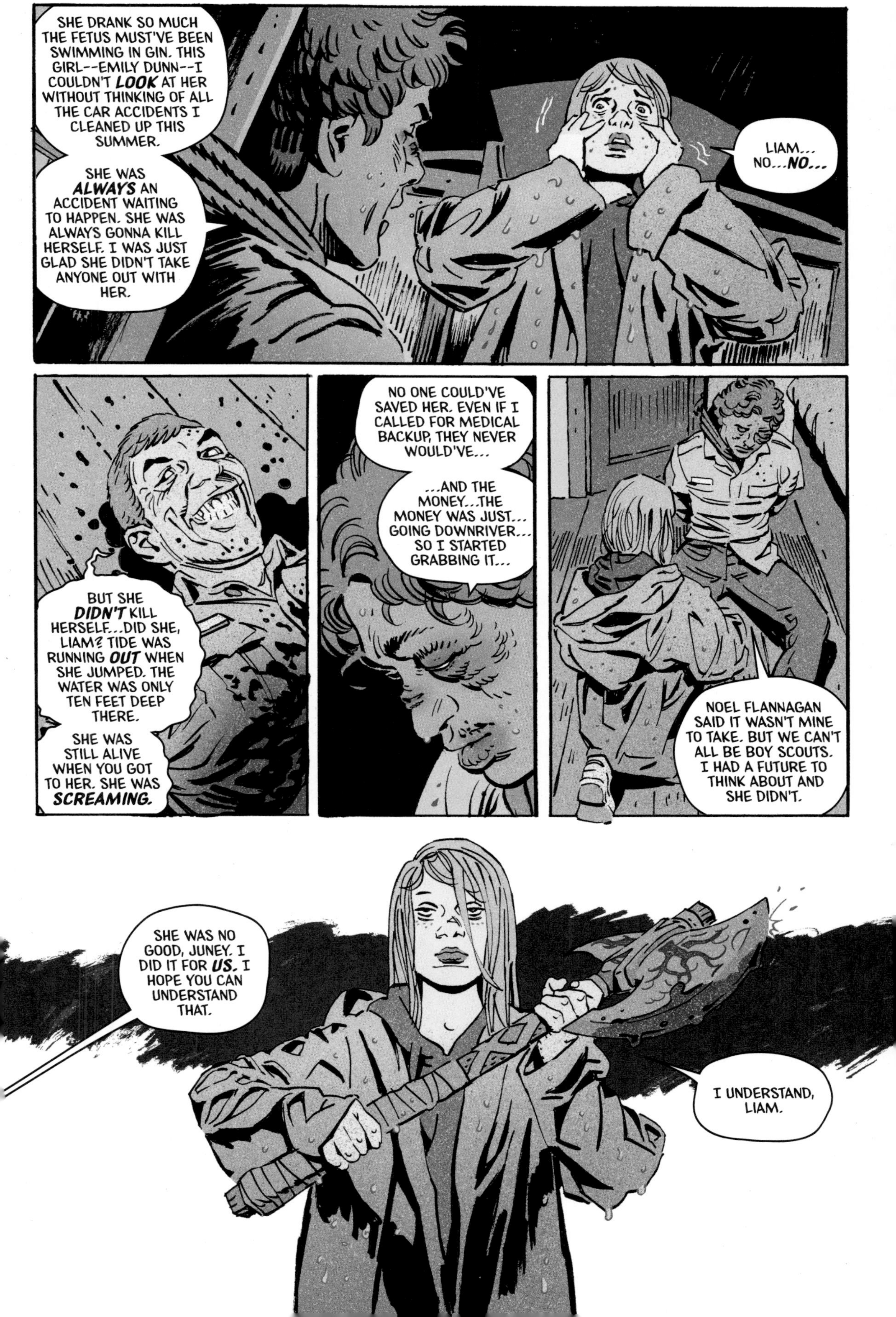
SHE DRANK SO MUCH THE FETUS MUST'VE BEEN SWIMMING IN GIN. THIS GIRL--EMILY DUNN--I COULDN'T LOOK AT HER WITHOUT THINKING OF ALL THE CAR ACCIDENTS I CLEANED UP THIS SUMMER.
SHE WAS ALWAYS AN ACCIDENT WAITING TO HAPPEN. SHE WAS ALWAYS GONNA KILL HERSELF. I WAS JUST GLAD SHE DIDN'T TAKE ANYONE OUT WITH HER.
LIAM... NO...NO...
BUT SHE DIDN'T KILL HERSELF...DID SHE, LIAM? TIDE WAS RUNNING OUT WHEN SHE JUMPED. THE WATER WAS ONLY TEN FEET DEEP THERE.
SHE WAS STILL ALIVE WHEN YOU GOT TO HER. SHE WAS SCREAMING.
NO ONE COULD'VE SAVED HER. EVEN IF I CALLED FOR MEDICAL BACKUP, THEY NEVER WOULD'VE...
...AND THE MONEY...THE MONEY WAS JUST... GOING DOWNRIVER... SO I STARTED GRABBING IT...
NOEL FLANNAGAN SAID IT WASN'T MINE TO TAKE. BUT WE CAN'T ALL BE BOY SCOUTS. I HAD A FUTURE TO THINK ABOUT AND SHE DIDN'T.
SHE WAS NO GOOD, JUNEY. I DID IT FOR US. I HOPE YOU CAN UNDERSTAND THAT.
I UNDERSTAND, LIAM.

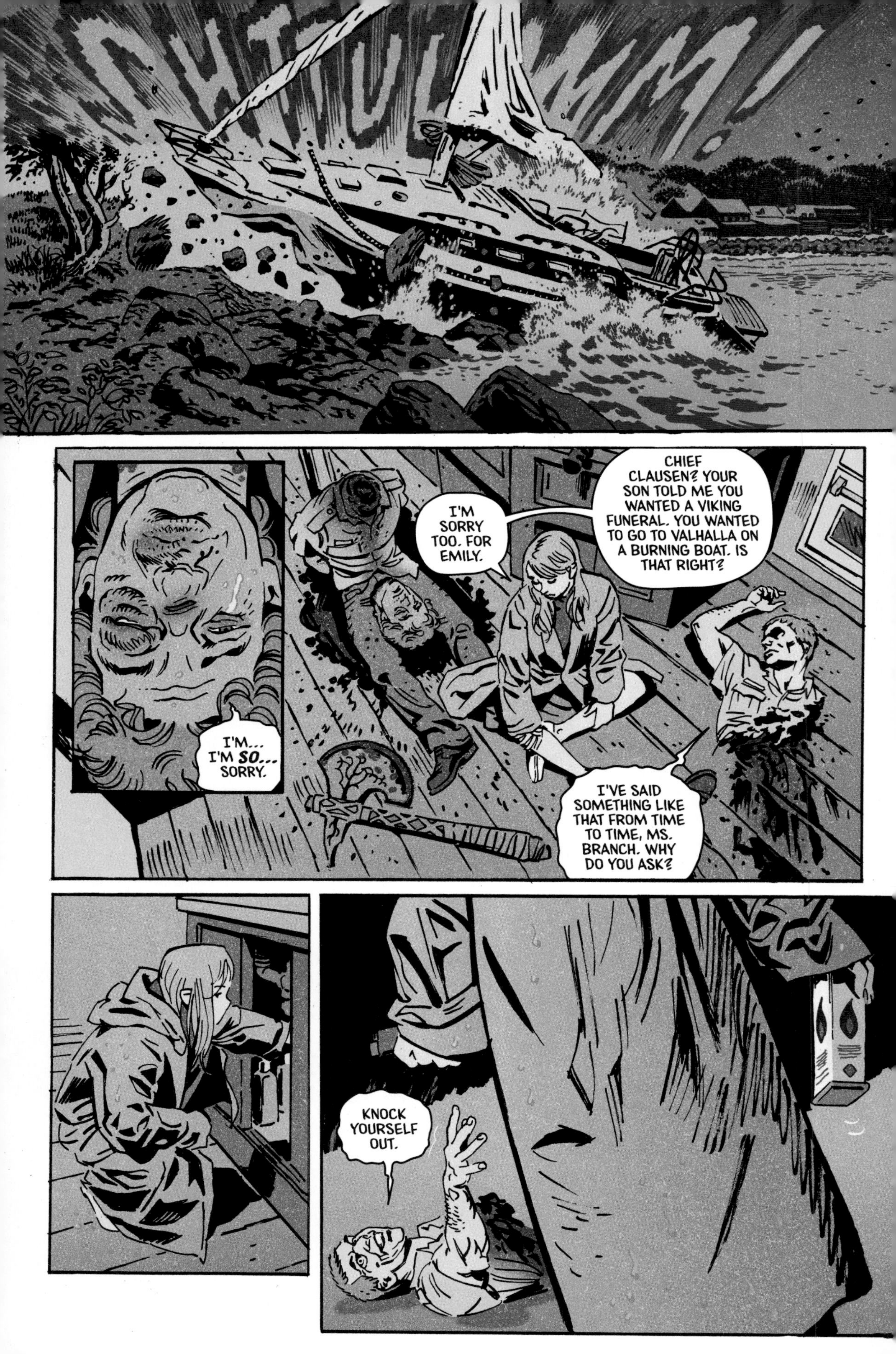
I'M... I'M *SO*... SORRY.
I'M SORRY TOO. FOR EMILY.
CHIEF CLAUSEN? YOUR SON TOLD ME YOU WANTED A VIKING FUNERAL. YOU WANTED TO GO TO VALHALLA ON A BURNING BOAT. IS THAT RIGHT?
I'VE SAID SOMETHING LIKE THAT FROM TIME TO TIME, MS. BRANCH. WHY DO YOU ASK?
KNOCK YOURSELF OUT.

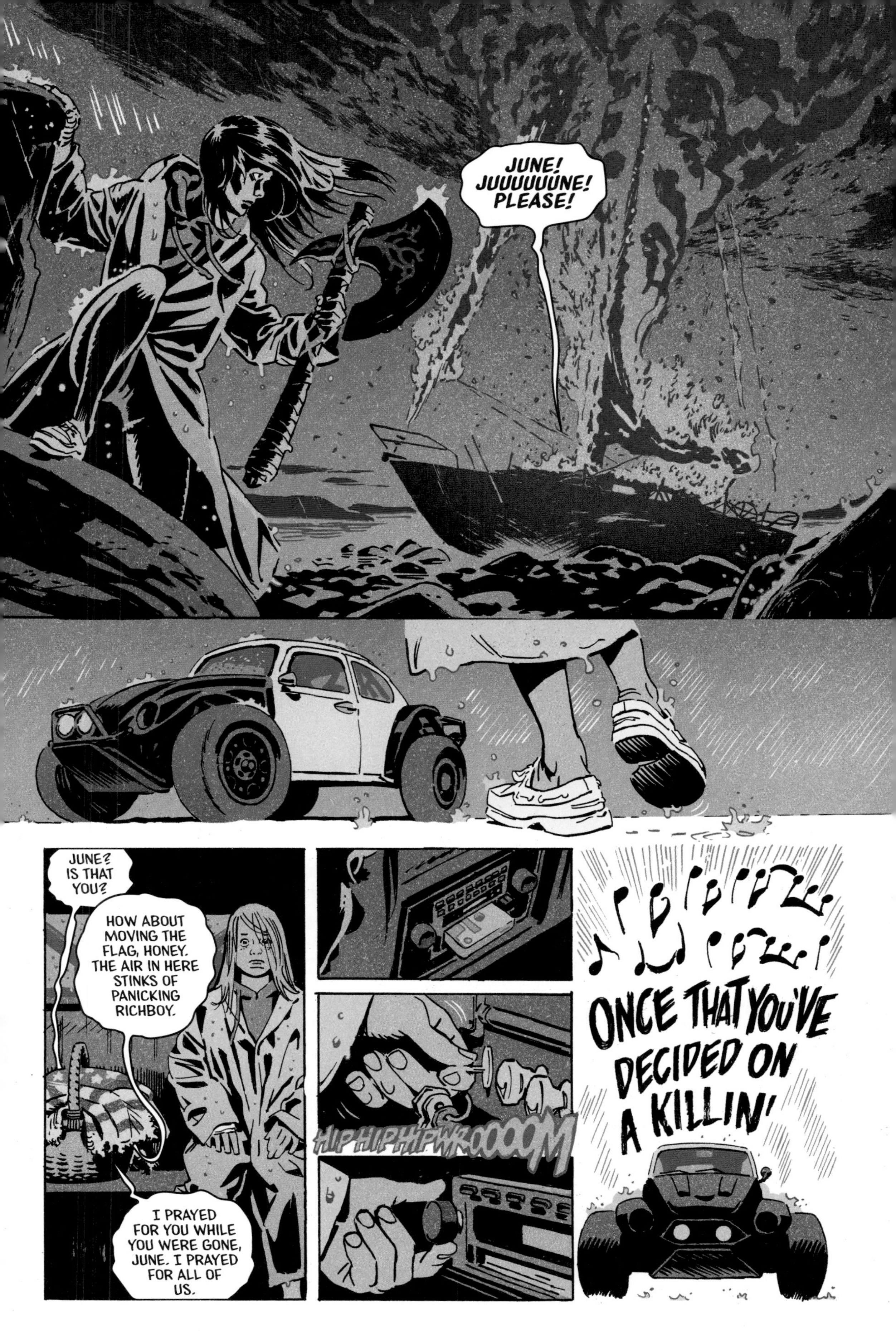
JUNE! JUUUUUUNE! PLEASE!
JUNE? IS THAT YOU?
HOW ABOUT MOVING THE FLAG, HONEY. THE AIR IN HERE STINKS OF PANICKING RICHBOY.
I PRAYED FOR YOU WHILE YOU WERE GONE, JUNE. I PRAYED FOR ALL OF US.
HIP HIP HIP WROOOOOM
ONCE THAT YOU'VE DECIDED ON A KILLIN'

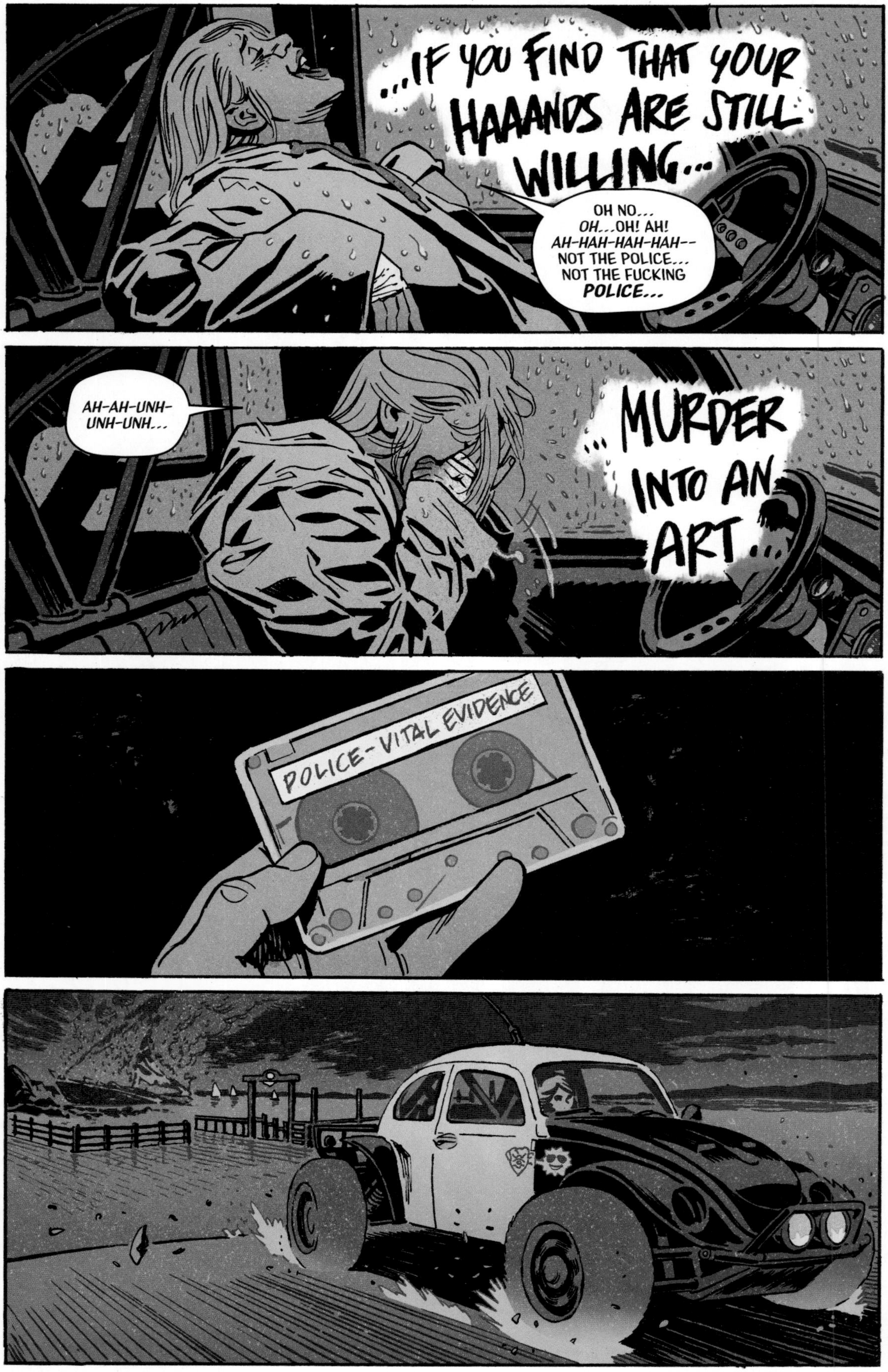
...IF YOU FIND THAT YOUR HAAANDS ARE STILL WILLING...
OH NO... OH...OH! AH! AH-HAH-HAH-HAH-- NOT THE POLICE... NOT THE FUCKING POLICE...
AH-AH-UNH-UNH-UNH...
...MURDER INTO AN ART...
POLICE - VITAL EVIDENCE

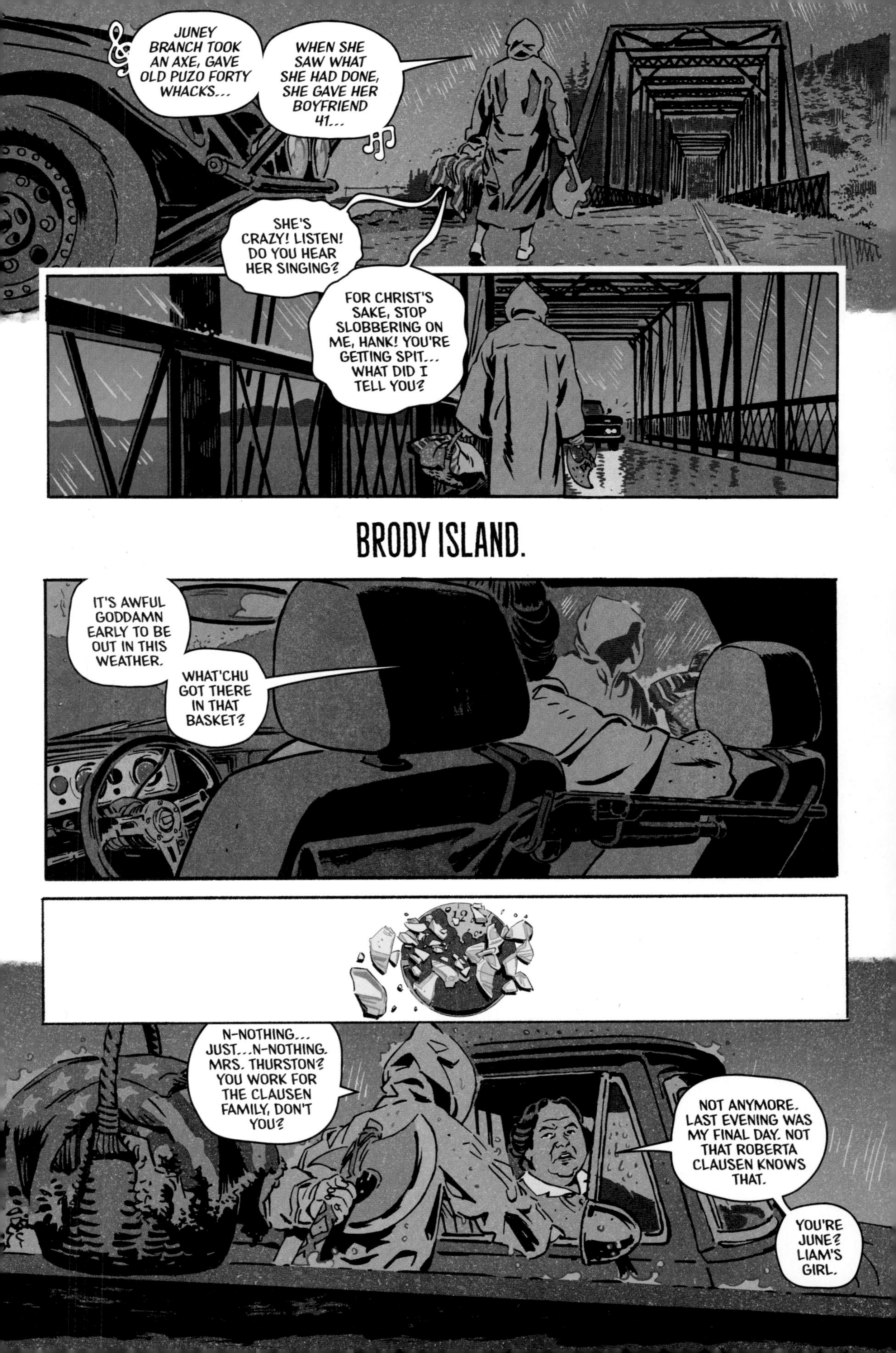
JUNEY BRANCH TOOK AN AXE, GAVE OLD PUZO FORTY WHACKS...
WHEN SHE SAW WHAT SHE HAD DONE, SHE GAVE HER BOYFRIEND 41...
SHE'S CRAZY! LISTEN! DO YOU HEAR HER SINGING?
FOR CHRIST'S SAKE, STOP SLOBBERING ON ME, HANK! YOU'RE GETTING SPIT... WHAT DID I TELL YOU?
BRODY ISLAND.
IT'S AWFUL GODDAMN EARLY TO BE OUT IN THIS WEATHER.
WHAT'CHU GOT THERE IN THAT BASKET?
N-NOTHING... JUST...N-NOTHING. MRS. THURSTON? YOU WORK FOR THE CLAUSEN FAMILY, DON'T YOU?
NOT ANYMORE. LAST EVENING WAS MY FINAL DAY. NOT THAT ROBERTA CLAUSEN KNOWS THAT.
YOU'RE JUNE? LIAM'S GIRL.

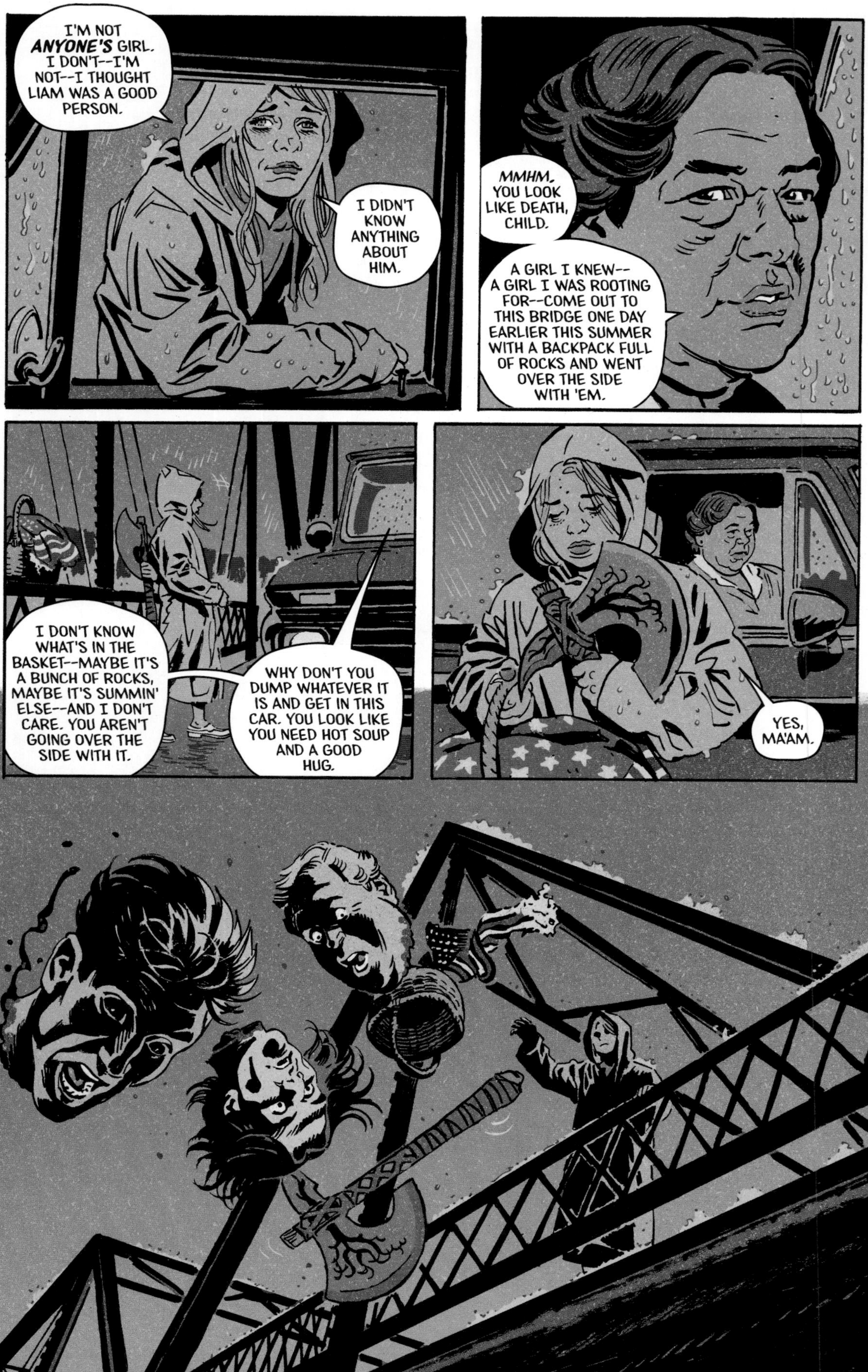
I'M NOT *ANYONE'S* GIRL. I DON'T--I'M NOT--I THOUGHT LIAM WAS A GOOD PERSON.
I DIDN'T KNOW ANYTHING ABOUT HIM.
MMHM. YOU LOOK LIKE DEATH, CHILD.
A GIRL I KNEW--A GIRL I WAS ROOTING FOR--COME OUT TO THIS BRIDGE ONE DAY EARLIER THIS SUMMER WITH A BACKPACK FULL OF ROCKS AND WENT OVER THE SIDE WITH 'EM.
I DON'T KNOW WHAT'S IN THE BASKET--MAYBE IT'S A BUNCH OF ROCKS, MAYBE IT'S SUMMIN' ELSE--AND I DON'T CARE. YOU AREN'T GOING OVER THE SIDE WITH IT.
WHY DON'T YOU DUMP WHATEVER IT IS AND GET IN THIS CAR. YOU LOOK LIKE YOU NEED HOT SOUP AND A GOOD HUG.
YES, MA'AM.

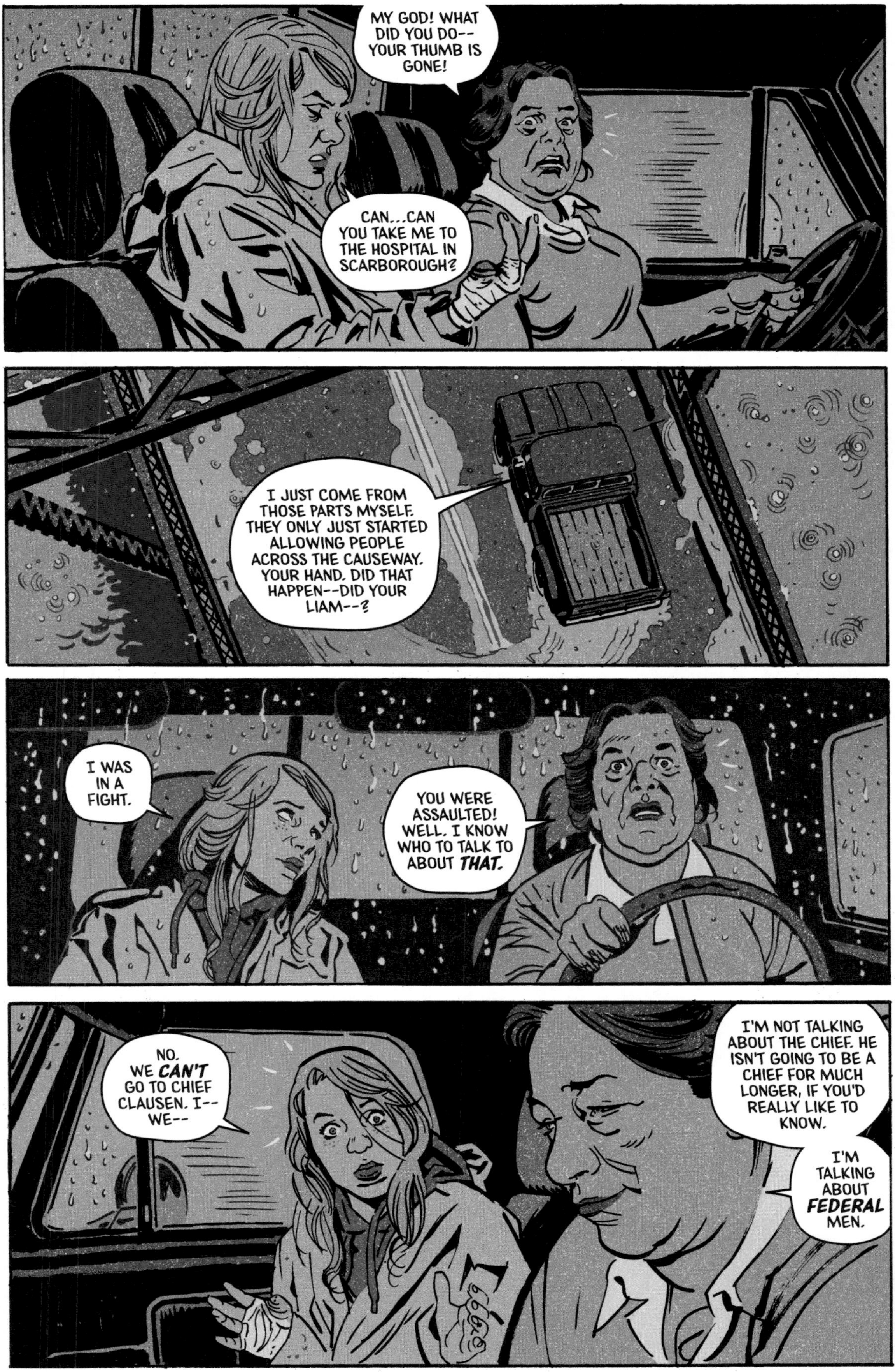
MY GOD! WHAT DID YOU DO-- YOUR THUMB IS GONE!
CAN...CAN YOU TAKE ME TO THE HOSPITAL IN SCARBOROUGH?
I JUST COME FROM THOSE PARTS MYSELF. THEY ONLY JUST STARTED ALLOWING PEOPLE ACROSS THE CAUSEWAY. YOUR HAND. DID THAT HAPPEN--DID YOUR LIAM--?
I WAS IN A FIGHT.
YOU WERE ASSAULTED! WELL, I KNOW WHO TO TALK TO ABOUT **THAT.**
NO. WE **CAN'T** GO TO CHIEF CLAUSEN. I-- WE--
I'M NOT TALKING ABOUT THE CHIEF. HE ISN'T GOING TO BE A CHIEF FOR MUCH LONGER, IF YOU'D REALLY LIKE TO KNOW.
I'M TALKING ABOUT **FEDERAL** MEN.

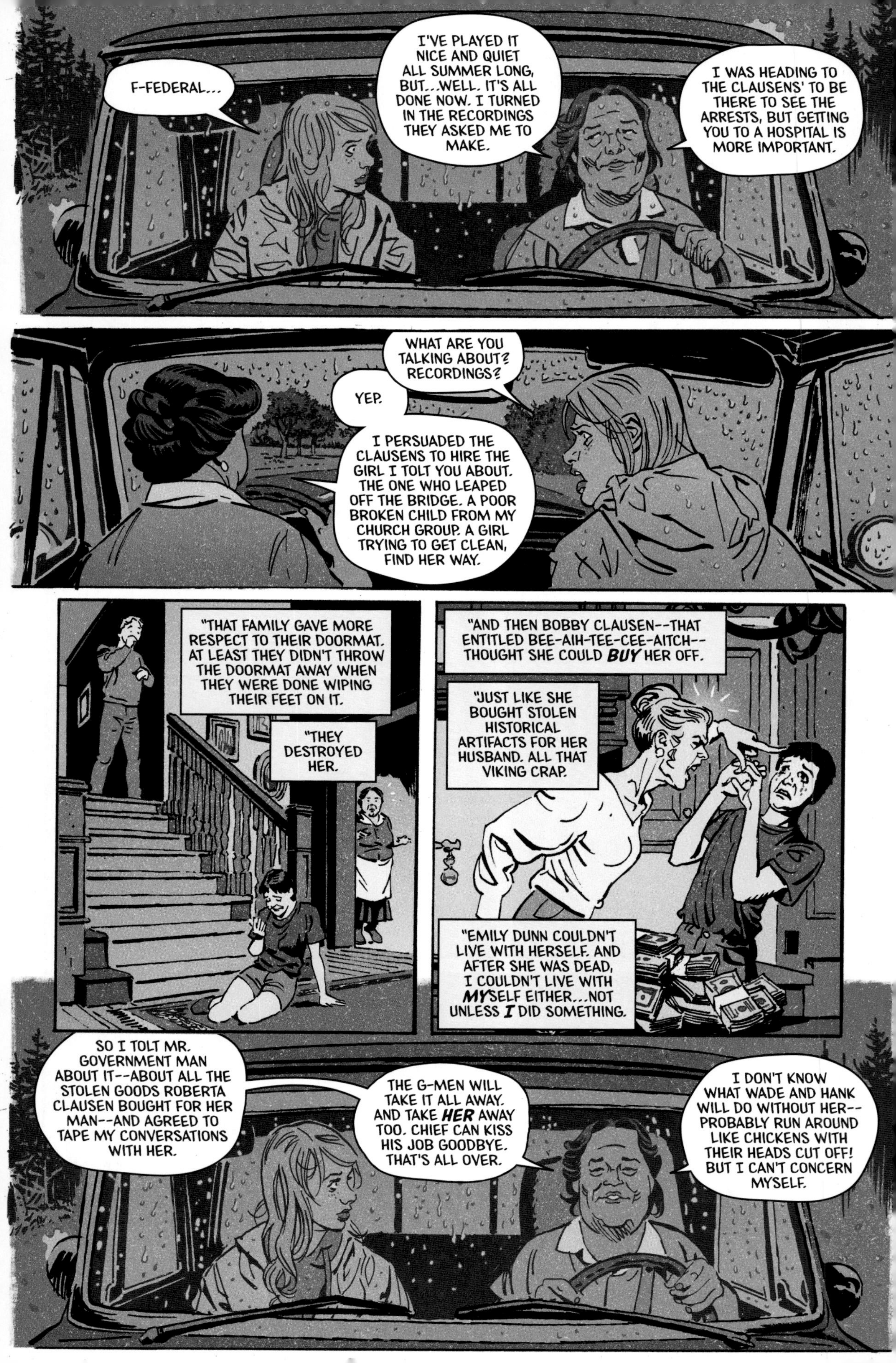
F-FEDERAL...
I'VE PLAYED IT NICE AND QUIET ALL SUMMER LONG, BUT...WELL. IT'S ALL DONE NOW. I TURNED IN THE RECORDINGS THEY ASKED ME TO MAKE.
I WAS HEADING TO THE CLAUSENS' TO BE THERE TO SEE THE ARRESTS, BUT GETTING YOU TO A HOSPITAL IS MORE IMPORTANT.
WHAT ARE YOU TALKING ABOUT? RECORDINGS?
YEP.
I PERSUADED THE CLAUSENS TO HIRE THE GIRL I TOLT YOU ABOUT. THE ONE WHO LEAPED OFF THE BRIDGE. A POOR BROKEN CHILD FROM MY CHURCH GROUP. A GIRL TRYING TO GET CLEAN, FIND HER WAY.
"THAT FAMILY GAVE MORE RESPECT TO THEIR DOORMAT. AT LEAST THEY DIDN'T THROW THE DOORMAT AWAY WHEN THEY WERE DONE WIPING THEIR FEET ON IT.
"THEY DESTROYED HER.
"AND THEN BOBBY CLAUSEN--THAT ENTITLED BEE-AIH-TEE-CEE-AITCH--THOUGHT SHE COULD BUY HER OFF.
"JUST LIKE SHE BOUGHT STOLEN HISTORICAL ARTIFACTS FOR HER HUSBAND. ALL THAT VIKING CRAP.
"EMILY DUNN COULDN'T LIVE WITH HERSELF. AND AFTER SHE WAS DEAD, I COULDN'T LIVE WITH MYSELF EITHER...NOT UNLESS I DID SOMETHING.
SO I TOLT MR. GOVERNMENT MAN ABOUT IT--ABOUT ALL THE STOLEN GOODS ROBERTA CLAUSEN BOUGHT FOR HER MAN--AND AGREED TO TAPE MY CONVERSATIONS WITH HER.
THE G-MEN WILL TAKE IT ALL AWAY. AND TAKE HER AWAY TOO. CHIEF CAN KISS HIS JOB GOODBYE. THAT'S ALL OVER.
I DON'T KNOW WHAT WADE AND HANK WILL DO WITHOUT HER--PROBABLY RUN AROUND LIKE CHICKENS WITH THEIR HEADS CUT OFF! BUT I CAN'T CONCERN MYSELF.

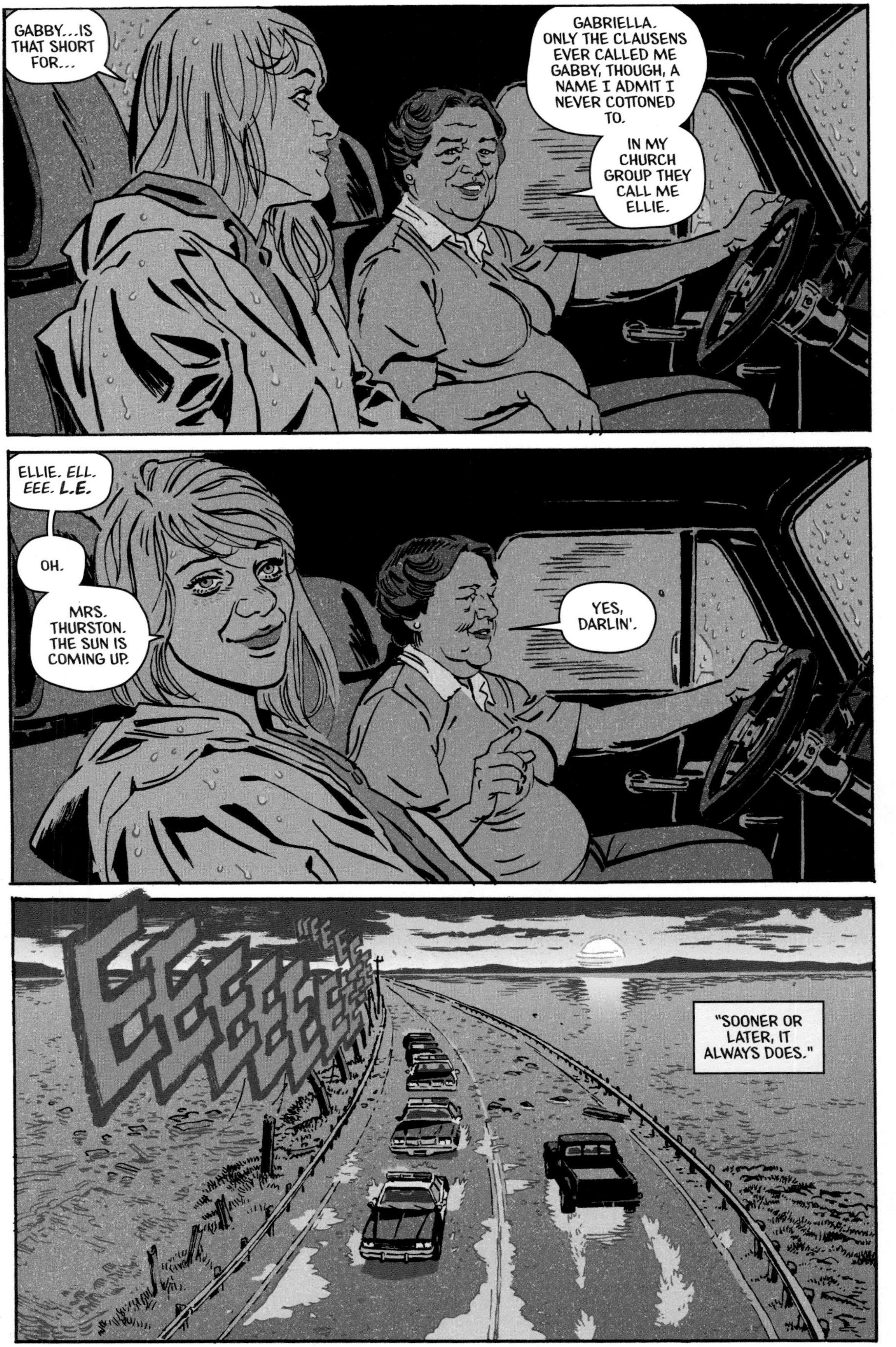
GABBY... IS THAT SHORT FOR...
GABRIELLA. ONLY THE CLAUSENS EVER CALLED ME GABBY, THOUGH, A NAME I ADMIT I NEVER COTTONED TO.
IN MY CHURCH GROUP THEY CALL ME ELLIE.
ELLIE. *ELL.* EEE. ***L.E.***
OH.
MRS. THURSTON. THE SUN IS COMING UP.
YES, DARLIN'.
"SOONER OR LATER, IT ALWAYS DOES."

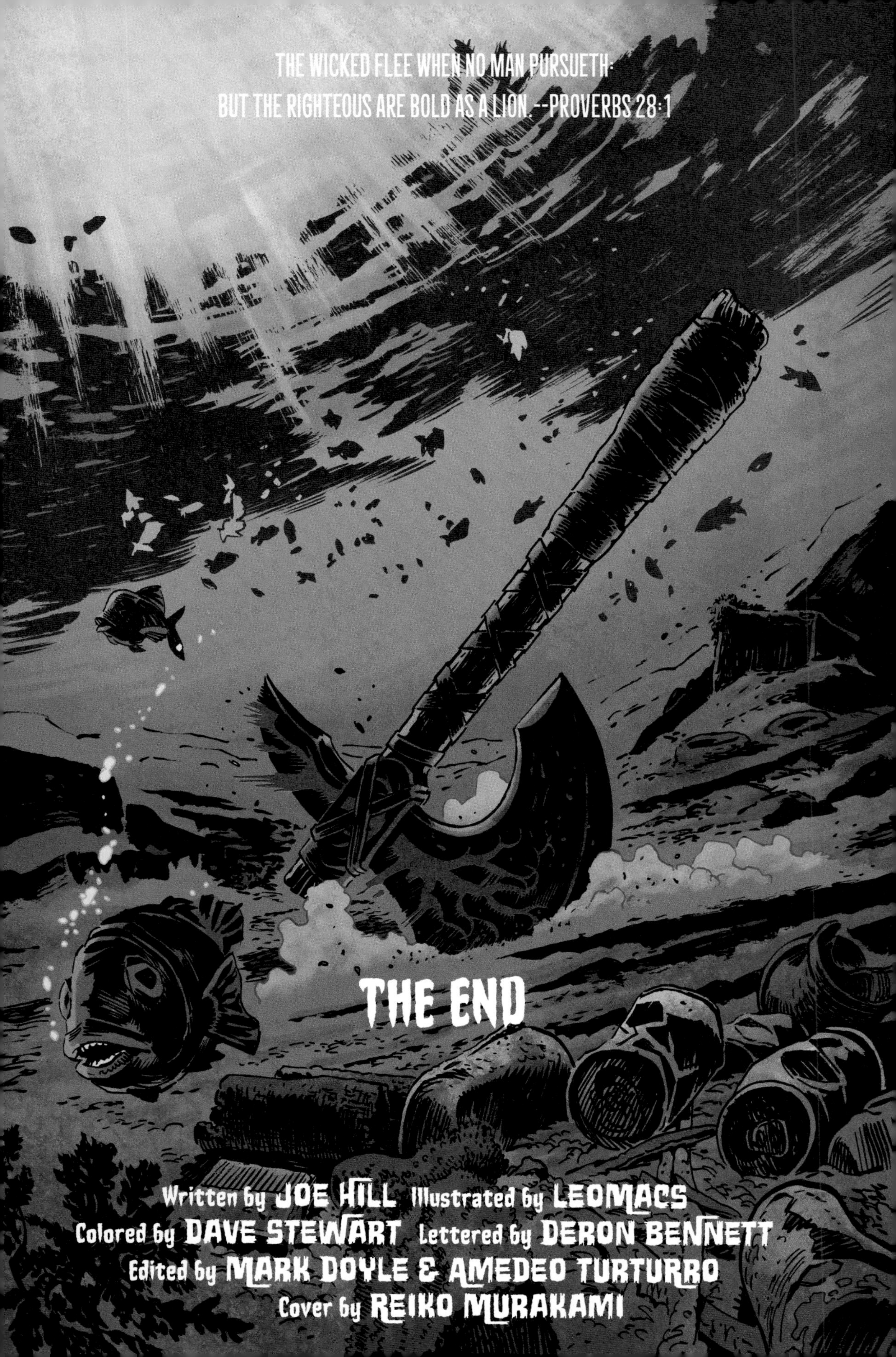
THE WICKED FLEE WHEN NO MAN PURSUETH:
BUT THE RIGHTEOUS ARE BOLD AS A LION. --PROVERBS 28:1
THE END
Written by JOE HILL Illustrated by LEOMACS
Colored by DAVE STEWART Lettered by DERON BENNETT
Edited by MARK DOYLE & AMEDEO TURTURRO
Cover by REIKO MURAKAMI

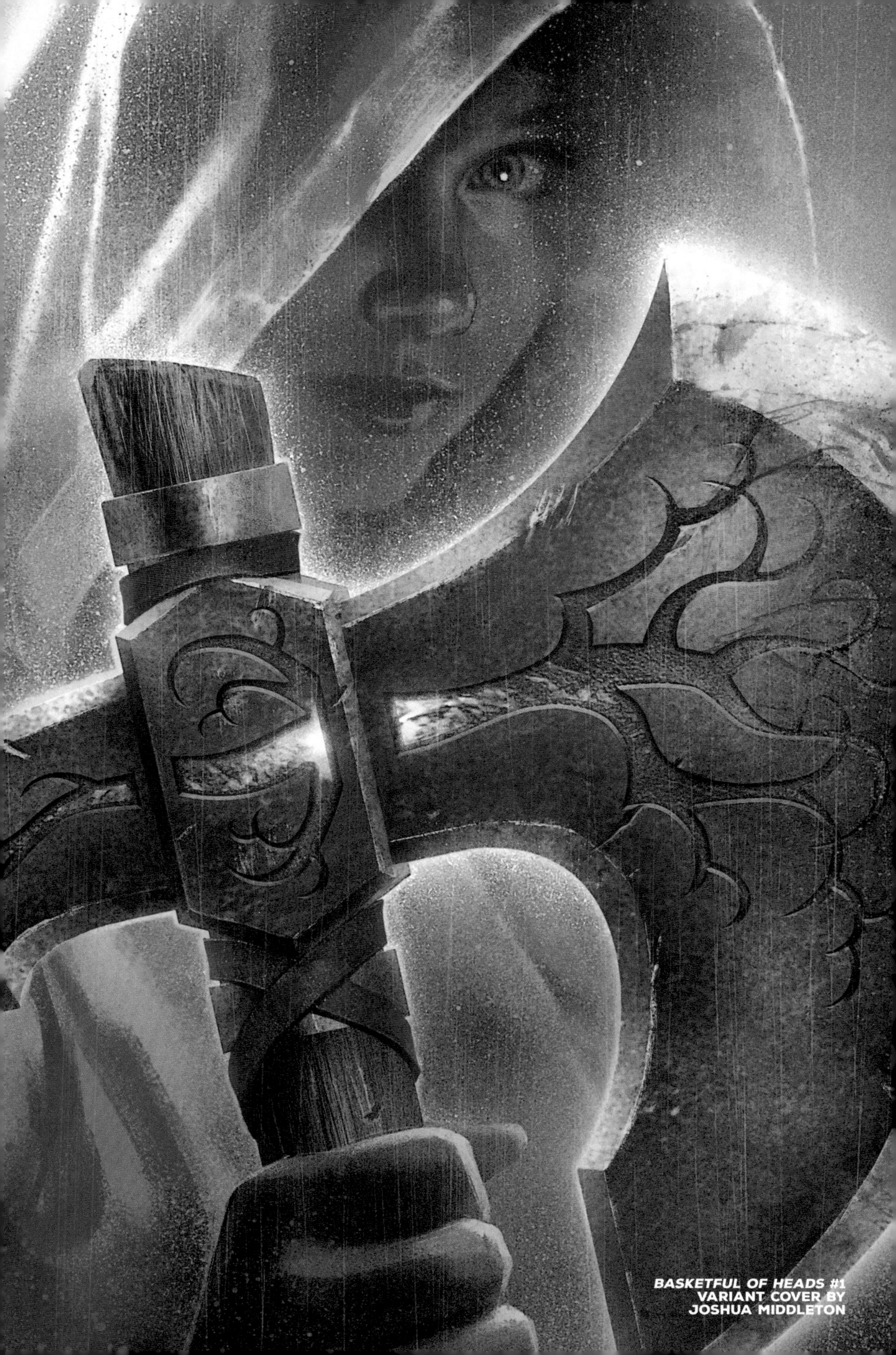

BASKETFUL OF HEADS #1
VARIANT COVER BY
JOSHUA MIDDLETON

BASKETFUL OF HEADS #2
VARIANT COVER BY CLAYTON CRAIN

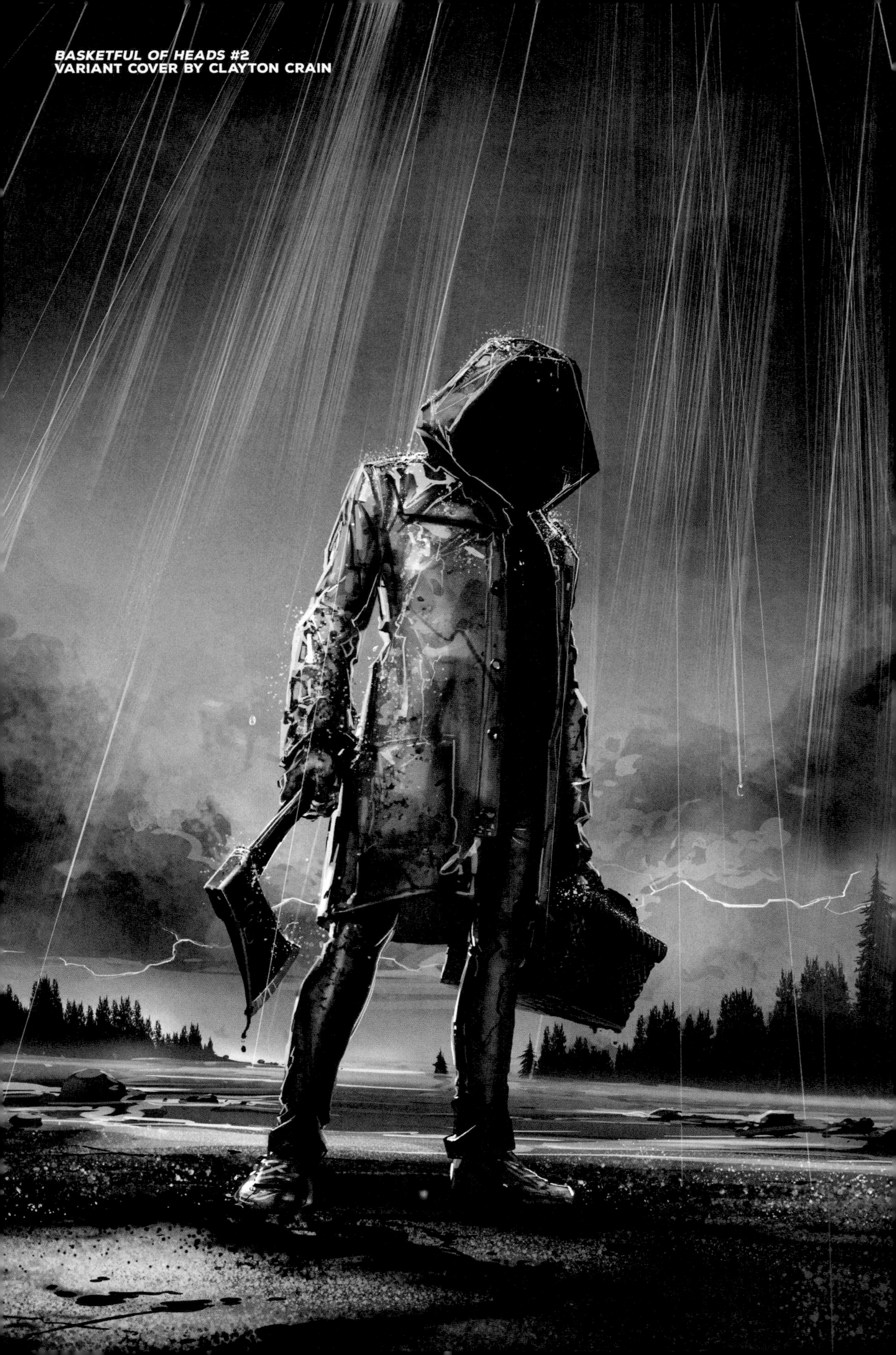

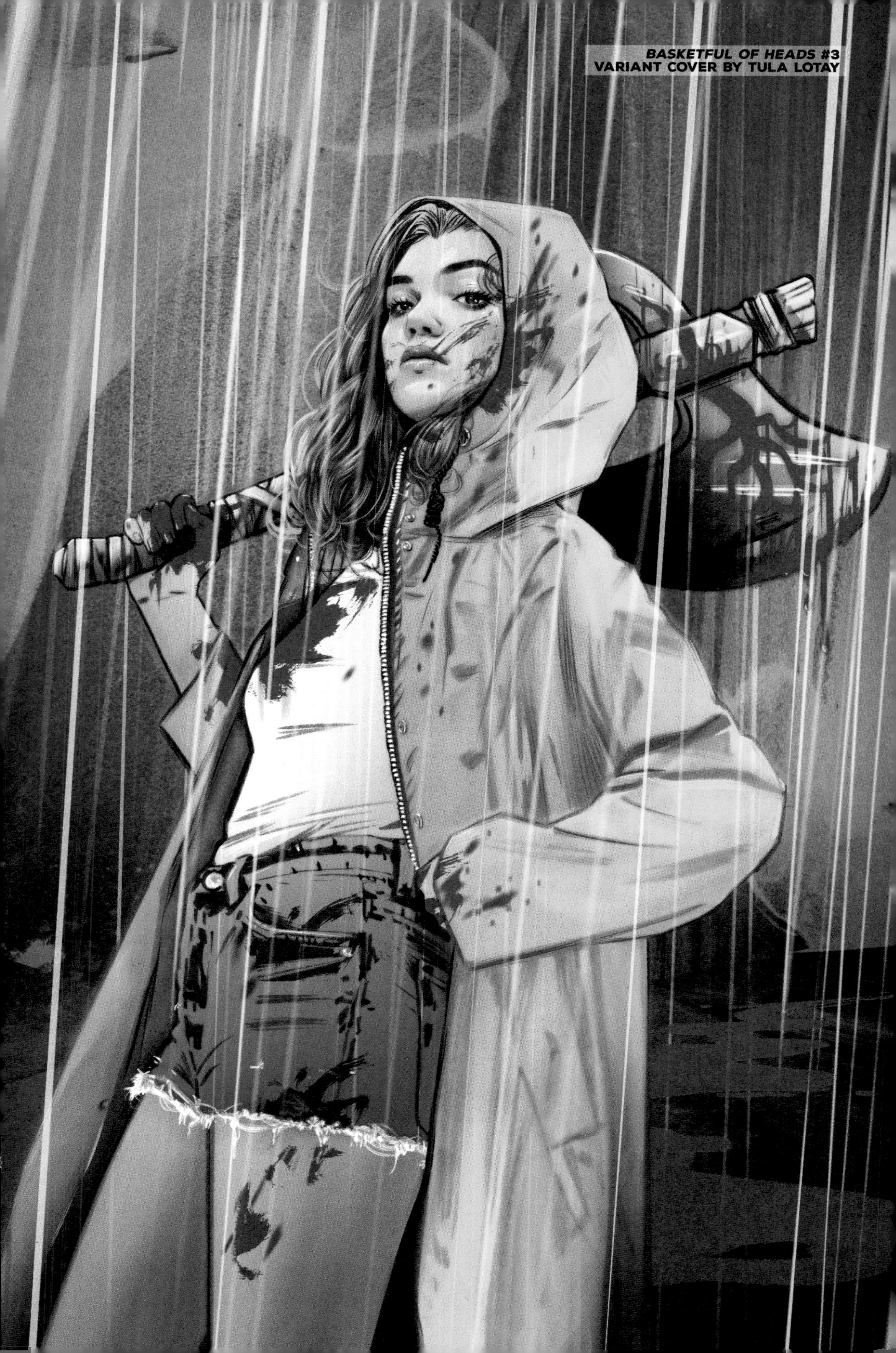

BASKETFUL OF HEADS #3
VARIANT COVER BY TULA LOTAY

BASKETFUL OF HEADS #4
VARIANT COVER BY BECKY CLOONAN

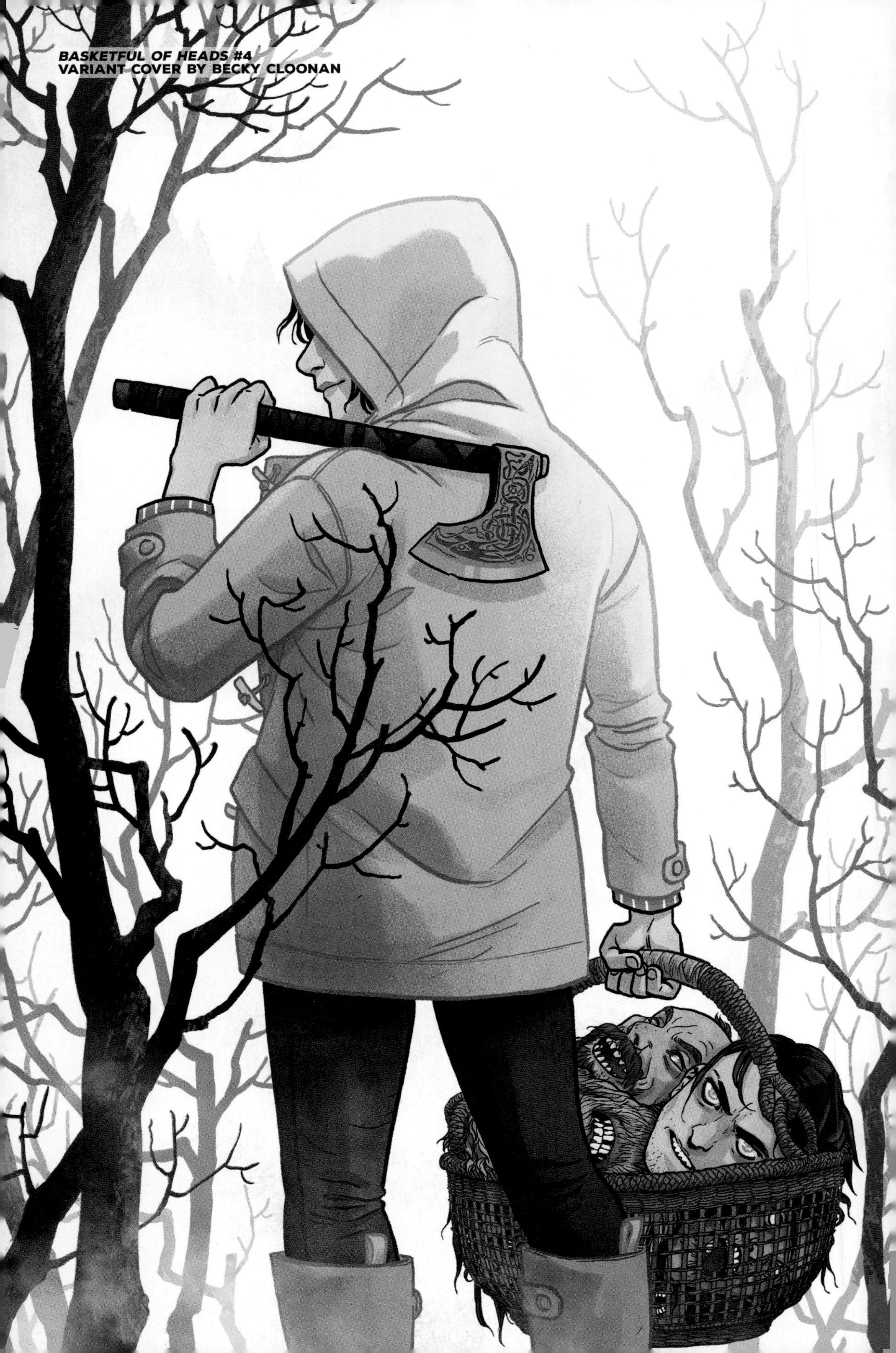

BASKETFUL OF HEADS #
BY MATTEO SCALERA AND

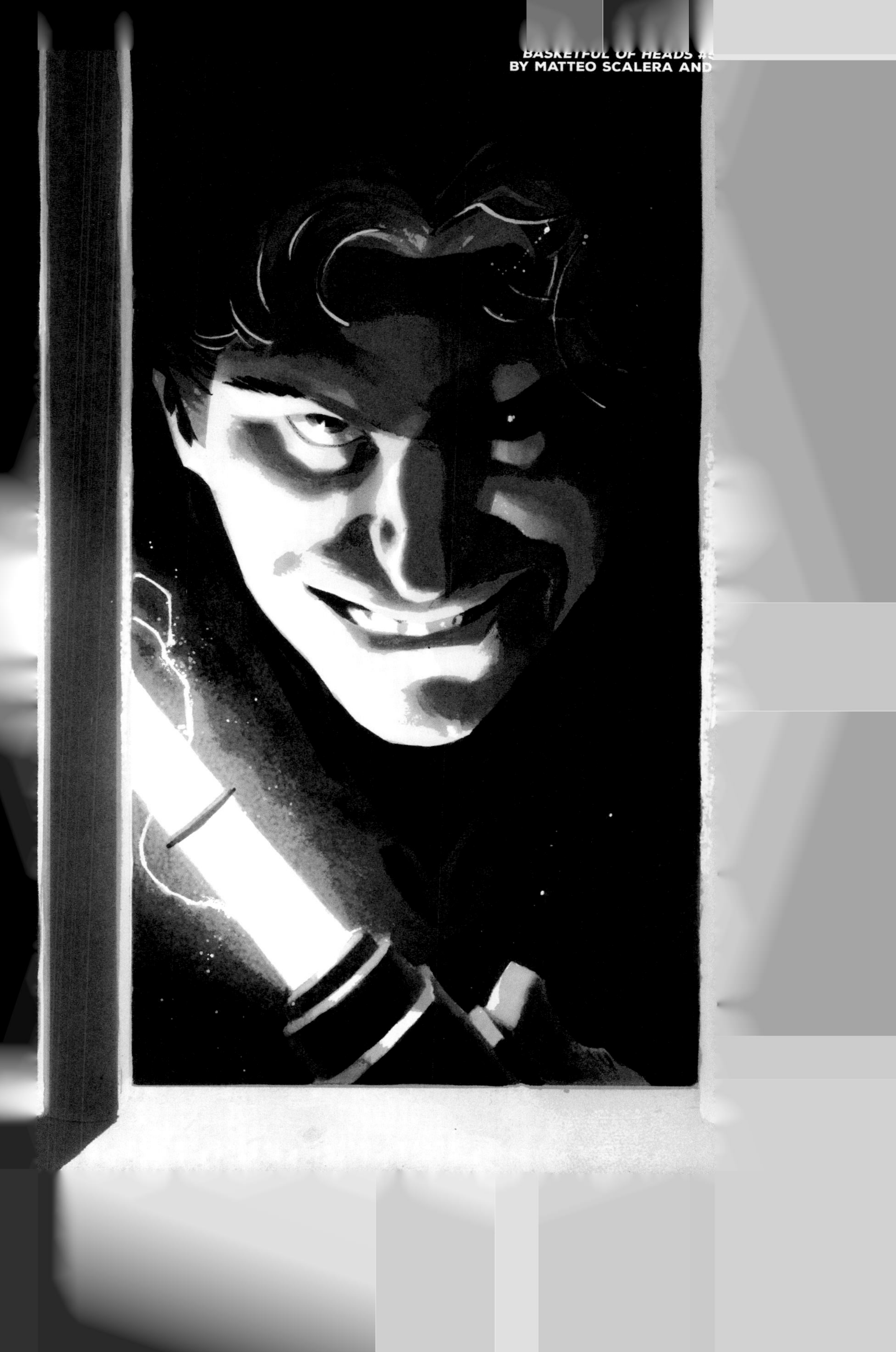

BASKETFUL OF HEADS #6
VARIANT COVER BY IGOR KORDEY

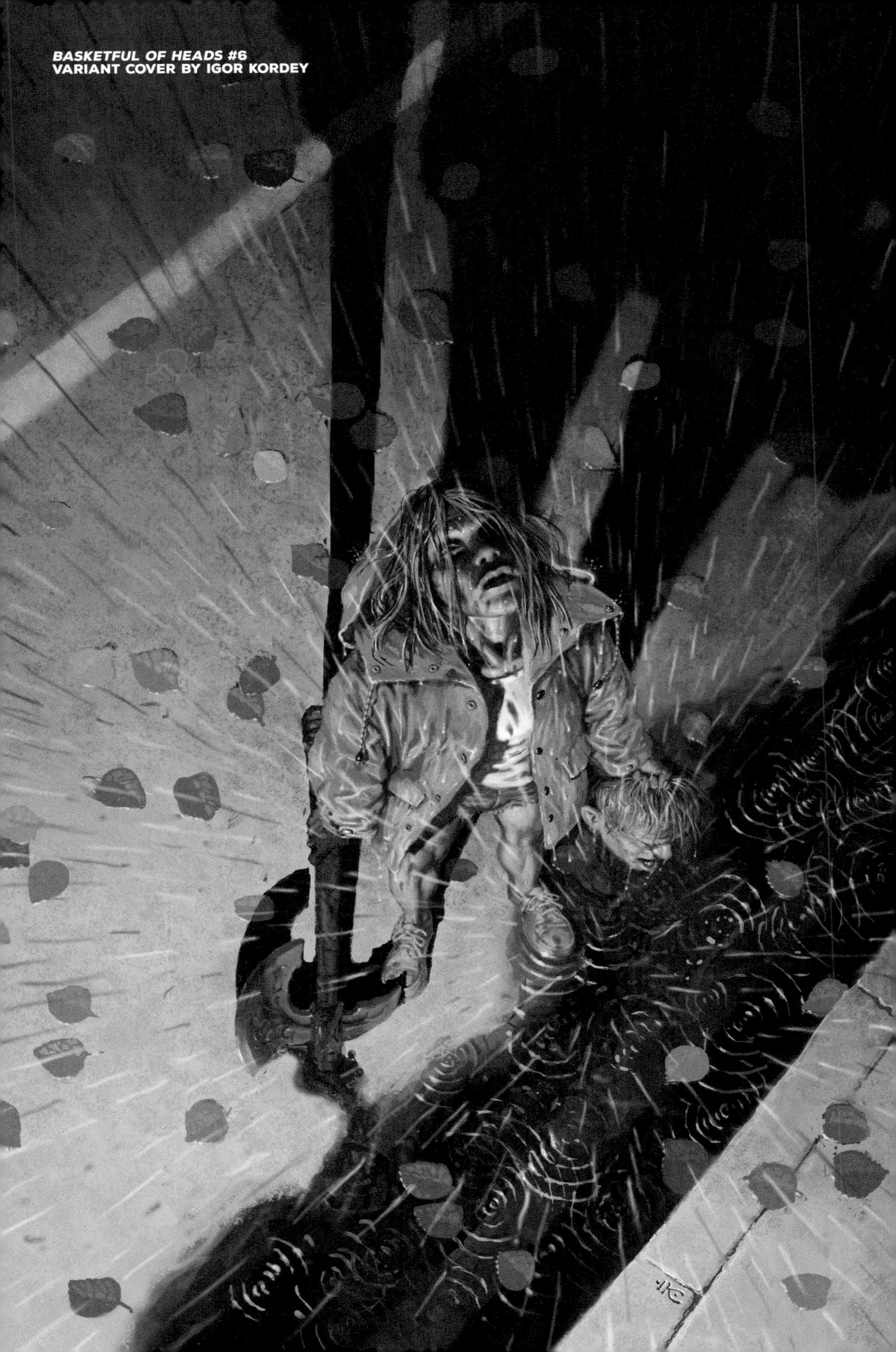

BASKETFUL OF HEADS #7
VARIANT COVER BY GABRIEL RODRIGUEZ

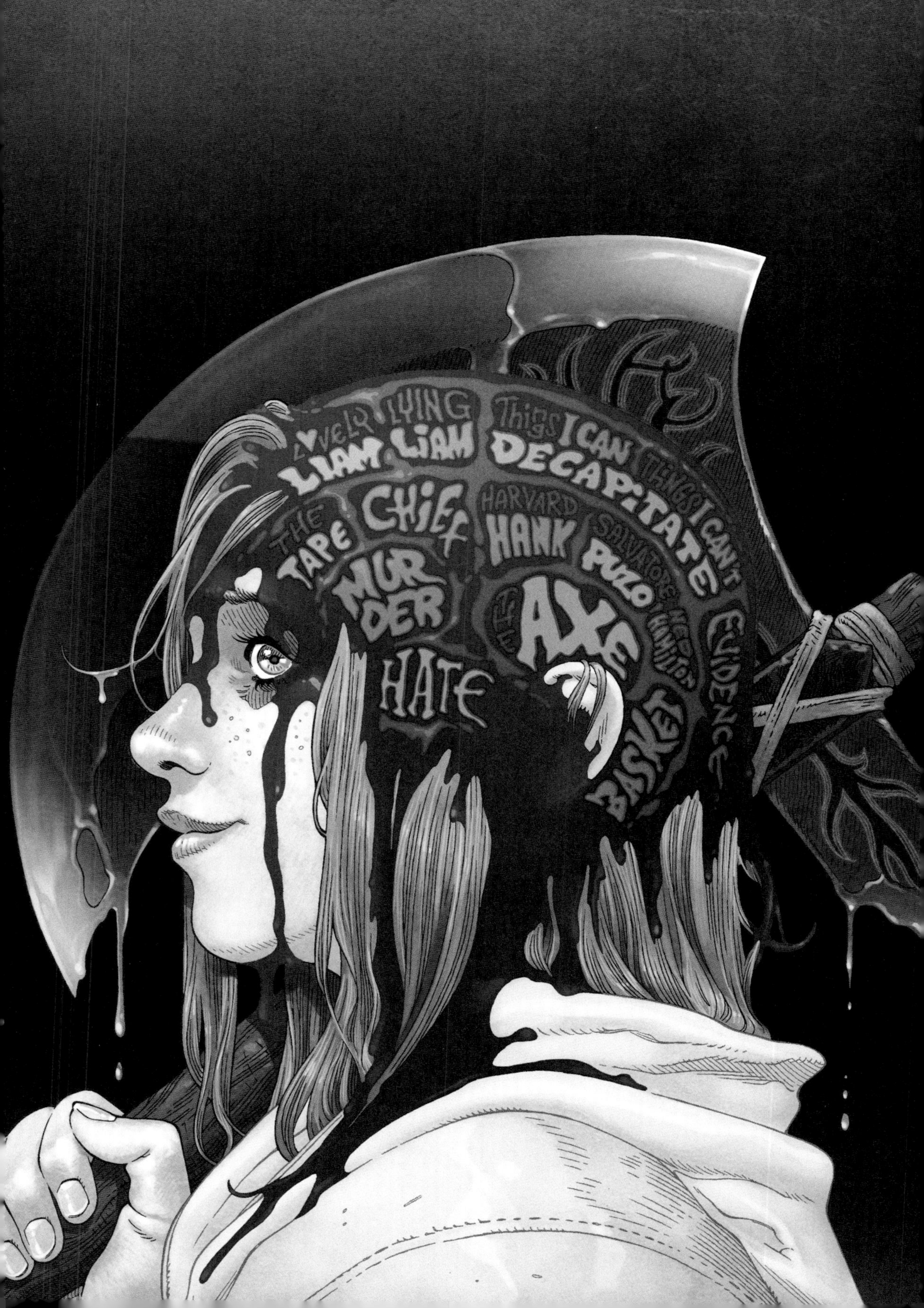
LIAM
LYING LIAM
Things I CAN DECAPITATE
THINGS I CAN'T
THE TAPE
CHIEF
HARVARD HANK
SALVATORE PUZO
MURDER
AXE
HATE
HAMILTON
EVIDENCE
BASKET

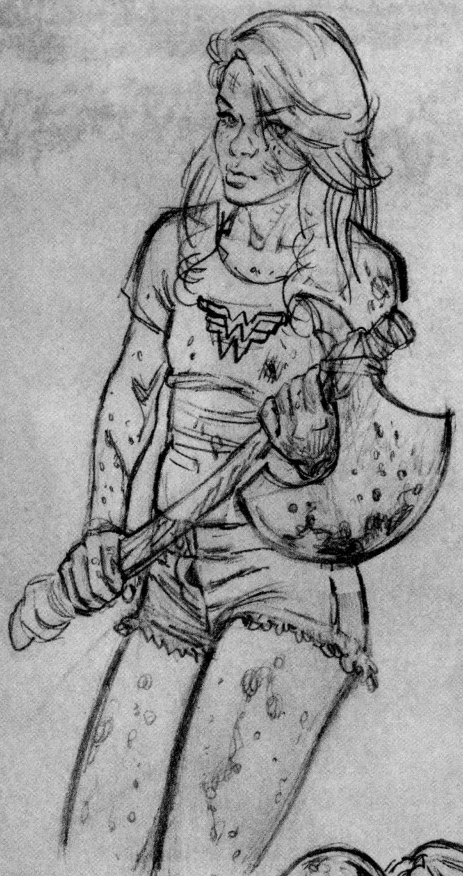

RED INK

INTERVIEW WITH JOE HILL
ALL CHARACTER SKETCHES BY LEOMACS

Joe, what makes *Basketful of Heads* the right series to kick off Hill House Comics and set the tone for the line?

I've had the idea for *Basketful of Heads* kicking around in the back of my mind for almost a decade. I even took a pass at the first script in 2011 or thereabouts, but it needed more time to brew. My subconscious stayed busy with it, apparently—the first four issues practically wrote themselves.

I wanted our first title to be insane, WTF, relentless reading: to script something that would blast along like an 18-wheeler going downhill with no brakes. These days, there's so much entertainment out there, there's so much distraction—if you want to cut through the noise, you've got to come out with both guns blazing. You have to do your best to deliver something that'll keep the reader flying through the pages.

What can you share about the main character, June Branch, and how she navigates the truly unconventional situation she finds herself in?

If writing *Basketful of Heads* has been a lot of fun, that's probably because I so like spending time with June. She's bright and sunny and open—someone we can love, someone we can root for—who also happens to be as flexible and sharp as a fencing blade. Her beloved, Liam Ellsworth, is snatched away by a gang of desperate men, for reasons she doesn't understand. She finds herself pursuing them with an eerie, occult axe and her own unique understanding of human nature. I won't say which I think is the more valuable asset.

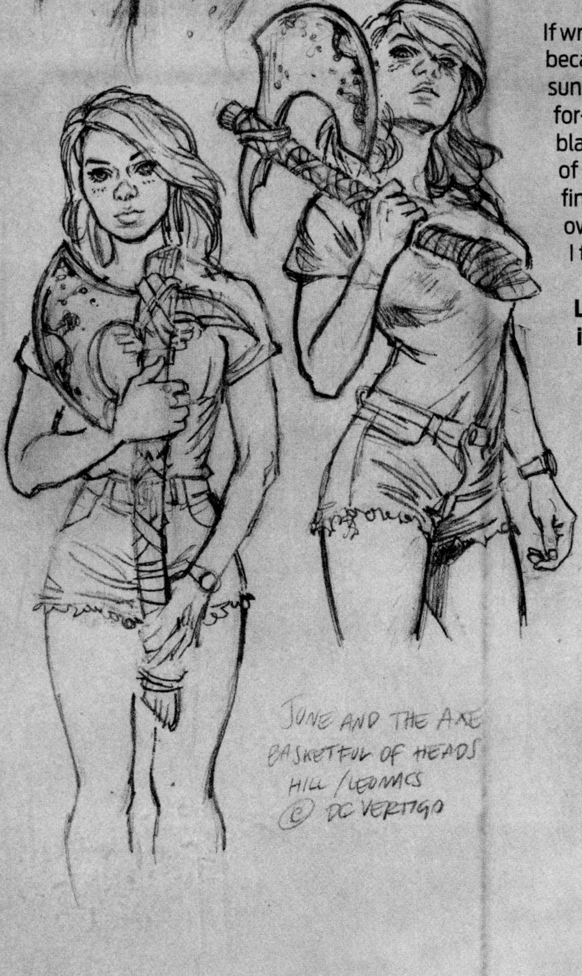
JUNE AND THE AXE
BASKETFUL OF HEADS
HILL / LEOMACS
© DC VERTIGO

Leomacs may not be familiar to a lot of DC fans—what's it like working with him bringing this story to life?

I'm so lucky to be working with this guy. Leomacs gets that even though this is a dark, suspenseful story, we're also setting out to have some good, gory, stomach-turning fun. He brings an anarchic, subversive energy to every panel. It's everything I was hoping for, and then some. I really wanted to tell a tale that was tense, funny, and unrepentantly grotesque—think of pictures like *Re-Animator* and *Evil Dead II*. "Tense, funny, and unrepentantly grotesque" is Leomacs's sweet spot.

RED INK
INTERVIEW WITH LEOMACS

Basketful of Heads is, as Joe Hill puts it, "tense, funny, and unrepentantly grotesque." Series artist Leomacs talks about his approach to each of those aspects.

What's been your favorite sequence to draw in *Basketful of Heads*?

In issue #2 when June is hiding in the laundry basket, and then later when she escapes from Puzo, after having taken the axe from the display cabinet. Both because that's when the tension levels begin to build up, and because I loved the change in atmosphere.

Horror comics have an incredible legacy, but can be a tricky genre to get right. How do you approach elements like the simmering tension in issue #3, when everything goes wrong between June and Mr. Hamilton?

My approach was not to create horror because it scares people, but rather to channel June's terror, her confusion after having to quickly adapt to this new reality that she's got caught up in, and her mounting adrenaline. All mixed together—fear, adrenaline, and her tiredness, in the darkness, under incessant rain—all that, if conveyed properly, will allow the horror to emerge. This is what was on my mind when Ned Hamilton meets June, who's just emerged from an ordeal. He looks like a beacon of safety, but soon she realizes he is not...

There is a lot of humor inherent in *Basketful of Heads*. How much fun are you having with that aspect of the series?

Oh yes, Joe's writing is like honey for a bear! Juicy and sweet and very energizing. I'm having a lot of fun, and it helps with telling the story. You go from having to create a very dramatic situation to suddenly being able to break that spell with a quip or a funny shot, like when June holds Puzo's severed head to clean his snotty nose. There is so much in that gesture; she's caring, funny, and the scene is so grotesque.

The characters in *Basketful of Heads*, as over-the-top as the premise is, immediately feel real. What was your process in bringing this cast to life?

Joe's descriptions of the characters were very precise and evocative. I committed the characters' faces to the page, so we knew what they looked like, in an array of expressions, and then I tried to fulfill Joe's description by characterizing the protagonists with their specific body language,

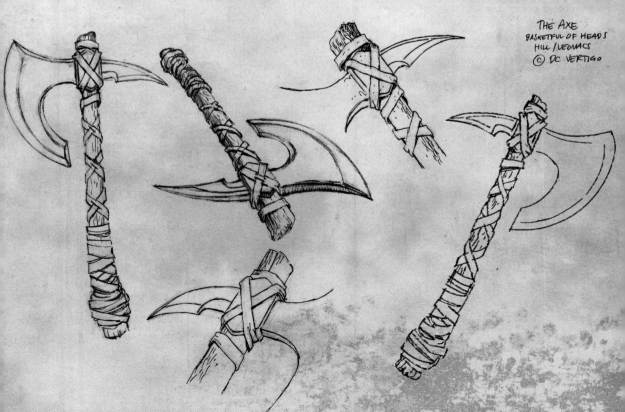

THE AXE
BASKETFUL OF HEADS
HILL / LEOMACS
© DC VERTIGO

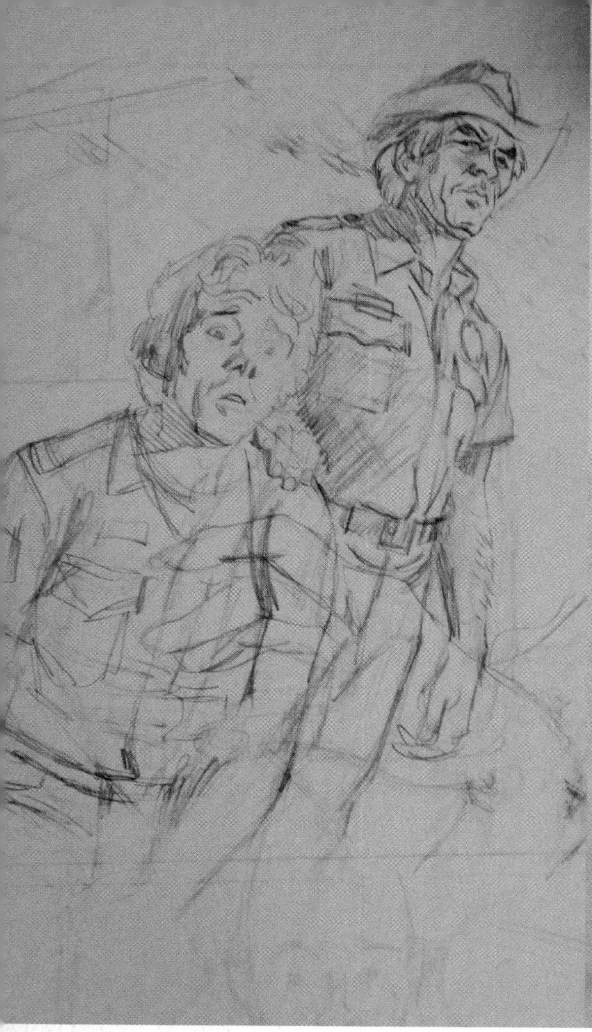

postures, and expressions that would make them feel real. June is a many-layered character, and as you read on, you discover a different aspect of her character. She seems like your average girl next door, but she will surprise you every time you turn the page.

What type of horror do you enjoy as a fan—be it movies, books, comics, etc.?

As a genre, horror normally works when it properly taps into our primal fears. Those are the stories that tend to attract my attention, when they are well-made, and sort of make me lose my sleep. I do, however, love films like *The Thing*, one of my all-time favorites, or *The Evil Dead*, because it is incredibly funny. *Rosemary's Baby* is blood-chilling, as far as I'm concerned. Another film I find very disturbing is *The Texas Chain Saw Massacre*—now that's a dysfunctional family! *Invasion of the Body Snatchers* by Philip Kaufman terrified me as a child. *Alien* is also a masterpiece—the atmosphere is incredible, and it's been copied but never really equaled, I think. Bergman's *Hour of the Wolf*, which I think is a real horror. Pretty much all of Alfred Hitchcock's productions!

In terms of books, how can I not mention Stephen King? *It* still scares the heebie-jeebies out of me. Kafka, Lovecraft, and Poe are my classic horror favorites. Richard Matheson, my girlfriend adores him, and if you read *I Am Legend* it will haunt you for a long time.

As for comics, Alan Moore's *Swamp Thing*, simply amazing. Jamie Delano's *Hellblazer* stories, *The Sandman* by Neil Gaiman, and EC Comics. I could go on, but you get me, I am a fan of the genre!

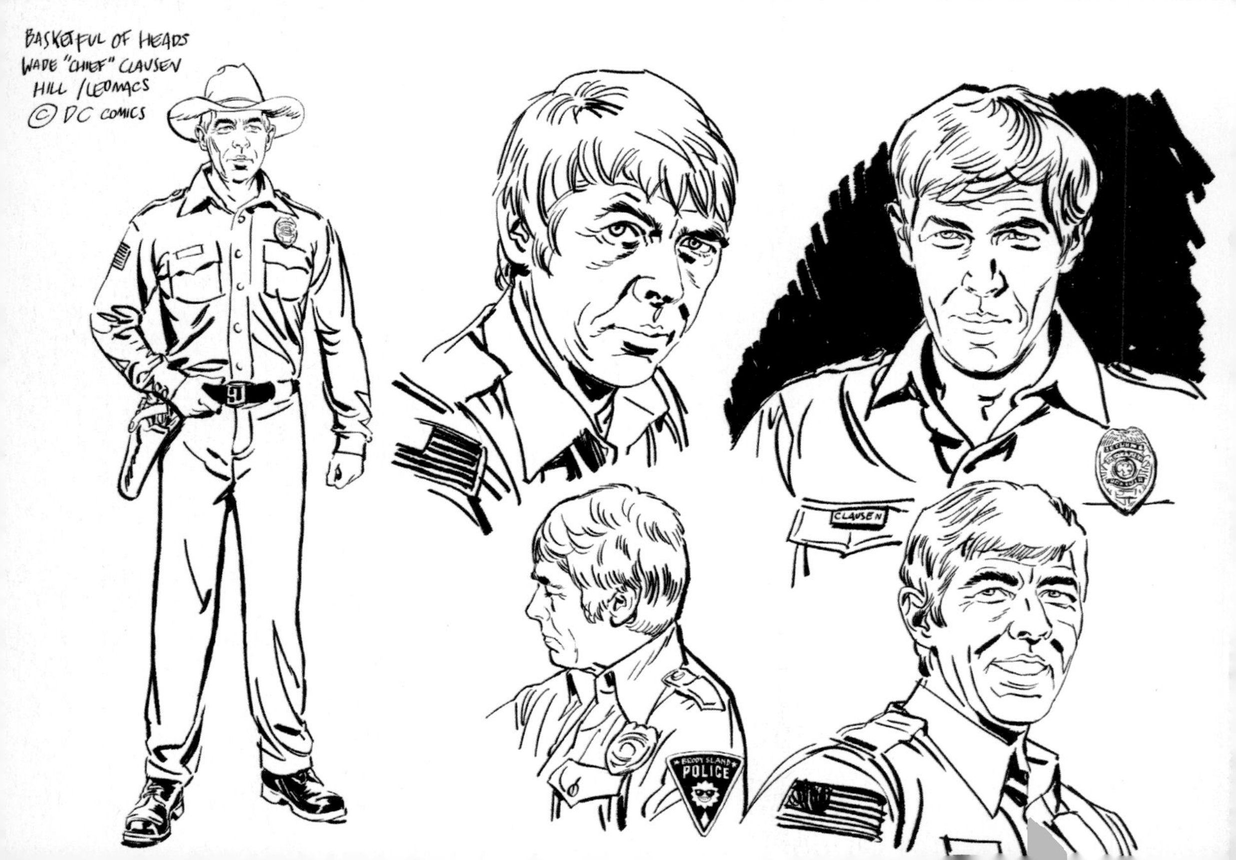
BASKETFUL OF HEADS
WADE "CHIEF" CLAUSEN
HILL / LEOMACS
© DC COMICS
CLAUSEN
POLICE